# THE LAST PETAL

### THE LAST PETAL DUET
### BOOK ONE

JANERA MOON

SLEEPYHOUSE PUBLISHING

*To the overthinker.*
*This is for every time you needed reassurance.*

# TRIGGER WARNINGS

This book contains the following that may be triggering for some readers:

- Detailed descriptions of torture from childhood to adulthood
- Attempted suicide
- Anxious thoughts/overthinking and spiraling
- Allusions to sexual assault, but it is not depicted
- One scene with dubious/assumed consent (does not include main characters)
- References to parental death

This book also contains descriptions of sex and should only be read by people age 18 and up.

If you read this book and believe any additional triggers are not addressed here, please contact me through my website: www.janeramoon.com.

CHAPTER

# ONE

"She's here, just like I knew she'd be," Mateo said, unable to keep the smile from coming to his face. He watched the woman he had been dreaming about for so long sitting alone at her table in the cafe in deep focus reading a textbook. Her face was decorated with freckles that were barely noticeable against her deep golden-brown skin and her thick, coiled hair was pulled into a crown on the top of her head.

"It's about time," Liam groaned. "We've been here almost every day at the same hour for the past month. You need to get a handle on your visions."

"Order seventy-two!" the barista chimed, setting two coffees on the counter. "Oh, it's you two again, professors Vazquez and Taylor. It feels like I've seen you almost every shift."

"It's quite convenient to campus," Liam replied. "Are you ready for the semester to begin next week, William?"

"Heck yes! Especially since I managed to get into your course on Comparative Approaches to Literature! I'm so excited to learn about-"

"Okay, I look forward to having you in my class again." Liam quickly cut William off to turn his attention to Mateo who was already heading toward the woman they'd been waiting ages to meet.

Mateo felt his heart race as he got closer to her. Before he reached her table, she looked up and made eye contact with him as if she'd sensed him approaching. Her brows pulled together and she tilted her head to the side, looking at him curiously when he finally got to her and Liam soon followed.

"May I help you?" she asked.

Mateo gave her his most charming smile. "Do you mind if we join you?"

The woman looked around the empty cafe, confusion decorating her face. After a few moments, she finally responded to Mateo's request.

"Sure." She returned Mateo's smile with her own, causing both his and Liam's hearts to flutter.

The men sat across from her at the table, taking in her image. She was even more breathtaking in person for Mateo. And Liam was floored by her beauty.

"Um... I'm Amara," she said awkwardly. She was beginning to rethink her decision to let the strange men join her with the way they stared without saying a word.

"Right, right... I'm Mateo."

"And I'm Liam. It's a pleasure to meet you." He smiled and leaned into the table. "Are you new around here? We frequent this cafe and we've never seen you before."

*Couldn't be more subtle, Liam?* Mateo thought.

"Oh uh... yeah, I just moved here a couple weeks ago, actually. I'm starting a PhD program in botany at Masoncrest."

"PhD? Impressive." Liam nodded approvingly. "You don't look old enough to be in a PhD program."

*Shut up, Liam. That's rude.* Mateo nudged him and joined the conversation. "So, we'll be seeing you around campus, I imagine? We both teach there."

"Really? Which departments are you in?"

"Both social sciences," Liam replied. "I teach literature and Mateo here does lectures on... Well, he can say for himself."

"I teach history and hold a few international relations seminars here and there."

Amara listened attentively while thoughts of her first impressions of Liam and Mateo filled her head.

*Okay, so Liam, the very confident one with the perfect jaw line, dark brown hair, and weirdly dark blue eyes teaches English lit. And Mateo, the one who first approached me with the lumberjack body, deep tan complexion that's only a shade or two lighter than my own, and almost black, curly hair, is a history professor. Great! They won't be around the Natural Sciences Department to distract me. How do men who look like this casually exist? I imagine they're very popular with students. They both look straight out of a hot professor fantasy.*

A gleaming smile grew on Liam's face and Amara couldn't understand where his sudden excitement came from.

Mateo noticed the way Amara seemed uneasy and nudged Liam again and cleared his throat. "So, botany? What made you choose that?"

Amara broke her eye contact with Liam and looked over at Mateo. "Well... It's always fascinated me how the earth nourishes and heals us, you know? And my grandma was kind of an herbalist. She raised me and was always teaching me these natural remedies using nothing but plants." She chuckled and shook her head. "I don't think I took any man-made medicines until I was a teenager, and..."

Amara stopped herself, wondering why she was speaking so freely with complete strangers. She looked down at her phone and realized she was already running late for her dance audition on campus.

She laughed nervously as she started packing her things. "I don't know why I gave you my life story like that. Anyway, I have to get going. It was nice to meet you, Mateo and Liam."

"The feeling is mutual." Mateo took out his wallet and pulled out one of his cards. "Here, if you ever have any questions about town or would like a tour, please don't hesitate to reach out."

"Yeah, sure..." Amara reached out for the card and when her hand grazed Mateo's, she felt a shock go through her system.

*"Look at how wet she is for us, Mateo."*
*Amara was naked and sitting with Liam on a bed, her back against his chest. His legs were wrapped to the inside of hers to keep her legs open while she was on full display for Mateo who sat across from them. Liam spread Amara's lips apart as if presenting her to Mateo and grazed his finger along her slit before slipping it inside. "Look at the way her body reacts to us..."*
*"Well, it only makes sense..." Mateo stood from the chair, beginning to remove his clothes as he approached the bed. "She is ours."*

Amara blinked several times as her mind came back to reality. She looked between the men and around the cafe and realized she was in the same spot and holding Mateo's card.

"Yeah, um sure... Okay... See you around." Amara's speech was awkward and her hand was shaky as she placed Mateo's card in the front pocket of her bag.

Liam tilted his head to the side and gave Amara a flirtatious smile. "I'm sure we'll be seeing more of you, Amara."

"Y-yeah." Amara scurried out of the cafe, almost tripping over herself as both men watched her leave.

"Shit." Mateo sighed. "When we touched, she saw one of my visions..."

"You say that like it's a bad thing," Liam replied. "Whatever she saw, it put her brain into overdrive and she was definitely turned on. It'd be much better if I could *see* thoughts rather than *hear* them."

Mateo stroked his beard thoughtfully as his gaze remained on the door. "She's doing natural sciences... It's going to be difficult to find an excuse to be around her more often."

"This is pointless," Liam grumbled. "We've been waiting to meet her for over a century and now we finally do and we have to to 'take our time,'" he said mockingly. "She is our Fated and this courtship shall be swift."

"Calm down and remember the speech patterns for this time," Mateo warned. "Lillian was right. It's like she was made for us. Down to her name and voice... everything about her is perfect."

"Which is exactly why I don't understand this pacing you and Lillian are so keen on. I heard her thoughts. She finds both of us attractive, just as we do her. It's simple. We take her to our home, we explain everything to her, and then we make lo-"

"It's not that simple and you know it, Liam."

"Whatever," he scoffed before turning to Mateo with a smirk and raised brow. "So... which vision did she see, exactly?"

# TWO

Amara was in high spirits following her successful dance audition on campus. To her surprise, the head of the Fine Arts Department who she auditioned with was so impressed that she immediately asked her to teach at least one workshop during the semester.

She lived in a decent-sized, three-bedroom home that was a ten-minute drive from the Masoncrest University campus. Amara shared the house with Evelyn Knight—a fortunate connection for her. Evelyn's cousin Cameron was Amara's closest friend, almost like a brother to her.

She took a deep breath before getting out of her car and going toward the front door. When Amara walked in, Evelyn was relaxing on the couch with a book in her hand. Her dark brown hair was in a short cut, the natural curls coiled tightly in small ringlets. The cut worked well with her bone structure—high cheekbones and a narrow chin. She turned her head toward the door to greet Amara with an inviting smile.

"How'd your audition go?" she asked.

"I got it!" Amara chimed.

"I'm not surprised. Cameron never shuts up about how talented you are and I've seen your film. Why didn't you just pursue dance?"

Amara shrugged. "I love botany as much as I love dance. And now, I think this means I'm set for the semester! I'll be teaching Biology 101, conducting my research, and hosting a dance workshop or two."

Evelyn nodded approvingly. "Sounds like you'll be sufficiently busy. But don't forget to find some time for fun here and there. It may be a small town but there are still things to do. I'll have to take you to some of my favorite bars. And probably a few weekend day trips here and there. Oh! And we can also go to my favorite nail spa in town. There's also a decent thrift shop that surprisingly doesn't get flooded with students."

"Oh, you don't have to do all that. I'm just appreciative that you took me in! It worked out that Cam had a cousin here."

"Nonsense! And you're still paying rent. I'll be happy to take you along on my regular trips to the bar. Trust me, you'll want a few drinks, especially with teaching a freshman course."

"Deal." Amara giggled. "Oh! By the way, I think I met one of your colleagues at the coffee shop this morning. Mateo? He teaches history and also does seminars on international relations."

At Amara's words, Evelyn lifted up from her relaxed position on the couch. "You met Mateo Vazquez?" she asked.

"Yeah, him and an English professor named Liam approached me this morning at the coffee shop while I was reading up on-"

"Liam Taylor? You were approached by Mateo Vazquez *and* Liam Taylor?"

Amara furrowed her brows. It was a small town with a university at the center of it. Meeting two professors at a local cafe didn't seem like a particularly odd occurrence, even if approaching strangers wasn't the most common thing to do. Though, the images that popped into her mind when she made contact with Mateo *did* seem strange. "Uh, yeah... It was actually kind of awkward."

"I'm gonna be real with you. Masoncrest is a *small* university and those two are probably some of the most attractive men on campus. At least top ten. The students aren't the only ones who crush on them. And they just walked up to you and joined you for coffee, or something?"

*Most attractive? I could definitely see that,* Amara thought to herself.

"It wasn't even five minutes! And I kind of blabbered before I realized I needed to leave for the audition. But, Mateo did give me his card and offered to show me around," Amara said as she pulled his card from the front of her bag. She was reminded of the scene that popped up in her mind when their hands grazed and heat came over her.

Evelyn was about to say something else, but before she could get it out, Amara was on her way to her room.

"I'm going to take a shower," she said abruptly. "I'll make dinner tonight, okay?"

Evelyn gave her a curious look and nodded. "Sounds good..."


MATEO SAT AT HIS DESK, playing with his pen in his hand as he stared off into the abyss, replaying each moment from the coffee shop in his mind.

He and Liam finally met the woman fated to be theirs and she was perfect to him in almost every way. From her eyes to her hair to her skin to her voice. Mateo never realized that voices could be attractive, but the softness of it, the smooth nature of her tone, was naturally disarming. And then her smile, even though the one she gave him was small, it nearly melted him. When her hand grazed his and she saw one of his visions, he wanted to invite her home with him and Liam to make it come true.

"And you should have," Liam said, interrupting Mateo's thoughts. "We could be in bed with her right now. Although, she was thinking something about being late for an audition."

"Oh right. She dances..." Mateo tapped his finger to his chin. "I just wish my visions weren't so spotty and inconsistent... Fucking Petra," he grumbled.

"We're lucky we retained any abilities after that. My telepathy still gets foggy at times. Though, the most annoying part is this inability to control it." Liam shook his head and ran his fingers through his hair. "But on to more important affairs... When shall we have Amara? My desire for her only intensified when we finally met and I know it is the same for you."

"Yes, it did," Mateo agreed. "As for growing the bond, shouldn't you know better than me? Somehow, you and all your siblings ended up fated to mortals."

"All except Samuel."

"Ah yes. It explains why he turned out... the way he did. It is almost unheard of to *not* have a Fated."

"Same as it is for anyone of our lines to be fated to a human. We just turned out to be a... unique generation."

"There might be some karma sprinkled in there, as well."

Liam huffed. "Is this where you begin placing your family on some sort of moral pedestal? As if we haven't had this conversation thousands of times?"

"Calm down." Mateo held up both hands, cautioning Liam. "I don't want to argue with you. Just an observation... It could explain why your mother hasn't initiated further investigation despite her obvious frustrations with who you Taylor siblings were fated to, and that one of you were not."

"You and I both know my mother well enough to know that 'karma' wouldn't be enough to calm her. She just has more important duties to attend to."

"Yes, and we know those duties all too well."

"Could we return to the much more important topic at hand?" Liam suggested, frustration clear in his tone. "We've been waiting for this time to come for so long and now that it's here, I am realizing that I don't know exactly what to do. I understand that we must now commence the courting—er... the *dating*, but how do we begin? Simply approach her again and ask for a date? Together? Or separately?"

"It'd absolutely have to be separately. We don't want to startle the woman. We need to spend enough time with her to strengthen the connection until she's drawn to us in the way we're drawn to her. And then, we date her together."

"But she's in the Natural Sciences Department. How can we find an excuse to go there? Especially with James." Liam rolled his eyes at the name. "And he can't find out who she is to us."

"It's a small university and a small town. I'm sure we'll have some opportunities. And besides, I've seen in my visions that we'll be together eventually, so it's only a matter of time."

Liam huffed. "I still don't understand why we must move so slowly. If we are meant to be, then we should be able to simply explain everything to her, she will understand, and we can be together. We've waited long enough. And we don't have much time with her as it is, relative to our own lives."

"I recognize your frustrations, Liam, and I have the same. But, we cannot risk scaring her away. Never underestimate fear's ability to change the fates."

"I know that, but she... we... It has been over a century, Mateo."

"Which means we can wait a measly few months more, especially if that short wait means being with her."

Liam let out a deep, exacerbated sigh and his shoulders fell. "Fine."

CHAPTER

# THREE

Masoncrest University was a small college—the population only about four-thousand students, faculty, and staff. Amara's academic advisor through her Master's program was surprised that she chose such a small school to pursue her PhD. However, it made sense to her. Masoncrest had an outsized biodiversity based on the size of the town, to the point where it seemed almost unnatural. Also, the name of the town had come up several times throughout her studies within notes on rare flowers she was researching early in her academic career.

Despite the biodiversity of the town, Amara had noticed in her first few weeks there that the university didn't show it off. They kept the grounds of the campus simple. Lush grass gracing the courtyards and brick walkways connecting the various buildings at the school. There was a hiking trail not far off campus where Amara found most of her opportunities to collect samples of the rare plant life that Masoncrest was known for.

It was short walk from her car to the Natural Sciences

building where she would be teaching Biology 101 for the semester. The lecture had about fifty students, who'd then split off into smaller classes for labs throughout the week that would be taught by two teaching assistants.

Once the room filled up, Amara stood at the front of the lecture hall to introduce herself.

"Hello, everyone! I am Amara Jenkins and I'll be instructing you this semester. To tell you a little about myself, I'm originally from Georgia, but moved here to pursue my PhD in botany. I'm looking forward to teaching you all about one of my favorite subjects! I've emailed the syllabus and have a few hard copies here. Your TAs are Gerald Aleman and David Keen. They won't be here for the lectures, but you'll see them in your respective labs. I do have office hours once a week on Wednesdays from one to four. Any questions?"

"If you're from Georgia, why don't you have an accent?" one student asked.

"Uh..." Amara hesitated, thrown off by the question. "Not everyone in Georgia is blessed with an accent and I happened to be one of the less fortunate ones. Next question!"

"How old are you? You look like you're our age."

"I'm twenty-five," Amara replied. "Questions about the course, please..."

"Are you single?" another student asked.

"Do you date younger guys?" a voice chimed.

"Okay!" Amara clapped to stop the onslaught of invasive questions. "If there are no questions about the class, we'll get started with course materials."

· · ·

"...Now that I've gone over the syllabus, are there any questions?" Liam turned to his small class of twelve students for his course on Comparative Approaches to Literature.

"So, our first assignment is due this Friday already?" a student asked.

"Correct," Liam responded curtly. "Next?"

"Professor Taylor, are you going to give us opportunities for extra credit?" another student questioned. *Like bending me over your desk?* she thought to herself and Liam internally rolled his eyes. He told himself he'd stop reading his students' minds, but after his and Mateo's debacle with Petra, controlling his ability became difficult.

"Your options are listed in the syllabus. Next?"

"A point of clarification on this first assignment," William, the barista from the coffee shop, spoke up. "If we're to outline our proposed..."

As William went on, Liam was distracted when he noticed a familiar, yet unexpected face outside the classroom, and faintly heard the thoughts that accompanied.

Amara was standing in the hallway looking back and forth with a piece of paper in her hand. *How did I get lost? It's not even that large of a building.*

"Professor Taylor?" William said, trying to get Liam's attention again.

"I'll be right back, William..." replied a distracted Liam as he went straight to Amara in the hallway.

Amara's face was tense as she looked at the signs on the wall and began in one direction. Seeing the numbers on the classrooms going down rather than up, she grumbled and turned to go back to where she started once again. She was startled when she turned and bumped into a firm chest. "Shit! Sorry, I'm lost and-" When she looked up and realized it was Liam, her words got caught in her throat. *Well, another awkward moment for my day. Now, I run into one of the men that I had that weird fantasy about that most definitely turned me on.*

Liam swallowed and looked down at her with pure desire in his eyes. "Amara, right?"

Amara cleared her throat as she nodded and averted her gaze. "Yes. And... Um Liam, it was?"

"Great memory. You said you are lost?"

"Oh yeah... I'm looking for room three-forty-two. I'm supposed to meet with Dr. Finch in Fine Arts."

"Really? I thought you were studying botany?"

"I am, but I'm also going to teach a dance workshop or two this semester. So, I'm going to meet with her about that."

"I see. Well... getting to that room can be a bit confusing. Allow me to walk you there."

*Fuck yes!* Amara thought, but she then noticed behind him a classroom door open with students looking at him impatiently.

"Oh! Are you in the middle of class? I don't want to interrupt. You can just point me in the right-"

"It's no trouble," Liam interrupted with a big smile. "It's the first day and they only have fifteen minutes left, anyway." Before Amara could object, he turned back to the class and dismissed them. "I'll see you all tomorrow! Don't forget the reading." Without asking further questions, the confused students hesitantly began packing their things and Liam turned his attention back to Amara.

She shook her head. "You didn't have to-"

"Like I said, it's no trouble," he chimed. "Besides, I was just taking some questions about the syllabus that they could always email."

"Oh, okay..." Amara still found it odd that this stranger would dismiss his class just to help her find an office. At the same time, there was something about Liam's aura that made her happy to be around him. "Did they at least stay on topic? My students were only asking personal questions."

"You're teaching as well? And what sorts of questions?"

"Yeah, just Biology 101 as part of my requirements. And the questions..." Amara chuckled. "They started by asking why I don't have an accent if I'm from Georgia and then I had to stop them when it got to a question about whether I date younger guys." She shook her head amused. "Those freshmen are going to be a handful. I can already tell."

"Well..." Liam cleared his throat. "Do you?"

"Do I what?" Amara raised a confused brow.

"...Date younger guys?" he asked.

"Oh, so I see the personal questions don't stop at the students," she teased. "No, I think I'd prefer older men. I mean, I don't have a lot of experience dating general. So, I probably can't definitively say... Shit. I'm doing that over-sharing thing I did in the coffee shop again." She laughed awkwardly.

"No, it's fine. I like it when you talk." Liam assured

"That's a relief." Amara exhaled and put her hand to her chest. She looked around and realized how deserted the hallway they were walking down was. "Oh wow, you weren't kidding about these halls. This is so strange." *People definitely have sex back here. There's no way people don't have sex back here. I wonder if Liam ever... Stop, Amara! What is wrong with you? Why are you having dirty thoughts about this man and the other one? You've never even enjoyed sex.*

"Wait, are you serious?" Liam blurted before catching himself.

"What?" Amara tilted her head as her brows knitted.

"Er- I mean. The building is fairly new and while Masoncrest is a small school, it's slowly expanding, so we're hoping to fill these rooms soon."

"I see..." Amara nodded thoughtfully. She looked at the numbers on the doors and realized that they were in the three tens. "Are you sure this is the right way?"

"Oh, you know what?" Liam feigned surprise. "This is the wrong hall. I think I know where I made the mistake. Let's go back to the last intersection and take the other one."

Amara followed Liam back down the deserted hallway. *I kind of wish he got us lost in this secluded hallway on purpose, but there's no way someone I met just a few days ago would be interested in me like that. What am I even thinking? Why do I want him to like me?*

Liam stopped in his tracks when he heard Amara's thoughts to give her a tense look, but his face immediately softened when he met her brown eyes. He stared at her, taking in her image. He allowed his eyes to shamelessly wander, his gaze going from her eyes, to her lips, to her form. He couldn't understand why she didn't think he could want her.

As Liam's eyes scanned over her, Amara was frozen in the moment. She felt like it should've been awkward—the two of them standing in the hall while he simply stared at her, but the interaction brought a heat over her that felt almost uncontrollable. She noticed the way Liam's Adam's apple bobbed when he swallowed as he stared at her lips. *He looks like he wants to kiss me? Does he want to kiss me? But we don't know each other! There's no way! But... I want it. Geez! What is wrong with me?*

Amara's thoughts met an abrupt halt when Liam

smashed his lips against hers. He wrapped his arm around her waist as he walked her back into a door before opening it and leading her into one of the unused rooms without breaking the kiss.

Amara instinctively wrapped her arms around Liam's neck as if were the most natural thing to do and when his tongue demanded entry, she let it in. Her breathing grew heavy as their lips moved against each other until Liam's mouth made its way down to her neck. Again, in a move that felt instinctive, Amara leaned her head back to allow Liam better access and his mouth grew more eager as one of his hands trailed down to grip her backside.

*I'm going to take you as many times as you want.* His voice echoed in her head, breaking Amara out of her trance.

"Wait. Stop!" She pushed him away and Liam stepped back. "What did you say?

"I didn't say anything, Amara. My mouth was busy with-"

"Wait! What just happened?"

"We were kissing..." He said casually.

"But we're strangers. I'm sor— no wait, you kissed me first, I don't-" Amara couldn't seem to get out any intelligible speech.

"You didn't want it?"

"Yes! I mean... No? I mean... it was nice. I liked it. But what was-"

"Calm down, Amara," Liam soothed. "We kissed, we both seemed to be enjoying it, but then you stopped. That's all. Do you want to continue?"

"Oh, um..." Amara bit her lip nervously. *I want to, but should I? I don't know anything about him beyond his name and occupation. But his lips felt so damn good. Like they belong with mine. But no— I shouldn't, right?* "No, I don't think we should..." she looked down.

Liam's jaw tensed with frustration knowing that she *did* want to kiss him, but for some strange reason, she told him she didn't. He respected her wishes and pulled her out of the secluded room to lead her to Dr. Finch's office.

"Dr. Finch is just down there and to the left," he directed when they reached the fine arts department's single hallway.

"Thanks..." Amara responded, avoiding eye contact with him and looking down the path she'd be set to follow.

"It's nothing to be ashamed of, Amara," he whispered. "I enjoyed it."

She finally looked at him again and his expression was one of pure confidence, which upset her. *I see. So this is something he just does. Look how comfortable he is, like it's just another Monday of kissing a random woman in a secluded hallway. He must do this all the time. He had a route and everything.*

Realizing how his actions could've caused Amara to have those thoughts, Liam attempted to recover. "I've never done something like that before," he said softly while rubbing the back of his neck. "So, would you like to go for coff-"

"I'm good," Amara interrupted before turning away and walking toward Dr. Finch's office. *I can't believe I got tricked by a player like that. I wonder how many women he's pulled that with.*

Liam grunted in frustration watching Amara walk away and muttered to himself, "Mateo isn't going to like this."

. . .

IN HIS OFFICE, awaiting Liam who said he needed to speak, Mateo leaned back in his chair with his eyes closed, reliving one of his favorite visions.

*Amara sat on the edge of Mateo's desk, looking down at him anxiously. He licked his lips as he opened her legs to reveal her core. He looked up at her, maintaining eye contact as he leaned in to have a taste of what he'd been craving for so long until Amara stopped him when she covered herself with her hand. "Wait," she breathed.*

*Mateo's brows tensed with concern. "Do you want me to stop?"*

*"No," Amara squeaked. "It's just that I've never... I mean no one has ever..." She took a deep breath. "I've never had someone go down on me before..." she finally got out. "I mean, I'm not a virgin or anything, it's just that I don't have a lot of experience..." She averted her gaze and swallowed.*

*Mateo smiled and kissed the inside of her thigh. "Then allow me to be the first." He took the hand she was covering herself with and put it on the back of his head. "You're in control here, Amara," he said before his tongue finally reached her lower lips.*

"Reliving your visions again, Mateo?" Liam interrupted from the doorway of his office. "All I hear is her name echoing in your mind."

Mateo cleared his throat and straightened up in his seat. "When did you get in here?" he grumbled.

"Just a few seconds ago. Anyway, speaking of our Fated... I may have upset her..."

Mateo put his hands on the desk and rose to his feet. "What do you mean you upset her?"

"I was helping her to the Fine Arts Department when I may have... kissed her."

"*May have?* Do you not remember what Lillian told us? We need to take things slow."

"Yes, but she wanted to kiss me. And I still don't agree with this concept of 'taking things slow' when she's destined to be ours. Besides, she wanted to kiss me and she enjoyed doing so."

"Did she use her words? Or were you reading her thoughts?"

"Well... She didn't exactly use her words at first. But, she kissed me back and then I think she may have heard my thoughts because she abruptly pushed me away and asked if I said something despite my mouth already being occupied and us being in an empty room. Anyway, she seems to assume I don't want her, so I assured her that I enjoyed the moment we shared and she seemed to take it the wrong way... "

"Wrong way, how?" asked an agitated Mateo.

"With her it felt so natural... And she interpreted my boldness as a sign that I kiss women in secluded areas often."

Mateo groaned and shook his head. "This is why we should move slow— Wait. You said she was looking for the Fine Arts Department?"

"Yes, she will be teaching a few dance workshops this semester."

"Was she meeting with Sarah Finch?"

"Yes."

His annoyed demeanor shifting, a smile came to Mateo's face. "That's perfect..."

When Liam realized what was on Mateo's mind, his face brightened too. "Excellent!"

# FOUR

A busy first week of the semester for Amara, she finally met with her PhD advisor for their first in-person meeting on Friday. Dr. James Minnow. They'd spoken over the phone several times prior to Amara coming to Masoncrest, but she'd never seen him in person.

He was much older than Amara—appearing to be somewhere in his early- to mid-fifties. His salt-and-pepper hair was cut in a short taper. His thick beard covered much of his facial features, though he had it neatly trimmed. His brown eyes scanned over the pages in front of him with Amara's latest plan for her studies. She couldn't decipher his expression while he read the materials, and they hadn't exchanged much beyond greetings when she first entered is office and handed him the papers.

Finally, he nodded in what looked to be a hesitant approval. "I see... So you think that the palisyfum lotus *does* exist and you can find it somewhere around here?"

Amara shook her head. "Not exactly. As you know, my research is going to focus on cross-breeding in plants. I know the palisyfum lotus is something that tends to come up in myths or old wives tales. However, based on how it is used in the stories, I think it might actually be the result of cross-breeding a number of medicinal herbs. Masoncrest has an incredible amount of biodiversity, and I imagine the rarer herbs that would end up creating the lotus could be found here."

Dr. Minnow pursed his lips. "I could see that, but it also sounds like something that'd take more than a lifetime to figure out. Even if you have hypothesized that the palisyfum lotus comes from a mix of medicinal herbs, you'd need to identify those herbs and then figure out the proper order and approach to cross-breeding them in order to affirm or reject your theory."

"Then I'll make sure my research is well-documented so the next generation can pick up from where I left off." Amara responded confidently. She'd been obsessed with the flower of legend since her grandmother began telling her stories about it. Despite it being the size of the average hand, the flower was supposedly made up of five-thousand tiny petals and seemed to have nearly magical properties based on the stories Amara heard growing up.

"Fair enough. Well, just keep me apprised on your research and we'll maintain these check-ins each Wednesday either before or after your own office hours. How has your first week been so far?"

"It's been fine. I'm still getting used to being in a new town on the other side of the country and at times it can feel a bit like culture shock, honestly."

"I'm sure you'll adapt soon enough. Are you living alone or do you have roommates?"

"I'm living with Evelyn Knight. She teaches history on campus."

"Oh Evelyn!" James' otherwise professional demeanor

perked up at the sound of her name. "She's great. We're in different departments but we have collaborated a handful of times. You know, biology and history go really well together, especially when we get into plant life. There's so much story to tell there."

"Yeah…" Amara's lips turned to a small smile. She was worried that Dr. Minnow would be a stiff from the way their meeting started. However, his excitement after hearing Evelyn's name was enough to improve her initial impression of him. "Evelyn is great. I'm glad we're living together."

James' informal posture continued. "And everything else is well? No one giving you a hard time or making you uncomfortable?"

"No. Everyone I've met seems nice."

"Well, if you do encounter anything… *strange*, while you're here just let me know. As your advisor, I want to make sure you're comfortable here."

"Right… Thanks, Dr. Minnow."

"Please, call me James."

Just then, Amara's phone began ringing. Embarrassed, she gave James an apologetic smile. "Sorry, I don't normally get calls at this time." She looked down at the screen and saw it was Dr. Finch calling.

"It's alright," he assured. "We are finished here."

Amara gave him a single nod and answered the call while she gathered her papers and packed her backpack.

"Hello, Dr. Finch? Is everything okay?"

"Amara! Yes, things are great! Would you be able to come to my office? There's something I'd like to speak with you about."

"Is this something we could cover over the phone?"

"I'd like to do this in person."

*That doesn't help my nerves,* Amara thought to herself. "Sure... I've just finished my meeting with Dr. Minnow. I could come by now."

"That's perfect!"

After leaving the Life Sciences building, Amara walked across campus to meet with Dr. Finch. On her way there, she went through several potential scenarios of what might unfold. Did Dr. Finch want to rescind the offer to teach workshops? Did she want to discuss changing what they had planned? Did she need Amara to teach more?

By the time Amara reached Dr. Finch's office, she'd overthought herself into pure nerves and her heart was thumping in her ears as she knocked on the door.

When Dr. Finch answered with a big smile on her face, some of Amara's anxiousness calmed, though she was still eager to hear what she wanted to talk about.

"Thanks so much for coming by! I know I was vague on the phone, but I really wanted to share this news in person!" Dr. Finch said cheerfully.

"Right, right... So, what's the news?"

"I'd like to hire you to teach a contemporary dance course this semester!"

"Oh!" Amara's eyes widened in surprise. "As in a full course? But the semester's already started. And I haven't taught a college dance course before. I haven't be able to plan what one would look like. What would I cover? And then there are my studies..."

"Oh, please! We're just a day in and one of the benefits of Masoncrest being such a small school is that we can easily add classes. As for planning the course, I can help you with that. We already have a syllabus we can use as a template and you'd just need to drop in the topics you want to cover. I'll be here to provide feedback and help you finalize it all."

"Well, I'd love to, honestly! I mean, dance has been such a big part of my life and I enjoy sharing it with people when I can. At the same time, I *am* already teaching a biology class and have my research."

"Don't worry! It won't be too demanding, I promise! Just two classes each week at sixty-five minutes per class. We'll have you choreograph a piece for the showcase, but the rest is the responsibility of the students and you'll be around to provide guidance. I'll do whatever I can to keep work outside of class at a minimum for you." Dr. Finch put her hands together as if begging. "Please! You will be compensated!"

Amara smiled, unable to resist the opportunity to do two of the things she loved while getting paid. "Okay, Sarah. I'll do it."

"Great! I'll email you some materials so you're prepared to teach starting two weeks from now! Right after I called you, it reminded me to check with Dr. Minnow, so I called him while you were on the way here. He seemed hesitant, but noted that you might have availability on Tuesday and Thursday afternoons? Would you say that's accurate?"

"Oh, uh... I guess that's fine?"

"Yes!" Dr. Finch yelped triumphantly. "Okay, I'll make sure everything is set for you in time. Thank you. Thank you. Thank you. Thank you! Have a great weekend!"

"Right... Thanks..." Amara replied before walking out the door.

A mix of confused and excited, she walked downstairs to the History Department to look for Evelyn. They had planned to get drinks together that day.

"Amara?" a familiar voice echoed down the hall.

She turned to see Mateo walking in her direction with a big smile. As he got closer, she noticed a glimmer in his honey-colored eyes and a single dimple on the right side of his face.

"Hi," she responded as her lips almost involuntary turned to a smile. She couldn't seem to form words beyond that single greeting when he finally reached her.

"Remember me?" Mateo pointed to himself. "From the coffee shop?"

"Yes, yes," Amara responded nervously, remembering the image she'd see when their hands touched before. "Mateo?"

His heart fluttered at the way his name rolled off her tongue. "What brings you to my neck of the woods?"

"Well, I'm looking for Evelyn Knight. We're supposed to go out for drinks to celebrate the end of the first week. It's been a long one."

"Amara!" Evelyn chimed, walking down the hall with three other people behind her. "It worked out that Dr. Finch wanted to see you and we could all meet here! A few of my other colleagues in the History Department will come too." When Evelyn noticed Mateo, she turned to acknowledge him. "Oh... Hi, Mateo! You just finished your last class of the day too, right?"

Mateo's eyes lingered on Amara before he finally turned to answer Evelyn. "Yes, I did. Where is it you all are going?"

"We're heading to Cade's bar so we can hopefully avoid running into any students. I thought about inviting you, but I know you don't drink."

"I'd love to join," Mateo said abruptly.

Evelyn tilted her head as she examined his face. "Even though you don't drink?"

"I don't, but I imagine you'd like a designated driver? I drive an SUV, so-"

"Sweet!" Eric Bledsoe, one of the History faculty, blurted. "Then I don't have to DD anymore. Lead the way, Mateo!"

Mateo waved a cautioning hand at Eric. "Actually, I should've been clearer. It's a compact SUV, so while roomier than a sedan, I doubt I could fit everyone. Also, if I recall, Evelyn and I are on the same side of Masoncrest while you, Alyssa and Daniel are on the other side, right?" Mateo then turned to Amara. "What about you, Amara? Which side of this small town are you on?"

Amara smiled up at Mateo, and it sent a fluttering straight to his chest. "I live with Evelyn."

"Excellent, so perhaps you and Evelyn ride with me and Eric can drive the others?"

"That sounds like a great plan to me!" Evelyn assured.

Amara, Mateo, Evelyn, and the three other professors from the History Department sat around a table at Cade's Bar a few rounds in, laughing at a joke Evelyn just told. Mateo was across from Amara, trying his best not to stare, but taking in as much as he could. He loved the way she slightly threw her head back and closed her eyes when she laughed and how animated she'd become when telling a story and would speak with her hands. Mateo's apparitions were rare and he'd only seen just a few snippets of what would be their future moments together, but he was already completely enamored.

Evelyn noticed the way Mateo kept stealing looks at Amara and remembered Amara's story about him and Liam approaching her at the coffee shop.

"Hey Mateo," Evelyn caught him just as he was taking another glance. "Amara is fluent in Spanish."

Mateo's eyes lit up and he turned his attention fully to Amara. "Really?"

"Yes, but I studied in Spain, so you'd have to excuse my lisp." Amara let out a shy laugh.

"En que parte?" Mateo asked, trying to hide his excitement that his Fated spoke his native tongue. *Could she be any more perfect?* he thought to himself.

A wide smile came to Amara's face when she recognized his accent. "Andalucia," she responded. "Vivía en Sevilla."

"En serio?" Mateo gawked. "Soy de Andalucia... de Granada."

Amara's face brightened even more. Continuing in Spanish, she explained how much she admired Granada for its history and explained that she'd visited the city multiple times during her time in Spain.

Mateo leaned into the table toward Amara as he listened to her go on about how much she loved is homeland, which gave him more assurance that she and him were meant to be connected to each other. As she continued to speak his mother tongue, Mateo was so enthralled by the conversation, that he hadn't noticed their colleagues looking at the pair until Amara stopped talking.

"Oh..." she said with a sigh before switching back to English and speaking to Mateo in a whisper. "They might feel left out."

The words broke him out of their moment and he cleared his throat, his expression turning from the one of excitement to neutral in an effort to hide his frustration that the others disrupted their moment. "Right. Well, I would love to talk to you more about my hometown. Maybe we could get coffee sometime?"

"Yeah, I would like that." Amara pulled out her phone and the two of them exchanged numbers.

Evelyn, who had tried and failed to distract their colleagues while Amara and Mateo spoke, had a satisfied smirk on her face looking between the two of them as they exchanged phone numbers. She'd known Mateo since she first joined the faculty three years ago and never once did he seem to show interest in anyone until she saw him with Amara tonight.

"I've never seen Mateo talk so much outside of work-related things," Eric said bluntly before his attention was then on Amara. "So Amara... How and why did you end up in our small town at our small university?"

Amara tore her eyes away from Mateo to turn her attention back to the group. "Well, since I'm pursuing botany, I wanted to find a place with plenty of biodiversity and when I heard about a small town in Washington with an unusual amount of it, I thought why not!"

"You speak Spanish. Why not somewhere like Costa Rica or Ecuador with rich wildlife and plant life?"

"You're right... The thing is, I was also drawn to this place for some reason. I can't really explain it, but I needed to come here. And the fact that my best friend just so happened to have a cousin here who had an extra room." Amara winked at Evelyn. "It all kind of worked out. And I'm happy to be here."

"Fair enough... Do you have a specific area of study within botany that you plan to specialize in?"

"Yeah, it's a flower called the palisyfum lotus. It's often mentioned in myths or old wives tales, but I think..."

Rather than his subtleness in stealing looks at Amara, Mateo's gaze was intent on her as she shared her theory about the palisyfum, and his heart sank at how wrong she was about it. *What business could she have studying that? Does she really plan to bet it all on the palisyfum?* He sighed. *When she learns our truth, I'll have to explain to her the real story behind palisyfum. And she'll see her time was wasted.* He shook his head.

"What?" Amara asked.

"Oh hm?" Mateo was so caught up in his thoughts, he didn't register the fact he was directly in front of her, staring at her while shaking his head. "Nothing... Sorry, I just drifted off a bit."

"Okay." Amara looked at him awkwardly before turning her attention back to the group and continuing to socialize.

The evening went on for a few more hours, though Amara and Mateo didn't speak much more one-on-one as the group spoke more generally about the new semester, students, and the non-existent happenings in Masoncrest.


Amara laughed hysterically as she watched Mateo help a passed out Evelyn out of the car. "I had no idea she'd get drunk like this. It's no better than the students!"

"No need to apologize," he assured as he picked up Evelyn like it was nothing. "This is exactly what a designated driver is supposed to do."

"You're right. I really appreciate it." Amara fumbled with her keys until she picked the one for the front door. "We can take her to her room and I'll just leave the door open so I can listen out for her."

Mateo followed Amara into the house and kicked off his shoes at the door while still holding Evelyn. Amara gave him a nod of approval and without saying anything, she led him up the stairs.

Mateo tried his best not to stare at her behind, but he couldn't help himself with the way her hips naturally swayed with each step she took, only triggering more memories of his sporadic visions.

Amara cleared her throat when she turned around and caught Mateo staring. Just like with Liam, rather than taking offense to his lust-filled gaze, Amara felt a warmness come over her at the sight of his heated stare.

"This is Evelyn's room." She gestured to the bed and Mateo gently put Evelyn down before Amara covered her with a blanket.

The two of them then went back downstairs to the kitchen. Normally, she would've walked him straight to the door to leave, but something about him had a hold on her that she didn't quite understand. She didn't want him to leave.

"Can I get you some water or something?" Amara asked hesitantly. "Er, I mean, I guess you probably want to get home."

"Water would be nice," Mateo replied with a warm smile. He watched her attentively as she reached up into the cabinet for two glasses, the way her shirt rode up to show her lower back, and then when she bent over into the fridge to take out the water pitcher, he got another brief look at her backside.

*Alone. With my Fated. In her home. And I can't act on anything,* he thought to himself. *Damn these mortals' arbitrary rules about courting. If she was of our world, we'd be in her room and she'd be clawing at my back while screaming my name right now.*

Amara interrupted his thoughts when she sat the water on the the counter in front of him. He finally tore his eyes away from her to look at the cup and bring it to his lips.

The two of them stood there in awkward silence for a few moments, drinking their waters. Amara felt the urge to speak to him, to get to know him, but she wasn't sure what exactly to say.

"So, Amara..." Mateo savored the feeling of her name coming off his lips. "You've chosen to study the palisyfum lotus?"

"Yes. Have you heard about it?"

"Only in fairy tales."

"Well, I have this theory that it's real and is likely the product of a very complicated crossbreeding process that was kind of a fluke the first time around when the flower was produced. My dream is to discover that process, replicate it, and breed the flower. Could you imagine having something with all those healing properties available to those who need it most? I know it sounds kind of like a pipe dream and maybe it won't happen in my lifetime, but hey, maybe the next generation or the one after that can figure it out. I mean... If climate change doesn't kill us all by then..." Amara trailed off when she caught herself beginning to ramble. "Sorry... I can get ahead of myself sometimes. And I guess you already heard this whole spiel at the bar."

"No, no... It's no trouble. I like listening to you speak."

Amara felt a smile coming to her face and her heart start to flutter. "Oh! All my talking and I didn't realize your glass was empty. Did you want more water? Or were you done?"

"Another cup would be lovely," he replied, handing her the glass. They hadn't touched at all that night, as Mateo was concerned she'd see another vision of his and they'd either end up making it come true, or she'd see one of his darker premonitions and be scared away. However, as he gave Amara his glass, their hands grazed, just as they had at the coffeeshop, and Mateo's face went blank.

*Amara lay on the couch unconscious in Mateo and*

*Liam's living room as an unwelcome visitor stood there staring down at her with pure greed in his eyes.*
*"She's a once in a millennium opportunity, brother. And you mean to tell me she's your Fated?" He released an entertained laugh and clapped his hands. "All this time, I thought you were the unlucky one. Maybe I didn't have a Fated at all, but you and the rest of our siblings were stuck being fated to mortals who'd be nothing but a blip compared to the length of your lives. However, it looks like I was wrong..."*
*The man leaned over and ran his knuckles over her cheek and Mateo's hand turned to a tight fist as his nostrils flared. "Her aura feels pure... Have the two of you not been performing well enough to corrupt her?"*
*He sneered. "Guess I'll have to be the one who-"*
*Suddenly, a bright light filled the room, blinding them.*

"Hey," Amara called, waving her hand in Mateo's face. "Are you okay?"

Mateo blinked several times and appeared unsettled. "I'm fine. Did you see...?"

"See what?" This time when their hands grazed, Amara didn't see anything.

"Oh," Mateo cleared his throat as he quickly stood up straight. "You know, I just realized I have a lot of work I need to get done tonight." He began making his way toward the door.

"Okay..." Confusion painted Amara's face as she followed him to the door to lock it behind him. "I guess I'll see you around."

"Sunday?" he quickly suggested, turning to look at her, but keeping enough distance as not to mistakenly touch her. "For that coffee?"

"Uh…" She couldn't decipher what had just happened, but she still wanted to see more of Mateo. "Sure. I think that could work."

"Great!" he beamed. "We'll discuss a time over the phone! I'll see you then, Amara," he said as he rushed to his car. He turned around and paused to look at the door as she closed it before getting into the car and calling Liam.

"Liam Taylor speaking," he answered.

"Do you want to tell me why exactly your brother would have an interest in our Fated?" Mateo asked through clenched teeth.

"What do you mean?"

"Just tell Lillian to expedite our request for a meeting. It's an emergency."

"Do you want to tell me what this so-called emergency might be that made you two throw me off schedule to come to this boring town?" Lillian chided as she entered Mateo and Liam's home.

"We requested your presence more than two weeks ago when we first came into contact with our Fated," Mateo complained. "What could possibly have you so busy?"

Lillian sighed as she rolled her eyes. "I know that coming from the Vazquez and Taylor families might make you think you should get special treatment all the time, but that's not the case with me. I have others I'm tasked with guiding as well..." she snapped her fingers and a table with three seats and cups of tea appeared in the large foyer. "So, what is it?" She asked as she settled into her seat and brought a cup of tea to her mouth. Mateo and Liam joined her at the table.

"Mateo had a vision..." Liam ran his fingers through his hair and took a deep breath. "It showed Samuel here and he wanted Amara."

Lillian's head jerked back at his words. "What? Why?"

"That's why we called you here," Mateo answered. "My visions are shit, so I only saw him in our living room. He said that Amara is 'a once in a millennium opportunity' and looked like he was about to take her away before my vision ended."

"That's strange. She's simply mortal. One-hundred percent human. The only thing abnormal about her is that she's a non-magical being who is fated to a Vazquez and a Taylor. But, that's not exactly impossible, given that all the Taylors except Samuel are fated to humans."

"There's something else," Liam added. "There seems to be a reaction when we make contact with her..." He looked to Mateo.

"The first time we touched, she saw one of my visions. And the second time, she triggered the vision I had about Samuel."

"And she was able to hear my thoughts, I believe, when we kissed."

Lillian gawked. "You kissed her? I told you to take it slow. If you move too fast, you could ruin it. The people of her world have no concept of a Fated and she could see it as some sort of forced arrangement. Not to mention the fact that she's fated to two men."

"Forced?" Liam asked with a hint of agitation. "It's nothing like that. Our souls are destined to become one and we're naturally drawn to her as she is to us. It's one of the purest and most beautiful aspects of our world. And who cares if she's with two men? We can give her everything she wants and more—two-fold."

"Must you Taylors be so dramatic, Liam? You're all such romantics... Except the heartless and Fated-less Samuel, for obvious reasons... Anyway, I am concerned about this reaction you seem to be having with her. Considering she's a mortal, it doesn't make sense for her to trigger or experience your abilities." She held her finger to her chin as she pondered. "Is there any chance you could get me a sample of her blood? I didn't sense anything when I visited her in her sleep. Perhaps she has something dormant."

"Mateo has a date with her tomorrow," Liam grumbled. "So perhaps he could help you."

"Oh?" Lillian raised an impressed brow. "See, Liam. Mateo asked her on a date, as a normal mortal would've done."

Liam rolled his eyes and crossed his arms. "I'll have my chance since she'll be just down the hall twice a week."

"I thought you two said she'd be in a completely different department from you?"

"Well..." Mateo rubbed the back of his neck. "The head of the Fine Arts Department seemed to really love her dancing and decided to hire her as an instructor."

"Sarah Finch hired a brand new teacher with no experience after the semester already started?" Lillian questioned, sarcasm clear in her tone. "Now, do you want to tell me the truth? What did you do?"

"Nothing too extreme... She already hired her to teach a few workshops, so it's not like we had to expend much energy on changing Sarah's mind to have her teach a course."

Lillian groaned. "You know after what happened with Petra, you're very limited. Why expend any energy at all?"

"She's worth it," Mateo added.

"Helpless..." Lillian shook her head at the two men before she snapped her fingers and two vials appeared. "Take those," she said as she rose from the table. "They should help repress those reactions that seem to be happening when you make contact with her."

Mateo and Liam quickly downed the vials.

"That tastes fucking disgusting," Liam griped. "And it burns like hell. Why must all potions be so unpleasant?"

Lillian shrugged. "Such is life for a pair of warlocks."

"I'm serious, Amara." Evelyn had a bright smile as she joined her on the couch to watch a movie. "I've never seen Mateo show interest in anyone until I saw the way he looked at you last night. I half expected to wake up to him here in the kitchen making you breakfast with nothing but a towel on!"

An amused smile came to Amara's face. "That is very... specific."

"What? He seems like the type of guy who cooks breakfast," she said before taking a bite of her sandwich. "Anyway..." Now talking with her mouth full. "When are you two getting that coffee?"

Amara hesitated before answering. "Well uh... We're actually meeting tomorrow."

"Tomorrow?" Evelyn nearly choked before swallowing the food in her mouth. "But you just exchanged numbers yesterday!"

"Oh..." Amara bit her lip. "Should I have not agreed? I don't have much experience with this stuff, to be honest. I mean, I did some dating back home, but no one's ever approached me the way he did..."

"Really?"

"Yeah, growing up with my grandma, she kind of kept me sheltered. I didn't really start interacting with many people until college," Amara smiled to herself. "That's when I met Cam and he became my first real friend... And then I went on some 'dates', if you can even call them that, here and there."

"I see, I see... Wait! Have you ever had sex? I'm sorry! I didn't even think about that when I was making those suggestions about Mateo. Are you... saving yourself or something?"

"Oh geez," Amara chuckled. "I have had sex before... Not much, but I tried it a few times and just didn't really enjoy it."

"Damn, I'm sorry..."

"Eh... It's whatever. I'll just spend the rest of my life being chaste or some day the right man might come along and maybe I'll enjoy it."

"Like Mateo...?" Evelyn said with a raised brow.

"Alright!" Amara clapped her hands together to signal an end to the conversation. "So, let's turn on this movie..."

CHAPTER

# SEVEN

Mateo's heart fluttered when he saw Amara walk into the cafe. She wore a burgundy corduroy skirt with a form-fitting long-sleeve black shirt that was tucked in. Its scoop neck showed off her collarbones and although it was one of the most innocuous sections of skin she could've been showing, the display turned his thoughts sinful as he was reminded of a vision of he and Liam covering the area with marks.

Amara entered the cafe a ball of nerves, trying to keep a cool demeanor. She looked around until Mateo's waving caught her eye. She nodded to indicate that she saw him and then gestured to the register to signal that she was going to go order. He shook his head and again waved her over to join him.

When Amara reached the table, Mateo stood to greet her with a kiss on each cheek. He felt the warmness of her face and figured she was probably blushing.

"Hi Mateo." She gave him a small smile. "I was just going to order something. I'll be right back."

"I already ordered," he said quickly. "Though, I'll admit

it was a bit of a hunch, so feel free to order something else if I got it wrong... My tab of course."

"Oh," Amara cleared her throat and sat across from him. "What did you get?"

"Order fifty-nine!" the barista announced.

"I guess you're about to find out." Mateo went to the counter to retrieve their order and returned to the table with two cappuccinos.

"Your hunch was right," Amara chimed. "This is exactly what I would've ordered. Are you a psychic or something?"

Mateo let out a chuckle at the irony. "I just might be," he said with a wink.

Amara felt butterflies in her stomach as she sat across from him. Without the distraction of other people like at the bar, she was able to focus on him without making it weird. Mateo's honey brown eyes had a glimmer to them and when his full lips turned to a smile, he had a small dimple on the right that was made even more subtle by the perfectly shaped stubble on his face.

"So, Amara... I'll have to admit. I may have brought you here under false pretenses," he confessed. "To be upfront with you now, I'd like to get to know you, Amara. Though, I am always happy to talk to you about my homeland if that will keep me in your company."

"Oh..." Amara felt her cheeks warm up even more. She took a sip of her drink to stop the large grin that she knew was coming. "What would you like to know?"

"Everything..." He continued his candidness. "Start from the beginning..."

"The beginning? Hm, let's see..." Amara tapped her finger to her chin and looked up thoughtfully before she spoke. "Well, I don't remember much about my childhood at all, honestly, other than being raised by my grandma on my dad's side who taught me everything she knew about herbal medicine up until she died when I was eighteen... But her lessons and the stories she told me about the palisyfum lotus put me on the path I'm on now."

"And your parents?"

"I never knew them and my grandma wouldn't talk about them. She said they died when I was very young and it always seemed like a sore topic, so at a certain point, I stopped asking questions. And I never met my mom's side. It used to be something that bothered me, especially when my grandma first died and I felt completely alone... She was all I had. But I went off to college and between meeting people and all the transitional things that happened, I forgot about those feelings of loneliness..." Amara paused, breaking eye contact with Mateo and looking down at the table. He could feel a somberness emitting from her. Sensing her unease, Mateo reached out hold her hands. *I'll make sure she never feels alone again*, he thought to himself. He was relieved that the potion worked—no visions triggered from touching Amara.

Just a few moments passed and Amara's posture eased. "Anyway, I didn't mean to get all gloomy. And I definitely overshared," she let out a small, nervous laugh. "What about you? Where did Mateo Vazquez begin?"

"There's no such thing as oversharing with me," he assured. "Well, as you already know, I'm from Granada and I spent a decent portion of my life there. Though, I also spent over a decade in Angola, where my mother is from. I have two other siblings and I'm the middle child. And when it comes to my parents, I don't get along so well with my father and my mother died when I was young." He looked down when he felt Amara gently squeeze his hand. They hadn't let go yet from when he reached out for her before.

"Oh!" Amara cleared her throat and pulled her hands away. "Sorry, I didn't realize what I was doing."

Mateo shook his head. "It was nice." He gave her a warm smile. "So, if I recall correctly, you dance?"

Amara nodded. "I started when I was young. I can't exactly remember how old, but I'd be in my grandma's backyard using the glass doors as makeshift mirrors and simply moving my body with the music... I absolutely fell in love with how liberating it felt and the fact that I'd have complete control over what I wanted to do. That freedom is what's so beautiful about the arts in my opinion... What about you? Any hobbies?"

Mateo couldn't get rid of the smile on his face, taking note of how attuned he already felt with Amara. "I play the guitar. Ever since I was a young boy. My mother actually taught me. She used to play the guitar for me and sing lullabies. To this day, I still play the songs that were passed down from her side of the family. But I've also made some of my own and I completely understand what you mean about the creative freedom. No pressure to fit into a certain mold or follow specific rules. You get to create what you want."

"Exactly!" Amara's eyes widened as she spoke eagerly. "I'd love to hear you play some day. Maybe we could share with each other sometime. I can show you some of my choreography and you could show me some of your songs?"

Mateo couldn't help the wide, toothy smile that grew on his face as he listened to Amara. "I would absolutely enjoy that."

The pair went on for another few hours talking about any and everything. She shared stories about her life—mostly after her grandmother's death when she went off to college and met her best friend Cameron. Mateo talked about his transition to life in the U.S., coding a lot of the explanations as the *real* transition was living life as if he were a mortal. His focus on their conversation was broken when he heard the grumbling of her stomach.

"Are you hungry?" he asked.

"Was my stomach that loud?"

Mateo chuckled. "I just pay attention. I know this pretty good diner that we could walk to from here if you'd like to get something to eat."

"Yeah, I'd enjoy that," she responded.

In his excitement, Mateo quickly left a tip on the table and led them out of the cafe to begin their path down the street to the diner.

As they walked side-by-side, Mateo was constantly fighting the urge to put his arm around Amara's waist or hold her hand. When they got to the diner and were eating dinner while sharing more conversation, he found it even more impossible to keep his eyes off of her.

*So this is the effect of a Fated... it's become even stronger the more time I've spent with her today.* As he sat across from Amara, watching her, even the tiniest actions either warmed his heart or turned him on. *How the hell am I turned on by the way she eats fries?* Mateo groaned internally. *If we don't complete the bond soon, this could become unbearable.* He also chided himself for not taking her to a nicer place for their first dinner, but promised himself he'd make it up to her, ten-fold.

Dinner had come to an end and Mateo paid before he reluctantly began the journey of walking Amara to her car. He didn't want their date to end.

They arrived to her car outside the cafe that was now closed and Mateo's car was just a few spaces over.

"We met at what? Like four-thirty? And now it's almost

nine?" Amara shook her head, seemingly in disbelief, leaned against her car. "I'm sure this is the longest da-" she stopped herself before completing the word.

"Date," Mateo finished. "You can call it a date, Amara. That's exactly what it was," he said as he walked in closer. "And I would like to go on more of these with you, if you would like to, of course."

The heat radiating from Mateo's body with his closeness to her caused Amara's heart to race. She wanted to touch him, wrap her ams around him and pull him in closer. She'd already thought about kissing him numerous times over the course of their date. "Y-yes. I'd like that too," she responded nervously.

Mateo took note as he leaned in closer to her that Amara's eyes were wide and there was a slight increase in the rising and falling of her chest. He gently placed his hand on her face and felt its warmness as he sensed the desire coming from her. "Amara..." he muttered. "May I kiss you?"

"Yes," she breathed and his lips immediately pressed against hers.

As much as he wanted to devour her right there, he continued to practice control, moving his lips gently before signaling with his tongue that he wanted more. Amara opened her mouth to let him in and with the way his tongue moved against hers, she was so turned on that she released a whimper against his lips.

And that was when Mateo lost control.

He moved the hand that was holding her face to the back of her neck, deepening the kiss while he pressed his body against hers as she leaned against the car. His mouth then moved from her lips, to her jaw, to her neck. Amara's breathing grew heavy and Mateo's body reacted to her. He completely forgot they were outside until they were interrupted by a car horn and obnoxious whistling.

"Heyyyyy, Professor Vazquez! Whose face are you sucking?" a clearly inebriated student called out. He was in the passenger seat of a car filled with other students that were looking at them.

Amara buried her face against Mateo's chest and he let out a deep, frustrated breath at the interruption.

"Is that you, Jason?" Mateo shouted to the car. "It sounds like you want a pop quiz Monday. I'll be sure to let your classmates know that you were the one who suggested it."

"No! Uh... Sorry professor, we're leav-" the car sped away before the student could finish his sentence.

Mateo looked down at an embarrassed Amara and lifted her head up by her chin to look at him. "Don't worry, Amara. They didn't see your face... Now, where were we?" he asked rhetorically before going back in for her lips.

Amara placed a hand on his chest stopping him. "I should go," she said softly.

"Amara..." Mateo wanted to protest, but he respected her request and let her go, feeling his heart drop as he opened her car door for her to get in. "I meant what I said," he whispered as she settled into her seat. "I would like to do this again sometime."

She looked up, smiling at him. "And I meant what I said, too. Thank you, Mateo. I do hope we can do this again."

Mateo tried to temper down the gleaming smile he felt growing on his face, but with no success.

"Let me know when you get home," he said, closing her door. He waited for her to drive off before going to his own car.

# EIGHT

"I'm not sure if this was our best idea..." Liam croaked. He swallowed once again as if it could get his heart out of his throat, but it was stuck there.

"Yes..." Mateo readjusted his pants. "I'm going to need that potion you brewed..."

The men watched through the window—trying their best to be inconspicuous—at Amara leading stretches for the dance class she was teaching. She had one leg extended to the side of her, resting on the barre and the other planted firmly on the ground. Facing forward, she eased lower and lower into a plié while her leg remained on the barre before easing back up again to straighten the supporting leg. She repeated the motion a few more times before switching sides.

"I mean, we knew she was a dancer, so of course she'd be... flexible."

"Yes, right. But seeing it now... It's giving me..."

"...ideas," the men said in unison.

Amara continued leading the class in stretches, this time away from the barre, she lifted her knee up to the side of her at almost chest level before further extending it above her head as her hand supported her calf until she was in a standing split.

Mateo immediately choked on his own saliva and Liam's throat dried when Amara took the position.

"I... I think we should go..." Mateo coughed out, pulling away a mesmerized Liam.

When the men reached Liam's office, not far down the hall from the dance class, they both took a potion to settle themselves.

Liam shook his head, trying to forget the image of Amara that was now burned into his mind. "Perhaps we should have considered her effect on us before *persuading* Dr. Finch to hire her."

Mateo grunted. "Maybe we were a bit impulsive on that decision. The pull of the Fated is quite potent. After our date Sunday, it's been impossible for me to think of anything but her. I'm trying to allow her to set the pace, but I feel like I'm going crazy having gone just two days without contact with her. How we waited one hundred thirty-eight years to meet her, I will never understand."

"Yes, and that concerns me as well," Liam said as he rubbed his temple. "As our Fated, shouldn't she be just as drawn to us? Yet she hasn't contacted you since your date. And I'm worried that when I try to intercept her in the hall today to apologize for before, she may not accept it."

"It worries me, but we must also take into consideration the way modern day mortals do this 'dating' thing. It's still baffling how complicated they choose to make a process that should be relatively simple."

"So, you believe she's thinking of you just as much as you are of her?"

"Maybe not as much, but I do believe she's thinking of

me. When we kissed, the connection was strong. If that fucking student didn't interrupt..." Mateo groaned and dragged his hands down his face. "Anyway, try your best not to mess up your apology today, yes? I am using every ounce of patience I can muster in this courtship and I will not hesitate in leaving you behind should the connection between Amara and I progress faster."

"Whatever," Liam grumbled. "I have a plan..."


AFTER SHE FINISHED TEACHING dance class, Amara packed her bag, smiling to herself and thinking about Mateo. *I can't get this man off my mind. And I don't want to. I haven't stopped thinking about him since Sunday. Especially the way he kissed me, I wonder if... I shouldn't think that far. Shit. I wonder if he's knows Liam and I kissed. I can't believe I kissed a pair of friends! Is that irresponsible of me? No. I am a single woman.*

Exiting the classroom, Amara started down the hall toward the stairwell to exit the building, but she stopped in her tracks when she noticed Liam walking in her direction. Just when Amara was about to turn around to walk the other direction in an effort to avoid him, he called out to her and she froze.

"Amara," his voice traveled down the hall. "May I speak with you, please?" he pleaded, doing a small jog to quickly approach her.

She crossed her arms and looked up at him skeptically without saying a word. It was her best attempt at a poker-face as she felt her cheeks warm at his mere presence and her heart raced with memories of how his lips and body felt against hers.

Liam swallowed before he spoke. "I, um, I wanted to

apologize for last week." He rubbed the back of his neck. "I didn't mean to blindside you and it was wrong of me..."

As he went on with his apology, Amara felt hypnotized examining his face—his unusually dark blue eyes, the way his jaw seemed to clench when he closed his mouth between thoughts as if searching for more words, and his lips that he seemed to lick each time before speaking again. *I would totally kiss this man again*, she thought to herself.

"... Sorry, I know I've gone on for quite some time, but I said all that to say that I wasn't playing some game or trying to take advantage of you. I never wanted to make you feel uncomfortable and I definitely don't want you to think..."

"I liked it!" Amara blurted before she could catch herself and covered her mouth.

"Oh?" Liam blinked several times, taken aback by her honesty.

In a failed attempt to recover, Amara stumbled over her words. "Er- I mean... I appreciate the apology?"

A smile pulled at Liam's lips as he looked down at his Fated. He found her awkwardness endearing. "Amara, would you be interested in spending some time with me?"

"Oh, um..."

"Apologies, I should clarify..." he reached out his hand to her. "Do you have time for me to show you something?"

"Uh... I mean, I have time, but..." Amara hesitated. While she found herself oddly trusting of him, logic told her that going somewhere alone with the man who kissed her out of nowhere just a week ago would likely result in more kissing or something beyond that. However, before she realized, her hand was approaching his.

"I promise I'm not taking you somewhere just to kiss

you again. Though, I wouldn't object if you'd be interested in that." He winked at her before turning to lead her further down the music hall to one of the rooms used for chorus practice. "Here…" Liam took Amara's bag off her shoulder and set it on a chair and pulled her with him to the piano at the center of the room.

As he stepped over to sit on the bench, Liam turned to see Amara's hesitant expression as she bit her lip. He gave her a warm smile and patted the spot beside him . "I promise I won't bite."

"I wouldn't be in your way? You know, like arm space or something…?"

"Of course not." Liam reached out for her arm and pulled her to the seat. Amara sat next to him with her legs on the outside of the bench. With her at his side, he turned back to the keys and took a deep breath before he began to play.

As Liam's fingers moved across the keys and a calming melody filled the room, the nerves Amara was feeling escaped her and she closed her eyes, enjoying the music.

Liam began to speak. "You know, despite being an English professor and lover of words, I'll admit I'm not always the best at using them." He swallowed before continuing. "I hope this doesn't make you feel uncomfortable, but I must admit: When we first met, I immediately felt drawn to you, Amara. I have a way of sensing things about people and what I sensed from you immediately pulled me in…"

"What did you sense?" she asked softly.

"Your aura. It has a warmness to it. A warmness that feels attuned to exactly what my own seeks. I can understand if something like that sounds strange, but it's the best way I know to describe it in this moment." He carried on playing as he spoke. "But I also sense something else in you, something a bit more bleak, a doubtful energy that I feel a need to get rid of, to get closer to you in the way that I feel —or at least hope—we could be someday." Liam released a slight chuckle as he continued the music. "Yes. I'm sure now that I sound strange saying all of this to you, especially given we don't know each other well."

Amara considered Liam's words. She agreed that what he was saying should've sounded strange. But it didn't. It sounded *right*. It made sense to Amara. Even if part of her was saying it shouldn't have. "It doesn't sound strange at all," she finally responded.

In a move that felt natural, she brought her hand up to hold his face, feeling its warmness to her touch. Her gaze switched between his eyes and his lips before she leaned in and closed the short distance between them. The music that was filling the room came to a stop. Even with the tenderness of the kiss, Amara's passion wasn't lost on Liam. Though he allowed her to take the lead, hoping to avoid a mishap like last time, until she showed some hesitancy in her movements and he heard her thoughts. *Crap, I didn't ask him to kiss, maybe I should stop.*

Liam pulled Amara into his lap and held her face to deepen the kiss, his tongue entering her mouth. As their lips moved against each other and their tongues danced, Amara felt her breathing begin to grow heavy.

*You can control yourself, Liam. You will not take her in this classroom. You will go on a proper date and then have her in your bed. But still...* His memories of seeing her lead the stretches in dance class got the best of him and Liam took one of Amara's legs and broke the kiss momentarily to bring it across them and place it on his side so she was straddling him before pulling her face back to his. He felt himself becoming strained against his pants and wondered if the potion wasn't strong enough or if this was the power of the Fated overwhelming it.

Amara released a whimper against his lips when she felt his erection pressed on her. Instinctively, she began moving her hips and Liam's kisses moved down to her neck while his hands started to wander until they reached her bare skin under her shirt.

*Self-control, Liam. Control. Patience,* he reminded himself and finally broke the kiss.

In a half-dazed state, Amara looked at him confused before her eyes widened and she realized what they were doing in a classroom. "Oh, god!" She winced. "I'm so sorry. I-"

Liam stopped her with a finger to her lips. "Don't apologize, Amara. The only reason I stopped is because I would much rather take you on a real date. And if it goes well..." he took her hand and brought it to his lips. "We'd continue this in a more private setting."

"Oh, um..." Amara tried to pry herself away from Liam and he helped her get up. "Y-yeah..." she averted her gaze, still embarrassed. She hadn't even considered stopping what was happening between them and forgot that they were in a classroom. "I think a date would be nice."

Liam held her chin and lifted her head to look up at him. "There's nothing to be ashamed of, Amara. In fact, I should apologize for now putting you in this type of position twice."

"No, no. It's fine. I've been a bit off lately..."

"How does Friday night sound?" he asked, pulling out

his phone and handing it to her. "There's this lovely French restaurant in the city if you're interested?"

"That sounds great," Amara responded as she put her information in his phone. "It's a..."

"Date," Liam finished before kissing her forehead. "And I'm already looking forward to it."

## CHAPTER

# NINE

Amara tossed and turned in her sleep, her heart racing at the vividness of the nightmare she was having.

*Amara struggled in the dark room with her wrists and ankles bound to the table. "Please!" she cried, her throat already raw and voice almost gone from the screaming she'd been doing for hours. "Not again! It hurts!" Her vision blurred as her eyes filled with tears.*

*A man whose face was covered by a cloak stood above her. All she could make out were his unnatural red eyes and the way they glowed as he scanned over her. "Amazing... She's already healed... Again," he ordered.*

*"No!" Amara wailed, pulling at the restraints.*

*Warm hands cradled her face and wiped the tears from her eyes. "It's alright, honey. This needs to be done," said a woman whose face was hidden by the shadows. Unlike the man, her eyes glowed purple. "You can do this."*

*Amara released a bloodcurdling scream as the blade was driven through her sternum and dragged down the center of her torso.*

Amara shot up in her bed, hyperventilating with a pounding headache and beads of sweat pouring down her face with tears filling her eyes. Her heart was racing and her body was in distress. Unable to breathe from the terror that had taken over her, Amara snatched the pill bottle from her nightstand. Franticly, she fumbled to get it open before finally dry swallowing the last capsule left. When her trembling calmed, Amara got up to turn on the light and pace her room.

She looked over to the clock and saw it was three-seventeen in the morning, but with her adrenaline-driven awakening, she knew she wouldn't be able to go back to sleep.

"I guess I'll just make more medicine..." Amara muttered to herself before making her way downstairs to the kitchen.

After gathering her jars of herbs, Amara began crushing and mixing them as she thought back to when her grandmother first taught her how to make the remedy.

*"AMARA," Glenda Jenkins called to her granddaughter. "Come, I'll teach you how to make this medicine for your nightmares."*

*Amara walked into the house with a basket full of freshly-picked herbs, looking at her grandmother curiously. "How did you know I was back?"*

*Glenda smiled without looking away from the the mortar and pestle she was using to crush a mix of herbs. "I always know where you are, dear. Now come, let me show you how to make this. It's very important that you take it any time you have nightmares, okay?"*

*"Yes, grandma," Amara responded, setting the basket down and approaching Glenda at the counter.*

"*Now, it's a simple mix and the most daunting part of it is stuffing just the right amount in these annoying capsules... So, you have lavender, chamomile, sage, and vervain. And if we're making, say, fifty capsules, we'll need about this much of each plant,*" *she explained as she set out the appropriate amount of each ingredient.* "*Once you're finished grinding and mixing them...*" *Glenda held up the mortar with the crushed herbs that she had already been working on.* "*You'll need to add a very special, very secret ingredient, Amara.*"

"*Okay,*" *the girl nodded attentively.* "*What is it?*"

"*Amara, I mean it when I tell you that you'll need to keep this part a secret, okay? You can't tell anyone...*" *Glenda pricked her thumb with a needle that she then handed to Amara, nodding toward her as a signal that she should do the same. When Amara followed the instruction, her grandmother put their two bleeding thumbs together and whispered something under her breath.* "*Do you promise not to tell anyone about this final ingredient, Amara?*"

"*Of course, grandma,*" *she agreed.*

*Glenda pulled their bleeding thumbs apart and held hers over the herbs.* "*The final ingredient is a single drop of either your blood or mine.*"

*Amara chuckled as a grin grew to her face.*

"*I'm serious, Amara. The medicine will not work if it's not enriched with my blood or yours. This is a remedy that has been passed down in our family for generations. I know it might sound strange, but it's vitally important. And even more important that you never reveal this secret to anyone, okay?*"

"*Yes, grandma.*"

JUST AS HER grandmother taught her all those years ago, Amara pricked her finger and finished off the mix with a single drop of her blood. She at first thought the practice was strange and didn't understand what difference it'd make for a mix of herbs to contain her or her grandmother's blood. However, she'd gotten so used to it when preparing the medicine that she added her blood out of pure instinct each time and never gave it much thought again.

Amara spent the rest of the morning packing the capsules, refilling the pill bottle for her room and setting aside more to keep in her bag for emergencies.

It was about six in the morning by the time she finished and the first thing she thought about when she picked up her phone was contacting Mateo.

She groaned. "It's too early... But, today will be the day that I contact him and ask him on a date. I can't keep letting fear hold me back."

Amara sat at her desk in the shared office for TAs and professors reading through her grandmother's journal full of notes on the palisyfum. She kept nodding, struggling to stay awake after a long day for her. Her phone ringing gave her a slight jolt of energy and she quickly pulled it from her pocket, hoping to see Mateo's name. She was let down when it wasn't him.

"Hey Evelyn," she answered. "What's up?"

"Amara, sorry, I know you're probably studying or working right now, but I'm at the grocery store. Do you want anything?"

Amara sighed. "No, I'm fine."

"You alright? You've had a long day, haven't you? I heard you up early this morning."

"I just had a bad nightmare that woke me up. I'm fine. I'll see you later."

"See you later."

After hanging up with Evelyn, Amara continued to stare at her phone, contemplating contacting the person she wanted to speak to most in that moment. She began scrolling through her contacts as she mustered up the courage she needed.

Amara nervously bit her lip as she clicked the call button beside Mateo's name. The line trilled and she took a deep breath trying to steady her nerves.

"Amara? I'm so glad you called." Mateo answered with a sense of relief in his voice. "I'm was afraid I may have scared you aw-"

"Do you want to hang out Sunday?" Amara blurted.

"Oh! I-"

"I mean, would you like to go on a hike... w-with me?"

"Amara, I would love to go out with you Sunday."

Amara could hear the smile in his voice when he responded and it gave her the assurance she needed, though she remained a bit nervous.

"Oh, great! Thank y— I mean, I'll send you the details for the trail."

"I look forward to it."

"Yeah, me too. I guess I'll see you then. Um... bye?"

"I'll see you Sunday, Amara."

After hanging up the phone, Amara punched the air triumphantly. "Yes!" she exclaimed.

"Um... Amara?"

The familiar voice reminded her that she was in a shared space and she turned to see David, one of her teachers assistants, looking at her curiously.

"Did something happen?" he asked.

"Oh, uh..." Amara awkwardly rubbed her neck. "Sorry, I didn't realize you came in."

"It's okay." He pulled up a chair across from her. "So, you said I'd be able to help you with some research on the palisyfum?"

"Right, right…" Amara picked up her grandmother's notebook from the desk in front of her and presented it to David. "I have some notes in here that I'd like your thoughts-" As she was handing him the notebook, she felt a sharp pain shoot down her arm and dropped it. "Whoops! Let me get that."

"It's okay, I've got-" When David reached down and touched the notebook, he felt an intense burning sensation and hissed at the pain. "Er…" He stood abruptly without picking up the notebook. "I should go."

"Oh, okay…"Amara furrowed her brows in confusion as she watched him rush out of the shared office, leaving the notebook on the floor.

As soon as he entered the hallway, David looked at his hand and saw an odd sigil burned in his palm.

"What the hell?"

# TEN

Friday had come and Amara was set for her first date with Liam. She nervously looked over herself in the mirror before turning to a smirking Evelyn behind her. "Are you sure I look okay?"

"If you ask me that one more time..." She shook her head while rubbing her temples. "You look good! Even better than good. You look sexy as hell! Actually, I'm a bit worried you won't make it to dinner," she teased.

With a smile, Amara turned back to the mirror to look at herself once again. She wore a black off-the-shoulder dress that hugged her form and fell right at her knees. Evelyn loaned her a pair of black pumps to go with it and she accessorized with gold jewelry and a clutch. Amara didn't find herself ugly, but she also didn't think of herself as particularly attractive. She found herself average and always thought that if she ended up with a man, he'd also be average. Yet, she somehow came across two men she found unbelievably gorgeous and they both showed interest in her.

"I can't remember the last time I felt this nervous,

Evelyn. My stomach is in knots and my hands are uncontrollably shaky. What if I have a panic attack before he even gets here? Or worse! I have it when he comes to pick me up!"

Evelyn walked up to Amara and rubbed her arms in a comforting motion. "You've got this, girl. That man has approached you on more than one occasion and now he's asked you out to some fancy spot in the city. Besides, *if* things don't work out with him, you don't have to worry about choosing between him and Mateo considering that Mateo is obviously completely smitten with you."

"You think so? I mean, I'm sure a man who looks like that has a ton of other options. Same goes for Liam! Then again, I shouldn't care about that, right? I don't even know why I'm thinking about it... I think it's the nerves. It has to be the nerves. I've never been in a situation like this before. Dating two men—especially ones who are friends—at the same time, I mean."

"Amara..." Evelyn wrapped her arms around Amara's shoulders in a friendly hug. "I know it's easier said than done, but relax and enjoy this weekend. You look amazing and you're spending time with two very nice men who've shown interest in you. Try to look at it that way without letting your mind get too far ahead. Be in the moment."

"I know, I just..." Amara looked at Evelyn through the mirror and smiled, holding onto her arms. "You're right. There's no point in worrying so much now." Her eyes went wide when she heard the doorbell and a big smile came to Evelyn's face.

"I'll get it," she said, walking out of the room. "We need to get the full effect of him watching your fine ass coming down the stairs to meet him."

Evelyn went downstairs to open the door for Liam. He

was in a dark blue button down dress shirt and black slacks. His brown hair was perfectly tousled and fell just above his eyes.

"Hi," he said to Evelyn with a tight smile. "I'm here for Amara. Is she..."

"Oh shit." Evelyn interrupted, raising an impressed brow and eyeing the rose in his hand.

"Is it not enough?" he asked. He took a potion to suppress his telepathy so he could enjoy his date with Amara and it was odd for him not to know what people were thinking. "I was about to bring a proper bouquet, but I thought it might have been too much."

"Oh no!" she assured. "I'm actually impressed. I didn't realize people still do flowers on the first date."

"Well," he rubbed the back of his neck. "I'm trying to make a good first- er at least *first date* impression. And you could say I'm a bit old-fashioned."

"I'd say you're off to a good start," Evelyn replied, finally letting him into the house. "Amara!" she called. "Liam is here."

A few short moments passed before they heard the clacking of her heels upstairs and she made her way down. As Amara descended the steps, Liam's heart jumped into his throat and his hands became shaky. The black dress hugged her curves perfectly and the off-the-shoulder look showed off more of her beautiful brown skin. Her naturally curly hair was down and fell just above her shoulders and she wore a burgundy matte lipstick.

Amara felt a warmness in her chest when she saw Liam standing at the bottom of the stairs with a rose in his hand staring at her adoringly. When she reached the final few steps, he rushed over to take her hand and help her down.

"Ms. Jenkins... To say you look stunning would be an

understatement." He softly kissed Amara's cheek and handed her the rose.

Her heart fluttered and her mouth went dry. Looking over Liam's face with him so close to her, all she wanted to do was kiss him again. "Hi," she finally choked out before bashfully averting her gaze and looking at the rose in her hand. "Let me just- um... I'll put this in some water." Amara walked into the kitchen and pulled out a thin vase to put the single rose in.

*Breathe, Amara,* she thought to herself as she returned to Liam by the door to leave for their date. You've kissed his man twice and you were dry humping in a classroom! What is there to be ashamed of at this point? No reason to be nervous now. Just. Breathe.

Evelyn, whose back was facing Liam winked at Amara as she passed by. "You've got this, girl," she whispered.

"Liam," Amara gasped, eyes wide with wonder when they reached the restaurant. It sat along the coast of the city with floor-to-ceiling windows that showed a beautiful view of the skyline lit at night reflected in the water. "Is this where we're having dinner?"

"It is," Liam confirmed, admiring the look on her face as he led her to the entrance.

When they were seated, Amara was still in awe at the restaurant, taking in the large space with white cloth covered tables that were far enough apart to provide the patrons privacy and dim lighting that created a more inti-mate ambiance, despite the size of the restaurant. Liam booked them a table by the window so they had a perfect view of the river.

"Welcome to La Maison," the waiter greeted Liam and

Amara. "Here are your menus and waters. May I get you started with anything while you decide on your meal?"

"Hmm, I think I'd like some wine..." Amara pondered, scanning over the wine menu.

"Red or white?" Liam quickly asked.

"Red."

"Do you prefer dry or sweet?"

"Eh... more of a dry, I guess."

"I know exactly what to get," he replied confidently before turning to the waiter. "She'll have a glass of this Chateau Canon from Bordeaux."

The waiter nodded. "Excellent choice. I'll get right on that."

When he soon returned with the wine, Liam stared attentively at Amara, waiting for her to try it. She brought the glass to her lips and sipped the red liquid with a thoughtful look her eyes as she took in the flavor.

A smile soon came to her face. "I like this one." She took another sip. "I like it a lot."

"You do?" Liam asked leaning in. "It's one of my favorites. I'd normally join you if I wasn't driving."

"Well, you've got great taste, Mr. Taylor," she complimented.

Dinner seemed to go on forever as the two of them spoke for hours, though to Amara and Liam, it felt like no time passed at all. Amara told him about her sheltered life growing up with her grandmother and why she decided to pursue botany and he told her about his love for music and literature. He paid close attention to everything she said, making sure to remember even the tiniest details of what she told him.

"...And what about your family?" Amara asked. "What are they like?"

"Well... My mothers are both into the fine arts. One of them paints and the other—like yourself—is a dancer. She does ballet. I have quite a few siblings who are spread all over the place. Three elder sisters and a younger brother... and I also have a twin."

Amara gawked. "Your family sounds big. So there are six of you? Wow! What was it like growing up? I always wanted siblings. And your twin? Were you two like attached at the hip?"

Liam chuckled at Amara's excitement. He grew up complaining about having such a big family and ironically, he hated how much he had to share with his siblings. "Well..." he rubbed his chin thoughtfully. "My twin Samuel and I actually were quite close growing up, almost inseparable, really. But then, when we reached our twenties..." He looked down with his brows tensed as he thought about his brother and their falling out.

"Oh." Amara reached out to squeeze Liam's hand. "I didn't mean to bring up a sore topic."

"No, no. It's fine," he assured. "You see, Samuel, he-Well, he... I don't want to go too far into detail, honestly." Liam swallowed his emotions. "He sort of emancipated himself from the family to pursue his own goals. When he left, it was... difficult. And it's been that way ever since."

"I see..."

Liam rubbed Amara's hand with his thumb before gesturing to call over the waiter. "Anyway, on to more exciting topics. How about dessert?"

"I could go for that!"

Not long after the pair ordered, the waiter returned with crème brûlée for Amara and molten chocolate cake for Liam.

Amara took the first bite of her dessert and moaned at

the flavor. "This is so good. You have to try it," she said, holding up the spoon to Liam.

A smile grew on his face when he realized she wanted to feed him. Holding her gaze, he leaned in to take a bite from the spoon and licked the rest of the custard off his lips. "That is good," he hummed. "Here, your turn," he said as he scooped from the molten chocolate cake and held it up for Amara.

Liam watched closely as she wrapped her lips around the spoon and took a bite of the dessert. Once again, she moaned at the flavor and Liam felt a twitch in his pants between the sight and sound. Amara felt a heat come over her when she noticed the way Liam's eyes flickered to lust and her breathing stopped when he reached out for her face. From the corner of her mouth, he wiped off some chocolate with his thumb and brought it to his mouth. "Delicious," he said, still staring at her.

Amara gulped, slightly embarrassed that such a subtle move turned her on and averted her eyes, looking down.

Liam noticed her flushed reaction and gently held her by her chin to lift her head so she could meet his gaze. "You don't have to be shy with me, Amara..." His lips turned to a suggestive smirk. "Trust me when I say that the feeling is mutual."

CHAPTER

# ELEVEN

"I can't believe we were there until the restaurant closed," Amara giggled, walking up to her front door with Liam behind her. "Our poor waiter! I feel so bad."

He chuckled. "I could tell with the way that you were practically emptying your wallet trying to leave an apology tip."

"It was the least I could do! Even though you wouldn't let me."

Liam moved in closer to her and wrapped his arm around her waist. "Don't worry, I left him a fifty percent tip for his trouble. Besides..." he pecked her forehead. "I couldn't allow you spend a dime on our date. Especially considering I'm the one who asked you out and you were kind enough to grace me with your company for several hours."

Amara looked up at him. "What was that you said before about not being the best with your words?" she tilted her head to the side. "I'm not sure if that was an accurate statement."

"I am an English professor. I do have to be effective with my words at least some of the time." Liam held Amara closer and looked down at her with a smile, pushing a piece of hair out of her face. Almost as if frozen in time, the two of them stayed in that position for several moments. Liam adored Amara's features, her dark brown eyes, wide nose, and full lips. And it wasn't just her looks that attracted Liam. A warm, pure aura emitted from her that was almost contagious and even though he at times felt nervous about making a positive impression on her, Amara's presence tended to put him at ease.

He held her face and leaned in to close the distance between them. When their lips met, Amara's breath was taken away as if it were their first time kissing and she wrapped her arms around his neck to hold onto him. Liam's lips massaged hers tenderly before he slipped his tongue into her mouth and Amara released a small, muffled whimper when their tongues began to tangle.

As the kiss continued both of their breathing grew heavy and connection of the Fated caused them a heightened sensitivity to each others' touch. Despite taking a larger dose of the potion to keep himself down, a tent still grew in Liam's pants. He lifted both of Amara's legs to wrap around his waist, causing her dress to ride up and his erection to press against the thin fabric of her panties. She moaned at the feeling and a shiver went down her spine.

"Liam," she breathed when he finally freed her lips and began placing kisses down her neck.

"Yes?" he whispered, his mouth still savoring her skin. He couldn't get enough.

"Do you want to come in?"

He immediately paused and looked into her eyes. "Are you sure?"

"Yes."

Liam was in a haze of his own desire on top of Amara in her bed. His lips made a trail down her neck, giving her soft kisses as he caressed the outside of her thighs and ground his erection against her core.

Amara felt herself grow wetter and suddenly her nerves hit her. "Liam..." his name came out as more of moan with the pleasure that was building up in her and his kisses became more eager.

"Wait, Liam..." Amara pressed her hands against his chest.

He immediately stopped and hovered over her with his hands on each side of her. "Are you okay?" When Liam noticed the discomfort in Amara's eyes, he pulled away further, leaning back so he was on his knees between her legs. "Sorry, I didn't mean to..."

"No!" Amara interrupted nervously. "It's not- it's just that... I'm not exactly... *experienced*." She bit her lip and looked down. "I haven't really been with a lot of men, so I'm not sure if I'll... I don't exactly know how well I can..."

He pressed a finger to her lips. Amara halting their interaction brought Liam back to his senses. As much as he wanted to have sex with her, he didn't want to go that far until he and Mateo told her the truth about them being warlocks and her being their Fated. "We're not having sex tonight."

"We're not?"

Liam moved his hand over to hold her face and rub her cheek with his thumb. "No, Amara. I don't want you to do anything that makes you uncomfortable. And besides, I would also like to wait."

A look of surprise crossed her face. "Oh..." Despite the nerves that had hit her, Amara's body was still on fire and she craved Liam's touch. "I mean- It's not that I don't... I *do* want you, Liam," she admitted aloud. "I don't want you to think that I don't."

"Like I said..." Liam took her hand and brought it to his lips. "It's okay." His gaze finally drifted from her face down her body and he realized that her dress had rode up to her hips. With him sitting between her legs, they were still wide open and exposed her pink underwear that were visibly damp with her arousal. Liam gulped. The sight alone had him practically bursting through his own pants as he continued staring at her body's reaction to him. "Besides, I can tell that you want me..." He placed her hand that he was still holding on his erection. "And as I said at dinner: The feeling is mutual."

Amara took a sharp breath at the feeling of Liam in her hand.

"Amara," he whispered, lightly caressing the inside of her thigh. "May I touch you?"

Without hesitation, Amara nodded. "Yes."

Liam carefully stroked Amara through her panties, moving the back of his hand up her core, allowing his knuckles to brush against her and then running his hand back down with the front of it touching her. His heart was racing—likely in sync with Amara's as he felt her pulsating against his hand and her core become wetter. "Fuck," he breathed, nearly coming undone himself knowing this was the effect he was having on her.

Light moans began to escape Amara with Liam touching her and he wanted nothing more than for those noises to get louder. He leaned back in to take her lips with his and his fingers moved up and down her slit. His kisses started a path back down to her neck and he gave attention to the parts of it he found most sensitive, pulling more sounds from Amara. Liam's tongue made a trail to her ear and he whispered, "Do you want more, Amara?"

"Yes," she said with a whimper as her arms wrapped around him and Liam moved his hand under her panties to touch her directly.

He groaned with pleasure of his own when he felt her slick wetness directly and started lightly massaging her clit. When Amara's moans against his ear grew more intense, so did his fingers and he felt her spasming around them.

Amara couldn't understand what was coming over her. It was like her senses were in overdrive and her sensitivity to Liam's touch felt unreal. Every bit of contact felt so *good* to her and she was already racing toward her climax.

"Liam, I'm going to co-" Amara was cut off by the strangled moan that escaped her lips as she buried her face into Liam's chest.

As she came down from her high, her body trembled and her breathing was ragged. She looked up and noticed that Liam's breathing was also heavy. He brought his fingers to his lips and sucked her essence off of them while holding eye contact with her. "Even better than dessert," he muttered with a knowing smirk.

He kissed her again, allowing her to taste herself before he reluctantly pulled away. Amara reached out for his belt and he stopped her with his hand around her wrist, causing her to look up at him in confusion.

"It's okay." He swallowed his embarrassment. "That was enough for both of us..."

Amara's eyes lingered down to his pants. When she noticed a very subtle spot on the fabric, she gulped. "Oh..."

CHAPTER

# TWELVE

I t was the middle of the day and David, Amara's TA who was also interested in the palisyfum, was at his favorite dive bar just outside of city—Joey's Tavern. *I've spent over a month working with her and I still haven't learned a single thing about the palisyfum outside of that idiot cross-breeding theory the human has,* he thought to himself. *I wonder if I were to tell her that magic is real, if it would unlock more theories for her, theories that would help me. Then again, that fucking journal of hers clearly has magic in it, so maybe there's something* she *is keeping from* me...

"Hey, I'm still here."

Despite his thirst, he'd nearly forgotten about the green-eyed blonde who was wrapped in his arm. He buried his face in the crook of her neck, breathing in her scent. She was already out of it, likely high on something, so it didn't take much for David to charm her.

The seal on Amara's journal didn't just repel him, there was some sort of residual curse that came with it too that had been weakening David and he found himself needing to feed more often.

"Absolutely delectable," he muttered against the woman he was holding before releasing his fangs and sinking his teeth into her.

The woman winced, but showed little resistance as he drank from her and his grip around her tightened.

He fed on her until her body went limp and he dropped her to the floor before making his way further down the bar to speak to the server.

"Hi there, Joey," he greeted, the red tint fading from his eyes. "I need something from you."

Joey turned to him and let out an amused huff. "Oh look, if it isn't David Keen," he said sarcastically. "Still looking for mythical flowers, are we?"

David scoffed. "Funny for a vampire to be talking about myths. You'll be looking like the fucking dumbass when I get ahold of the palisyfum and all the power that comes with it."

"Ha!" Joey shook his head with an entertained smirk. "I think you've been feeding on too many addicts. The palisyfum—if it ever did exist—went extinct ages ago, well before you even tasted your first drop of blood."

"Whatever... Anyway, I am here to buy. Do you have anything that can counter a protection spell? Particularly one that might also have a curse attached to it."

Joey sat down the glass he was drying and leaned into David. "What type of protection spell are we talking about, exactly?"

David revealed his palm to Joey, showing the sigil that burned into his skin when he tried to take the notebook from Amara.

Joey analyzed the symbol with his face scrunched before his eyes went wide. "Oh shit... What type of witch are you dealing with? This seal is..."

"Extremely complex and likely done by an incredibly skilled witch with either centuries of experience or from a strong bloodline?" he said impatiently. "Yes, I know that. Now, do you have anything I can use to break it?"

"You didn't answer my question... Who is this powerful witch you're dealing with?"

"Not a witch. She smells purely of human and looked completely baffled when I couldn't touch the notebook she was trying to give me—which I'll add that she was very excited to share. I don't think it was her. So, do you have anything that can get rid of the fucking seal?"

"I might have someone who could help you with it... A warlock for hire. But it'll cost you a pretty penny."

"I'm willing to pay any price."

"Excellent. I'll make contact."

Mateo looked at Amara with a wide smile of adoration on his face as he watched her pick up more herbs on the side of the trail and put them in small jars. As usual, even her most minuscule actions warmed his heart and made him admire her even more. Each time she clipped a plant from the ground, she would whisper something under her breath as she touched the dirt where it once lived. Then, she carefully placed it into a jar, sealed the jar, and looked at the herb one last time before putting it in her bag.

"Are you positive you don't want me to carry your bag?" he asked Amara for the fifth time.

"Yes!" she exclaimed with a smile. "Besides, it looks like you've got enough to carry yourself... When I said hiking, I didn't mean some hardcore trail that'd require you to bring a ton of stuff." She chuckled. "You probably could've left whatever you have in there in your car."

Mateo shook his head. "Nope! Trust me, this is absolutely necessary for our hiking activities today."

"Okay..." Amara raised a suspicious brow. Mateo seemed particularly giddy since picking her up for their hiking date, holding a big grin on his face the entire time, even when they were met with tougher inclines or had to climb over large boulders.

They made their way up yet another hill and the exhaustion began to creep up on Amara. Despite her ability to dance for hours on end and as much as she loved hiking, it was one of the few activities that truly tired her out. And although she was happy to spend time with Mateo, she was also looking forward to going home and soaking herself in a warm bath to sooth her muscles.

When they reached the peak of the incline, there wasn't much to see except more woods, but when Amara started descending on the other side, Mateo took her hand to stop her.

"What is it?" she asked.

"May you come with me? There's something I'd like to show you."

"Oh, um... Sure," she replied skeptically. She'd been hiking the same trail every week since she moved to Masoncrest, often using it to study the plant life, though she never found anything particularly interesting about it outside of the plants.

With her hand in his, Mateo led Amara off the beaten path through the elevated part of the forest until they hit a clearing that sat at the edge of it, overlooking the landscape.

"Oh my..." Amara stopped in her tracks, gaping at the campsite. At the center of it was a campfire with a grill rack over it and a log seat with makeshift cushions sat at the front, facing the horizon. On the side of the campsite, there was a large open tent filled with pillows, blankets, and cushions and lined with string lights at the entrance and along the top.

Mateo looked back at Amara with a bit of nerves in his eyes. "Do you like it?"

Amara was still gawking at the scene, unable to answer him, only causing his nerves to get worse.

"I'm sorry," he said quickly. "If you don't like it, it's perfectly fine. I wasn't sure what-"

"I love it!" Amara blurted, interrupting what was likely to turn into a long rambling by Mateo. "It's beautiful," she said breathlessly, finally moving her feet to walk further into the campsite.

Mateo let out a deep breath of relief and led Amara to the campfire. From his bag, he pulled out food that he had already prepared. Chicken skewers stacked with vegetables, pita bread, and tzatziki sauce. "Everything is mostly cooked except for the chicken skewers," he said as he lit the fire. "And they shouldn't take too long, so we will be eating soon."

Amara was speechless, watching Mateo get them set up for dinner. When he noticed her silence, he turned to her. "Are you okay, Amara?"

She looked up at him with glossy eyes, still stunned. "Yeah... This is just... It's- I've never had someone do something like this before."

He released a low chuckle, approaching her to take her hand. "You deserve a lot more than this," he assured before kissing her knuckles.

As promised, it didn't take long for the chicken to be grilled and Mateo set up a small table in front of the log seat facing the horizon so that they could watch the sunset as they ate dinner.

"How did you know that I like anything that requires tzatziki sauce?" she asked softly, eyeing the food Mateo had set out.

"You said it yourself on our date... Or it could just be that I'm a psychic, remember?"

Finally relaxing, Amara giggled and shook her head. "I guess I'll never know your secret."

Mateo sat next to her and wrapped an arm around her waist to pull her in close to him. "In due time," he replied. "So, I did get the recipe from a Greek friend of mine and I'm desperately hoping it's to your liking." He dipped a piece of pita bread in the tzatziki sauce and held it up to her.

When Amara took a bite, her eyes immediately widened at the flavor. "This is perfect!" she beamed. "Are you sure you cooked this yourself?" she teased.

"Yes!" he feigned offense. "In fact, to prove it to you, perhaps you could come over one day and I'll cook the same meal for you again, right before your very eyes."

Amara smiled and leaned against his shoulder in an affectionate gesture. "I'd love that."

As dinner went on, Amara and Mateo shared more banter and conversation and ended up feeding each other until the sun finally set. He took notice of the way she kept eyeing his guitar expectantly and finally pulled it into his lap.

"I would like to play you something, if you'll allow me. It's one of my favorites."

"You would?" Amara leaned in toward him as her eyes widened in excitement.

"I would..." He rubbed the back of his neck nervously.

"Admittedly, this song is quite old, so I'd understand if you're not familiar with it." He strummed his guitar to the rhythm before he started singing.

"Por alto que este el cielo en el mundo.
"Por hondo que sea el mar profundo.
"No habrá una barrera en el mundo.
"Que mi amor profundo no rompa por ti.
"Amor es el pan de la vida.
"Amor es la copa divina.
"Amor es un algo sin nombre.
"Que obesesiona al hombre por una mujer."

Mateo went through the entire ballad and Amara was glossy-eyed by the end. The feeling with which he sang the song as he held her eyes the entire time had Amara momentarily wondering if he felt those things about her, but she quickly reminded herself of reality that they'd just met.

"Okay, now I'm actually starting to believe you're a psychic because that's one of my favorite baleros."

"Wait, so you do know it?" The song was one of his favorites as well—having seen it performed live soon after it was written—but he had no idea that Amara would've been familiar with it, as he'd never heard it in his few visions of her.

"I do!" Amara nodded excitedly. "I know its from what? Like the nineteen-thirties? But my grandma had these old records she used to collect with music from all over the world and she actually had one with this song on it. It's actually one of the reasons I started learning Spanish—I *felt* this song when I heard it, but I wanted to know what the lyrics meant as well."

"And when you understood the lyrics, what did you think?"

"Beautiful."

The two of them spent hours at the camp site. They talked more about Amara's love of botany and her curiosities about the palisyfum. And Mateo told her more about his background—his years of traveling and studying histories.

Neither of them realized how much time had passed until it became noticeably dark outside.

"I'm still amazed..." Amara said softly. "How did you manage to set this up?"

"Would you believe me if I told you it was magic?"

"At this point? I'm not sure I'd exactly doubt it," she giggled. "It all seems so perfect that it feels surreal. So maybe there *is* some magic going on here." She gestured with her hand between the two of them.

"I hope you're still talking about the setup," Mateo replied. "Because there's no magic necessary in recognizing an amazing woman who is deserving of everything I could possibly give her."

Amara choked at his words and her body tensed against his. She was afraid of how strongly she had been feeling for Mateo since their first date, but with his words and actions tonight, she was happy to learn that she wasn't alone.

"Sorry," he said softly as he rubbed her arm and she immediately relaxed again. "I didn't mean to come off too strong. I hope that didn't bother you."

"Not at all."

"Amara..." Mateo swallowed, wanting to reveal everything to her, but not wanting to ruin their moment.

"Yes?"

"I wish we could be like this forever... but I don't want

to be the cause of you having a rough morning since we'll have to get back to work tomorrow..."

"I don't want to leave yet." Amara whispered, laying her head on his chest. "Thirty more minutes?"

A big smile came to his face and he stroked her shoulder. "Of course we can."

CHAPTER

# THIRTEEN

*I think I'm going insane,* Amara thought to herself. She was supposed to be reviewing her studies so far on Masoncrest plant life, but focus was elusive as her mind always went back to Mateo and Liam. *It doesn't make sense to feel so strongly about a person in such a short period of time, let alone two.*

She shook her head. Amara had men in the past who she liked but absolutely nothing compared to how she felt about both Mateo and Liam. Friday with Liam and then Sunday with Mateo were two of the best days she'd experienced in years and she wondered if it was right to feel that way. It was like both men were made for her. They were kind, attentive, musical, and direct regarding how they felt about her.

And then the parts where they seemed to differ satisfied two separate sides of Amara. Liam was more playful and not as subtle in his flirtation. She enjoyed their banter and his sense of humor. Mateo seemed more composed, but at times—especially with the way he kissed her—Amara wondered if he were still that way in the bedroom.

*I'll see Mateo later today, at least. That might be part of the reason I can't stop thinking about them, too.* She'd accidentally left her hiking boots in Mateo's car Sunday, so she would have to stop by his office to get them.

"Focus, Amara," she muttered to herself as she tried to turn her attention back to her notes on the palisyfum and analyzed the various charts she'd made on her cross-breeding theory.

Whispering to herself, Amara outlined what she knew. "Okay, so I know that sunlight and warm temperatures are key, but I also need to figure out exactly how many plants may have had to been crossbred as I build out this chart. There's also the issue of how the crossbreeding occurred, given that lotuses are typically in ponds. Obviously plants or herbs that grow in water are part of the process, as well as those that often grow close to bodies of fresh water, but I wonder just how far out I should go from where the lotus would grow..."

Days like this, Amara wondered if she made the right decision to focus on the palisyfum, especially considering that its existence had never been confirmed in modern times. The stories her grandmother told were always set centuries ago. But there was something inside Amara that told her the flower just had to be real and she needed to figure out its secrets.

*"GRANDMA, what is this palis... palisyf... palis- How do you say it?" Amara finally asked after struggling to pronounce the name.*

*"Palisyfum. Pal-ees-see-fum," Glenda sounded it out for her. "Why do you ask, dear?"*

*"I see the name in your journal a lot, but then next to it, you*

have characters that I don't understand, like it's in another language?"

"Well, I'll have to teach you how to read Latin sometime, won't I?" Glenda approached her twelve-year-old granddaughter sitting at the counter reading through the large book that had been in her family for centuries. "Go get your own journal so we can take some notes."

Amara's face brightened and she bolted to her room for the journal that her grandmother had gifted her a year prior. It was already filled with notes on herbal remedies, but she still had plenty more room to add to it.

"I'm ready!" she chimed as she pulled back up to the counter.

"So, the palisyfum was one of the most powerful ingredients to any remedy that could be conjured in earlier times. People describe it as a lotus the size of a human hand that has five-thousand petals. And each petal represents a different property that makes up the lotus as a whole..."

Amara nodded excitely and took notes while her grandmother explained.

"According to lore, the palisyfum has been used not only to cure various ailments, but also in remedies that have other effects, serving purposes of control, elimination, creation, and enhancement..." Glenda leaned in with a smirk and lightened her tone. "In fact, there is one myth that says the palisyfum can even be mixed with a number of other ingredients to achieve immortality."

"No way, grandma," Amara giggled at the last part.

"Um, yes way," Glenda retorted with a chuckle of her own. "You will learn in due time... Anyway, what shall we have for dinner tonight? Would you like to go into town?"

"Really?!" Amara beamed. She and her grandmother lived in a very rural, almost isolated community in Georgia and she rarely ever had the opportunity to go into town.

*"Yes, dear. Why don't you go ahead and get ready?"*

AFTER SPENDING MOST of her day reading more about the plant life in Masoncrest, various theories in crossbreeding, and as much as she could on lotuses, Amara packed her bag and made her way to the humanities building to pick up her boots from Mateo.

LIAM SAT in his office on the phone with his mother, trying to pass the time more quickly until he could go to Mateo's office where the both of them would see Amara.

"So, how did your first date go with your Fated?" Penelope Taylor asked her son, her enthusiasm leaking through the phone.

"It was absolutely perfect, mother. It really couldn't have gone any better," Liam beamed. "She loved the restaurant, the food, the wine. Our conversation was enthralling and it's incredible how much we seem to have in common despite the fact that we're of two different centuries and two separate worlds."

"That makes me so happy, Liam. I can tell she's already having quite the effect on you. I don't think I've ever heard you with this level of excitement in your voice!"

"I cannot wait for you to meet her, mother. Not only is her beauty ethereal, but she has an energy to match. Her thoughts feel like clouds or something akin to them and she has a gentle, warm aura about her that is contagious."

"Well, I look forward to meeting her. Hopefully sooner rather than later." When Penelope first learned that her son would be fated to a mortal, she thought it was bad luck. Not only would he have to wait over a century to meet her after learning he would have a Fated, but whenever they did get together, he and Mateo would have to watch her grow old and die while they stood still in time. However, since meeting Amara, Liam already seemed to be happier than Penelope had ever seen her son.

"I hope the same! And my other mother? How is she?"

"Scarlett is great," Penelope responded. "You know how my Fated can be. She's always the busy one with the Assembly and what not."

"Of course. Always Assembly business going on..."

The Assembly was the governing body of the magical world, and Liam's mother Scarlett, the one who was a Taylor by birth, was one of its five members. There was a familiar hint of resentment in Liam's tone, but it was no secret how him and his siblings felt about the group. Scarlett often chose her Assembly duties over her family.

"Well, Liam, I know Scarlett is excited to meet Amara as much as I am. When do you think you and Mateo will tell her everything?"

"We're still trying to figure that out. Her being mortal makes it more complicated. Not just when it comes to the existence of our world, but the concept of being Fated. It could be difficult for her to understand, so we're still coming up with ways to describe it."

"Hm..." Penelope pondered with a hum. "Why not explain to her it's the same concept as soulmates? Mortals are obsessed with that and it is technically the same, though very much an oversimplification."

"Yes, we've considered that route as well. We know that we will need to explain it soon. If the effect of the Fated is having anywhere near the impact on her as it has had on us, then I imagine she might feel as though she's losing her mind."

"She'll realize she's not once she learns and accepts the truth of it. It's a beautiful thing, the Fated."

"Even though all of your children are fated to mortals, mother?"

"I'll admit that, that part is... unfortunate, but there is no point in lamenting it. It is not something that can be changed."

"Mother, do you think that if Samuel had a Fated, even if that Fated were also likely to be mortal, do you think he would've turned out... different?"

"Again, my son, there is no point in lamenting that either. Samuel chose his path. And he's made clear to us that there is no changing it."

"You're right..." Liam began thinking about his twin. Samuel was once just as gentle and characteristically sensitive as the other Taylor siblings. But at some point, a point Liam couldn't quite identify, there was a shift. Samuel became brash, hot-headed, cruel, and obsessed with collecting his own wealth, despite the wealth that existed with their family. He went on to become a mercenary and severed his connection with the family. It felt so abrupt to Liam. And each time he tried reconnecting with his twin, it seemed to drive a deeper wedge between the two of them.

"How is Mateo doing?"

Penelope's question broke Liam out of his musings.

"Mateo is well. He's just as taken with Amara as I am. I didn't think he and I could get any closer, but since meeting Amara, we've managed to do just that. In fact, I am going to his office shortly so that I'm there when she visits him. It will only be brief, but I'd like to see how she reacts to sharing a space with both of us at the same time, now that we've each gone on dates with her."

Penelope giggled. "I see... Well, don't scare the woman, please."

"Never," Liam assured. "And please tell Scarlett that her son would like to hear from her sometime on topics unrelated to the Assembly. Perhaps a simple checking in as you do, mother?"

"I will be sure to remind her of it. I love you, son."

"Love you too."

Liam soon made his way to Mateo's office to see him sitting at his desk grading papers. He looked up at him and said, "She's on her way now. Try your best to act casually when she arrives. I know we are testing her reaction to being around us both now, but please don't push it. Our Fated can be quite the nervous one."

"Why not?" Liam asked with his head tilted to the side. "I acknowledge we should treat this delicately, but we can't keep moving at such a slow pace. I'm sure the bond of the Fated is pulling her just as hard as it's pulling us. I also think we should tell her our truths sooner than later. She should know."

"Yes, yes. You make fair points. And I agree that our truths shouldn't be kept from her for too long, but I still worry about overwhelming her. Also..." Mateo crossed his arms and leaned back in his seat, looking away from Liam. "Perhaps we should see if there's something that can be done about our... *sensitivity* to her as well."

"Ha!" Liam clapped. "And you had the audacity to laugh at me when she had the same effect on you. At least I was touching her when it happened to me."

"Shut up... Those leggings she wore on the hike were quite thin and the friction was rather... *deep*."

Liam raised an amused brow. "Because of you losing a bit of self-control..."

"Those erotic sounds she makes and knowing the effect I'm having on her do nothing to help me in tempering my urges..." Mateo shook his head with a groan. "And then she went and put her mouth on my neck and... Anyway, at least she didn't notice."

"Well, now you understand. Actually, what if we take the opportunity to tell her now? She'll be teaching dance class after, so she can clear her mind."

Mateo's head jerked back and he glared at Liam. "*Or*, she could be a total wreck afterward and unable to teach... What if she faints? Could you imagine not being of our world and then suddenly learning that you are fated to be with not one, but *two* immortal warlocks? It's not something we can just spring on her a few minutes before she needs to teach a class."

"Fair enough, then what about after-"

Liam was cut off by a light knock on the door and knew it was Amara. A smile came to both his and Mateo's faces when they sensed her presence.

"Come in," Mateo practically sang.

Amara slowly opened the door and a gasp crossed her lips when she saw both men in Mateo's office together.

"Oh," she choked out. "If you're busy, I can just come back..."

"No, please come in." Liam greeted her with a kiss on the cheek and pulled her into the office, closing the door behind her.

Mateo walked around his desk to peck Amara on her other cheek. "You've come for your hiking boots, right? Let me go get them."

She was speechless looking between the two men that she'd gone on dates with over the weekend who both casually kissed her in front of each other. Her mind began to rack over her current predicament.

*No way. This is not normal. And they're friends! They seem close, too. So they obviously know I'm seeing both of them... What if they do have some kind of sex bet going and I'm in the middle? They don't seem like bad guys, but I've been tricked before... I hope they're not bad guys. I like both of them so much. Then again... maybe if one of them is bad, it'll make it easier if I have to chose between them. My mind is getting ahead of me again... Stupid brain.*

When Liam heard her thoughts and Mateo sensed her distress, both men felt a sinking in the pit of their stomachs.

"Here, Amara..." Liam took her hand again and guided her to sit in the chair in front of the desk. "We should probably talk about this."

Mateo brought over Amara's freshly cleaned hiking boots and sat them down beside her before he leaned against the desk across from her alongside Liam.

She looked up at the two men nervously and was visibly shaking. *What did I get myself into dating two men that are obviously friends? And falling for them at that! What if it has nothing to do with a bet and they just want to break things off? That would really, really suck. But it'd be my fault... and I wouldn't want to cause a rift between—*

"Amara," Liam called, breaking her out of her quickly devolving thoughts.

She froze and looked at him with pure anxiety in her eyes until she noticed the gentle smile on his face. When she took a peek at Mateo, she noticed he was smiling as well.

"As I'm sure you've already gathered," Liam continued. "We're both aware that the other is seeing you..."

"And we're both okay with that fact," Mateo added. "As long as you are also okay with it... With seeing both of us, I mean."

Amara's anxiety turned to confusion. After hesitating for several moments, she finally swallowed and took a deep breath before speaking. "Y-you're okay with me seeing both of you? At the same time?"

"Of course we are!" Liam chimed. "We both think you're a wonderful woman..."

"And we both enjoy spending time with you..."

"So, if it's fine by you, we'd both like to continue seeing you. Now that the three of us are all aware, it'll hopefully make things less awkward?"

"Oh! Um..." Amara fidgeted with her hands. "Y-yeah. It's fine with me. I enjoy spending time with the two of you as well."

"Excellent!" Mateo beamed. He looked at the clock and realized Amara would need to get to class soon, so he picked up the hiking boots that he sat beside her and her gym bag. "Would you like one of us to walk you to class?"

"Oh, no... I'm fine," Amara muttered, taking her bag and boots from his hand, when she looked down at the boots, she realized how clean they were and furrowed her brows. "Did you... wash these?"

"I did," Mateo responded with a grin.

*These men are perfect,* she thought to herself as a smile came to her face and she calmed down. "Thank you, Mateo." *This is nice, like really nice... But what will happen when or if things get serious and I have to choose one of them? I can't have two boyfriends at once.*

"Of course, cariño." Mateo pecked her on the cheek.

"I'll see you soon, I hope," Liam said before Mateo walked Amara out of the room.

CHAPTER

# FOURTEEN

Weeks had gone by since Amara started dating Mateo and Liam and she began seeing them more regularly as they integrated each other into more of their routines. She and Mateo would often grade papers together at least a each week.

As Mateo awaited Amara's arrival, he visited Liam's office and the two spoke about the prospect of telling her the truth about them.

"Yes, as soon as midterms are over, we'll sit her down and tell her everything." Mateo leaned by the door, checking his watch for the seventh time as he anxiously awaited the hour he'd get to see Amara.

"And not a day later," Liam added. "Things are only becoming more difficult."

"Who are you telling? I could probably drink a gallon of that potion and it wouldn't be enough to keep me... settled."

"Yes, yes... but she's also starting to question whether we're truly attracted to her considering we keep initiating things and then stopping when she wants to... reciprocate."

"What?" Mateo's head jerked back. "Did she say-"

"No," Liam interrupted. "Those times when I don't take the potion or it wears off in the middle of a date, I can hear her doubts. Each time I reject her, she wonders if there's something wrong with her, but she doesn't say it aloud or press it further as not to pressure anything."

"I see... Then perhaps we should tell her sooner. I can't bare to have her feeling even the slightest bit that we don't want her."

"Well, it can't be this weekend. Her friend Cameron is coming into town and she's incredibly excited about it."

"Then we'll tell her as soon as he leaves."

Liam nodded. "Agreed. Now, I need to finish writing this exam for my students. Go enjoy your time with her. I hope it's... productive."

Mateo scoffed. "Please. I'll just go home and *actually* grade papers afterwards like I always do. It's impossible for me to do anything but think about her, but *want* her when we're together. I don't know how I've managed to last this long without bending her over my desk."

"Try to keep yourself in check, please. It won't be much longer."

Mateo hummed his agreement before leaving Liam's office.

AMARA AND MATEO sat in his office with their coffees grading papers and preparing midterm exams for their students. They both had a difficult time focusing while alone together, but Mateo's self-control had been depleting by the day and he couldn't seem to take his eyes off of Amara. If he thought her subtlest movements turned him on before, it was even worse now.

He watched carefully as she brought her coffee to her mouth, to the movement of her throat when she swallowed it, to the way that she would lick the small remnants of the drink from her full lips that he couldn't get enough of. Every thirty minutes or so, she would stretch with her arms extended above her head while arching her back and it took everything in Mateo's power not to take her right here.

He could count on one hand his visions of her, but his fantasies were immense. When she stretched in that way that turned Mateo on so much once again and this time moaned at the relief it gave her, he audibly groaned.

"What?"

Mateo didn't bother to hide the lust in his eyes when he responded to Amara. "You are... distracting," he admitted.

"Oh!" she replied nervously. "Did I-"

"No, it's nothing you did. At least... not on purpose." Mateo interrupted as he rose from his chair to approach Amara. He took the books and pen from her hand and set them off to the side of the desk and pulled Amara from her seat so that she was standing between his legs while he leaned against the center of the desk, holding her by her waist. "It's your existence, Amara... You are exquisite... And you cause my mind to... go places."

"Oh?" she questioned with a smirk, looking up to him. "Places like where?"

He moved a piece of hair out of her face and bit his lip as he analyzed it. "Do you really want to know?"

Amara nodded with a shy smile. She was very sexually attracted to both Mateo and Liam. While Liam was more forward, Mateo's sensuality tended to be more subtle. And Amara wanted to see more from him.

"Well, other than thoughts of taking you on this desk..." He brought her in for a kiss that had him savoring her lips, only pulling away to whisper in her ear. "The look on your face as you come undone while I'm deep inside you."

Amara took a sharp breath as heat rushed straight to her core.

He took her earlobe between his teeth before releasing it to speak again. "The sound of you screaming my name as your nails dig into my back..." He buried his face in the crook of her neck and breathed in her scent. "... And the feeling of that flower between your legs spasming around me as you reach your climax," he finished, reaching under her shirt to touch her bare skin.

What Mateo said to Amara didn't make up a fraction of his desires and he avoided sharing the details of his fantasies—feeling it was too soon and he didn't want to scare her away.

Mateo's mouth moved down to place kisses along Amara's neck and shoulders while his fingers gently caressed the bare skin of her lower back, sending chills up her spine. Amara and Mateo had never gone further than heavy groping, but he quickly learned exactly where to touch, kiss, or lick and with how much pressure to get a rise out of her.

However, Mateo wasn't the only one who learned quickly.

With him occupying her neck with his lips, Amara couldn't return the favor to Mateo just yet, so she rubbed her hand up his chest until her fingers lightly traced along his jawline down to his neck and she leaned more of her body against him as small whimpers escaped her mouth.

Mateo's hands traveled down from Amara's lower back, under her pants to firmly grab two handfuls of her bare backside as his tongue trailed up from her neck to her lips and he growled against them. Amara jumped at the aggressiveness of the move and it only made her wetter for him.

"Mateo," she gasped and he looked down at her with a devious smirk.

"Do you like it, Amara?" He muttered as one of his hands moved further down to stroke the wetness between her legs. "It feels like you do."

She took the opportunity to begin placing soft, wet kisses against his neck and he groaned with pleasure at the feeling while the tips of his fingers lightly stroked her.

When he couldn't handle it anymore, he turned them around and placed Amara on his desk.

"Amara," he whispered in her ear.

"Hm?" she hummed.

"May I taste you?" he asked before his kisses along her neck resumed.

"What do you mean by-" Amara was cut off and her breathing hitched when Mateo's hand went down the front of her pants and he stroked her soaking slit. He eased a finger inside before pulling it out to bring it to his lips.

"I mean more than just this," he said after licking her essence off his finger.

Amara's eyes were wide and full of desire watching him. "Yes." She nodded lightly and that was all Mateo needed to remove her pants and crouch down in front of her. She looked down at him anxiously as he licked his lips while he opened her legs to reveal her wet pussy. He looked up at her, maintaining eye contact as he leaned in to have a taste of what he'd been craving for so long until Amara stopped him when she covered herself with her hand.

"Wait," she breathed.

Mateo's brows tensed with concern. "Do you want me to stop?"

"No," Amara squeaked. "It's just that I've never... I mean no one has ever..." She took a deep breath. "I've never had someone go down on me before..." she finally got out. "I mean, I'm not a virgin or anything, it's just that I don't have a lot of experience..." She averted her gaze and swallowed.

Mateo smiled and kissed the inside of her thigh. "Then allow me to be the first." He took the hand she was covering herself with and put it on the back of his head. "You're in control here, Amara," he said before his tongue finally reached her lower lips.

Amara's body trembled as soon as she felt the first lick and as Mateo continued, involuntary sounds began to escape her. She used her free hand to cover her mouth while the other tangled in Mateo's hair. The feeling of his soft tongue moving up and down her inner lips before flicking against her clit was a pleasure she'd never felt before and even as she tried to cover her moans, they were still growing louder.

A muffled squeak sounded through the room when Mateo added a finger and lightly pulled Amara's clit between his lips. While he'd grown more accustomed to her, Amara still had an intense effect on his body and if her moans weren't being suppressed by her own hand, he surely would've come by now—he was barely hanging on with her taste alone. But still, he wanted to hear the sounds he could pull out of her uninterrupted.

Reluctantly, he stopped eating her out and returned to his feet to meet her flushed face and glazed eyes. He admired the way she looked like she was in a daze knowing he put her there.

Amara blinked a few times and gave him a confused look before the anxiety hit her. "Oh gosh," she cringed. "Do I taste bad or someth-" She was cut off when Mateo smashed his lips against hers and captured her in a deep kiss, allowing Amara to taste herself.

"You are delicious…" he whispered when he finally pulled away. "I could eat you all day, but I can't have those beautiful sounds you make muffled because I didn't have the decency to do this in a proper setting."

"What do you mean?"

"Will you come home with me, Amara?"

# FIFTEEN

Liam sat in his office trying his best to focus on lesson planning and finalizing the midterm exams for his students, but it proved difficult as his mind kept going back to Amara. He'd never been the type to get nervous until he met her. Now, he was overflowing with anxiety thinking about the weekend and then what would come after. First, he and Mateo would have to meet Amara's closest friend Cameron and win his approval. After that, the two of them would sit down with Amara and explain everything.

He worried that Cameron might not like him and Mateo. Or even worse, he'd like one, but not the other. But, the absolute worst case scenario on Liam's mind was Amara rejecting him and Mateo. Even if they were Fated and Mateo had already seen the three of the them together, Mateo's visions had become unreliable after their debacle with Petra—something they weren't sure they'd ever be able to fully recover from.

Liam pushed his papers to the side and ran his fingers

through his hair as he leaned further over his desk. He'd seen and heard plenty about the experience of the Fated and even that didn't prepare him for how utterly invested he would be in Amara. She caused him a happiness he didn't think possible, he'd already loved her deeply, and along with that love, came intense feelings of fear—fear of losing her, fear of seeing her hurt, fear of being rejected by her. Should anything happen to her that would cause her to no longer be in his life, Liam wasn't sure what he'd do; the idea of existence without her sounded unbearable.

His thoughts were interrupted when his ears started ringing and his head pounding.

*Oh hell... Mother?* he thought, rubbing his temples. *Is that you?*

"*Yes,*" Scarlett Taylor's voice echoed in his mind. "*The distance between us makes the link a bit less pleasant.*"

*So why not call on the phone? It's one of the more useful advancements that have been made throughout history.*

"*Because, my dear son, what I need to discuss with you should not be said over the phone.*"

*What do you mean? Is everything ok—*

"*It's Petra, she's on the move again.*"

LIAM PULLED up to his and Mateo's home, figuring Mateo went there after parting ways with Amara, but as soon as he reached their door, Liam learned that was not the case. He felt a heat come over him and blood rush to his member before even crossing the threshold of the house. And when he did, his suspicions were confirmed.

Entering the home, he heard the intoxicating sounds of Amara's moans echoing in the hall and began to curse

Mateo. The men had both agreed not to take her until they told her everything. They wanted to have sex with her without those two huge secrets hanging over them.

Liam started walking toward Mateo's room—which was right across from his—when he noticed the door was cracked and got a peek at what was happening.

Amara was without pants and Mateo had abandoned his shirt. He laid on his stomach with his face buried between her legs while she was on her back, chest heaving, eyes squeezed shut and fingers tangled in his hair as he feasted upon her.

She was already completely undone and based on the cloudiness and incoherent nature of her thoughts, Liam figured she had already climaxed more than once. And with the pure, carnal desire leaking from Mateo's mind, Liam knew that he was not even close to finished eating her out.

*Oral sex is still sex, Mateo,* Liam thought to himself as he rolled his eyes.

Liam reluctantly tore his eyes away from the erotic scene, knowing it'd be wrong to continue watching without Amara's consent. However, he couldn't bring himself to close the door the rest of the way and went into his room just across the hall, Amara's moans still loud and clear.

It wasn't just Amara's hazy thoughts that let Liam know she was in sexual ecstasy. The effect of the Fated given his proximity to her caused him to feel a certain level of pleasure from Amara's and it was the same for Mateo.

Laying in his bed, Liam released his painfully erect dick from his pants and held it in his hand. It twitched when he heard an outburst from Amara and he knew she was hitting another orgasm.

*Three.*

Liam heard Mateo think and shook his head. *Of course he's keeping count.*

To the music of Amara's pleasure, Liam began to stroke his length, visualizing as if he were in the room with them.

Amara's mouth was wide open as a breathless moan escaped her lips and she continued to bathe in the euphoric state that Mateo put her in. His tongue and lips moved so skillfully on her core that she was sure she was losing her mind to the bliss that came with it.

"Mateo," she whimpered, her legs shaking uncontrollably as he pulled from her yet another orgasm. Vibrations traveled through her pussy when he released a satisfied hum without letting up on the way he devoured her.

*Four.*

The precum leaking from Liam's hardened member at the sounds of his Fated being pleasured in ways she had never experienced was enough to lubricate his shaft as his movements picked up pace.

Amara's back arched and she cried out yet another erotic melody as Mateo sucked her clit and curled his fingers inside of her. No matter how much she rotated her hips with her body's natural reaction, Mateo's grip on her thighs and the connection between his lips and her lower ones were unwavering. She didn't know it was possible for her body to feel so good.

*Five.*

Using her noises as a guide and the look on her face when he momentarily saw it from the crack in Mateo's door, Liam visualized how it might be twisted in pleasure at that moment and pulsed his hand while he stroked his length faster.

The only things on Mateo's mind as he ate Amara were

her pleasure, her taste, her moans, and her hands pulling at his hair with the intensity of the experience he was giving her. By Amara's second orgasm, he had already come in his boxers, but he still couldn't get enough. He'd probably never get enough.

"Oh my god!" Amara bellowed and her entire body vibrated at yet another orgasm. She panted and struggled to breathe with its intensity. Finally, she started pushing Mateo away rather than pulling at his hair, and he stopped to look up at her, realizing she'd had enough.

*Six.*

"Oh my god!"

Liam heard Amara come once again and could no longer hold himself back, coming at the sound of her outcry. He took himself by hand, but the climax was intense and he laid there for several moments, trying to collect himself before getting up to shower.

Amara was still catching her breath as Mateo kissed his way back up her body. Her eyes fluttered open to see him hovering above her and his short facial hair glistened with her essence. She pulled him in for a deep kiss and her hand traveled down his body but he stopped her and broke the kiss.

She gave him a confused looked. "You don't want me to...?"

"Not just yet," he said softly. "Besides... I can tell that you're a bit exhausted."

And about that he was right. Amara was drained from what felt like were endless orgasms that he gave her. It was unlike anything she experienced and her body was tired.

Mateo kissed her on the cheek before he got up to go to his dresser for a pair of shorts she could wear.

"Thank you," she muttered as Mateo put the fresh pair of shorts over her bare bottom half.

In no time, she drifted off to sleep and Mateo sat there for several moments analyzing her peaceful face before getting up to clean himself.

"DON'T LOOK SO JEALOUS," Mateo teased, walking into the kitchen with Liam. "You're the one who told me to be more forward in the way you were."

"Shut up," Liam grumbled. "And stop fucking thinking about it. I have something important to tell you."

"Liam, you know better than I do that I won't be able to stop thinking about that, especially considering it concluded not twenty minutes ago. I'm considering asking her for more when she wakes-"

"It's about Petra," Liam interjected.

Mateo's released a deep, agitated sigh. "What?"

"Petra," Liam repeated. "My mother told me that the Assembly received word she's on the move."

"What? How? She should still be in a weakened state... But I guess this is good news since it means she won't be wherever the hell it was she was hiding before. What else do you know?"

"Well, the last sighting of her was just outside of Tirana and she seemed to be heading north..."

"That's it?" Mateo asked, a tinge of irritation in his voice.

"I know... it's virtually useless... But at least we know she's on the move and currently on a different continent at least."

"That won't make much difference if she's able to get her power back. We need to-"

"She's coming," Liam interrupted with a whisper and the men changed the subject.

Amara walked into the kitchen wearing her teeshirt from earlier, but a pair of Mateo's gym shorts given that her own bottoms were no longer an option. Her eyes went wide when she noticed Liam sitting across from Mateo at the kitchen table and she visibly cringed.

"Right, so I was explaining to the class-" Mateo stopped and feigned surprise, turning to Amara as she entered the kitchen. "Already up from your nap?"

Amara was stilled looking between the two men. She knew that they lived together, but Liam normally worked late on Wednesdays. Although the men had expressed they were okay with her seeing the both of them, it didn't change the awkwardness she felt, especially after what she and Mateo had just done.

"Y-yeah," she finally choked out. "I'm not the best with naps... I mostly just close my eyes for a few minutes." Thoughts began to fill her head. *How long has he been here? Did he hear me? I feel like I was loud... But I couldn't help it! I really hope he didn't hear anything.*

"It's okay, Amara." Liam broke her out of her thoughts, giving her a warm smile as he reached over to pull her between his legs while he remained seated. "Like we told you before, we're both aware, and it's okay."

"Right..." A confused Amara made quick eye contact with Mateo, who was giving her a lustful smirk before she was taken by surprise when Liam brought her down into his lap.

He was still deeply turned on, remembering the sounds of her from before and pulled her into a kiss. The taste of her very faintly lingered on her mouth from when Mateo kissed her after his face was covered in her essence. Liam deepened the kiss, trying to taste more and his hand instinctively began trailing up the inside of her thigh. Amara whimpered against his lips. She thought she was completely spent from Mateo, but feeling Liam's lips, his touch, had her turned on all over again. Until she remembered that Mateo was sitting right there across from her and Liam and she broke the kiss.

"Oh gosh, sorry. This is weird," she cringed. But her eyes widened with surprise when she noticed that Mateo was looking at them intently and full of desire.

"Is it?" the men asked in unison.

Mateo walked around from the other side of the table to where Amara and Liam were sitting and he pulled her up from Liam's lap to press his lips against hers. At first, Amara kissed him back and melted into him in a move that felt natural until she broke their moment.

"Wait... You kissed me," she pointed to Liam. "And then you kissed me right after," she pointed to Mateo. "You two seem really okay with this..." Amara drifted off in a state of pure bewilderment before Liam spoke up, now standing behind her while she faced Mateo.

"Amara, we are really okay with this," Liam said as he snaked his arms around her waist. "In fact, we had talked about something and we were wondering..." He looked to Mateo.

Mateo's eyes flickered from Liam to Amara. "How would you feel about dating the two of us exclusively?"

Amara furrowed her brows. *I'm already dating the two of them exclusively. I mean... two men is enough and they seem to be the only two I'm interested in seeing anyway,* she thought to herself.

"What we're trying to say is..." Liam continued. "What do you think about the three of us being in a relationship?"

"Oh!" Amara gasped. *I didn't realize they could've been dating each other also. That's such a heteronormative assumption to ma-*

"What we mean is..." Liam interrupted her thoughts before he and Mateo spoke in unison.

"We'd like to share you."

# SIXTEEN

After picking up Cameron from the airport, he and Amara caught up on their way to her and Evelyn's house. She hadn't shared as many details about her separate relationships with Mateo and Liam over the past few weeks.

"They asked if they could share me," Amara told Cameron.

"What?" Cameron's gaze snapped over to Amara in the driver's seat. "The hell does that mean?"

"Well, they said that the three of us would date exclusively... But they wouldn't be dating each other...? I would be their girlfriend, I guess. Both of theirs."

"I don't know about that," he responded, sinking into his seat. "From what you told me about them, they sounded like great guys, but that type of proposition usually is not done in good faith... just passing you back and forth like that? And something about the phrase 'sharing' you just doesn't sit right with me."

"It does sound strange," Amara agreed. "But they seem

genuine about it. You'll understand when you meet them. They don't give off even the slightest negative vibe."

"I'll see about that... What about you? What do you think about it?"

Amara smiled to herself. "I mean, I'm already seeing both of them exclusively, so the only change would be like maybe the three of us would go on dates together? And maybe do other things together..."

"Amara?" Cameron gasped.

"What?" she giggled. "After saying I would think about it, I may have made out with both of them... at the same time."

"My goodness..." Cameron crossed his arms. "What happened to my dear, sweet innocent Amara?"

"I am a woman, Cam," she countered with a playful smirk. "I have needs."

"Yeah yeah..." Cameron rolled his eyes. "Well, I look forward to meeting Liam and Mateo."

"I'm so excited!" Amara beamed. "I really do think you'll like them."

"I hope so."

"What about you? What's your love life looking like these days?"

"Same old, same old. Just some casual dating, but nothing serious."

"Well, we are going out tonight, so maybe you'll find someone here..." Amara's face brightened. "And if you do meet someone, maybe you'll visit more often!"

Cameron chuckled and shook his head. "You're getting ahead of yourself, Amara. Besides, you just moved here a few months ago and I wanted to let you settle in before visiting. I'll be sure to visit more often."

"I still missed you like crazy, though. I mean, I'm happy

to be living with Evelyn, but I don't think you and I have ever been apart for this long since we met."

"I know what you mean... But it was about time for you to spread your wings and it looks like you're doing fine! You're getting along well with Evelyn and your colleagues and you're out here dating."

"You're right! I just never imagined a life like this... Growing up with my grandma, I didn't really know many other people. It was just me, her, and our pet rabbit that died when she did..." Amara stared off at the road ahead as her thoughts drifted off to memories of her grandmother.

*"GRANDMA, when we go into town today, do you think there will be other kids there?"*

*"Maybe..." Glenda finished the final plait in Amara's hair and secured it with a bow.*

*Amara turned to look up at her grandmother with the plea in her eyes. "Do- Do you think I could play with them today?"*

*"I don't know about that, Amara. They're usually out with their parents shopping. It's not really a time to play."*

*"Bu-But what if... Could I maybe talk to them?"*

*Glenda looked down at her granddaughter skeptically. "I don't kn-"*

*"Please," Amara uttered with a pout, her bottom lip quivering. "I just want to make some friends other than you and Xivan..."*

*"And what's wrong with having your grandmother and pet rabbit as your closest friends?" Glenda teased. "We'll never betray you and we're not as cruel as children can be."*

*Noticing the way Amara's face fell, Glenda lifted her chin up and gave her a warm smile. "I guess I don't see anything wrong with you doing some conversing."*

*Amara smiled before she squeezed her lips together and twisted her mouth. "Grandma... Why can't I go to school like other kids?"*

*Glenda let out a deep sigh. "I told you before, Amara. The world is a... difficult place. And I want to prepare you for it myself before you go out into it."*

*"But I still don't understand why that means I can't go," Amara whined. "Other kids go to school even though the world is difficult and I don't see why-"*

*"Because you're different!" Glenda snapped before she could catch herself. "Er- I mean... What I'm trying to say is that we have certain traditions in our family, certain ways of learning... And it's important that those values are carried along with you."*

*Amara looked down, fighting back the tears that were coming to her eyes. She loved her grandmother and Xivan, but loneliness still plagued her. She never understood why she couldn't at least make friends of her own, and when she did interact with people on the outside, her grandmother would often interrupt.*

"Amara!" Cameron shouted and she slammed on the breaks. Amara was met with the sounds of horns around her as her car came to a screeching halt. She looked around and realized that she was stopped in the middle of an intersection and had just missed getting into an accident.

"Are you okay?" Cameron asked urgently. "What happened? You just zoomed through that stoplight. Do you want me to drive?"

Amara looked at Cameron and blinked several times. "Sorry about that... I'm fine." She put the car back in gear to drive out of the intersection and continue on their route.

"Are you sure? I haven't seen you blank out like that in a while..."

"Y-yeah... I'm fine. Sorry about that."

CAMERON EXAMINED himself in the mirror after he finished buttoning up his black shirt. He removed his glasses to put in contacts over his hazel eyes and he used a hair sponge to define his dark brown coils as he finished his look.

He, Amara, and Evelyn were preparing for a night out in the city where Cameron would meet Mateo and Liam for the first time at a lounge downtown. Amara was in the bathroom getting dressed while he and Evelyn were in her room.

"How have you been, Ev?" Cameron asked.

"I've been alright. Classes are going well. My students this year aren't annoying the hell out of me. Teaching three hundred and four hundred level classes are where it's at. I'm gonna get into teaching grad students in a few years too."

"And personal life?"

Evelyn shrugged. "It's fine. I knew not to expect much moving to this tiny town. Though, things have been getting interesting these past couple of months."

"Oh? How so?"

"I've been seeing someone. I mean, we had a subtle flirtation thing going for a while, but we barely saw each other outside of larger faculty meetings since we're in different departments. Recently, though, we've been getting coffees and he's made an effort to visit my side of campus."

"Tell me about him. What's his name? Which department does he work in?"

"James… He's in Natural Sciences… And he's… Amara's advisor."

Cameron's head lunged forward. "What?"

Evelyn held up her hand. "Listen, this has nothing to do with Amara. In fact, we don't even talk about her. It's just a coincidence. And like I said, we knew each other before Amara even moved here."

"Okay, okay. How serious would you say the two of you are?"

Evelyn tilted her head side-to-side as she mulled it over. "Not really serious. He's good looking and a nice guy. You'll actually meet him tonight. He's meeting us at the lounge."

"Great. So, I'll be the…" Cameron counted on his hand. "The sixth wheel since Amara's… *boyfriends* are coming."

"First off, I have James bringing a friend with him for you. And why do you say 'boyfriends' like that? I've worked with Mateo for years and he's a good guy, and I've got a pretty good impression of Liam."

"Yeah, yeah… I just don't know about this whole 'sharing' thing."

"It's her choice. You need to trust her judgement."

"I just don't want anyone taking advantage of her," Cameron lamented. "I worry about her."

"As any big brother would. But you also need trust that you helped her get the tools she needs to be okay without micromanaging her relationships with people."

"Fair enough." Cameron sighed. From the corner of his eye, he noticed Amara entering the room. "Oh! So you're trying to give these men heart attacks, I see!"

She wore a form-fitting royal purple cutout dress that left her hip and most of her mid-section exposed. It came just about halfway down her thighs and she wore it with black platform heels.

"You think they'll like it?" she chimed, smiling as she analyzed herself in the mirror. "I've never worn anything so revealing before, but I'm in the mood to look sexy."

"Geez, what am I gonna do with you now?" Cameron groaned. "I'm not sure if these men are having the best influence."

"Oh, they are having the *best* influence," Evelyn commented, admiring Amara's outfit. "You look good, girl!"

Cameron walked up to Amara and looked her in the eyes with his brows tensed. "Are you wearing this for *you* or *them*?"

"Cam!" Evelyn interjected. "I told you. She's a grown-"

"I've got it, Evelyn," Amara spoke up. "I'm wearing it for myself *and* for them, Cam. I know you see me as your little sister, but we are the exact same age!"

"I know... I just don't want anyone taking advantage of you."

"Liam and Mateo are doing anything but taking advantage of me. They are really good guys, Cam, I promise you."

"But that whole 'sharing' thing... I'm still not sure."

"You're stuck on that one word."

"Because it sounds like they're objectifying you."

"They're not! They're actually oddly chivalrous..." Amara paused with her finger to her chin. "Chivalrous to the point where it doesn't feel real! Aren't you going to trust me, Cam? They're good men. I know it. "

Cameron took a deep sigh. "Well, I guess I'll be finding that out tonight, then. Won't I?"

# SEVENTEEN

"You're keeping your telepathy on tonight, right?" Mateo asked Liam as they sat in the section of the lounge they reserved.

"Yes, of course," he answered. "One benefit of this pesky ability is I can at least know most mortals' true intentions and impressions. I should be able to quickly read what Cameron thinks of us."

"Good. This Cameron, he's like a brother to Amara and we'll need to win his approval or it could make the decision more difficult for-" Mateo paused when he saw Amara enter the lounge and his throat went dry when she removed her coat.

"Fuck..." Liam breathed out the word when he noticed her too.

"Is that woman trying to give me a heart attack?"

"If we weren't immortal, we'd surely be dead right now..."

"Just give me more of the fucking potion," Mateo whispered sharply. "She is making this impossible."

The men knew that Cameron and Evelyn were at her

side, but they couldn't take their eyes off of Amara. The cutout dress she was wearing hugged her body perfectly and exposed much of her smooth brown skin. Mateo and Liam had touched her before, and Mateo had been up close and personal with the place between her legs only days ago, but something about the exposure of her body in that dress had them barely keeping it together.

Amara's eyes scanned the room until they landed on Mateo and Liam and a wide smile came to her face, causing their hearts to flutter. She rushed up to the two of them—Cameron and Evelyn following not far behind—and wrapped both men in a tight hug. They maintained their decency while they greeted her with innocent pecks on her cheeks.

"Amara, you look..." Mateo started before he gulped and looked over her again.

"... Stunning." Liam finished.

"Ehrm," Cameron cleared his throat loudly, breaking both men out of their lustful trances.

Mateo and Liam jumped and straightened themselves up.

"Oh, right... I'm supposed to be introducing you guys!" Amara said cheerfully. She stepped back from the men and pulled Cameron beside her. "This Cam! And Cam, meet Mateo and Liam. I've already told you all about each other, so I'm not sure what else to say..."

Mateo stepped forward with a bright smile and reached out his hand. "It's a pleasure to meet you, Cameron. Amara talks about you often."

"She says good things, I hope," Cameron quipped as he took Mateo's hand.

After their greeting, Mateo stepped back next to Liam who hadn't moved or said anything yet and nudged him.

When he was still unresponsive, Mateo turned to look at Liam and realized he had a puzzled expression on his face, simply staring at Cameron.

In turn, Cameron's brows knitted, looking back at Liam.

*You're offending him, Liam,* Mateo thought and nudged Liam again.

Finally, he came to his senses and stepped forward to greet Cameron as well. "Oh, yes... It is a pleasure to meet you. Thank you for coming out tonight."

"Yeah..." Cameron shook Liam's hand while his expression remained indecipherable.

Amara's face was still alit seeing the men finally meet. "I'm so excited for tonight!" she said before looking around with confusion in her eyes. "Wait... Where did Evelyn go? She was just beside me."

Mateo pointed toward the door where Evelyn was greeting James and another woman. "It looks like she may have invited James." Mateo had noticed that the two of them were spending more and more time around each other recently as well as some flirting, but he didn't expect her to invite James out. He also wondered who the other woman might be, as he had never seen her on campus before.

Evelyn walked up to the four of them with James and his guest behind her.

"I hope you don't mind that I invited two more guests!" she said, presenting them. "Amara, I know that you already know James, but to Cam, Mateo, and Liam, James is in the Natural Sciences Department."

"Hi everyone," James greeted with a warm smile. "And this is my cousin, Clara, who will also be joining us. She works as a mechanic in town."

Clara looked around the group and her the side of her

mouth ticked up slightly when her eyes landed on Cameron. "A pleasure to meet you all."

Following their greetings, the seven of them went to the reserved lounge area where they drank, exchanged stories, and talked about the lore behind the city of Masoncrest.

"You know, Cam convinced me to move to this tiny town for a treasure hunt," Evelyn explained as the group continued talking about Masoncrest's myths. "Told me I'd have all the riches in the world in just a few years."

Cameron burst out laughing. "I didn't tell you shit close to that."

"You did!" Evelyn countered playfully. "You said there's some large treasure under the city of Masoncrest and something about an assembly that put it there."

Liam and Mateo—both of whom had been focused on Amara's squirming between the two of them the whole night—immediately turned their full attention to Evelyn. Meanwhile, Clara and James exchanged a look.

"Tell us more about this treasure," Clara urged. "I'd love to quit working at the shop. Maybe I can help you find it."

"Well..." Evelyn cut her eyes over to Cameron with a smirk on her face. "You wouldn't expect it because he's such a tame guy, but Cam is really into conspiracy theories and is *deep* in online forums. So, when I was trying to figure out what to do next for my academic career, he pitched me this small town-"

"Okay, Ev," Cameron interrupted. "It wasn't like that... *You* explicitly asked me if I had any ideas on places you could find adventure. And stop acting like I'm some conspiracy nut. The Masoncrest thing was just fresh on my mind."

"Fine, then *you* tell it, Cam."

"Fine." Cameron rolled his eyes in an exaggerated

motion at his cousin. "Ev wanted a change of pace and I'd recently come across a super niche forum about eight strange locations—Masoncrest being one of them—around the world that apparently recorded high levels of unexplained occurrences. Supposedly, under each of those towns lies some sort of treasure, but people in the forums were saying it's not the type of treasure 'mortals' commonly think of. It was... weird. And Ev sounded like she needed more weird in her life, so I suggested she come here."

Cameron looked around the group to see that they were all listening to him attentively, with James leaning in as if he were urging him to continue.

"And there was mention of an 'assembly' of people," Cameron went on. "They supposedly plant these places under random cities, or something? I don't know. It's been years since then. But after telling Ev about it, she was pretty much convinced to come here. I remember asking her a few months after she moved to Masoncrest, if she made any progress on finding the treasure and of course as soon as she got here, she got distracted..."

"Distracted how?" James asked.

Cameron leaned back in his chair just as his third drink was delivered and took a sip of his whiskey. "Not my business to tell."

Evelyn gave Cameron a somber glance before she shrugged and looked down at her own whiskey in hand. "I fell in love," she said nonchalantly. "Or so I thought. Anyway, I kept hitting dead ends when I *was* trying to find out about this alleged treasure. So, at some point, I gave up."

"You could always try again, Ev," Cameron responded

before finishing off his drink. "It's never too late. No such thing as quitting when you have the option to try again."

Again, Evelyn's face slightly fell and her lips turned to a frown at Cameron. "Are you sure you want to keep drinking?" she asked him softly.

Cameron cut his eyes at her. "I'm fine."

Evelyn's gaze swept over the group, then back down to her drink. "Right... Sorry. I was just asking because I feel like I've had enough, you know?" Her gaze then went to Amara. "What about you, Amara?"

Amara, whose eyes had been on Cameron, looked back to Evelyn. "I think I could go for one more. But first, I need to go to the bathroom."

Evelyn nodded. "You know what? Me too. I'll come with you."

After the two of them left, James turned his attention to Liam and Mateo and asked the question that had been on his mind all night. "You two seem rather affectionate with Amara... What's going on there?"

"Well, yes," Mateo responded flatly. "We're both dating her."

Clara's brows raised and she leaned in toward the two of them. "And you're okay with that? Aren't you friends? Are you sharing her or something?"

"That's the goal," said Liam, his tone just as candid as Mateo's. "We both adore her and polyamory, although still seen as taboo in some circles, is a valid option."

"And you truly care for her?" Cameron asked. "Because using a term like 'sharing' makes her sound like an object. And to be honest with you guys, I don't like that."

Liam and Mateo both nodded, taking in Cameron's words.

"You're right." Mateo was the first to respond. "And I

assure you that we don't think of Amara as an object. When I say we're sharing her, I mean sharing her affection, attention, admiration. Though, I see how the term, especially when used in reference to her, can come off."

"Agreed," Liam added. "I just want to be clear that we are entering this with Amara with the utmost respect for her. We'll strike that term from our lexicon when describing our relationships with her."

Mateo nodded his agreement.

Cameron also nodded with a hum of approval, impressed with how quickly they adjusted based on his concerns, which gave him a bit more comfort around the thought of Amara seeing both of them.

They'd settled it just in time for Amara and Evelyn to return, Amara taking her seat between Mateo and Liam, and Evelyn sitting next to James.

As the night went on, Amara, Mateo, and Liam were a mess. Liam had to constantly readjust himself in his seat to hide his erection as he listened to Amara's deeply sinful thoughts and sensed how much she wanted him and Mateo. *What a useless fucking potion*, he thought to himself as he held his arm that wasn't on Amara across his crotch.

Mateo's finger traced figure eights on Amara's hip and he would periodically lean in to kiss her shoulder or neck or cheek and whisper something subtle in her ear.

Amara reached a point where she couldn't take it anymore. She looked around at the group and saw that Evelyn was entranced with James and Cameron was deeply engaged in conversation with Clara. Placing each of her hands dangerously far up Liam and Mateo's thighs, Amara whispered to the two of them.

"Can I go home with you?"

The men didn't need anymore prompting than that and

the three of them quickly rose from their seats and said their farewells to the group.

"Are you sure you guys are good?" Amara asked Evelyn and Cameron for the third time as they finished their goodbyes.

"Yes! Now, go!" Evelyn exclaimed.

Cameron eyed Mateo and Liam again for several moments as if analyzing them and took a deep breath. "I'm good, Amara... You can go home with your men," he assured with a wink.

Amara smiled brightly and wrapped her arms around Cameron's neck to bring him in and pepper kisses on his cheek. "Thank you, thank you, thank you!"

"Geez, Amara," Cameron choked out as he peeled her arms off of him. "You didn't need permission!" He chuckled. "Now go on."

Liam gave Cameron one last curious glance before turning around and leaving with Mateo and Amara.

*THIS DOESN'T FEEL NORMAL*, Amara thought to herself sitting in the backseat of the car while Mateo and Liam were in the front. *I have never in my life wanted someone so bad and now I want both of these men really, really bad, and they want me too, but I wonder if it's this intense for them too.*

Hearing her internal ramblings, Liam reached back and placed a hand on Amara's knee. "Sorry if we seem distant. We're just trying to make sure we get back safely. We'll be home soon..."

"R-right, okay..." she answered. *It's like he can read my mind sometimes, I swear.*

*Liam*, Mateo thought. *You've seemed a bit tense all night and I know it's not just because of your nerves about Amara. Did it have something to do with James or Cameron?*

Liam leaned his head against the window as they continued the ride. When they arrived at his and Mateo's home, the two led Amara to Liam's room and she sat at the end of the bed while the two of them stood in front of her.

*Okay, now I'm starting to feel awkward. They haven't touched me since we left... Should I be the one to initiate?*

"Amara, can we get you something to eat or drink?" Liam asked, breaking her out of her thoughts.

"I could go for some water."

"Coming right up," he responded with a warm smile.

"You know, I could go for some water too," Mateo said. "I'll go with you."

The men left the door open as not to seem even more suspicious, but as soon as they got into the kitchen, Liam's eyes went gray momentarily and the air in the room grew slightly thicker.

"Okay, with this veil up, she won't be able to hear us."

"So," Mateo started. "Do you want to tell me what happened tonight? Why were you so tense? Did it have anything to do with James? I had no idea Evelyn was bringing him. And that woman with him, I don't think she was an average mechanic."

"Well, it's a good thing we never told him about our abilities because his thoughts were unrestricted. He is suspicious of our intentions with Amara and thinks we are getting involved with her to learn more about the palisyfum 'lotus'. As for Clara, she also knows about it. She and James have similar... beliefs."

"Is that what had you uptight? They'll be disappointed to find out that our plans for Amara have nothing to do with the palisyfum. It's clear they don't know the true story behind it either. Anyway, on to more important topics. What does Cameron think about us?"

"About that..." Liam gulped. "I couldn't read his thoughts."

Mateo gasped. "What do you mean?"

"I mean pure silence. Absolutely nothing. I couldn't even get a sense of the texture of his thoughts."

"What the hell?"

"We'll figure it out later," Liam assured. "Now, can we please tend to our Fated? I can't stand for her to think that we are neglecting her."

CHAPTER

# EIGHTEEN

"Here's your water," Liam said as he handed a glass to Amara. She was still sitting in the same spot at the edge of the bed when they returned to the room.

"Th-thanks," she replied softly without looking at him. She took the drink with a shaky hand and looked down at it. *This went differently in my head... It's like one minute, they can't keep their hands off of me and the next, they pull away.*

Liam, hearing her thoughts, and Mateo, sensing her distress, joined her on the bed. They sat on each side of her and returned their hands to the spots they'd been most of the night—Liam caressing the bare skin of Amara's back while Mateo, with his arm around her, traced shapes into her hip.

Amara took a sip from her cup and tried to steady her breathing as the heat that accompanied their touch started to come over her again.

"Are you okay?" Mateo asked.

"Yeah," Amara gulped. *I'm just not so sure what I was*

*thinking would happen when I asked to come home with you. Damn hormones.*

Liam held back a chuckle and kissed Amara's cheek. "Do you remember what we did the other day?" he questioned. "After we asked about both dating you?"

"Yes," Amara breathed as the memories of it began to fill her head. *Making out with just one of them at a time already felt good enough, but making out with both was out of this world.*

"How about we pick up from there? Would you like that?"

"I would!" Amara responded without hesitation. *Hormones!* she internally chided herself.

"Are you finished with this?" Mateo gestured to her cup. When Amara nodded, he took it from her hands and went to set it on the nightstand while Liam moved his hand to her torso and pushed her to lay down on the bed.

In no time, Mateo joined and Amara was on her back, sandwiched between the two of them. Their hands ran over her body and their mouths were practically glued to her. When one man released her lips to place kisses on her neck or shoulder, the other would immediately take them.

"We really, really like this dress, Amara," Liam whispered, running his fingers along her thighs while her lips were against Mateo's.

"Fuck," Mateo breathed when he broke the kiss, his hand now far enough up her leg to feel the heat coming from her core. He nearly bursted through his pants when she released a small whimper at the feeling of Liam rubbing her through her panties. "Are you wet for us, Amara?"

She gulped and nodded timidly.

"There's no need to be shy about it," Liam muttered

against her neck, his fingers still moving up and down her slit along the thin fabric.

"Don't you remember that I devoured you only days ago?" Mateo asked as he caressed the inside of her thigh. "I'd be happy to remind you."

Amara's breathing hitched and she felt herself twitch at the flashbacks that flooded her mind.

"If we're being fair..." Liam held Amara's gaze. "I do think this turn would be mine."

Mateo paused from peppering kisses along her collarbone. "What do you think, Amara?"

"W-wait... you mean right now? Like, in front of you?"

"Yes, cariño," he replied with a smile. "We're both with you, which means..."

"We'd do things like this together," Liam finished. "How about we start with something a bit more... mundane," he suggested as he raised her dress. Both men audibly groaned when they looked down at Amara's exposed underwear and saw from them how wet she was.

"I-is everything ok- oh..." Amara was cut off when she felt both men's hands rubbing her through her panties before they worked in unison up to her hips to tug at the fabric.

"We're going to remove these," Mateo whispered against her ear as they pulled the panties off of her.

Liam turned Amara's head to face him and he took her lips with his while he gently rubbed her clit and Mateo lightly sucked her neck as he eased a finger into her pussy. Amara gasped against Liam's lips and her breathing grew heavier with the pleasure that came over her.

"So wet..." Mateo muttered, sinking in a second finger and speeding up his movements in sync with Liam.

Amara broke her kiss with Liam and released another

moan before Mateo turned her head to face him to press his lips against hers. Liam toyed with the neckline of her dress and without breaking her kiss with Mateo, Amara tugged at the fabric to signal to Liam he could pull it down.

As soon as he freed one of her breasts, Liam took Amara's nipple between his lips as his and Mateo's fingers continued to work her. Amara broke away from Mateo and threw her head back into the bed as her back arched and her body shook at her release. As she came down from her high with labored breathing, she watched as both men licked her essence from their fingers before she pulled each of them into kisses.

While her mouth was against Mateo's again, Liam's lips began to trail down Amara's body until he was between her legs. Amara jumped when she felt him give her one long lick and she pulled away from Mateo to look down at Liam who had a mischievous smirk on his face.

"How many times was it the other day, Mateo?" he asked slyly.

Amara's brows knitted. "What do y-"

"Six," Mateo replied confidently.

"That should be easy to beat," Liam sneered.

"What are you talk- oh shit!" Amara blurted when Liam's mouth latched onto her core and his lips and tongue moved against her.

The sounds that escaped her were loud and shameless as wave after wave of pleasure rolled through her body and a second climax hit her instantly. Not wanting to disrupt the melody of her pleasure, rather than taking her lips again, Mateo's kisses moved down Amara's body and he released her other breast. He took one into his mouth as he toyed with the other using his fingers all while Liam was still devouring Amara.

Her body trembled and her speech turned unintelligible. She thought the experience that Mateo gave her just a few days ago was the most intense she'd had, but what she was feeling in this moment being pleasured by both men put her on an entirely different level. She didn't know how many times she came, unsure where one orgasm ended and the other began. It wasn't until she felt her leg twitching uncontrollably and that her core was overly sensitive, practically on edge from even the tiniest lick from Liam that she mustered enough strength to push his head away.

"Seven," Liam chimed when he lifted himself from her.

Amara's chest was heaving and her breathing ragged as she was coming down from the euphoria that the men put her in. When Liam came back up, he pulled her face against his to give her deep kiss.

"You are exquisite, Amara," he muttered when he finally broke the kiss.

Before she could respond to Liam, Mateo pulled Amara into him and he released a satisfied hum against her lips at the taste. His kisses made a path to the corner of her mouth and then her jaw, until he was right by her ear and whispered, "We're going to have to work you up to more than just seven."

"He's right," Liam added. "Because I'm still hungry."

Amara's eyes went wide and she squeezed her thighs together, grappling with conflicting feelings of being spent from coming so much and deeply turned on by their words. "T-technically, it w-was eight..." she corrected before her hands began to trail down to each of the men's erections. However, they both grabbed her by her wrists as soon as she reached the front of their pants.

"Why do you always stop me?" The defeat was already in her tone.

The men paused for several moments before Mateo finally spoke up. "We just want to wait, Amara..."

Amara swallowed and her mouth slightly twisted. "Why are you always doing things to me if you don't want me to do anything to you?"

"It's not that," Liam said, taking her face in his hand. "We just want to make sure you know what you're getting into..."

Amara snatched her face away before she sat up in bed and huffed. "What does that even mean?"

Mateo and Liam exchanged a concerned glanced, unsure what to say to her.

"I don't want to pressure you guys," she said softly as she put herself back in her dress. "It's just... Maybe we should be more fair about this..."

"What does that mean?" Mateo asked, sitting up to meet her face. His heart sunk when he saw the distress in her eyes.

"If you want to wait, I'm fine with that. But I'm not comfortable with you doing all these things to me if you're not ready for me to reciprocate..." Amara hunched over, looking at her hands as she fidgeted with them. "I don't want you to interpret this as me pressuring you, it's just that I don't want to keep being in this position and I don't want to keep putting you in the position of rejecting me."

"But Amara, we're not rejecting you," Liam protested as he lifted himself up. "It's just that there's something we need to tell you..." He took a deep breath and held her hand. "Mateo and I, we're-"

"Somnum," Mateo said with a snap of his fingers and Amara suddenly fell back into the bed and closed her eyes.

"What the hell was that?" Liam whisper-yelled. "Did

you seriously use magic on our Fated and put her to sleep in the middle of me talking to her?"

"You were about to tell her that we're war-"

"What just happened?" Amara sat back up and the two men looked at her completely bewildered. "We were just talking and then I swear I passed out... Did something happen?" she massaged her temples and blinked several times.

Mateo's mouth was agape as he stared at her in disbelief. *What the hell? That should've put her into a deep sleep for several minutes at least.*

"N-No," Liam finally choked out. "You must just be sleepy."

"Right..." Amara dragged out. "I guess it has been a long night." She took a deep breath and looked between the men when she remembered what they were talking about. "You were about to say something, right, Liam?"

"Y-yes. I was um... apologizing for causing you to feel this way, Amara. I can assure that we are not rejecting you and that we are very attracted to you." He gestured to the tent in his pants.

"We're both sorry," Mateo added. "And we want to discuss this further, but maybe now isn't the best time since emotions are high?"

"Right," Liam agreed. "Perhaps we try Wednesday evening? Here at our home?"

Amara's face scrunched with confusion, still in a daze after feeling like she'd gone unconscious for a few seconds. "Oh, okay..."

"How about we take you home, eh?"

"Y-yeah, okay."

. . .

LIAM AND MATEO walked Amara to her door and she stood there looking up to the two men as they said their good-byes. The fifteen-minute car ride on the way to her house from theirs was virtually silent.

"Well, I guess I'll see you Wednesday?"

"Wednesday!" the men chimed in unison with bright smiles.

"Oh, Amara," Mateo called out to her as he nervously rubbed the back of his neck. "I meant to ask you about this, and I don't mean to be intrusive. I'm just curious about Cameron... Evelyn said something about him and drinking. Is it something he struggles with?"

Amara's mouth twisted when he asked the question and she nervously rubbed her chin as she thought about Cameron's history with drinking and the story that Evelyn told her. "It's not really my business to share..." she replied.

"Right, right... Fair enough. We'll see you on campus Monday, right? Perhaps the three of us could get coffee?"

Mateo and Liam's hearts dropped when Amara didn't immediately answer and she averted her gaze. "Yeah... maybe another time. It's actually kind of a busy for me since Cameron is leaving that night."

"Yes, of course."

After kissing both men goodbye, Amara turned and went into the house without looking back at them again.

When the two of them got into the car, Liam hit his head against the back of the seat and Mateo slammed his fist on the dashboard.

"I hate putting her through this!" Mateo shouted. "This is inhumane for all three of us!"

"It is... I can hear it in her thoughts. As if her anxiety wasn't bad enough before, she is terrified and confused as to why what she feels for us is so strong."

"Just a few more days and she'll know everything... Let's just hope that she will accept us."

"Speaking of which, why didn't your spell work? Did you hold back or something?"

"I didn't want to expend too much, so I *did* hold back, but it still should've kept her down for at least a few minutes. It's like it barely affected her... Could it have something to do with the connection of the Fated?"

"Maybe," Liam noted. "We still haven't gotten around to getting a sample of her blood. The drive is Tuesday, so let's ask her to come with us..." He groaned and rolled his eyes. "We'll have to make up an excuse as to why we can't give blood, though."

"I hate lying to her," Mateo griped. "But between my vision of Samuel before and what happened tonight, we should check just to be sure."

"Yes, though if she was of our world, she'd understand completely what is going on and would be able to sense our magic."

"You're right... and at the very least, she would've told us, I'm sure about it."

"There's also the possibility that our unfortunate bond with Petra is starting to fuck with our powers even more now that she's on the move again. So that could be the reason your magic failed as well."

"Shit," Mateo spat. "We'll need to hunt her down and deal with her eventually."

Liam nodded. "Yes, but Amara will take priority. Now, onto Cameron. He is still a curious case, but now we have something to start with as far as theories go... Based on Amara's thoughts it seems that in high school, he struggled with alcohol addiction. When he was eighteen, he got into a drunk driving accident that should've killed him, but he somehow survived and it was like he was miraculously cured of his alcoholism."

"Interesting..."

"There's more. Amara then thought something about the week of his accident being traumatic for both of them, but it was a strange thought considering they didn't meet each other until months later when they were at university. I'm not sure what it means."

"Strange indeed." Mateo stroked his beard as he pondered. "Do you think he might have some sort of demon deal going on that kept him alive?"

"No, I don't think that's it. Something like that wouldn't affect my ability to read his thoughts. What about a living corpse?"

"That would explain the blankness of his mind, but he has to have a soul considering his relationship with Amara. I can sense that he cares for her. And he doesn't give off that awful scent that living corpses normally do."

"How strange... We'll need to investigate further."

# CHAPTER
# NINETEEN

Amara stood in the shower, deep in thought as the water ran down her body. Since the day she met them, Mateo and Liam caused her some of the deepest confusion she'd ever experienced—even more than when she left her home in Georgia after her grandmother died and Amara entered the 'real world'.

The men seemed to truly care about her and Amara never felt like they had bad intentions, but she didn't understand why whatever they needed to tell her had to wait until Wednesday and why it needed to be done at their home. She felt like she could trust the two of them, but the times that they acted strange around her worried Amara that she may have judged them wrong.

Growing up, Amara's grandmother always told her that she couldn't trust anyone and even after she died, Amara was overly cautious about interacting with people until she met Cameron.

. . .

YOUNG AMARA WAS *in her backyard dancing when she heard a car pull up to her grandmother's home. They almost never had visitors other than the rare times that someone would come to pick up a remedy or receive treatment from Glenda every few months. Curious about who the visitor could be and knowing that her grandmother was busy upstairs, Amara walked around the house to see who it was.*

*As she rounded the corner of the home, the first thing she noticed was a black car with North Carolina license plates. She wondered why someone from an entirely different state would be visiting her grandmother.*

*"Hello, little one," said a woman with a velvety voice.*

*Amara jumped. She'd been so distracted by the car that she completely forgot that a person had to have come in it. She looked up at the brown-skinned woman whose hair was braided in individuals that fell down to her waist. Her full lips were painted with a burgundy lipstick and she gave Amara a wide smile, flashing her perfectly-aligned white teeth. Most of her face was hidden behind large shades, but something about the woman felt familiar to Amara.*

*Noticing the fear in the young girl's eyes the woman crouched to meet her at eye-level, but avoided removing her shades. "Amara, I'm here to see your grandmother."*

*"Amara!" Glenda shouted as she rushed over to her grand-daughter and grabbed her by her shoulders, scaring the girl. "What did I tell you about talking to strangers?"*

*The woman stood straight up again and scoffed at Glenda's words.*

*"Sorry, grandma! I knew you were busy and I-"*

*"Let's go, Amara," Glenda interrupted as she yanked her arm and led her toward the house. She turned back to glare at the mysterious woman. "Please, have a seat on the porch. I'll be*

back down shortly." Despite the courteous nature of her words, Glenda practically spat the sentence with agitation clear in her tone.

"Grandma, who is that?" Amara asked as Glenda dragged her up the stairs. "She knew my name and there's something familiar about her. If she's your friend? Can I have friends too?"

"That woman is not *my* friend," Glenda snapped. "In fact, she is not even someone that I trust enough to be near you. Now, go to your room."

"But grandma, she didn't look like a bad person."

"Amara! I told you that deceivers can come in any form, whether that be friends, neighbors... even lovers. So how do you think that would apply to a stranger arriving at our door?"

"But she seemed-"

"It doesn't matter what she 'seemed', Amara! You can never really know people's true intentions and you should always be cautious."

Amara's eyes teared up, confused as to why her grandmother was scolding her so harshly. "I-I'm sorry, grandma."

Glenda's face softened when she saw Amara's distraught expression and immediately felt the guilt come over her. "In your room, Amara," she said softly. "I'll come get you when she leaves."

Amara did as she was told and not long after her grandmother closed the door, she rushed to her window to look down toward the front porch and watch the woman and her grandmother speak. While most of their conversation was barely audible, she did catch a tense exchange between the woman and her grandmother.

"Of course I haven't told her about her parents," Glenda snarled at the woman. "She is not ready."

"She will resent you, if you don't. And you need to tell her what she is."

*"That's very interesting coming from you," Glenda replied sarcastically. "Yes, I'll tell her about her parents and then I'll let her know why you looked familiar."*

*"Are they talking about me?" Amara whispered to herself. Suddenly, the shaded woman's head turned up to look at Amara sitting in the window as if she'd just heard her and Glenda's head snapped in her direction too. Amara saw her grandmother mouth something, wave her hand and suddenly, everything went blank.*

STILL DEEP IN THOUGHT, Amara got out the shower, put on her pajamas and went to her room. She was startled when she saw Cameron sitting up in bed with the lamp on.

"Cam! Don't scare me like that. You were fast asleep when I got home."

"You're not exactly quiet when you're rummaging through your things and mumbling to yourself," he teased. "So, how was your evening with Liam and Mateo?"

"Oh! It was..." Amara averted her gaze. "Nice," she replied unconvincingly.

Cameron's eyes followed her as she walked over to the bed and got in next to him. "What happened?" he asked. "You know you can't lie to me, Amara."

She swallowed the lump in her throat and stretched her arms above her head. "It's just that they confuse me sometimes. I don't understand them."

"What do you mean?"

"Well... I don't want to get into the details of it, but when we're... *intimate*, they never let me reciprocate and when I finally confronted them about it, they said it's because there's something they need to tell me first. I don't get it. What secret could they *both* have that's keeping them from letting me..." Amara caught herself. "You know..."

"That is odd," Cameron replied as he held his finger to his chin thoughtfully. "Why didn't they just tell you when you confronted them?"

"I don't know! And now they're saying that they want me to come over Wednesday night and they'll tell me everything. It's all so strange..."

"Damn, I'll already be gone by then..." he paused and his brows tensed. "What did you say their last names were again?"

"I didn't tell you because I didn't want you trying to stalk them before meeting them," Amara quipped. "Mateo's last name is Vazquez and Liam's last name is Taylor."

Cameron took a sharp breath when he heard the names. "Vazquez and Taylor, you said?"

"Yeah..." Amara tilted her head to the sided while examining Cameron's expression. "Why do you look like that?"

"Oh, nothing!" he chuckled and laid back down. "I'm just excited to do my stalking now."

"Weirdo," Amara grumbled before she fell back into her pillow.

They were silent for several moments, the two of them unable to immediately fall asleep, until Cameron spoke up.

"Amara... have you noticed anything weird since moving to Masoncrest? Like things you can't explain?"

"Other than the fact that you're not the first person to ask me that question?" she replied. "Well, I'm currently dating two men that I already have really strong feelings for who want to 'share' me and every time I try to reciprocate their sexual favors they reject me, so nope! Nothing weird at all about that. Totally and completely normal!"

"Asshole," Cameron scoffed. "But seriously, do you ever feel like something is pulling at you or anything like that?"

"And I repeat: weirdo... But to answer your question, other than Mateo and Liam, nothing that weird has happened. I'd say the biggest change is that I get those nightmares I told you about slightly more often, but I think it's just because I'm in a transitional phase."

"Damn, I'm sorry to hear that. Have you been taking your medicine that you make for it?"

"Yeah, I have..."

"Has it been helping?"

Amara took a deep sigh. "Yes, but I'm worried I'm building an immunity to it. I mean, I have been taking it since I was young, so it's only natural, I guess. But I will admit that some of the things I see in those dreams still haunt me."

"Do you want to talk about it? Like we used to when the nightmares got bad?"

"Yeah, I guess saying it aloud will help. Though, there's not a ton to say, it's more like the way I feel when I'm in those dreams..."

"What do you mean?"

"I'm a combination of panicked, terrified, heartbroken, angry... But most of all, I feel anguish in those dreams. The pain is so intense and then I hear the sounds of a man screaming and he sounds so familiar for some reason to the point that I get chills just thinking about it even when I'm awake. And then there's..." Amara blinked several times, trying to avoid tears rushing to her face. She took a deep inhale and audibly exhaled. "And then I see these red eyes that horrify me and then a pair of purple ones that sadden me."

"Well..." Cameron gulped. "Just remind yourself that none of it is real."

"Yeah, you're right." Amara yawned and turned over to lay on her stomach. "Good night, Cam. Love you."

Wide awake and staring blankly at the ceiling Cameron replied, "Love you too, Amara."

CHAPTER

# TWENTY

"It is absolutely baffling!" exclaimed a frustrated Liam as he threw down another book. "What could Cameron be? We've spent all day reading through the lore and nothing makes sense."

"It doesn't help that we're not working with much information about Cameron," Mateo replied. "Perhaps we should get Lillian involved..." He looked down at his phone for the tenth time that hour and sighed when he saw it was still without notifications.

"Waiting to hear from Amara too?" Liam asked, raising a knowing brow. "She usually texts or calls, but today, it's absolutely nothing."

"This entire situation is incredibly frustrating and I am both eager and reluctant to tell her the truth about everything," Mateo griped and buried his face in his hands. "What if she doesn't accept us?"

"I know... It scares me too. But it must be done. And once we explain to her what it means to be Fated, at least she won't feel like she's going crazy when it comes to her feelings for us."

"I just worry about overwhelming her. Let's at least hold off on telling her about the palisyfum. I'm afraid she'll be devastated to learn the truth. I just hope she won't think all her studies were a waste of time..."

"They weren't! She is an incredibly talented botanist and I'm not saying this just because of how I feel about her. Amara is as good with herbs and remedies as an elite witch..." Liam suddenly froze and fell into deep thought. "Wait, do you think she could be..."

"A witch?" Mateo leaned his head forward with his brows raised.

The men were silent for several moments.

"Nooooo..." they said in unison after the long pause.

"Even if she were a witch, that's no reason for her to have resistance to my spell. It's worked on you before. I also never saw any signs of it in my visions."

"Yes, but your visions are so sporadic now and they've turned unreliable after the debacle with Petra."

"You do have a point," Mateo agreed. "And considering the fact that my visions of Amara before we met her came to me differently from the way I usually have premonitions, it is fair to be skeptical. Normally, it'd take physical contact and deep concentration to see a future, but hers came to me randomly, kind of like the way my mother experienced her visions."

"Right. But you haven't had anymore come to you in that way since we've met her, right?"

"No, my vision of Samuel came to me when I touched Amara, so that was a relatively normal case."

"I see..." Liam contemplated for a few moments. "Maybe you should lay off of Lillian's potion for a while and we could do a proper reading with her. It could help determine if she actually is of some supernatural background."

Mateo twisted his mouth and swallowed. "That's something I'd rather avoid..."

"Why? Don't you- oh..."

"I can't run the risk of seeing her death, Liam. I don't know what it would do to me. When my mother... When I saw..."

"Right, of course." Liam placed a comforting hand on Mateo's shoulder. "We'll figure this out another way."

"Okay," Mateo cleared his throat. "Now back to theories... So, the likelihood of her being a witch is rather low since it wouldn't explain her resistance to my spell."

"Yeah, unless she were from some bloodline more powerful than either of ours..."

"And those are long gone," Mateo finished. "It is a much higher chance that the failure in my magic has to do with the current inconsistencies in our powers."

"Wishful thinking on our part," Liam sighed. "If she were a witch, she'd have the potential to become immortal like us... And then we wouldn't have to think about the inevitable."

"Right." Mateo looked down, trying to fight back thoughts of what it meant to be an immortal fated to a mortal. "And we wouldn't have to worry about her accepting the world that we come from." He ran his fingers through his hair anxiously when he looked down at his phone yet again and there was still no text.

Liam pulled his phone from his pocket and opened his text conversation with Amara. "Perhaps we should just-" He was cut off when he received a notification from an unknown number and heard Mateo's phone chime as well.

"What the...?"

This is Cameron. It is important that I speak to the both of you. I'll be on campus tomorrow while Amara is teaching.

Mateo held his phone up to Liam, showing a message from Cameron. "Did he…"

"Message me too?" Liam finished. "Yes, the same thing."

"As if things couldn't get any more strange," Mateo grumbled.

Liam huffed, shook his head, and typed a response to Cameron.

Of course! How about you meet us in my office on campus? I'm two floors up from Evelyn's office.

I'd rather meet in a more visible location. How about the bleachers by the athletic fields? We will meet during Amara's 9AM class.

The men exchanged a confused glance with each other.

"He asks for 'a more visible location' as if he's threatened by us… Do you think he knows what we are? But even then, if he *does* know we're warlocks, he'd know that being in a more visible place wouldn't make that much of a difference."

"Perhaps it's just a precaution," Liam replied before sending his message.

Yes, that is fine. We will meet you there. Ahead of that, could you tell us what it is you would like to discuss?

No. I will see you then.

Liam muttered a series of expletives under his breath and stuffed his phone back into his pocket. "He must have taken our numbers from Amara's phone. Why the hell couldn't he at least say what this is about?"

"I believe it has to be one of two things: Either he's behaving as the protective big brother and wants to give us a warning not to hurt Amara or something. Or... This has to do with you not being able to read his thoughts. It's possible he's figured out we are warlocks."

"Shit! What if he assumes the worst about us and tries to put a wedge between us and Amara? He has a lot of influence over her."

"Let's hope that's not the case. This is only growing more and more stressful, Liam. Also..." Mateo leaned back in his seat, clasped his fingers together and placed them on his head. "With everything going on, I think we should consider the possibility that Amara is might be some type of magical being, even if she isn't a witch..."

"You're right," Liam nodded. "Something is definitely up with Cameron and these strange occurrences with Amara seem to keep mounting."

"Yes, it is odd that we need to take a potion to keep from her hearing your thoughts or seeing or triggering my visions. And that premonition of Samuel haunts me. You really can't track him?"

"No. He has somehow found a way to cut off his connection with everyone in the family. My mother can't even reach him through her mind links anymore. Him being a collector and damn good at it, I imagine he found some type of tool or spell to sever our bond. Also, you seeing him here to take her... It could've been Samuel playing one of his fucked up games with me rather than it having to do with Amara herself."

"Add that to the pile of shit we may have to deal with." Mateo rolled his eyes and sat back up to rest his chin on his fist. "Let's table the Cameron research for right now since we're speaking to him tomorrow. As for Amara, let's go through the lore again with a focus on what she could be—if she's anything at all. We'll also need to convince her to participate in the blood drive on Tuesday."

"Agreed. If she's anything, let's hope that it's relatively minor given that we can't detect any energy from her. She probably has the blood of an imp or fairy or something along those line from deep in her family tree."

"Plausible." Mateo shrugged. "We'll know for sure once we get her to do the blood drive."

"Are you sure you'll be okay alone on campus, Cam?" Amara asked. "Your flight leaves tonight and I would've been fine taking off of work so we could spend the day together."

"I'll be fine! And it's not like you're working all day. You just have the one lecture, right?"

"That's right. It'll be for an hour and fifteen minutes and then I usually spend another fifteen minutes after class answering students' questions."

"See! That doesn't even make up a full two hours. I'll just pass the time exploring campus. I know Evelyn is in classes or office hours all day."

"Okay, this parking lot is like a five-minute walk from the building where I'm teaching. Meet me right back here by ten-thirty and we'll spend the rest of the day together before I need to take you to the airport."

"Deal." Cameron nodded. "I'll see you then!"

After the two of them parted ways, Amara started her

brief journey to the building. Mid-terms had just finished and the air on campus seemed calmer. Walking past the quad, where there were often activities going on, Amara saw what appeared to be a pet adoption event at the center of it. She decided take a detour to see the animals available —there were dogs, cats, rabbits, and hamsters. Amara had recently been considering getting a pet, but Evelyn was allergic to almost anything with fur.

She smiled to herself when she stopped to look at the cages of rabbits on display, thinking about her only friend growing up besides her grandmother.

*"GRANDMA, Xivan won't do any tricks." Amara pouted. Over the past several months, she'd been trying to train the rabbit to go through an obstacle course that she built, but he was painfully stubborn and refused to go through even the first tunnel.*

*Glenda approached her granddaughter who was sitting on the ground in the backyard petting the rabbit's dark gray fur and joined her in the grass.*

*"Hm..." she pondered aloud as she joined them in the grass. "Well, Xivan is very, very old, Amara. And he's been through a lot..."*

*"A lot? Like what?"*

*"Well, you know Xivan had a whole family before, two kittens, a grand kitten, and his own mate."*

*"Kittens?" Amara asked skeptically. "How could Xivan have cats?"*

*"No," Glenda chuckled. "Baby rabbits are called kittens."*

*"But you said two kittens and a grand kitten? I thought rabbits have more babies than that at a time... Like a whole litter."*

*"Always so smart." Glenda patted her granddaughter's head*

*with a smile. "Xivan's mate was special and gave birth to one very special kitten... and that kitten also gave birth to a single kitten."*

*"Oh, okay... And Grandma?"*

*"Yes, dear?"*

*"Did I ever have a bunny? Like, when I was really young? One with black fur?"*

*Glenda's tilted her head to the side curiously. "Wh-why do you ask that?"*

*"I don't know... for some reason, I vaguely remember having a rabbit. And I had a dream the other day about this black rabbit that seemed so familiar, I could almost feel it."*

*"Was it one of your nightmares? Have you been taking your medicine for those?"*

*"It wasn't a bad dream, grandma. I was somewhere outside, playing with the rabbit and she even had a name. It was Chel and..." Amara drifted off when Xivan started to show distress, distorting his body and releasing cries that sounded like that of another animal. "Is he okay?" she asked urgently.*

*Glenda took the gray rabbit and cradled him in her arms. "He will be..." She muttered something under her breath as she stroked his fur and Xivan began to calm down until the rabbit was sound asleep.*

*Amara gasped. "How do you do stuff like that, Grandma? You manage to calm anyone down."*

*"I'll teach you one day," Glenda replied with a wink.*


"AMARA?" David called, breaking her out of her daydream.

Amara shook her head and blinked rapidly before turning to her TA. "Hi, David. How are you?"

"Thinking about getting a pet?" he asked with a warm smile.

"No, I was just looking. They remind me of the pet rabbit I had growing up." Amara tilted her head and gave him a curious look. "I almost never see you on campus around this time, David. Are you going to sit in on the lecture today?"

"I am! My lab students have been great, but I just want to make sure I'm completely aligned with you on all the materials."

"That makes sense! And it's good to hear that all is well with your students. You'll see in lecture that they can at times get a bit off topic."

The two of them started walking toward the building together and David would peek over at Amara occasionally to see if he noticed anything strange. "So, um... how has your progress been on studying the palisyfum?"

"Eh... It's been alright. I've been hitting a lot of dead ends lately."

"Oh? How so?"

"Well, the more I read through my grandma's notes, the longer the list of potential plants involved in its creation. But then, it seems almost impossible for that many plants to combine into one, don't you think?"

David pondered. "Yes, but since—like you said yourself—its properties seem almost magical, it makes sense for its creation to sound beyond the bounds of possibility."

"You're right. It's just so frustrating. One of my theories that stresses me out the most is that with the lore saying the flower has five-thousand petals, I fear that could be figurative and mean it is the result of mixing five-thousand different plants. But that sounds ridiculous!"

"Hey, hey... Don't get so frustrated," David assured. "I'm sure you'll figure this all out. Just keep it up! And like I said,

I'm also interested in rare plants like the palisyfum, so I'm happy to help you anytime."

"Oh yeah... What happened last time when you came to help me that time? You left so abruptly. Was everything okay?"

"Oh, that? Y-yeah. I just started feeling kind of sick..."

"That's weird." Amara raised a skeptical brow. "You seemed fine when you first arrived and then you suddenly got all pale. Have you been to the doctor about it? It could be something serious considering the abruptness of it."

"It's fine!" David snapped before catching himself when he noticed the surprise on Amara's face. "Er- I mean, thank you for your concern, but I'm okay."

"Okay." Amara shrugged and entered the lecture hall.

CHAPTER

# TWENTY-ONE

Liam bounced his leg anxiously as he and Mateo sat on the bleachers by the athletic fields waiting on Cameron.

"Where the hell is he? Do you think we should text him?"

"Let's give it five more minutes," Mateo replied. "And then we will try to contact him."

Several minutes passed and just as Liam pulled out his phone, they saw Cameron walking toward the bleachers. Mateo and Liam stood from their seats and went down to meet him.

"Hello, Cameron," Mateo greeted, reaching his hand out. "How are you?"

Cameron looked at his hand skeptically before finally taking it. "I'm well," he responded.

The three men stood there silently for several minutes after the greetings as if measuring each other up when Liam finally broke the silence, clearing his throat. "So, you wanted to meet with us about something?"

"Yes, I did..." Cameron paused for a few additional

moments, only making the men more anxious. "Amara told me that your last names are Taylor and Vazquez. Is that correct?"

"Yes, those are our last names," Liam said.

Cameron walked in closer to the men with a sharp glare and stared the two of them down. Liam and Mateo were both frozen and felt like his eyes were examining their very souls with the intensity of his gaze.

"You are warlocks," he stated plainly.

Both men kept cool composures despite the panic and bewilderment in their thoughts.

"And what makes you think that?" Liam questioned.

"Okay, no need for your little show or whatever it is you put on to avoid people learning your secret, if you can even call it that with your famous names. The Vazquez and Taylor families are practically magical royalty along with the Vallis family."

"They're also both very common names, so what makes you think we're magical or whatever you called it?"

"Let's see..." Cameron didn't hide his sarcasm as he pretended he was mulling over a complicated equation with his eyes turned to the sky, lips pursed, and finger tapping his chin. "You barely flinched when I started talking about magical families, you're extremely close and happen to have those last names, and you're seemingly unfazed by the idea of dating the same woman. It's pretty obvious to me."

Mateo gulped and clenched his teeth while Liam crossed his arms across his chest and looked at Cameron defensively.

"I bet you're wondering why I would know things like this, aren't you?" Cameron challenged. "And I imagine you've already detected somehow that I am not your average human?"

Both speechless, the men continued to stare at Cameron.

"Okay, I feel like considering who you two are, you should be able to play this a bit cooler, but it seems that is not the case..." Cameron took a deep sigh. "Can't get into my head, can you, Liam? What about you, Mateo from the family of seers? Do your eyes work through time or space?"

Mateo and Liam's eyes went wide. Although the Vazquez and Taylor families were famous among the magical world for their immortality, the details of their hereditary abilities were not widely known beyond the upper echelons.

"What the hell are you?" Mateo asked through his still clenched teeth.

"I can't tell you what I am other than the fact that it's a very unusual, almost unheard of, case."

"The hell is that supposed to mean?" Liam snarled. "You tell us that you're not an 'average human' and then refuse to explain what you are. You're the one who called us here! Did you just do it to confuse us even further?"

"No. I came here to speak with just the two of you without Amara. I imagine you haven't told her that you're warlocks, have you?"

Despite Cameron's calm demeanor, the tension between the three men was suffocatingly thick, mostly due to Mateo and Liam.

"Why the hell do you get to ask all the questions without answering any of ours?" Mateo blurted.

Cameron groaned and massaged his temples. "Because, I know what questions you're going to ask me and there's a very low chance of me being able to answer them. In fact, I may not even be able to give you very useful hints."

"And why is that?"

"I am bound through a mutually agreed upon blood promise not to release certain information and it also prohibits me from combining certain words or signals that would hint as to what I know about Amara in addition to my own origin. Even if I tried, I wouldn't be able to get anything out."

Mateo and Liam exchanged frustrated glances before glaring back at Cameron.

Liam was the first to speak up again. "What questions do you think we were planning to ask you?"

"Well, you already asked me what I am, so that's one. Then, you'll probably want to know my intentions with Amara. Finally, you'd likely ask me if she is your average mortal."

"And you mean to say that you can't answer any of those, Cameron?"

"The second question, I could, but for the others, the closest I might be able to get are rather vague references to the answers you seek. But first, you must answer a question of mine..."

"Not like we have a choice," Mateo grumbled.

"Go on," Liam gestured.

"Are you two fated to Amara?"

Mateo and Liam cut their eyes at Cameron and straightened up before nodding to answer his question. "Yes," the men said in unison.

"I see," he stroked his chin thoughtfully. "I felt it when we first met at the lounge the other night. There is an inherent bond between you three."

"So…" Mateo crossed his arms and leaned against the gating of the bleachers. "You know of the Fated?"

"Of course I know of the Fated," Cameron answered. "Souls destined to find each other and then become one. It's poetic." He paused and his gaze cut to the ground as he clenched his teeth. "… When things work out."

"Why do you say it like that?" Liam asked angrily. "Things will work out between us and Amara."

Cameron's eyes came back up to meet Liam's intense gaze before his lips turned to an assuring smile. "Yes, I hope that they do. And I really mean that."

Mateo cleared his throat to break the staring match that seemed to have started between the two. "Now it's time for you to answer our questions as best as you can, Cameron. What are your intentions with Amara?"

Cameron broke eye contact with Liam to turn his attention back to Mateo. "They were once to protect and watch over her. Now, simply to ensure she's on the right path. Next question."

"Right path to where?"

"I cannot answer that."

"This is frustrating," Liam huffed and rolled his eyes.

Mateo sharpened his gaze at Cameron. "Is Amara human? Is she mortal?"

"Amara is human. You two are technically human. I am technically human."

"Can we get anymore details? What all can you tell us about Amara?"

Cameron teetered between his heels and toes as he looked down at his feet contemplating which words he could put together that would be of some use. "Amara is human. She was sheltered growing up, which made her transition to the real world a bit difficult, though I helped her as much as I could. I do strongly wish that her grandmother who raised her was more open to allowing Amara to explore the world as well as her own identity. But unfortunately, she was not."

"What else you can give us?" Mateo pressed. "You're not telling us anything that we don't already know."

Cameron stood silently in deep thought for several minutes, only making the men more nervous. His blood promise made it nearly impossible to reveal much about his origins or Amara's. "Here's something: She is your Fated. Isn't it unusual for an average mortal to be fated to two immortal warlocks from the Vazquez and Taylor families? Isn't it odd for there to be such major power differences between Fated? Aren't they usually from classes where they are likely to cross paths naturally?"

"That's it?" Liam snapped. "We already know that and our liaison checked her out thoroughly and found absolutely nothing!"

"Okay." Cameron shrugged.

"What the hell?" Mateo exclaimed. "You can't say things like this about our Fated, knowing what a Fated is, and expect us to just let you walk away without going further into detail."

"I already told you that I can't," Cameron replied calmly.

Mateo took a deep breath in an effort to settle his tone. "Please, Cameron. No matter how small or vague. Anything else you can give us would be much appreciated."

Cameron hummed thoughtfully and clasped his hands on the top of his head. His nose twitched several times when he returned to his contemplative state before he finally spoke again. "Although I'm the one who pushed Amara to come to Masoncrest, after meeting the two of you and now learning that you are her Fated, it's confirmed that she was destined to come here even without my intervention."

"Fucking speaking in riddles like an ancient," Liam griped. "But he is definitely not one of those... Next question: Is Evelyn human?"

"Yes, and she has no idea what I am, nor does she know about the existence of this world... None of the Knight family knows."

Mateo and Liam exchanged a knowing glance before turning their eyes back to Cameron.

Mateo pushed himself off the gate and walked up to Cameron, looking him up and down as he analyzed him skeptically. "Are you truly Cameron? Is that whom you were born as?"

"I can only say that I am currently Cameron."

"Fair enough," Mateo nodded thoughtfully. "So, why'd you send Evelyn here?"

"Because I had plans to send Amara here a few years later and I knew she'd need as much support as she could get. The Knights are a good family and Evelyn is a trustworthy person."

"Does this have anything to do with that 'treasure' you mentioned to Evelyn? You know about that? How?"

Cameron took a step back from Mateo and looked between him and Liam. "I'm sorry, but I've said as much as I can say. I sense no malice from you two and even if I did, as you can tell from what you sense of me—or lack thereof —I'd be no match for either of you. All I can do is trust that my judgements and Amara's are correct."

"However," Cameron continued. "I do have powerful friends and Amara is protected. If she or I have judged wrong, we'll have nothing to worry about because if you try to harm her, that will be the end of you and everyone you love. Immortal or not."

"What is that supposed to mean?" asked an agitated Liam. "First of all, we would never do anything to hurt Amara. And second, you sound quite confident about an effective retaliation should we try the unthinkable. What protection is Amara under and who do you know?"

"Like I told you, I've said all I can say about Amara. And as far as my allies, there's no need for me to give you that information..." Cameron turned and started walking away. "I'll be back here to visit Amara toward the end of November for that odd holiday about genocide. She and I have committed to spend that week together each year no matter what— hm... I guess that could be another hint as well."

Mateo brushed his palms against each other horizontally and his eyes flashed green. Cameron was stopped in his tracks by some invisible obstacle and couldn't advance further.

"Why should we let you go after all of this?" Mateo questioned.

Cameron huffed and answered him without turning around. "What good would it do you to keep me? I've told you everything I can. Also, imagine how Amara would feel if I went missing or if you two were to continue exacerbating the tension between us. There is no reason for you to feel such hostility toward me, I thought I had made that clear."

There was a long pause and Mateo and Liam exchanged a series of glances, communicating nonverbally before the obstacle in Cameron's way was gone.

"Fine," Mateo surrendered.

"You make a valid argument," Liam added. "But that

doesn't mean that we won't be keeping tabs on you moving forward."

"I shouldn't expect anything less from Amara's Fated," Cameron replied. "Speaking of whom, I should get back to the parking lot to meet her. I do hope that the information I've shared with you can be of use."

Once Cameron was finally out of earshot, both men's shoulders relaxed as they exhaled.

"How do we know we can believe him? It'd be so much easier if I could read his mind."

Mateo looked down in deep thought as he ran through their conversation in his head. "What reason would he have to lie? And if he did, why have this meeting that would only make him seem more suspicious?"

"Yes, those are fair points. Now that it's practically confirmed she has some sort of magical properties, we should focus all our energy on investigating Amara and figuring this out."

"Agreed. But let's not mention any of this to her until we learn exactly what she could be. For now, I think revealing to her the existence of our world and explaining the concept of being fated will be enough information to drop on her this week."

"Of course," Liam nodded. "As soon as we're finished with classes today, we'll go straight home and lock ourselves in the study."

AMARA, Cameron, and Evelyn stood by the check-in counters at the airport saying their goodbyes. Of the three of them, Amara was visibly the most emotional with tears running down her face and her bottom lip quivering uncontrollably. Having Cameron there—even if only for a few days—reminded Amara of just how much she missed him. She knew that as adults and as individuals, it was important that they lived their own lives, but she still had an innate attachment to him that she had felt since the day they first met.

"Welp, cousin..." Evelyn reached out to hug Cameron. "I guess this is where we say goodbye!"

A deep frown on her face, Amara asked, "Why couldn't you stay longer?"

"Don't worry!" Cameron placed a gentle hand on Amara's cheek and gave her an assuring smile. "I'll be back here next month!"

"I know, but..." Amara rubbed the tears from her eyes. "I'll just miss you." She threw her arms around him and buried her face against his chest.

"Amara!" Cameron chuckled. "You're getting tears and snot on my shirt!"

"Don't be like that, Cam." Amara's voice was muffled against him.

He smiled and rested his chin on her head as he returned her embrace. "I'll miss you too, Amara."

Once they finally parted ways and Cameron made is way to the security check, he took one last look at Amara, hoping he made the right decision to trust Mateo and Liam. Based on what he could sense from them, it seemed they only had good intentions with Amara and after learning that she was their Fated, it also gave him a bit more calm.

*It's a big risk, but it needed to be done,* Cameron thought to himself. *It makes sense that she's fated to two warlocks from powerful families. Maybe it was supposed to line up like this all along so that they can help her discover the truth. And hopefully, they'll find it soon because she needs to know... I just really, really, hope I'm not wrong about them...*

"Glenda would have my head if she were still alive."

CHAPTER

# TWENTY-TWO

"Shit." Liam sighed. "It's going on three thirty in the morning. We've been reading non-stop since getting home. How about we assess our progress."

Mateo lifted his head from the book he was reading to look at Liam sitting at the desk across from him. "So, let's think about it..." he started. "Whatever she is, Amara is unaware of it and Lillian couldn't detect it."

"Right." Liam scribbled in his notebook the facts that they knew about Amara. "When we touched her before we started taking that potion, it's like we were able to share our abilities with her. And then there was this weekend when your spell seemed to barely have an effect on her."

"Yes, yes." Mateo nodded. "The undetectable nature of whatever she might be and the lack of effect of my magic indicate that she's probably under some sort of protection spell, which is likely what Cameron meant when he said Amara is 'protected.'"

"That makes sense. And if *she* doesn't know what she is, it is likely there's some type of binding on her that is keeping whatever it is inside of her suppressed."

"Which only worries me further because it adds validity to my vision of Samuel here with the intentions of taking her from us. It may not be one of his odd games to fuck with you. If Amara is not of some rarity, then why go through these lengths to hide her supernatural properties from Amara herself and shield her from people?"

"And given her sheltered life growing up..." Liam took a sharp breath and his head snapped up to look at Mateo. "Her grandmother! It had to have been her grandmother who did all of this!"

"Of course!" Mateo snapped his fingers. "We're making progress! That only makes sense considering what Amara has revealed to us about her upbringing. With the strength of the binding and protection, it's clear that her grandmother was a very powerful witch. Which means..."

"Amara is a witch!" both men exclaimed with excitement.

"That means she is part of our world and she'll accept us! We could make her immortal too!" Liam beamed before his face fell when he looked at a visibly disturbed Mateo. "What's wrong? This is excellent news."

"Liam... Amara's grandmother was likely a powerful witch and she was a highly skilled *herbalist*, as is Amara... Growing up, she told Amara about the palisyfum '*lotus*' and kept her sheltered from the rest of the world... as if hiding her."

Liam's eyes went wide and he stopped breathing. Slowly, his mouth opened and his brows tensed. "Impossible," he finally choked out. "They are extinct!"

"I always heard rumors of stragglers and all signs point in that direction." Mateo pinched the bridge of his nose and closed his eyes. "It would also explain why Cameron pushed so hard for Amara to come to Masoncrest rather than go to another place."

"But how?"

"There's a small chance that I've come to the wrong conclusion, but think about it... What other explanation could there be given everything that we know?"

"Shit!" Liam shot up to his feet and slammed his fist on the desk. "Why can't there ever be purely good news? Now this complicates things... In any other case, I'd say we remove whatever seals are on her and tell her what we think she could be."

"But it's likely safer for her that she remains sealed... It would help her avoid being detected by any of the vampires or other beings on campus and around town. We don't know if they know the true story about the Palisyfum and we can't risk it."

"Agreed, but she should know the truth if this is indeed the case."

"We'll start with telling her our truths this afternoon. We'll pick her up immediately after dance class and bring her here."

"But she has office hours Wednesday afternoon and then she usually meets with James."

"Yes, but considering what we are thinking she could be, we should at least tell her immediately what we are and why the bond between the three of us is so strong. Hopefully, she will accept us and it will remove some of her current uneasiness, because considering this theory that we have, one of us needs to be in her proximity at all times. I'd hate to pull her away from office hours and the meeting with her advisor Wednesday, but it has reached a point of urgency."

"It's a good thing we met with Cameron before encouraging Amara to do the blood drive..."

"The timing couldn't be any more perfect," Mateo agreed. "Sharing a sample with Lillian would've resulted in a disaster."

"If our suspicions are confirmed on this, or even if she ends up being something else, when should we tell her?" Liam questioned. "It's a pretty large revelation to make to someone that they are not an average human. We should be cognizant of her other commitments in our approach."

"Thanksgiving break," Mateo suggested. "Cameron will be here again too, so it might just be the perfect time."

# TWENTY-THREE

Amara tossed and turned in her bed, shivering from the cold sheets wet with her sweat. Her heart was pounding and her face kept twitching. Tears leaked from her closed eyes and her body was behaving as if it were trying to wake her up, but Amara's mind remained in her dream.

*Amara cried out when she was cut again from the fold of her arm down to her wrist and the blood escaped her, pouring onto the table and funneling into a cup.*

*"It's amazing!" the red-eyed man beamed. "So long as we don't bleed her dry, she'll just heal and I can drain more from her every few days."*

*A woman with purple eyes and a hopeful smile looked up at him. "I did a good job, didn't I, sir?"*

*"Yes," he replied. "Now, I have the three of you for as long as I want. Though, the man is causing problems." His ruby gaze cut to Amara and he looked at her skeptically. "This one is young... Has she been trained at all?"*

*"No, sir!" the woman answered confidently. "She'll be nothing like him. No problems at all."*

*The man, whose eyes were still on Amara, nodded approvingly. "That's good to know. Considering all the trouble he's caused, I will bleed him dry myself and we can just depend on you and the girl," he said before turning away to walk toward the door.*

*"No!" Amara yelled as loud as she could. "Don't! Please! Why are you doing this? Please stop! Don't do it! Let us go!" the girl's pleas were ignored by the man who continued on his path as if he didn't hear her. She looked up to the purple-eyed woman as the tears blurred her vision. "How could you do this to us?"*

*Guilt appeared to flash across her face before her expression turned calm again. "I am doing what needs to be done, honey," the woman wiped tears from Amara's face. "It is for the best."*

*"And they always say vampires are the villains," a woman with a rather distinct voice said from across the room. Something about it naturally soothed Amara, despite the predicament she was in.*

*The purple-eyed woman's gaze snapped up to glare at the woman with the velvet voice. "What the hell is that supposed to mean?"*

*"It means that we're not the only ones who are villains considering what you've done here," she replied flatly.*

*"What I've done is for the greater good!" the woman snapped, removing her hands from Amara's face and storming up to the vampire. "If what I'm doing is so wrong, then why aren't you doing anything to stop me?!"*

*"I never said that I wasn't a villain. But I'd also be lying if I said watching you try to comfort the girl didn't disgust me," the vampire spat.*

*"You sound bitter. Is it because Alistair is keeping us to himself while you continue to work so hard for him for nothing in return but whatever scraps he passes your way?"*

*"It's better than being livestock." The vampire shrugged. "You're a pathetic excuse for a mo-"*
*"Don't you dare finish that fucking sentence, Haze!" the woman shouted.*
*Suddenly, a man's screams could be heard from the other room with an agony so intense that Amara felt it herself.*

"No!" Amara shouted to the top of her lungs and sat up in bed, tears running down her face and her breathing heavy. She scrambled to get her pills out of the nightstand drawer and took two of them.

Just when she was getting out of bed, Evelyn bursted through her bedroom door in a panic.

"Amara! Are you okay? What's going on? What happened?"

Amara, still slightly distraught, fell back into her bed and took deep breaths. "I'm sorry... It was a nightmare."

Evelyn placed a calming hand over her chest. "Geez, another one? Are you sure you don't need to see the doctor about that? Especially considering the physical symptoms you seem to be getting from them?"

"No, no... I'm fine. These capsules work, I might just need to up the potency or my dosage."

"Are you sure?" Evelyn questioned.

"Yes, I'm sure. Sorry I woke you up."

"It's okay. I'm just glad you're fine." Evelyn sat on the edge of Amara's bed. "Do you want me to stay in here with you?"

"No, I'll be fine... I'm sorry again for waking you up."

"Right..." Evelyn replied with uncertainty in her tone. "I'm going to try to get a few more hours of sleep. But call me if you need me, okay?"

Amara nodded. "Yes, of course."

After Evelyn left the room, Amara stayed in the same spot on her bed staring at the ceiling for what felt like an entire hour before she gave up on going back to sleep.

She sat up and got her phone off of her nightstand and when she looked at it, she realized she had a text from Liam.

> Amara, I hope this message doesn't wake you. Mateo and I have decided we'd much rather tell you what we needed to today. Could you come home with us this afternoon after you finish teaching dance?

Amara bit her lip when she read the text message. The mix of excitement and nervousness his message gave her distracted Amara from the residual anguish she was laying in from her nightmare just moments ago.

> Yes, I can.

Immediately after she responded, her phone chimed again.

> Please don't take this the wrong way, but could you bring an overnight bag? Just in case you fall asleep here?

Amara noted the odd message, but didn't think too much into it.

> Amara: Sure. See you later.

As she was packing extra clothes in her gym bag, Amara couldn't seem to take her mind off of the nightmare she just had. They seemed to be getting more frequent and vivid than before. The face of the purple-eyed woman caused a sharp pain in her heart. And when she saw her arguing with the other woman, in her mind, she knew that other woman was a vampire. Both women's voices were familiar to her, though she found it strange that the vampire's voice brought her peace, while the purple-eyed woman's voice—despite the way she'd cradle Amara's face in her hands or try other comforting gestures—only caused her more distress.

Usually, Amara only remembered bits and pieces of her nightmares, but recently, more and more details remained in her mind. The two names spoken in her dream: Alistair and Haze. She figured Alistair was the red-eyed man whom she also for some reason knew to be a vampire, and Haze was the female vampire arguing with the purple-eyed woman. She continued trying to convince herself that it was just a dream given that vampires weren't real, but Amara couldn't seem to shake how familiar, how real it all felt. As if she'd actually experienced it.

"Packing extra clothes?" Evelyn questioned from Amara's open doorway, interrupting her thoughts.

"Oh! Um. Yeah…" A small smile pulled at Amara's lips thinking about what her evening might hold despite her nerves. "I'm going to stay with Mateo and Liam tonight. We're going straight to their place after I teach dance this afternoon."

"On a Tuesday? Are you sure that's a good idea? What if you have trouble walking tomorrow?"

"Evelyn!" Amara exclaimed.

"Hey, I'm just saying…" Evelyn shrugged. "Anyway…

That works out for me because I planned to have James over tonight."

"Oh? And you were talking about me? You and James seem to be getting along really well. I remember when we had our first meeting and I mentioned that I was living with you. His face lit up when he heard your name."

"We've been flirting for a while and things have recently started to pick up between us."

"Do you like him?"

Evelyn looked up and thoughtfully tapped her finger to her chin. "Maybe. I like spending time with him and he's fun to be around. We get along really well. But I can't say for certain if I have feelings for him. I'm just going with the flow."

"Well, I like him. But, I *am* biased because he's been such a supportive advisor. He doesn't make me feel like I'm crazy for studying the palisyfum. In fact, he proactively asks me about my research and seems really into learning more about the palisyfum himself."

"Mhmm," Evelyn hummed. "He is quite the gentleman. So, what are you wearing tonight to Mateo and Liam's?"

"What do you mean?" questioned a confused Amara. "Probably something like what I have on now. I mean, it'll be after dance class, so I'm obviously going to shower as soon as I get to their place and then change into..." She drifted off when she noticed Evelyn raising a skeptical brow at her. "What?"

"I mean what are you wearing *under* your clothes?" she asked with a suggestive smirk.

"Oh!" Amara gasped. "I didn't even think about that..."

"It's okay!" Evelyn interrupted. "We both have time to run into the city before we need to be on campus. Let's get you something that will have those men salivating over you

more than they already do! What do you think?"
Amara's mouth opened to a wide grin. "I'd love that!"

# TWENTY-FOUR

At Joey's Tavern just outside of Masoncrest, a man covered in tattoos from the neck down sat at the bar awaiting David's arrival. He ran his fingers through his dark brown hair as his deep blue eyes scoured the pages of his notebook. *It works out that this new job is in Masoncrest...* He thought to himself. *Two birds, one stone.*

"You have the jawline of a model," commented a woman with eyes red as blood as she scanned over his side profile before her gaze landed on the bite marks on his neck. The man ignored her, not even turning his head to meet her eyes.

"You smell of warlock, but it appears you have a thing for vampires." She settled herself in the seat next to him and reached for the mark on his neck. "And those tattoos are sexy. Did you come here looking for some fun-"

The woman was cut off when he abruptly grabbed her wrist and held it tight before her hand could reach his neck. "I can see the images in your mind of what you want to do to me," he said, still without looking at her. "Trust me, you can't compete with the *only* vampire who has ever had the privilege of feeding from me."

Suddenly, the woman let out a bloodcurdling scream as her hand began to dissolve. It wasn't until she tried to fight back that she realized she could no longer move her arms or legs.

"No need to struggle, this won't take long," the man assured, still intent on his notebook. "And please, be quiet," he added before his eyes flickered gray and the woman's screams turned soundless.

Joey approached the two shaking his head just as the female vampire's hand finished dissolving. "Those are rather distinct marks on his neck, Christina..." he said to her. "You don't know who they came from?"

The man let go of Christina, leaving her without her right hand. "I suggest you leave before I finish the job," he warned. And with that, the terrified vampire quickly exited the bar without making another sound.

"Did you really have to scare away one of my customers like that, Samuel? If you had taken your eyes off that notebook, you would've seen that she was actually attractive."

Samuel finally looked up from his notes on Masoncrest to meet Joey's gaze. "It doesn't matter to me. I'm here strictly for business. And I'm beginning to get pissed off already. Where is this David who you claimed needed my help and would pay well?"

"He should be here soon." Joey eyed Samuel's neck. "I thought you were a no-go on vampires, Samuel. But it looks like a certain someone has changed your mind," he raised a knowing brow. "What happened to that thing about elites like you not allowing vampires to feed from them?"

"You've clearly never felt the inside of Haze's cunt if you had to ask that," Samuel whispered sharply.

"Very few have had the chance," Joey replied before looking up at the door and waving someone over. "Anyway, looks like David has arrived," he said before walking off.

"Considering your scent, I assume you're Samuel?" David asked from behind him.

Samuel continued to face forward. "You must be David. You're three minutes late. This better be worth my time."

"Straight to business, I see." David sat next to Samuel and put his hand on the bar with his palm facing up. "Is there any way you can break this residual curse and the protection spell that caused it?"

Samuel cut his gaze to analyze the marking on David's palm. His eyes momentarily went wide before his expression returned aloof. "You pissed off one powerful witch or warlock..."

"Neither," David replied. "A non-magical human with a book that seems to have a protection spell put on it by a powerful witch."

Samuel turned to look him in the eyes for the first time since he approached. David was immediately unsettled by the natural darkness behind his gaze. "If a 'non-magical human'—as you describe it—has a book with a protection spell that is also embedded with a residual curse with them, you don't think it's possible they might have magical properties themselves, especially if the book has no effect on them?"

David scoffed and shook his head. "I work with her often. I would've sensed something by now. Anyway, I'm not hiring you to play detective. Can you just break this curse?"

Samuel's jaw tensed and his nostrils flared. If David wasn't paying so well, he would've taken his head off at that snide comment. "On the contrary, you may actually want to hire me to play detective... I hear that you're looking for the palisyfum. I think we could help each other out. Considering you're in Masoncrest of all places on your search, I imagine you're not too much of an idiot."

David's brow twitched, but he kept his composure, remembering that Joey warned him about Samuel's temper and taking note of the way agitation flashed across Samuel's face at his previous comment. "Is that so? You believe the flower exists as well?"

"Hm, a flower..." Samuel pondered aloud. "I see. And who told you that it's still around? It's rumored to be extinct."

"It appears you know her well already..." David eyed the distinct bite marks on Samuel's neck. "Haze," he answered.

Samuel raised a curious brow. "Why would she give you such valuable information?"

"She had no choice. I witnessed her using her power. And although her eyes normally don't change, she just happened to be in a life threatening situation, even for a vampire. And she was forced to take stronger action than usual."

Samuel attempted to decipher a few of the images that came up in David's mind. "A life threatening situation you put her in, I imagine?"

"Yes." David shrugged nonchalantly. "Haze has this reputation for being all powerful and I was curious about the validity of that... So, I may have framed her for the robbery of the home of a warlock along with the death of his Fated."

Samuel scoffed. "You went through all that just to test if those rumors were true?"

"Of course! I am a scientist, after all... Anyway," David continued. "I shared with the warlock information on her whereabouts and worked with him to lure her into a warehouse by some docks in Lenrod City." A devious smirk came to David's face as he remembered the event. "Haze, being the fearless vampire she is, came alone as expected only to be met with a very powerful, very angry warlock who had no interest in hearing her out."

When he saw the images populating David's mind of Haze in action, Samuel had to hold back a sneer of his own and readjust himself in his seat.

"So," David sighed. "She defeated the warlock rather easily. But what was important to me was that glimmer in her eyes when she did it. The color they glowed... I knew from what I had read before that it was associated with the palisyfum and it made sense given her abilities."

"And you mean to tell me that you actually approached her after pulling all that shit?"

"I slipped out before she could sense me, but a few weeks later, I showed up to her office with thirty grand and confronted her about it, asking her for the secrets of the palisyfum."

"Wow." Samuel scoffed. "I would've killed you, if I were her."

"And risk pissing off my family? It was easier if she simply gave me the information. So, she doubled the price to sixty grand and told me as much as she could. She said that since Masoncrest is a former central office of the Assembly, I could find more information, and possibly the flower itself, here in the archives that were left behind."

"I see..." Samuel nodded thoughtfully. "And Haze said it was a flower you seek?"

"That's correct. Just like what the small bit of lore that's out there on it says."

"Have you visited the archives below the town?"

"I'm unable to do that. There are guards up against vampires and other 'undesirables', as the Assembly labels us. I'd probably have a better chance of accessing it if I were human at this point. Which is why I'm hoping this notebook will give me what I need. Are you suggesting you'd go down there for me?"

"Fuck no," Samuel spat. "I already know what information is down there."

"So, you're willing to share it with me?"

"Perhaps... But you'll need to tell me about your lead first. Who is it that owns this notebook with the palisyfum information you seek?"

David pulled back and leaned his arm on the bar. "Like I said before, someone I work with."

"Name?"

"I'm not giving you that until you give me at least a piece of what you know about the palisyfum lotus."

"What does this person look like?" Samuel asked, ignoring David's initial refusal.

"I told you, you're going to need to share something with me too."

A smile came to Samuel's face when he saw the image that came up in David's mind after he asked about the person's appearance. David unknowingly gave Samuel all he needed to pursue the palisyfum on his own.

"You know what? I've changed my mind. I'll just focus on removing this curse of yours and that protection spell."

"What?! You can't-" David paused, startled by the way Samuel's gaze sharpened as if he were going to kill him. "I mean, yes... Fair enough. How long will it take?"

"The materials I'd need to gather for that particular type of curse and the protection spell will likely take me three weeks time to procure."

David's eyes widened and just before he was about to have another outburst, he caught himself. "Fine... I'll get the first half of the payment wired to you."

"Excellent."

# TWENTY-FIVE

Mateo and Liam were both full of nerves sitting in silence at their kitchen counter as they waited for Amara to finish her shower. Both men were mentally running through their plans for explaining everything to her, still in disbelief that the day had come for them to tell her their truths. Finally, Liam abruptly rose from his seat at the counter and looked around anxiously, trying to figure out what to do with himself before settling on making a pot of tea.

"How much time does she need to get ready?" Mateo grumbled as he tapped his thumb on the counter. "We told her she could wear something comfortable as she would at home. It should be relatively quick after her shower, right?"

"Well..." Liam cleared his throat and swallowed. "The last thought I heard from her was, 'I hope they like the set I bought.' So I imagine she is putting that on..."

"Oh hell," Mateo groaned. "By 'set', do you think she meant..." His throat went dry when Amara entered the room and he immediately regretted telling her to dress as she would at home. The athletic shorts she wore were dangerously short and the crop hoodie she had on left much of her midsection exposed.

"We should've told her to wear an oversized sweatsuit," Liam whispered sharply. "How the fuck are we going to concentrate now?"

Amara noticed their intense gazes as she approached and wasn't sure what to decipher from them. While she could admit that what she had on was rather skimp, both men had seen, touched, and had their mouths on the most intimate parts of her, so she didn't expect it to be a big deal.

"Wait." She looked down at herself and then to the men. "Is this too casual? Er... too little? I was going to put on jeans, but when you said to wear something comfortable like I would at home, I just pulled this out."

After several moments of the men staring without answering her, Amara turned around and went back to her gym bag to change into jeans, but kept on the cropped hoodie.

"Sorry," she muttered when she returned.

"No, it's fine," Mateo replied, finally speaking up and walking over to guide Amara to sit at the counter beside him. "Please don't apologize for what you wear when you're with us. And I'm sorry we made you feel like you needed to change."

"Thank you for being willing to come home with us tonight, Amara," Liam said as he handed her a cup of tea and joined her and Mateo at the counter.

She nodded. "Yes, of course. So, what's this secret you've been wanting to tell me?"

"Well..." Mateo began. "We had a few ideas on how we would tell you this and it's not really the easiest thing to say or explain to you..." He stroked his freshly-trimmed beard and looked down thoughtfully. "So, we decided to present a-"

"We're warlocks!" Liam blurted and Mateo cut his eyes at him.

"What?" Amara's head jerked back as she looked between the two men before a big grin grew on her face and she bursted out laughing. "Okay, that was a funny one, guys. But seriously... Please tell me. I've been anxious for days to know."

"He's telling you the truth... Liam and I are warlocks."

"Guys..." Amara said impatiently. "I'm serious. You can stop playing around now." *What could it actually be that they want to tell me? Oh no! Do they have kids? Like a secret family with a wife and everything or something?*

"No, Amara. We don't have kids or a secret wife," Liam replied.

*Did I say that aloud?*

Liam gave her a warm smile and took her hand. "No, you didn't say it aloud. I can read your mind."

*What? He can? Is this a trick?*

"It's not a trick."

Amara's eyes got wide and her mouth went agape. *Shit! So he could hear my embarrassing thoughts all this time?*

Liam rubbed Amara's hand with his thumb. "There's no need to be embarrassed."

*This is insane. Wait...* Amara turned to look at Mateo. *Can Mateo hear my thoughts too? Can you hear me, Mateo?*

Liam chuckled. "Mateo is not a telepath."

"I am a clairvoyant, amor," Mateo said with a smile.

"You see the future?" *What the hell is going on? I can't believe I'm saying or even thinking this stuff.*

"Yes."

"Wait, how does that even work? Did you see this conversation before it happened?"

"No, no... It doesn't work like that."

Amara sat there gawking, looking between the two of them as her mind went a million miles per minute.

*Warlocks? Like magic and stuff? It's real? So that means there are witches, too? What would be the gender neutral term? Are they good or bad warlocks? But they're so kind, they can't be bad, right? Wait! No way! What the hell am I thinking? I'm losing it. These men have officially driven me crazy. I knew it from the day we met. They've been having me throw all logic out the window since then. I haven't even seen them do magic. But it did seem like Liam was reading my mind just n- shit! Liam, can hear all of this!* Amara shifted her eyes to Liam and gave him an awkward glance.

"Here, let us show you something." Liam's eyes turned gray for a split second and Amara's cup of tea began hovering.

Amara looked apprehensively at the cup floating in front of her. She waved her hands over and under the mug, looking for some type of string or other contraption that would be making it float, but she felt nothing.

"Oh my god," she gasped.

Following Liam's lead, Mateo snapped his fingers and his eyes flashed green before the tea kettle floated over to them to top off Amara's cup.

"M-magic..." She gulped, laying her hands on the counter. "It's real?"

"Yes," the men said in unison.

"Magic," she murmured to herself. "They just..." Her words drifted off and her body tilted to the side and off the bar stool, falling into Mateo's open arms.

"Damnit. We've gone and made her faint," he groaned as he carried her to the couch in their living room.

"It could've been worse." Liam shrugged. "She didn't seem upset, just in shock, which is to be expected."

"That is fair," Mateo agreed. "But we won't know for sure until she wakes up. How long do mortals normally pass out?"

"Less than a minute, I think? She should be up soon... even if she isn't an average mortal."

As soon as the words left Liam's mouth, Amara's eyes fluttered open and she looked up at the two men hovering over her in a state of pure bewilderment. She blinked several times before she immediately sat up with a loud gasp.

"Don't move too fast," Mateo cautioned as he took one of her hands in his and Liam took the other. "Do you want some water? Are you dizzy?"

"You're warlocks!" she exclaimed looking between the two of them. "You did magic! You made my cup float and then the teapot to refill my cup! Liam..." Amara turned to him. "You can really read my mind? Have you been reading it all this time? And Mateo..." Amara turned again. "Did you know we were going to meet? Wait! Did you see me naked before we even met?"

Both of them had amused smiles and took note that Amara hadn't snatched her hands away from theirs—it was enough to give them some comfort.

"How about we discuss this in our office?" Mateo suggested. "We've got things set up in there."

"What? Your office? Set up? Are you going to give me a presentation or something?" Amara questioned playfully.

Again, the men exchanged a look and then met Amara's eyes.

"Wait... I was being sarcastic! You really made a presentation for this?"

Liam rubbed the back of his neck nervously. "We thought it would be the quickest and clearest way to give you all of this information... And we are professors, after all."

"Are you okay to walk to the office? Should I carry you?" Mateo asked.

"No, I'm fine. I can walk." Amara got out of the couch to follow the men to the office. *It's all just getting weirder and weirder. I can't believe they made a presentation for something like this, but I have to admit that it's kinda cute—Shit! Liam, can you hear me?*

Liam turned back to flash a knowing smirk and nodded.

*This isn't fair, how am I supposed to control my thoughts? I can't believe you've heard them all this time. It's embarrassing.*

"If it's any consolation, I'd often take a potion to suppress my telepathy prior to our dates, so I didn't know what you were thinking *all* the time," Liam clarified. "There's nothing to be embarrassed about. I normally hate my telepathy—I honestly think it's one of the cruelest 'gifts' to be given, but when I hear your thoughts, the way they feel, it makes me happy to have this ability."

*These men are so sweet. They're so perfect, of course magic is involved. Damnit! Liam, you can still hear me...*

"If you want me to take the potion to suppress it, I can."

"No, it's fine..." *I don't know what it means for my thoughts to have a 'feel' to them, but if you like it, I don't see why not... At least in this moment. You've been hearing them all this time anyway.*

Liam's face brightened and he gave her a gleaming smile.

Mateo looked between the two of them, feeling more

relaxed. "I'm not sure what you're thinking about, Amara, but it's making Liam happy." *This is going better than I expected, honestly*, he thought to himself, and so Liam could hear. They entered the office and Amara sat on a chair in front of a projector screen while the two men stood on each side of it.

"Let's get started, shall we?"

# TWENTY-SIX

Amara was a combination of intrigued, confused, and entertained at the fact that she was dating two warlocks and they were currently giving her a presentation on themselves and their world as if she were in a class. She paid careful attention as they went through explanations of their abilities.

"I am from the Vazquez family," Mateo started. "And we are a family of 'seers' which means that we can 'see' through time or space, typically. For myself and my little sister, we see through time. She sees pasts and I see futures. My elder brother, however, can see through the 'space' that exists between our world and others—into parallel dimensions."

"Wow," Amara breathed. "And your parents?"

"Well, my mother could also see futures, though her visions came differently than mine. They were often at random and would hit her in the form of fainting spells. My father is not a seer because he married into the family. But he is still a warlock."

"I see..."

"The Taylor family is known for our ability to get into people's heads," Liam began his explanation. "I can hear thoughts, while my twin Samuel can see them. My three elder sisters inherited the ability to mind link others from our mother, while my younger brother can quite literally get into someone's head and see all their thoughts and memories as if he's there by touching them and concentrating hard enough."

"Whoa..." Amara gawked before her face turned pensive as she remembered the first time she met the men. "When we first met in the cafe, Mateo and I's hands brushed and I saw this um... scene. It was as if I could almost feel it. And we were uh... intimate. Did that have anything to do with your powers? Did you put that in my head or something?"

"No," the men replied quickly.

"Er- it kind of had to do with my abilities," Mateo clarified. "That was actually one of my visions that you saw. We would never purposely plant something like that in your head. At least not without your consent."

"But then how did I see it? You didn't share it with me?"

"No. It wasn't like that. It was involuntary when we first touched. I'm still not one hundred percent sure how or why it happened."

"Okay..." Amara then turned her attention to Liam. "And Liam, the first time we kissed, I heard your voice in my head even though you couldn't exactly have been speaking at the time. Is it like what happened with Mateo and I?"

"Yes." He nodded. "We believe so."

"That is so strange. Er— I guess even stranger than what you've already told me. But I don't mean that in a bad way!" she exclaimed. "I just mean that it's... new."

Liam nervously bit his bottom lip. "We have more that we need to tell you..."

"Hm? What more could there be?"

"I'll just com out and say it..." Mateo took a deep breath and anxiously ran his fingers through his hair. "We are immortal... Liam and I are one hundred fifty-six years old."

"Oh. My. God. I thought you were in your early thirties!"

"We are. Technically," Liam clarified. "Our families are two of three known for immortality. To keep it brief, there is a ritual that we go through at a chosen age to sort of 'activate' our immortality, for lack of better term."

"Well, at least if you're immortal, I don't have to worry about coming home and finding you dead," Amara said softly, looking down at her hands in her lap. *I can't go through that again*, she thought. "Sorry. That was morbid."

"No need to apologize," Liam approached and took one of her hands. He wanted to ask her what she meant by 'again', but told himself he'd ask at a more appropriate time. "I know you have a lot of questions, and we are prepared to answer every single one of them."

"You say that now, but I'm not sure if you'll feel the same way after twelve hours of interrogation because that's how long all of my questions will probably take."

Liam chuckled. "Like I said, we'll answer every single one of your questions. We just have one last thing to add."

"More?" Amara gasped.

"Yes, but this is that last one, we promise," Mateo assured. "Amara, do you believe in the existence of certain bonds between people? Such as bonds that are inherent?"

"What do you mean?"

"Things like soulmates," Liam added. "People who are fated to be with each other."

"Hm..." Amara looked up at the ceiling thoughtfully as she contemplated for several moments. Cameron was the first person who came to mind and then she thought of Mateo and Liam. "There are people in my life who I feel are meant to be part of it. Is that what you mean?"

"Exactly!" Liam chimed.

"Ever since we've met, you've felt particularly comfortable around us, haven't you?" Mateo asked.

"Yes, that's true," Amara replied.

"As if there's a natural connection between us, right?"

"Yes…"

"In our world," Mateo began. "There is this concept that we refer to as 'Fated' and it's very much like that. There exists this innate bond between certain people, and those people are meant to be together."

"Right," Liam continued. "And that bond is so strong that those who are Fated are drawn to each other in a rather intense manner."

Amara nodded. "Okay…" *Are they saying this 'Fated' thing is why I feel such a deep connection with them?*

"That's exactly what we're saying!" Liam confirmed. "With us being Fated, it is already written in our destinies that we are meant to be with each other and Mateo and I are fated to you and you to us, Amara. It is one of the purest, most beautiful things about our world. And it's why you feel such a deep connection with us, as we do with you."

Amara looked down as her eyes moved rapidly, scanning over the floor. Her mouth twisted with hesitation before she spoke. "It doesn't sound voluntary… Is it forced? By whomever is writing these destinies?"

"No! It's not like that," Mateo replied urgently. "It's just like soulmates—almost the exact same thing. The only difference is that we know ahead of time with whom we're meant to be. You see, one hundred thirty-eight years ago when we turned eighteen, we were informed by an ancient—think of them as oracles—who showed us an image of you and said that we would meet in Masoncrest in the year two-thousand ten. As the year approached, Liam and I moved here in two thousand three. That was when I started getting visions differently. They normally require that I touch something belonging to the main subject of the vision and concentrate, but in this case, visions of you and us would come to me randomly."

Visibly unsettled, Amara shifted in her seat. "When I think about it... It sounds kind of cruel, doesn't it? To tell you you're meant to be with someone you won't meet until more than one hundred years later and then for that person to be mortal while you two are immortal... Relative to your life, I'd only be around for a short period of time and you'd just watch me grow old and die."

"Admittedly, we and our families thought the same thing," Mateo confessed. "But then when Liam and I met you for the first time, all the waiting was worth it. Being fated to you is anything but cruel. It feels more like a blessing."

"That doesn't sound like you have much of a choice, though," Amara countered. "If you're told ahead of time that you're meant to be with a specific person, you're automatically biased in favor of them, right? Did you ever try dating other people? What if there's someone else? Someone who can do magic and is immortal like the two of you who would be a better fit?"

"Impossible!" Liam uttered. "We had one hundred and thirty eight years of trying to see other people—separately and together—but none of them had the effect on us that you have, Amara Jenkins!"

Her eyes immediately shot up to Liam's and then

Mateo's. Both of their hearts dropped when they saw the tears running down her face.

"It just doesn't seem right," she said softly. "As if we didn't choose each other, but someone else did."

"No! It's not like that," Mateo attempted to explain. "It's not a single person or a group of people or anything like that who chose, Amara! It is fate that brings us together."

"The three of us are meant for each other, Amara. It's a beautiful thing." When Liam tried to squeeze her hand, Amara pulled it away and started massaging her temples. Her mind was moving so quickly with questions and prowling over all the information that they had given her that even Liam couldn't keep up with her thoughts.

Her eyes fell to the floor again and she tugged at her hoodie. "This is... a lot to take in," she said between sniffles. "Can I... have some time... to think?"

"Yes, of course," Mateo affirmed. "We have a room..."

"No," Amara interrupted, still looking down. "I mean... time to think by myself... at home."

Mateo immediately choked and Liam felt his bottom lip begin to quiver.

She slowly stood up, avoiding eye contact with the men and starting toward the door. "I'll get my bag." Amara was stopped in her path when Liam gently grabbed her arm.

"Please." It came out as a wince that he quickly tried to cover up by clearing his throat. "We love you, Amara..."

Amara's head quickly snapped back to look at them in pure disbelief, analyzing their faces looking for signs that what he said wasn't serious. She gulped when she noticed the pleading in their eyes and more tears flowed from hers as she snatched her her arm away from Liam.

*Do they really think that they love me? I mean, what I feel for them does seem all consuming. Like maybe it could be... No. It's too soon. And why the hell would he tell me like that as if it's such a casual thing to say to someone? Is love not serious in their world? This Fated thing is only seeming more involuntary... Where's the consent? Who falls in love in a matter of months...?* She paused when she noticed Liam's eyes begin to water, reminding her that he could hear everything she was thinking. *I'm sorry, Liam. Maybe you should've taken that potion. You shouldn't have to listen to this.*

Mateo looked between them and noticed Liam was even more distraught than he was and worried about what may have been going on in Amara's head to shake him up so much.

"Okay," Mateo choked out. "We'll drive you home."

"Thank you," she mumbled before leaving the office to gather her things.

It was another silent drive to Amara's home just as they'd experienced over the weekend. Liam decided to take the potion so he wouldn't have to listen to any more of Amara's thoughts as the ones she had earlier already had him crumbling.

They wondered if it was the right thing to tell her. They wondered if there was a better way they could've revealed things. They wondered if it was possible to go on without Amara if she decided she didn't want to be with them.

Once they arrived at her house, Amara quickly got out of the car and the men followed. She clasped her hands together in front of her and looked at the ground, knowing she'd have a full on breakdown if she were to meet their eyes again.

"Thank you," she whispered.

"Amara." Mateo sighed. "I'm sorry that I have to say

this. I know you have enough to process... But what we've told you, it has to be kept-"

"Secret. I understand," she replied before quickly turning around and walking toward the house.

Liam and Mateo were speechless as she walked away from them. They were worried that the image was the last interaction they would have with her.

"Mateo..." Liam sniffed and held his chest once Amara closed the door behind her. It was the first time he'd spoken since they were in the office and he told Amara that they love her. "This really hurts..."

"I know." Mateo gulped and placed a comforting hand on his friend's shoulder. "But now, we must give her time and hope for the best."

# TWENTY-SEVEN

It was the following Tuesday. One week had passed since Liam and Mateo revealed everything to Amara and her mind hadn't slowed down since. She had been doing well at avoiding the men. This Tuesday, she arrived an hour before class was supposed to start so she could dance on her own, hoping to ease her mind

*Immortal warlocks,* Amara thought to herself as she danced in the dark studio. *I still can't believe it. It's even more unbelievable that that is the part I'm least worried about. The comparison of Fated to soulmates makes sense. The idea of an innate bond isn't exactly uncommon. In fact, it's in our nature...*

*But still.*

*Is it really that natural to feel a bond this strong? And so quickly? At what point do we throw our survival instincts—the instincts with which we protect ourselves—out the window for these types of phenomena.*

*Grandma warned me that I shouldn't trust people so easily and I've learned the hard way before... But there are good people out there who can be trusted easily.* Images of Cameron and Evelyn appeared in her mind.

*Could Mateo and Liam be like them too? They're both kind and they haven't given me a reason not to trust them. I can understand keeping the secret about being immortal warlocks.*

Tears fell from Amara's eyes as she allowed her body to follow the music. She'd never been so confused in her life. Her mind was consumed with the conflicting feelings of wanting to be with Mateo and Liam along with the fear that they were somehow forced to want her.

*However, whether or not they're good or trustworthy doesn't matter for the issue at hand. This overwhelming bond that I feel with them—this 'Fated' thing—it concerns me. Liam said that they love me, but could that be true? And if it is true, is it even okay? Would it count as some sort of coercion... being forced in some way? How can I—in good conscious—accept something like that?*

Consent was incredibly important to Amara, and she worried that the concept of having a Fated disrupted that.

*But again... the soulmate comparison... How different is it from the idea of having one?*

Samuel walked through the underground club, a place frequented by vampires, lower-ranking warlocks and witches, and other supernatural beings. The front was set up as a simple lounge—smoke filled the room that was characterized by the sounds of conversations while a live band played smooth jazz in the background. When Samuel approached the door leading to the next room of the club, he was met with a large vampire that towered over him despite Samuel already being tall standing at 6'4" himself.

The guard looked down at Samuel in what would've been a glare before he realized who was before him.

"Oh uh, Samuel?" he said, softening his face to one of nerves. "Back again already?"

"That's right, whatever-the-fuck-your-name-is," he replied impatiently. "Now move."

Without another word, the large vampire stepped out of his way and allowed Samuel to pass into the next room. In contrast to the lounge at the front, this room appeared as a more traditional club with upbeat music, strobe lights, and gogo dancers. Vampires fed openly, warlocks and witches entertained themselves and others with their magic, and fairies walked or floated around with their wings freed. Samuel continued on his path, already knowing exactly where to find whom he was looking for.

When he finally reached his destination, he saw the vampiress just where he expected—in her secluded section toward the back of the club. She sat on a wide couch with her arms stretched across the back of it and her legs crossed, full of rightful confidence given that she owned the place. Her hair was braided in individuals that fell at chest length and her brown skin had a golden tint to it. She wore her signature burgundy lipstick, but tonight, it was in matte. A low-cut black dress hugged her body and fell well above her knees, putting her long legs on full display.

Her eyes snapped up to Samuel as soon as she caught his scent and a smirk came to her face. Uncrossing her legs, she stood from her seat and walked toward a door a few feet away from her section that led to a back hallway. Without hesitation, Samuel followed her down that hall until they reached a door at the end that led to her large office.

When they got inside, she leaned against the desk with her hands on each side of her as she eyed him curiously.

Samuel stayed in the doorway with a snide look on his

face. "I was sure you'd bring me to your bedroom, Haze. It's only next door."

"What do you want, Samuel?"

"Other than to be buried in your cunt again?" he said as he strolled up to Haze and relaxed into the chair in front of her. "Do you remember a vampire by the name of David? I met with him recently and now I have questions for you."

She scoffed and rolled her eyes. "You say that as if I'm somehow inclined to answer any questions you have for me. You think just because we've fucked a few times that I'm going to give you information for free?"

"By my count, it's a lot more than 'a few'," Samuel sneered.

"Cute that you're keeping count..." Haze approached and straddled him in his seat. Using her index finger, she trailed her sharp nail down the center of his chest over his shirt. "Perhaps we could set a new record tonight..."

Samuel grabbed her wrist to stop her and looked into her mysterious brown eyes. "First question: What do you know about the Palisyfum?"

Haze huffed her frustration and snatched her wrist out of his firm grip effortlessly. "I never said I'd answer your questions." She returned her nail to his chest. "You know... one of the things I do enjoy about being a vampire has got to be these heightened senses. Your blood... I know exactly when it begins rushing and which direction it goes." Her eyes followed her finger as it traveled down his body before she stuck out her tongue and ran it across her lips. "And something tells me that those questions aren't your primary goal here..."

After taking a sharp breath, Samuel clenched his teeth and his jaw tensed as he tried to temper his desire. "You think that I don't know why I can't see what's going on in that head of yours, Haze? Or why when *you* wound me I don't heal as quickly?" His questions came out as challenges and she sharpened her gaze. "You must have forgotten who I am and what I've brought out in you..." Samuel caressed her thighs that were sitting on each side of him. "I make you come hard enough and your eyes flicker to that very distinct purple color. I know you hold the power of a Palisyfum."

"And what does it matter to you?" Haze countered, pushing herself off of Samuel and returning to her position standing against her desk in front of him, now with her arms crossed. "The flower went extinct ages ago."

"Ages ago, you say? Haze, I know you're not that old of a vampire... You were turned in the seventies. So, how exactly did you come across a 'flower' that was supposedly extinct long before that?"

"Honestly," Haze replied with a sigh. "It's none of your fucking busine-" She was cut off when Samuel shot to his feet and wrapped his hand around her neck.

"Don't lie to me, Haze," he growled. "We both know that the Palisyfum is not a fucking flower."

A devious smirk pulled at her lips. "This... can't... kill me..." she choked out.

Samuel analyzed her face and there wasn't an ounce of fear in her eyes. She didn't struggle and her lust-filled gaze into his eyes was unwavering. Suddenly, he pulled her in and smashed his lips against hers while his hand remained wrapped around her neck.

Haze pushed him back into the chair and returned to her position straddling him while their mouths still moved against each other. As she felt him hardening against her core, Haze moved her hips instinctively and then broke the kiss. Samuel tried to pull her back in, but she held her ground and pushed him back to keep him in place, this time, wrapping her hand around his throat as the other trailed down his chest.

"Now, what was it that you said you wanted before?" she whispered as she used her nail to pop off the first and then second button of his shirt.

"To be buried in your cunt again," he responded unabashedly and reached behind Haze to grab two hand-fuls of her backside as she continued to grind against his growing erection.

"You see…" she started, tracing her finger around his bare chest. "When you first came in, I really liked the sound of that. But now, you've pissed me off and I'm not so sure I'm in the mood anymore."

"Lying to me again?" he asked with a raised brow. "I may not be able to get into your head, but I know you want to feel me inside of you just as much as I want to be there."

"Oh Samuel," Haze sighed. "Always the blunt one…" She leaned into him closer so that their lips lightly brushed against each other. Each time he tried to close the distance, Haze held him in his place and slightly pulled her head back, denying him what he wanted.

His grip on her behind tightened and Samuel raised his hips to meet Haze's core as she ground against him. "How long are you going to play this game?"

"What game?"

In the blink of an eye, Haze and Samuel were on the couch toward the front of her office and he was on top of her. "You're right," he replied. "What game?" His lips were soon against her neck and eagerly working their way down as he began tearing at her dress.

Again, they were repositioned and Haze was back to straddling him, now in the couch. "You're not the only one with magic…" She tore the rest of his shirt open to reveal his tattoo-covered torso. "You're also not the only one who can tear fabric."

Samuel's lips returned to Haze and there was one final tear before her dress was completely removed from her body. He raised one of his hands and slammed it back down on her ass, then pulled one of her nipples into his mouth.

Haze snapped her fingers and Samuel's shoes, pants, and shirt were removed, leaving him in only his boxers. "That's better," she cooed.

His eyes flickered gray and they were suddenly in Haze's bedroom, but held the same position with her straddling him while he sat up against the headboard of the bed.

"If the Palisyfum don't exist anymore, why are you still telling lies about their nature?" Samuel asked.

"Are you really going to fuck up the mood?"

"Who said anything about stopping?" He pulled her panties to the side and started playing with her clit. "Since you lied about that. I think Palisyfum are still around— even if only a few stragglers."

"I don't know… what you're… talking about," Haze breathed through light moans.

Samuel flipped them over so that she was on her back and wasted no time in spreading her thighs wide open and tearing off her panties. "I think you do," he muttered against her core before slipping two fingers inside of her. "And considering you have their power…" He lightly flicked his tongue against her clit while his fingers pumped in and out of her. "I know you've fed from them," he added before his mouth and tongue began to work her in sync with his fingers.

"Not… your… business- Shit!" she uttered when Samuel

pulled her clit between his lips and growled on her. "This won't... persuade... me."

"I know that and there's no need for you to talk..." he said when he broke his mouth away and curled his fingers still moving inside of her. "I'm just sharing what I know and that is-" He was interrupted by an outburst from Haze as her body shook from the pleasure.

"Fuck!"

A satisfied smirk came to his face knowing what he was bringing out in her. "My theory is that you must be keeping them to yourself..." His mouth returned to her clit as his fingers continued to move, pulling an orgasm from her. After allowing her to ride out her climax, he freed her core from his lips and spoke again as he crawled up to meet her gaze. "But now you have competition..."

"David is not any compet-" she was cut off when Samuel roughly grabbed her face and his eyes bore into hers.

"Do not say another man's fucking name when I'm in bed with you," he snapped. "*I'm* your competition," he sneered. "I'm going Palisyfum hunting."

"Fuck if I care." Haze turned them over so that she was on top and her kisses trailed along his neck until she reached the spot where she last fed from him. "I see my mark is still here." Her tongue traced over it and Samuel released a groan. "It makes you more sensitive, doesn't it?" she whispered as she tore the boxers off of him.

With the way she concentrated on that one spot, Samuel knew what she wanted and he had no interest in denying her. Leaning his head to the side, he gave Haze better access to his neck. She released a low purr of satisfaction before freeing her fangs and sinking them into him.

Pleasure rippled through Samuel and he grunted when

Haze held his dick at her entrance and slowly eased down without releasing his neck. As she rode him while feeding, Samuel was already on edge. He normally prided himself on how long he could last, but that didn't apply to Haze. When she released his neck and licked off the remaining drops of blood, Samuel immediately came deep inside of her.

"Don't tell me that's it," Haze taunted, licking his blood from her lips. "I could've sworn that you last longer." She was abruptly flipped on her back and her calves placed on Samuel's shoulders, feeling him immediately harden again inside of her.

"Not even fucking close."

# TWENTY-EIGHT

Liam took a sip of his whiskey as he and Mateo sat in their home office still brooding over what happened with Amara. "I don't know how much longer I can do this, Mateo. It has been an entire week without seeing her, without so much as communicating with her. We haven't been apart this long since we first met her."

"I know," Mateo gulped. "But we have to let her be the one to decide. And we need to respect her wishes for space, no matter how much it hurts."

"How the hell are you so calm about this?" Liam snapped. "How are you not in constant distress? And your thoughts have been a lot calmer than mine... Do you not feel as strongly for her?"

Mateo lunged toward him and grabbed Liam by the collar. "You think just because you can read my thoughts that you truly know how the fuck I feel?" he shouted. "Not everyone has been as privileged as you to have never known heartbreak. Some of us cope in different ways, Liam! And you forgot that we've known each other most of our lives. I know how to control my thoughts around you when it's necessary."

"You think I've never experienced heartbreak because I've never lost a parent like you?" Liam countered, pushing Mateo off of him and grabbing *his* collar. "Have you forgotten that I've lost a sibling? My twin brother at that! At least your mother didn't betray you. At least she's not out there lurking somewhere still alive while you're acutely aware of the fact that she doesn't want to be saved."

Mateo's eyes went green and Liam flew across the room, hitting the bookshelf and causing the texts to tumble down. "You are completely wrong! Don't talk to me about saving a loved one! My mother didn't want to be saved either. She didn't even let me-"

He was cut off when a gust of wind threw him into the bookshelf on the other side of the room. Mateo looked up to see Liam's gray eyes with tears pouring from them.

"How are you able to keep so calm? We might be losing her!" he wailed.

Suddenly, he was wrapped in a tight hug with Mateo. "We can do this, Liam," he assured. "We don't have a definitive answer just yet, so keep hope alive."

Liam returned his embrace and they stood there for several moments until both of their phones went off and the men quickly broke from each other to see what it was.

Are you guys home now?

In sync, they took sharp breaths and exchanged a nervous glance.

"You respond," Mateo told Liam.

> Yes, we're here. Did you want to come over?

> Yeah, I'm actually just five minutes out from your house if that's okay. I was hoping we could talk.

> Of course it's okay! You're always welcome here, no matter what.

> Thanks, I'll be there soon. And Liam... I'm sorry to ask this, but could you take that potion?

> Yes, I can do that no problem. We'll see you soon.

Liam rushed into the kitchen to get a vial of potion and immediately downed it. He and Mateo's hearts were pounding and they expended more of their magic to clean up the office that they made a mess of with their fight.

Liam huffed. "Oh hell, I think I'm going to vomit from the nerves."

Mateo was pacing back and forth in the foyer, anxiously running his hands through his hair.

Both men were a wreck, but they immediately froze and straightened themselves up as soon as they heard Amara pull into the driveway. Mateo rushed to the door and opened it to see her getting out of her car. When she turned and saw the men at the entrance to their home, she had an indecipherable expression on her face as she approached.

"Hi guys," she greeted. "Thanks for letting me come over last minute like this."

"Like I told you, you're always welcome here," Mateo said, giving her a warm smile.

"Would you like water or coffee or tea or anything?" Liam offered.

"N-no. I'm good." Amara swallowed. "Thank you."

"You said you wanted to talk, right, Amara? How about we do so in the office."

"Sure." She nodded and followed the men to the room where they explained everything just a week ago.

As soon as they got into the room, Amara took a deep breath and said, "I have a lot of questions about the things you told me, but what I want to start with is the part about us being Fated…"

The men looked at her attentively as she began.

"The more I've thought about it and the comparison you made with the concept of soulmates… I think it makes sense. Innate bonds and things like them—they do exist. If we are beings with souls, I do think that souls interact with each other in certain ways. And since meeting you, I feel like our souls have been interacting with each other.

"And when it comes to souls, I don't think a soul can be 'forced' to do something. Beings yes, they can be forced, but souls… their purity— er, even ones that could be considered impure, I think they're one of the few parts of us that can't be controlled by others… Not even by magic or some other supernatural ability. What do you think?" She looked between Mateo and Liam. "And please, be honest with me. Does there exist something that could manipulate a soul and would be forcing this 'Fated' bond between us?"

The men stood there for several minutes pondering her question until Mateo finally spoke up. "People of our world question if the ritual we go through to become immortal might affect the soul, but it really depends on your beliefs. We believe the soul is eternal, so only the body is affected by the ritual. However, to my knowledge, nothing that manipulates the soul exists. Liam?"

"No, I've never heard of any item or spell that could do that. However," Liam's shoulders rose and then fell with the breath that he took. "For the sake of being honest, which is what we always want to be with you, Amara, just because we are unaware of the existence of such things, it doesn't mean that they don't exist."

"All that being said," Mateo added. "What we feel for you is not forced. In fact, it feels more liberating than anything—the way our emotions seem to flow freely when we're with you."

"I see..." Amara paced in front of them for what felt like an eternity to Liam and Mateo.

Finally, she stopped in her tracks and turned to face the two of them. "What I feel for you... This bond we have... I don't want to let it go. I don't want to let either of you go... Honestly, I can't imagine life without you and I don't want to," she finished with a smile.

Both men nearly collapsed when the words left her mouth.

"Does that mean...?" Liam drifted off.

"Are you saying that you accept us, Amara?" Mateo asked.

Amara quickly nodded, the smile still on her face.

"Amara, may we-" Before Liam finished, Amara jumped into his arms and pulled him in for a kiss before repeating the same move with Mateo.

Still wrapped in Mateo's arms, Amara turned around to meet Liam's eyes. "There is one last thing I should be honest with you two about. As much as I care about you and as strongly as I feel, I'm not exactly ready to say those three words..." Her gaze fell to the floor.

"That's no problem at all," Liam assured without hesitation. "We'd never want you to do anything you're uncomfortable with and we most definitely do not want to put any pressure on you. In fact... I regret the way in which I made the confession. You deserve much better than a panicked utterance."

Amara giggled and her body relaxed against Mateo. "You two are so good to me."

"It comes naturally."

"I can't believe I spent days thinking this was forced," she said softly. "How could something that feels this comfortable ever be forced?"

"The farthest thing from it..." Mateo rasped. He moved a piece of her hair out of the way and placed soft kisses on her neck. "It's natural. You noticed from the first moment you met us, didn't you?"

"You realized something was different..." Liam said as he closed the distance between them, taking Amara's face in his hands while Mateo's began to wander over her form. "And it wasn't just the way you felt so comfortable around us. There was a pull as well, wasn't there?"

"You want us..." Mateo added. His tongue made a trail to her ear and he pulled her lobe between his teeth.

"...Just as much as we want you." Liam finished before he pressed his lips against hers.

While Liam had Amara captured in an intense kiss, Mateo's hands wandered while his lips scoured her neck and shoulders. As soon as Liam released her lips, his eyes flickered gray and he and Mateo instantly switched places.

Amara jumped when she realized what happened. "It's so... seamless?"

"Is it okay?" Mateo asked. "For us to use our magic in this way with you?"

"Yeah, as long as you're not using it on me, I guess. I think it'll take getting used to."

"Of course, mi alma," Mateo muttered before taking her lips. While his mouth occupied Amara's neck, Liam's hands roamed her body before they reached under her shirt to caress her bare skin.

"Wait," she breathed and both men froze, pulling their lips away to listen attentively.

"Can we go to one of your rooms?"

"Are you sure? We don't want you to feel any pressure, especially since this warlock business is new to you..."

"I'm absolutely positive," she assured.

The men exchanged a glance. "We'll go to my room," Mateo said. "But first, could you give Liam and I some time to... freshen up?"

"Oh, um... Of course."

"In the mean time, just stay here. We will not keep you waiting long, I promise."

Both kissing her one more time, Mateo and Liam left Amara in the office and rushed to Mateo's room.

"We'll do it in here," Mateo explained while Liam urgently prepared the potion that the two men used to diminish their sensitivity to Amara. "And we need to be gentle. We have— Liam! Are you listening?"

"Here." Liam handed Mateo a large vial of potion while he held one of his own. "I've prepared enough to keep us going into the morning."

"We can't do that."

"What do you mean we can't do that? This is our first time with our fated and we will make love to her until the three of us can no longer move."

"Liam," Mateo sighed. "We both have over one hundred years worth of fantasies... We need to be careful to not get out of hand and wreck havoc on her body. She's also inexperienced. We cannot overwhelm her."

Liam groaned and rolled his eyes. "Fine… But we should at least take enough so that we don't come before even getting inside of her."

"Agreed. And remember… We need to be gentle."

"That sounds more like a warning for yourself than for me, Mateo. I'm not the one we need to worry about in that department…"

"Which is exactly why you will take her first," Mateo grumbled. "Now, let's quickly clean up and get back to her. We already made her wait too long the second we left her in the office."

# TWENTY-NINE

Amara fidgeted with her fingers as she paced Mateo and Liam's office awaiting the men to return. Although she wanted to be with the two of them —and she had for a long time—she was also still nervous about her first time with both of the men.

"Okay, Amara," she whispered to herself. "You can do this. They're good guys- er warlocks? Warlock guys? Guy warlo- whatever. They won't be mad if I'm not good at this, right? And they already know that I'm not super experienced. And I've wanted this! It'll be fine. I'm glad that I didn't leave this set at home. I wasn't one hundred percent sure how today would end up, but best to come prepared, right? Shit! I didn't bring condoms. Do they have condoms? They should, but would that mean- whatever. It's fine. Everything is going to be alright... But they've made me feel so good. I hope I can do the same for them..."

"Amara, are you ready?"

Her attempt at a hushed pep talk was interrupted when Liam called and she turned to see him and Mateo standing in the doorway.

Mateo's brows tensed when he sensed her nerves. "Are you sure you want-"

"Yes!" Amara squeaked, cutting him off. "I want this..." she said as she approached the men. "And I've been wanting this for a long time."

As soon as she was within arm's reach, Mateo pulled her body against his and captured her in a deep kiss. She heard Liam snap his fingers and they were in Mateo's room. Amara tugged at his shirt and he wasted no time in removing it before Liam turned her around to bring her in for a kiss while Mateo's lips scoured where they could of her exposed skin.

After Liam's shirt was removed, the men went to work undressing Amara—Mateo unbuttoning her pants and Liam removing her top. When they separated to allow her to step out of her pants, both men nearly came undone when they got a good look at what she was wearing under her clothes.

Amara wasn't sure exactly how to decipher the looks on their faces. She wore a pink lace bra with a matching thong. It was her first lingerie set and she didn't yet feel comfortable with the other outfits that Evelyn and the woman at the store suggested, so she settled on something that was at least an upgrade from what she was used to wearing.

"Do you like it?" she asked nervously. "I know it's simple, but-"

In the blink of an eye, Amara was sandwiched between Mateo and Liam again and their hands and mouths were practically glued to her.

"We love it," Mateo whispered in her ear as he caressed her sides.

"A bit too much," Liam continued, running his fingers

along the fabric of her bra. "I'm not sure if I want to remove it."

Mateo played with the waistband of Amara's thong. "He's getting carried away because this is absolutely coming off."

Trying to ignore her nerves, Amara started placing kisses along Mateo's neck—something she learned was a weakness of his—as her hands trailed their way down his body to unbutton his pants. It was the first time she made the move without being stopped. Once Mateo's pants fell and he was in nothing but his briefs, Amara turned to Liam to pull him into a kiss. She knew that he liked it when she sucked his bottom lip and she ended their kiss with that as she undid his pants as well. She felt both of their erections grinding against her and she began to release light moans

While his lips were at the base of her neck, Mateo's hands came up to massage Amara's breasts through her bra. Liam cupped her over her panties and nibbled at the other side of her neck. She let out a light moan and suddenly the three of them were on the bed.

Liam's hand moved from Amara's pussy to under her bra and one of Mateo's slipped down into her panties. Amara reached down into their briefs to stroke both of them and they grunted trying to keep themselves together, feeling her touch directly for the first time. Her heart was racing and her body was aching for more, but Amara's nerves still lingered.

"Let us take care of you." Mateo's assuring words helped ease some of the tension.

"You trust us, right?" Liam asked. When Amara nodded, his hands reached back to unlatch her bra and he kissed his way down to her breasts while Mateo gently rubbed her pussy.

"We crave you, you know that, right?" Mateo muttered, his fingers traveling her folds.

"Allow us to show you how much," Liam added, fully removing her bra.

In no time, her panties were also pulled off and her legs were wide open with Mateo and Liam side-by-side between her legs. She looked down at the two of them anxiously.

"What are you... oh god!" she shouted when Mateo's mouth met her lower lips. His tongue moved up and down her inner lips before he spread her apart with two fingers and flicked his tongue on her clit while using his other hand to push two fingers inside of her. At the same time, Liam kissed and sucked the inside of her right thigh.

The way Amara pulled at his hair only encouraged Mateo and his mouth moved more eagerly until he pulled an orgasm from her that had Amara's body shaking. As soon as she rode out her first release, she felt Liam's mouth latch onto her while Mateo's lips and tongue were against her left thigh and he reached a hand up to fondle her nipple. She threw her head back into her pillow as she came on Liam's mouth before Mateo started eating her out again.

The men devoured her to music of her erotic sounds composed by the pleasure that they were giving her. Amara was coming completely undone with the way Mateo and Liam were taking turns until they finally came up to each share kisses with her.

"Did you enjoy that?"

A still recovering Amara nodded before she began tugging at both men's briefs and they didn't need anymore prompting than that to remove them. It was her first time seeing Mateo and Liam with her own eyes. She was thankful that neither of them were massive, but they were still larger than anything she'd experienced.

Shaking herself out of her daze, Amara's eyes finally went up to meet theirs. "You guys have condoms, right?"

"Of course," Mateo replied as he took two from the nightstand and the men rolled them on.

When they rejoined her in bed, Mateo pulled one of her nipples between his lips while lightly pinching the other one and Liam's lips moved fervently against hers as he massaged her clit.

Already sensitive and her senses in overdrive with the connection of the Fated, it didn't take long for Amara to hit another climax. Coming down from her high, she looked between Liam and Mateo and it didn't take any abilities for them to know what she was thinking.

"It's okay," Mateo said softly as he continued to toy with her nipples. "Liam will take you first. He is... gentler."

Her eyes turned to a smiling Liam whose fingers were already working her core. "Is that okay with you?" he asked.

"Yes," she whimpered and in no time, Liam was sitting between her legs with his dick positioned at her entrance. He spit on his fingers and slowly rubbed her clit as he eased himself inside of her until Amara released a loud moan. Mateo remained at her side, switching between kissing and sucking her neck and doing the same to her breasts.

"Fuck," Liam shuddered, trying to keep himself together. Between being inside of his Fated for the first time and her spasming uncontrollably around his dick, he wasn't sure he'd be able to last long.

"Are you okay, Amara?" Mateo asked.

"It feels... really... good," she replied between labored breaths. Amara's body was in a frenzy, already on edge from feeling Liam inside of her for the first time.

Noticing that Liam hadn't even started moving yet, Mateo gave him a curious look.

"Amara," Liam grunted. "Take... deep... breaths. Try to... relax."

Amara tried and failed to calm her body—each time she took a deep breath, it only seemed to make things more intense. Realizing that she was too far gone and was going to keep pulsating around his dick, Liam accepted his fate and began giving Amara long, slow strokes, hoping he'd be able to last a bit longer.

But when her moans grew more persistent as her walls closed around him, he was done for.

Knowing he was about to come himself, Liam's movements grew faster causing Amara to cry out his name and that was all he needed to push him over the edge, releasing inside the condom. She pulled him into a kiss that had them savoring each others lips until Liam could gather himself.

When they finally broke the kiss, Liam pulled away from Amara and went to dispose of the condom before Mateo was on top of her. Studying her face, he asked, "Are you okay, cariño? There's no pressure to keep going if you ca-"

"Please Mateo," she interrupted and her hand wrapped around his member. "I want to take you too."

He didn't need anymore prompting than that and he had just the position in mind as he remembered watching her lead stretches in dance class. Mateo lifted one of her ankles to his shoulder while pushing her other leg to her side before driving his length into her.

Amara belted Mateo's name at the feeling of taking him from that angle and when he was inside of her, Mateo understood why Liam couldn't last long at all. With the way Amara was tightening around him, Mateo knew he'd soon come and wasted no time in beginning to pound her while playing with her clit.

She was saying Mateo's name through loud moans and when Liam walked in, he hardened once again at the sight. He approached and crouched by the bed in front of Amara to meet her glazed eyes and flushed face.

"Do you like this position, love?"

"Yes!" she cried out just when she hit yet another orgasm and Mateo came with her, releasing a drawn out groan as he finished inside the condom. When he pulled out of her, Amara's body was trembling, but that didn't stop her from wrapping her arms around him and bringing him in for a deep kiss.

Once their lips finally separated and Mateo went to the bathroom to dispose of the condom, Amara was in Liam's arms and she felt that he was hard again already.

"Liam," she murmured. "Can I ride you?"

There was a breeze of wind and Liam, fully erected, was already in bed with her and wearing a new condom.

Amara straddled Liam with one hand on his chest and the other holding him at her entrance. She exhaled as she lowered herself on him and Liam nearly came as soon as she did it. Slowly rocking her hips, Amara held his gaze, both of their mouths wide open with breathless moans. When Mateo returned to the room and saw Amara riding Liam, his erection was instant.

Amara turned to look at Mateo. "I want... to do this... to you... too." She choked out a strangled moan, even more turned on with the look in Mateo's eyes as he watched and the feeling when Liam began thrusting into her as he approached his release. With one hand on her hip and the other gripping her breast, Liam moved his hips to meet

Amara's movements, stroking her deeper until her walls were closing in around him once again.

By the time Liam hit his climax, Mateo was laying in bed next to them and without missing a beat, Amara was on top of him. She knew Mateo enjoyed taking control and that's exactly what he did. Holding her hips, Mateo's guided Amara until she was bouncing up and down his length and he lifted himself up to pull one of her mounds into his mouth.

"Mateo," Amara cried out. "It feels so good... oh fuck!" she blurted when he moved his hands from her hips to grab two handfuls of her ass and his thrusts became faster. Amara threw her head back while her nails dug into Mateo's shoulders at the intensity of her orgasm and he came in unison with her.

Amara collapsed between Mateo and Liam, sharing lazy kisses with them as they caressed her body before Liam pulled away and snapped his fingers and Mateo picked her up out of the bed to carry her to the bathroom.

"Here, mi alma. We'll give you a bath."

# CHAPTER
# THIRTY

"So, you're going Palisyfum hunting?" Haze questioned causally. She sat up against the head-board while Samuel was at the edge of the bed with his back to her reading through his notebook. Looking at his back, she admired the scratch marks she left on him. "Is that why you met with David?"

"Oh," he scoffed without turning around. "Now you want to talk?"

"What's that supposed to mean? We've done a lot of talking over the past twenty-four hours, have we not?"

"Very funny, Haze. And why do you ask? Would you like to join my little hunt? We do work well together."

"Ha!" Haze clapped. "What happened to your accusation that I have a few Palisyfum stragglers hidden away somewhere? Why would I join you if that were the case? And didn't you say you were my competition?"

"I clarified that it was just a theory. Or was your mind a bit too occupied while I had my fingers inside of you and you missed that part?" he asked, turning back to her with a raised brow. "So, how does it feel, Haze?"

"How does what feel?"

"Being an all powerful vampire and probably the only one in existence who holds the power of the Palisyfum? Don't most of your kind die when they feed from one?"

"I am going to rip David's head from his body and burn him to dust, I swear it..." She shook her head and massaged her temples. "Not as fun as it sounds... And I don't know why or how my body took to it. Anyway, you should under-stand... given that you come from the 'all powerful' Taylor family and now you're what? A thief and occasionally an assassin for hire as if you don't have enough money?"

Samuel huffed. "The power is great, but I hated the fucking politics of it all."

"Sounds like a rich boy sob story if I've ever heard one," Haze mumbled. "So, back to my question. You're helping David find the Palisyfum?"

"No. The idiot still hasn't figured out that the Palisyfum isn't a even fucking flower. Amazing how changing a few words in the lore threw so many people off. He just needs help breaking some curse and he pays well."

"You're a greedy one, Samuel. So if your hunt for a Palisyfum isn't for David, then who is looking for one?"

"That's the fun part... Petra."

Haze's head jerked back in disbelief. "Petra? I thought she was dead. And you trust her to pay you? The bitch is probably broke."

"Petra pays in power. She has plans for a whole new world... And the blood and flesh of a Palisyfum is the key."

Haze snorted. "Someone always has plans for a 'new world.' No matter what, it's always gonna be shit."

"So I take it you're not coming with me?"

"Why would I? It sounds like extra work and I have no need for a Palisyfum. I've already had my fill."

Samuel, still looking at Haze, sharpened his gaze. "I thought you enjoy a good challenge? Plus, we could go on a trip. I need to travel to some mountains deep as fuck in the Caucus region to retrieve a special amulet. It'll be fun. Like Indiana Jones or some shit."

"Amulet, you said? And you're hunting Palisyfum..." Haze looked down thoughtfully before she gasped and her eyes returned to Samuel. "Those are still around? I thought they were all destroyed?"

"The same way people think the Palisyfum is some extinct flower rather than a possibly extinct race of beings created from magical experiments?"

"Fair enough. Perhaps I will join you on your little adventure. You've sparked my curiosity."

"That was easy." Samuel sat his notebook on the night-stand beside the bed and turned to look Haze directly in her eyes as he held a snide look on his face. "And I still haven't told you the best part of this job."

"Oh? And what is that?"

"I already know the identity of our target."

Haze tilted her head to the side as she grabbed Samuel's face. "You already have a fucking target and you came here to interrogate me, anyway? Why must agitating me be fore-play for you?"

Samuel reveled in her tight grip, his lips stretching to a smile that strained against her finger tips. "Not only do I already know my target, but there's an added bonus that makes this job even more interesting than it already is. In fact, I'd say it's almost personal."

"Could you get to the fucking point, Samuel?"

"The Palisyfum that we're hunting just so happens to be my twin brother's Fated."

CHAPTER

# THIRTY-ONE

Mateo admired Amara's face as she slept peacefully between him and Liam. With the way her head rested on the pillow, her full lips were slightly parted and small snores came from Amara as her body expanded and contracted with her breathing. Their first time with her was better than either of them could've imagined and they hadn't gone to sleep until the early hours of the morning.

"We should make breakfast," Mateo whispered to Liam.

"That's a great idea," Liam nodded. "I'll have French toast and she likes-"

"Blueberry pancakes, I know," Mateo replied sharply. "And why the hell are you putting in orders? You're going to help me."

"But why? I don't want to let go of her."

"We will only be eighty-three feet away in the kitchen. And we'll be cooking for her. It's the least we can do after last night. I'm sure she is hungry. Now, come on." Mateo gently kissed Amara's forehead and reluctantly pulled away from her to get out of bed. She stirred in her sleep and snuggled up closer to Liam who in turn looked up at Mateo with the plea clear in his eyes that he wanted to stay in bed with her.

"We could just summon a large breakfast with a snap of our fingers."

Wanting to scold Liam without disturbing Amara, Mateo resorted to thinking what he wanted to say. *No! We have been using too much of our magic already as if it's unlimited. We need to figure out how to sever our connection with Petra and regain our full strength. For now, when it comes to tasks we can do without magic, we should just do it. And besides, it is better if we put in the work of making it ourselves. It's the absolute bare minimum we can do for her.*

Liam rolled his eyes and exhaled deeply. "Fine, but give me ten minutes."

*Whatever*, Mateo spat internally before leaving the room to start breakfast. He felt a tinge of guilt that he and Liam had kept Amara up almost all night. Although he did hold back, Mateo was afraid he still may have been a bit too rough with her. He thought the least they could do was was wake her up to her favorite breakfast rather than simply a sore body.

"What was that you said yesterday about not wrecking havoc on her body?" Liam teased when he finally joined Mateo in the kitchen.

"I wouldn't call what we did 'havoc.' But I do think we did get slightly carried away." Mateo handed Liam a bag of bread. "Here, you can make your own French toast."

"She seemed to be enjoying it." Liam sucked in his bottom lip and shook his head as flashbacks of last night came to his mind. "Those sounds she makes alone could do me in."

"Yes, and between those and the way it feels to be

inside of her…" Mateo groaned and dragged his hands down his face. "I hope she isn't too sore when she wakes up. But she kept wanting to go as well."

"As amazing as last night was, imagine how it'll be once she is used to us and we to her… Which reminds me, we should show her the other room."

"Liam!" Mateo exclaimed with agitation. "We just got through the warlocks and Fated conversations. We do not need to overwhelm her further by saying that we've already got a room in our house for the three of us. Give it some time…"

"But she might like it."

"*Or*, she might freak out again. Now, let's hurry and finish cooking before she wakes up."

"Fine," Liam grumbled as he started preparing the French toast.

It didn't take long for the men to finish a large spread for the three of them for breakfast and Amara was coming out of the room just as they were setting up at the counter.

"Wow," she gasped. "Is all this really for the three of us?" In addition to the pancakes and French toast, Mateo and Liam prepared scrambled eggs, sausage, bacon, an assortment of fruits, and coffee.

When the men turned to look at her, a smile came to Liam's face, while Mateo gulped and stared at Amara intently. She was wearing his shirt and while he knew it should feel rather mundane, something about seeing *her* wearing it with likely nothing else underneath caused blood to rush straight to his dick.

"Oh, sorry…" Amara cringed when she noticed how intense Mateo's gaze was on her. "I didn't have anything to wear and so I just grabbed your shirt out of the dresser. I hope you don't mind."

"No," Mateo cleared his throat and approached her. "Don't apologize. You can take anything you want from me, mi alma. Here…" He led her to the counter. "I'm sure you're hungry."

"I am!" she said as she scanned over the breakfast spread. "I know that we had dinner at some point last night, but it feels like we burned it off so quickly."

"Sorry about that." Liam gave her an apologetic smile. "I hope you can understand why we may have gotten a bit… carried away."

"Please don't apologize! I'm fine." *I kept going too. If I didn't get so tired, I wouldn't have stopped*, she thought to herself as she sat in her seat between the two men at the counter. Liam had his hand at the small of her back while Mateo's fingers caressed dangerously high up her thigh. *Oh gosh, Liam, I forgot you can hear me.*

"It's okay, Amara. I'm just glad that you don't feel over-whelmed." Liam cut his eyes to Mateo as he said that last word almost mockingly, but Mateo's gaze was glued to Amara as if he didn't notice anything else going on.

"Everything looks too good. There are blueberry pancakes!" she beamed. "How did you do all of this? Do you like snap your fingers like you did when you were switching place last night? Or like when you ran the bath right before we went into the bathroom?"

"We actually made this by hand."

*Perfect! These men are perfect! Are all warlocks this perfect? Yikes! I'm going to have to get used to knowing you can hear me, Liam.*

"It's fine," he replied with a chuckle. "Do you want me to take the potion to suppress my ability?"

"No! It's fine."

Liam took Amara's hand and brought her knuckles to

his lips. "Thank you for giving me the privilege. Here..." he picked up two large blueberry pancakes and put them on her plate. "Dig in."

"Thanks! Oh, you have French toast too, I know that's your favorite..." Amara searched the table to see if they may have made crepes, which were Mateo's breakfast of choice and they were notably absent. She also noticed that he hadn't said anything since they sat down. When she turned to him, Mateo's eyes were still on her body, but she didn't notice until she followed his gaze that three of the bottom buttons of his shirt she was wearing were undone.

"Mateo," she called and it took several moments before he seemed to shake himself out of his trance and return his gaze to her eyes.

"Shit, I'm sorry. My self-control has been dwindling..."

"Do you want me to take it off?" Amara challenged with a smirk. "I wouldn't want to mess up your shirt, I mean..."

Mateo muttered a series of expletives under his breath. He was already struggling to keep himself from taking Amara right there, and she only seemed to be challenging him further.

"You... should... eat..." Mateo struggled to get the words out through clenched teeth only for Amara to test him further.

"Are you sure you don't want me to take this off?" she asked, undoing another button. "What do you think, Liam?"

"I think you should take it off," he agreed, moving his seat closer to Amara. "Would you like some help?"

"If you don't mind..."

Liam didn't need anymore prompting than that. "Why don't you face Mateo, while I help you?"

Amara turned in her seat to face Mateo. Her core was

already exposed to him from when he unbuttoned the bottom buttons of the shirt since she wasn't wearing any panties and all that was left to reveal were her breasts, her hard nipples already pressing against the shirt.

From behind her, Liam wrapped his arms around Amara and started undoing the final few buttons while placing kisses on her neck.

*Fuck, have we already corrupted her?* Mateo thought to himself as he watched Liam slowly unbutton the shirt.

*What is going through Mateo's mind?*

"He's wondering if we've corrupted you. You're not often so... forward."

"Oh, that... There is something I realized last night." Amara held her hands over Liam's to signal him to stop and Mateo blinked several times before his eyes met hers.

"Is everything okay, Amara?"

"Yeah," she assured. "Its just that... It's... I don't really know a subtle way of saying this, but I can't seem to get enough of you two. Sex never felt good to me before, but last night was... amazing."

"Good," Liam responded and kissed her shoulder. "We intend for every time you're with us to be 'amazing' if not more."

"He's right," Mateo said with a low rasp. "Which is why you should eat your breakfast... you'll need the energy," he finished with a suggestive smirk.

"Don't you two have work?"

"We're calling out sick..."

When Amara dropped her hands, Liam finished unbuttoning the shirt, fully revealing her to Mateo who had almost a primal look in his eyes. The intensity of his gaze alone was enough to cause heat to rush to Amara's core. Liam's finger tips caressed her form before he brought both hands up to massage her breasts, playing with her buds between his fingers while his lips and tongue continued to trail along her neck and shoulder.

Amara didn't realize it was something she was into, but the way Mateo watched while Liam touched her only seemed to turn her on more. Her breathing grew deeper and she leaned her head against Liam's shoulder, but was still able to look into Mateo's eyes.

"Open your legs for us," Liam whispered. "I want to touch you."

Mateo licked his lips when Amara parted her legs and one of Liam's hands traveled down to her core. He slipped one finger inside of her and took a sharp breath when he felt how wet she was already.

Amara released a light moan when Liam dragged his finger that was wet with her arousal back up to gently rub her clit.

"Does it feel good?" Mateo asked. His pants were severely strained as he drank in the image before him—Amara with her legs wide open, holding eye contact with him, while Liam's fingers worked at her core and his other hand played with her nipple.

"Yes," she moaned. Her sounds grew more persistent as Liam continued pleasuring her. They became louder when he moved the hand that was on her breast down to massage her clit while using the other to pump two fingers in and out of her.

Liam felt the way her walls were spasming around his fingers and he picked up his pace. "Are you about to come, Amara?"

She nodded against his shoulder just as she reached one hand back to tangle her fingers in his hair. Mateo could see very clearly the way Amara's body was trembling as the climax grew inside of her.

Amara's eyes temporarily dropped from Mateo's to look down at the large bulge in his pants and the sight brought her closer to her release as her thoughts grew even dirtier.

"Don't worry, we have plenty of ideas for that," Liam said when he heard what she was thinking.

"What was that?" Mateo questioned. His fingers dug into his legs as he keep his eyes on Amara.

"She was wondering why you weren't touching yourse-"

Liam was cut off by an outburst from Amara when she came. Mateo nearly lost it as he watched the way her hips moved on Liam's fingers and her chest heaved while she rode out her orgasm.

"Would you like to taste yourself?" Liam muttered against Amara's ear as he pulled his digits out of her and brought them to her mouth. She held eye contact with Mateo as she sucked her essence off of Liam's fingers.

As soon as she finished, Mateo brought Amara in for a kiss to taste what was left of her. Knowing he was about to get carried away, he pulled his lips from her and retook his seat.

"Eat, Amara..." It came out as more of a command than anything. "And then I want you on my face."

"Now that sounds fun," Liam gleamed as he finally buttoned the shirt back up and let go of Amara. "Let's finish breakfast quickly, shall we?"

CHAPTER

# THIRTY-TWO

"Mateo!" Amara cried. Her body quivered and she felt like she would soon collapse. She straddled his face while his mouth worked at her core as his eyes remained on hers the entire time. Mateo enjoyed taking in every bit of Amara's reactions to the pleasure that he gave her.

"I still haven't had my turn, so don't 'overwhelm' her," Liam warned, continuing to use the 'overwhelm' term mockingly considering that Mateo was the one who set the rule, but didn't let Amara finish breakfast after giving in to her teasing and taking her to the couch. When Liam realized Mateo's state of mind, he gave up his efforts to join, knowing exactly what was about to happen.

After riding out yet another orgasm on Mateo's face, Amara was placed on her back and before she realized, her ankles were on his shoulders while he was sitting up straight and aligned with her entrance. He slid himself into her with ease given how wet she was and immediately started pounding her—the sound of their bodies slapping against each other filling the room.

Amara clawed at the couch with the immense pleasure that was coming over her and Mateo grunted with his strokes. Liam was just a few feet away, trying and failing to distract himself by cleaning the kitchen and monitoring Amara's thoughts to make sure Mateo wasn't becoming too much for her.

"Fuck!" Amara bellowed when Mateo leaned in to stroke her deeper. He kissed and sucked her neck before wrapping his hand around it and nibbling at her ear. It wasn't lost on Mateo the way she spasmed at the move.

"Do you like it when I choke you, amor?"

Amara nodded as she held his gaze and he was set off once again. They were repositioned so that she was straddling him on the couch and he roughly grabbed her ass while thrusting up into her and Amara's body bounced at the intensity of it while her arms wrapped around Mateo's neck. He caught one of her nipples in his mouth and his strokes remained relentless while Amara's core only grew wetter.

"Oh. My. God!" Amara cried out at yet another climax and Mateo slowed his movements when he felt himself approaching his own, not wanting to come yet. She looked behind the couch at Liam in the kitchen and as soon as their eyes met, he abandoned cleaning the space and returned to the pair.

Mateo sensed Liam's presence and for a third time, he and Amara were repositioned. She was on all fours while Mateo took her from behind and Liam sat at the end of the couch near her head.

When Liam heard what Amara was thinking, he held her chin up to look into her eyes. "Are you sure that's what you want?"

Amara nodded and Liam immediately removed his pants and released his member, positioning it at her lips.

While Mateo's strokes were still slow as he gathered himself, Amara was able to focus on Liam and his dick twitched as soon as he felt her tongue on his shaft. She licked him several times from his base to his tip before taking him into her mouth. Liam had been staring down at her, admiring her every move the whole time, but as soon as he felt her lips wrapped around him, his head fell back and he tangled his fingers in her hair. Amara's head bobbed up and down as she worked Liam's length, taking him further with each turn.

Suddenly, Liam felt the vibration of Amara squealing while she had him down her throat, followed by the sound of Mateo's body slapping against hers along with her wetness as he started pounding her again.

"Fuck," Liam moaned as he felt himself racing toward his release already.

Mateo was rapidly coming undone himself as he watched the way Amara's body accepted him while he fucked her from behind. He lifted his hand from one of her cheeks and slammed it back down, causing her to jump at the move and let out another squeal against Liam.

"Te gusta bien duro?" Mateo teased before smacking her ass again. With Liam's length filling her mouth, Amara couldn't answer, but Mateo didn't need her to—he felt exactly how her body was reacting. "Creo que si..." he said, his voice raspy as he spoke between his grunts. "Your pussy is so wet, Amara. Are you about to come again?"

Amara answered Mateo through muffled moans and when she felt Liam's balls tightening in her hand, she knew he was about to come too. Not wanting to release his dick,

Amara gave an answer to his question before he needed to ask.

*You can come in my mouth,* she thought and the words alone were enough to push Liam over edge and he did exactly that.

Amara soon came again herself and the way she spasmed around him triggered Mateo's climax. He quickly pulled out of her and released all over her ass before Amara's body gave out and she lay down on her stomach.

"Shit…" Mateo exhaled through labored breaths. "Did I… hurt you?"

Amara shook her head lightly with her eyes closed.

"Don't worry, she's telling the truth, Mateo," Liam assured after hearing his worried thoughts. "She liked it."

A smile etched into Mateo's face and he lifted Amara from the couch. "I'm sorry for the mess, mi alma. Let's clean you up."

AMARA WAS SPRAWLED out between Liam and Mateo asking them questions as the three of them lay on a large comforter and bed of pillows in the middle of the living room.

"Think of Lillian as sort of our handler in a way," Liam explained.

"She's been a guide for us as we've learned more about the practices of the mortal world so we could more easily adapt," Mateo added.

"Is your world really that different?"

"Yes and no. We still have comparable politics and jobs, but there's always the magical elements that you don't have. It was particularly difficult with this Fated bond between us. You see, while not everyone has a Fated in our world, it's still a widely-understood concept, so when you come into contact with yours, things move pretty quickly from there."

"And with you, we had to pace ourselves... or at least as best as we could. We were afraid to come on too strong too soon. Even though you felt the bond too, we had to keep in mind that your reaction would be different from ours."

"Wow, there is so much to consider..." Amara pondered aloud before turning her attention to Liam. "And your mom is part of something called the Assembly?"

"Yes," Liam nodded. "Think of the Assembly as sort of a government for witches and warlocks."

"Hmmm... So like they make laws and enforce them?"

"Correct. They also develop ways for us to advance as a people and try to keep peace between all of us."

"Oh! Does that mean you guys have wars and stuff? Er — I guess with any group there's bound to be conflicts to a certain extent. But what would a war between people with powers be like?"

"Not as exciting as you would think," Mateo replied through a slight chuckle. "They usually manifest in smaller battles or covert actions... It's very rare that you'd see entire armies of our kind going at it with each other. It's just not our style."

"Hm... Is it weird that that gives me some comfort? Humans without powers are already destructive enough."

"I don't blame you for feeling that way."

Amara hesitated as she twisted her mouth and looked between the two men. "I did have another question and I hope it's not too intrusive..."

"There's nothing you can ask us that is too intrusive," Liam assured. "Go ahead."

"With the three of us being Fated and you two knowing

for over one hundred years... Did you ever think you might be fated to each other as well?"

"Liam and I are fated to be with each other and with you. We are meant as three."

"I don't think she meant it that way, Mateo... Are you asking if Mateo and I have ever had a romantic relationship?"

Amara nodded. "Yes."

"Oh. I misunderstood. We tried it, but it didn't work out." Mateo shrugged casually.

"Mateo and I work well together and we have an incredibly strong bond, but romantically and sexually, we just don't seem compatible."

"At least when you're not involved," Mateo clarified. "Liam and I are partners, but the relationship we have with each other is different from what each of us has with you and you with us. But those different types of relationships occurring simultaneously between the three of us is exactly why this works."

"I see..." Amara replied. "I have one last um... sensitive question."

"Go for it."

"Well, um..." Amara hesitated. "I know you explained that once you reach a certain age is when you go through this ritual to become immortal, but both of you have told me about members of your family who have died. If you're immortal, how can that happen?"

"Well," Mateo began. "Immortality for us means that we won't die of natural causes and we're a lot more resilient than average humans—we heal quickly and wounds that might be fatal for most mortals, we generally survive."

"However," Liam continued. "Immortals can be killed if we are beheaded or severely injured repeatedly faster than we can heal. Also, as simplistic as this might sound, there are some immortals who wish to cease their existence and so they have their immortality removed, though the process is quite excruciating from what I understand."

"Immortality isn't glamorous, to be honest."

"I can imagine," Amara said softly. "Does it get frustrating?"

"Frustrating how?"

"I mean, don't you have to witness firsthand the way we mortals make the same mistakes over and over and over throughout history? That has got to get annoying."

Liam chuckled and rubbed Amara's leg. "It's not too different in our world either."

"I still can't believe that all of this is real."

"You'll get used to it, love."

# THIRTY-THREE

It had been two weeks since Mateo and Liam revealed everything to Amara and she was practically living at their house when she wasn't on campus. Learning that she was fated to two immortal warlocks and of the existence of supernatural beings was still surreal to her.

Amara was also becoming increasingly frustrated with her research on the palisyfum. Every time she thought she was making progress, she'd hit another dead end. While she'd made interesting discoveries in various cross-breeding processes, her lack of any breakthroughs on the palisyfum disheartened Amara.

She sat at her desk in the shared office space in the natural sciences building flipping through her notebook that contained all of her notes on the palisyfum when she cut her finger on one of the pages. Suddenly, her head began pounding and when she closed her eyes, she saw herself in her childhood bedroom.

. . .

*A*MARA WOKE *up in the middle of the night to the sound of whispers downstairs.*

*"It's not fair what you're doing to her, Glenda."*

*The voice said Amara's grandmother's name, but it was unlike any voice she'd ever heard before. It was deep and distorted and while it spoke words she registered as human, it didn't sound human.*

*"Listen to me. She is not ready, but I will tell her everything eventually, at least once she turns eighteen."*

*"She should know sooner. You need to teach her so she can protect herself."*

*"I told you, no!" Glenda raised her voice before she immediately hushed her tone. "Think about the type of trauma she went through. You weren't there when I retrieved her. You didn't see the conditions..." she choked up and Amara could hear almost a sob from Glenda.*

*Hearing her grandmother in distress, Amara ran down the steps calling to her. "Grandma! Grandma! Are you ok?" When Amara reached the bottom of the stairs, she noticed a figure flash past her with almost inhuman speed. She couldn't quite make out the shape, but with how quickly it went by, she assumed that it was something else as her mind still hadn't caught up to her awakened state.*

*Glenda was sitting on a couch with two cups of tea on the coffee table in front of her and looked up at her granddaughter startled. "What are you doing down here? I thought you were asleep."*

*"I was, but then I heard you and you... you seemed..." Amara stumbled over her words, trying to put together exactly what she heard. "It sounded like you were arguing with someone and then you were crying. I just wanted to see if you were okay."*

*"I am fine, Amara," Glenda replied curtly. "Thank you for your concern. Now, please go back to bed."*

*Amara paused, looking over the room. She didn't understand why Glenda had two cups of tea and she could've sworn that there was another voice speaking earlier. However, there were no other signs that someone else was with her grandmother. She noticed Xivan hopping back into the room toward his cage and tilted her head curiously.*

*"You let Xivan out?" she questioned. "I can't believe he's up so late..."*

*"He just needed to stretch a bit before going to sleep, which is exactly where you should be going as well, Amara."*

*"Why do you have two cups of tea? Is someone else here? I thought I heard you talking to someone."*

*"The two cups of tea are for myself. It's just Xivan and I here, Amara."*

*"But-"*

*"But nothing!" Glenda snapped. "Now, do as you're told and go to sleep or you'll be regretting it when I wake you up early in the morning."*

*Glenda's words didn't register to Amara as the young teen reviewed in her head the pieces of the conversation that she heard. "You kept using 'her' and talking about letting 'her' out. Were you talking about me? Are you going to let me go more places? I really want to go to school."*

*"No!" Glenda shouted as she rose to her feet. "It's too dangerous, now go to sleep!"*

*"No!" Amara countered, echoing Glenda's tone. "You always say it's too dangerous for me to go anywhere, but everywhere is dangerous, grandma. Even here! Why does it feel like you're hiding things from me? And you're always keeping me locked up here. It's not fair. I want to meet other people! I want to be normal! I'm fourteen years old and I can't even have friends or interact with people my age!"*

*Glenda took a deep breath and her voice was softer when she spoke again. "Amara, the world is a dangerous place and you cannot trust people!"*

*"If I can't trust people, would that include you?" Amara spat. "How can I trust you, grandma, if you keep me here like some prisoner? And you never give me a real answer whenever I ask you why! It's always 'it's too dangerous.' Why won't you tell me the truth? Stop fucking lying to me!"*

*"Language!" Glenda warned. "Amara Rosalind Jenkins, if I have to tell you one more time to go to bed, you will be grounded!"*

*"Then ground me! I don't care," Amara snarled. As her anger grew, there seemed to be a slight trembling of the house. While Amara was too wrapped up in her argument with her grandmother, Glenda realized what was happening. "What difference does it make if I'm grounded? I'm already stuck here, anyway! I'm a prisoner already!"*

*Glenda reached her hand forward toward her grand-daughter and muttered something under her breath. When Amara continued to stand there stubbornly and the rumbling in the house persisted, bewilderment flashed across Glenda's face. She muttered the words again and still, nothing happened as Amara stood her ground.*

*"What are you saying?" she questioned when she heard Glenda's murmurs.*

*Suddenly, Glenda's eyes turned purple and everything went blank.*

"WHAT THE HELL WAS THAT?" Amara whispered, looking down at the blood that was coming from the paper cut on her thumb before she brought it to her mouth and sucked it away. "I don't remember anything like that happening? But it *felt* like a memory." When she looked at the wound again, it appeared to had stopped bleeding immediately and the tiny cut was closed.

Amara ran her fingers through her hair as confusion about what she just saw flooded her. She didn't understand how or why such a vivid memory popped into her head so suddenly. She never recalled that event, but what occurred didn't seem like something forgettable, especially considering the purple color of Glenda's eyes. They reminded her of the woman's eyes in the nightmares she'd been having.

However, despite their eyes being the same, Glenda and the purple-eyed woman looked different from each other—they didn't even appear related. Still, Amara felt just as connected to the purple-eyed woman as she did to her grandmother and she didn't quite understand why. She wasn't related to the woman a far as she knew.

Amara took out the notebook she'd been using to track her dreams and jotted down notes about her memory. As of now, the only things the dreams and her new memory had in common were how vivid they felt. The pain Amara experienced in her nightmares, both physically and emotionally, felt real to her as if she'd gone through it in real life. It was the same for the sensations she felt with the memory that hit her.

At the center of it all were a set of distinct purple eyes.

"What is wrong with my brain?" Amara muttered to herself as she added to her notes. "My reactions to these nightmares and memories are turning more and more visceral... I wonder if I should start going to therapy again. Maybe its all the stress from these dead ends or something."

After closing her dream and herbal notebooks, Amara packed them in her bag and started heading toward the door when she was intercepted by David. She had noted a shift in his attitude over the past several weeks since the incident with the notebook. He'd gradually become more unkempt and his skin often looked dry with chapped lips. There was also something about his aura that Amara couldn't quite put her finger on that gave her discomfort.

"Hi, Amara! Are you going somewhere? I was hoping to rejoin you on this palisyfum research."

"Oh, David! Yeah, about that... I've hit another dead end and it's just so frustrating, so I decided to take a break and get back to it tomorrow. Would you like to join me then?"

"Yeah, absolutely! And where are you heading for your break? There's this really cool bar just outside of the city that I could show you."

"No, I'm actually going home." She was going to Liam and Mateo's house, but Amara didn't want to explain why to David.

"Aw, are you sure? This place is really cool..."

"Yeah, I'm sure," Amara nodded before continuing down her path. "But I'll see you tomorrow?"

"Wait," David reached out and grabbed her arm. He was able to touch Amara herself without feeling any effects as it only seemed to come from the notebook. "It'd be really, really nice if you came."

Amara suddenly felt a waft of something hit her and then breeze past like a light wind and her body calmed. For a split second, she was about to say yes to going with him and it almost felt involuntary, but the trance was momentary and she quickly emerged from it.

She shook her head. "Nope. I'll see you tomorrow."

Amara pulled her arm from his grip and quickly walked away.

David watched her escape completely confused about what just occurred. He used his vampiric ability of charm on her, but it seemed to have no effect at all.

# THIRTY-FOUR

"I'm ridiculously stressed," Amara groaned, falling onto the couch in Liam and Mateo's living room. "I keep hitting dead ends on the palisyfum. Maybe the flower is really just a myth... I know that I keep saying my studies primarily focus on cross-breeding plants with the idea that the palisyfum could be a perfect example of the benefits of cross-breeding, but I was really hoping to have more leads on it by now."

Mateo joined Amara on the couch, placing her head on his lap and stroking her curly hair while Liam went to the kitchen to brew her some tea.

"Don't get too discouraged, mi alma. Like you said, cross-breeding is the core of your studies and even if the palisyfum doesn't turn out to be a flower, there's still so much that can be done with other discoveries you make."

"Why did you word it like that?"

"Like what?"

"You said 'if the palisyfum doesn't turn out to be a flower' rather than saying it doesn't exist. Do you think it might be something else?"

"I think Mateo's words just got a bit jumbled," Liam interjected as he joined the two of them on the couch and Amara sat up to take the tea he made.

"Right..." Mateo agreed. He started kneading the back of Amara's shoulder with his thumb and realized how much tension she was carrying.

*We'll need to reveal the truth to her eventually,* Mateo thought to Liam. *Keeping this a secret from her is killing me. I can't wait for Cameron to visit.*

Mateo moved behind the couch so he could give Amara a proper massage. "You're so tense. Is it really stressing you out that much?"

"It's just so frustrating, you know? But maybe it's my fault." She sighed. "Why am I so worried about a flower that's only come up in tall tales?"

"You shouldn't be ashamed of your interest in the palisyfum," Liam assured. "You'll learn more about it soon, I'm sure of it."

"Yeah, you're right, it's just..." Amara drifted off as satisfied moans escaped her and she closed her eyes relishing in the massage.

Although Liam and Mateo were growing more accustomed to her, they were still abnormally sensitive to many of her actions—especially the noises she would make.

Liam looked between Amara who was clearly enjoying the massage and Mateo who was clearly as turned on as he was in that moment.

"We can help you... *relieve* some of that stress, Amara. How about we try something new today?"

"Hm?" she hummed.

Mateo leaned down closer to her ear. "May I watch you with Liam?"

"Don't you two already do that? When the three of us have sex..."

"This way would be different. It would be just you and I while Mateo watches."

She turned and looked up at Mateo. "I'd like to try it."

BOTH STRIPPED down to their underwear, Amara was on top of Liam in the bed and Mateo sat in a chair just a few feet away from them. Grabbing two handfuls of her ass, Liam guided Amara's movements as she ground against the growing tent in his pants.

While Liam would often take the lead, understanding that Amara was still growing into her sexuality, Amara learned in her time with him that Liam seemed to like when she took control. Allowing her desire to guide her movements, Amara ground harder against Liam and bit his bottom lip, earning a groan from him. She grazed her teeth against his neck before lightly sucking it and allowing her kisses to trail lower down his body.

Mateo's eyes were intent on Amara, paying attention to how she appeared more comfortable with herself in the bedroom and he wondered if she'd soon be ready for more with him and Liam.

When Amara reached Liam's erection and freed it from his briefs, he knew exactly what was on her mind, but he was cautious of his continued sensitivity to her, even if it wasn't as potent as before. He took deep breaths while Amara worked his length with her mouth and tongue, but it wasn't long until she was flipped on her back, her panties were removed, and Liam was eating her pussy.

Mateo watched as Liam's head was buried between Amara's legs while he ate her out. Her fingers tangled in

Liam's hair while her eyes remained on Mateo. Between the sight and Amara's sounds, Mateo was severely strained against his pants, but he wasn't ready to touch himself just yet.

"Oh god!" Amara shouted when she hit her first climax and Liam held her legs tight as he took every bit she had to give him. She turned her head to look down at him while his mouth continued to work her core until she let out a breathless moan and her body trembled.

Liam slowly worked his way up Amara's body until he met her lips. They lay there in an intense kiss as their tongues tangled and they moaned softly against each other.

After separating from Amara to put on a condom, Liam returned to her in bed and positioned her on her side so she was facing Mateo while Liam lay behind her. He lifted her leg up so that she was wide open in perfect view for Mateo before Liam eased his length into her.

Mateo licked his lips and finally pulled himself from his pants while watching the way Liam gave Amara slow strokes, going deeper each time until she could take him fully. One of his hands toyed with her nipple between his fingers while the other rubbed her clit and it didn't take long for Amara's moans to begin filling the room.

Mateo spit on his hand and started stroking himself at the scene before him. Each time Liam's strokes into Amara sped up, so did Mateo's hand.

It wasn't lost on Liam the way Amara's body reacted and how she kept watching Mateo, watching them.

"So... you do... like him... watching?" Liam whispered between labored breaths.

"Yes," Amara shuddered and Liam's strokes stopped.

"Let's give him a good show, shall we?" he said before repositioning the two of them so that he was on his back and Amara was on top of him also facing the ceiling. She placed her hands on each side of him to hold herself up so she could continue looking at Mateo and Liam drove his length back into her. With the position they were in, Amara's body was in perfect view for Mateo and he could see very clearly her pussy being pounded by Liam.

"Show Mateo how you touch yourself while I'm inside of you," Liam muttered and Amara reached down to rub her clit while he continued moving in and out of her.

Mateo grunted at the sight as his hand sped up watching the two of them. Based on the aura in the room, he knew that they were quickly approaching their climaxes and he was nearing his own as well.

When Liam cupped under Amara's knees to bring them up so he could stroke her deeper, the move set all three of them off. Amara cried something unintelligible, Liam moaned her name, and Mateo groaned with pleasure as the three of them came in unison.

Liam slowly pulled out of Amara while she was still catching her breath and set her on the bed so he could go dispose of the condom while Mateo removed his shirt and wiped himself off with it before throwing it to the side. Amara reached out for him and he joined her in bed.

Amara rested on his chest and looked up at him with a subtle smirk. "Did you like it?" she asked softly.

"The best show I've ever seen," he replied and pecked her on the forehead. "You and I are going to have to give Liam one sometime too."

# THIRTY-FIVE

Sleeping over at Mateo and Liam's home had become a regular part of Amara's week, splitting her time between her and Evelyn's house and theirs. They'd often go between Mateo or Liam's room and share the bed the together while they slept. Tonight, Amara was tossing and turning between the two of them as she was hit with another intense nightmare.

*"I hate you!" Amara snarled at the purple-eyed woman. "I hate you! I hate you! I hate you! I hate you! I hate you! I hate you!" The eight-year-old repeated the words until her throat was dry, and continued the chanting through coughs. The purple-eyed woman showed signs of distress, but she maintained her resolve and avoided Amara's glare.*

*"Look at me!" Amara gestured to her mangled arm and legs covered in scars. "How could you do this to us? You're supposed to be my mom! And what about dad?"*

*"I told you, honey," her mother finally turned to look Amara in the eyes. "It's for the greater good. Our blood and flesh can change the world."*

*"No!" Amara shouted. "I hate you. I wish you weren't my mom! Why did I get stuck with y-"*
*"The girl has been growing more angry with each day..."*
*Alistair, the red-eyed vampire who'd been keeping them hostage appeared out of nowhere, standing next to Amara's mother.*
*"Victoria, did you tell her of her father?" he asked, keeping his eyes on Amara as if examining her.*
*"No," Victoria replied softly.*
*A snide smirk came to Alistair's face and he tilted his head before speaking to Amara.*
*"Your father is dead, little girl. I killed him."*
*Amara didn't know what came over her, but it went beyond rage. She no longer felt she was in control of her body and suddenly lunged toward Alistair. In a split second, she found herself fighting against her mother's hold and one of Alistair's arms was removed from his body and on the ground.*
*"Give me back my dad!" Amara wailed as she clawed at her mother's flesh until she drew blood.*

"Give him back!" Amara shouted to the top of her lungs, startling both Liam and Mateo who were sleeping on each side of her.

"Are you okay?" Mateo questioned, holding her face.

"What's wrong?" Liam followed, taking her hand.

Amara pulled them off of her and scrambled to get out of bed, going for her bag. "My medicine. I need my medicine." She was hysterical, tears running from her face and in a panic. Her breaths were shaky, along with her trembling body. "Medicine. My medicine," she repeated as she urgently searched through her bag.

She nearly had another meltdown on top of her ongoing one when she found her pill bottle and realized it was empty.

"Herbs!" she cried. "I need to make the medicine. Please!"

"Okay, okay," Mateo said franticly. "What do you need?"

Amara's mind was moving faster than her mouth and in no time, Liam summoned the lavender, chamomile, sage, and vervain she needed with the exact measurements as well as a mortar and pestle for her to make her medicine.

The men felt helpless, watching Amara's panicked movements as she made her medicine. Liam hated that his ability was limited to only the words that went on in her head and Mateo was frustrated that he had no idea what was going on other than assuming she'd had a nightmare.

When Amara finished grinding the herbs and pricked her finger to put a drop of blood into the bowl, both men's eyes went wide.

Still in a flustered state, Amara continued to plead for materials. "Capsules! Please, I need to put this in capsules."

At the snap of Mateo's fingers, the herbal mix was put into capsules and Amara immediately downed two of them. She raised her hand to signal the men not to approach her as she took deep breaths and centered herself.

Amara finally looked up at the men and the terror was clear in their eyes. "I'm sorry... I get these nightmares and they're really, really bad. Very graphic. Too graphic, really. I didn't mean to scare you."

Liam shook his head. "Please don't apologize, Amara. We're more worried about you than anything. What did you see?"

Amara hesitated as she tried to remember exactly what happened in the dream. She'd been recollecting more and more of her nightmares lately, but she was still unclear on many of the details.

"There was a purple-eyed woman, a red-eyed man, and a lot of pain... Physically and emotionally. Despair would be an understatement. And anger. It was like pure rage, but it felt so concrete. Like it manifested into something solid. There was also something about my dad. Something bad. But, I can't remember exactly what it was."

Mateo and Liam exchanged a glance before turning their attention back to Amara. She was still coming down from her panicked state, but Liam read from her mind and Mateo sensed that she didn't want to be touched.

While they remained in her proximity, at least staying present while she gathered herself, Mateo mentally communicated his concerns to Liam.

*She said she saw purple and then red eyes in her dream. This concerns me. It could be a premonition, especially given that it comes with physical symptoms. And the medicine—lavender, chamomile, sage, and vervain—all four of them have cleansing properties in addition to healing, stress reduction, and protection. And did you see when she pricked her finger at the end? But she clearly doesn't know anything about the truth of the Palisyfum. How could she know to add her blood? And why is she doing it?*

"Amara," Liam called when her breathing was finally steady and her body relaxed. "Why did you add blood to your medicine?"

"Oh, I..." Amara tried to explain to the men that it was something her grandmother taught her and it turned into a very strange habit, but she was physically unable to get the words out. Her lips twitched, and when she again tried to tell them, what she *did* say felt involuntary. She shrugged. "I don't know."

Liam looked at her curiously because even her thoughts seemed to be going toward an explanation, but just as her words, they came to an abrupt halt before all delivering an "I don't know."

"Sorry, I think I'm just off," Amara said nervously. "My mind is all over the place. This is a difficult week. It's been seven years since grandma... And Cam's accident too. Even though we didn't know each other then, I think it still affects me similar to grandma. I feel bad that I won't be able to see him the moment he gets into town tomorrow. I'm excited about teaching the dance workshops, but wish they didn't conflict with his arrival."

"We understand there's a lot going on," Mateo replied. "Liam and I will be sure to keep Cameron entertained after we pick him up from the airport."

Amara smiled wide and approached Mateo and Liam to wrap them in a tight hug. "Thank you for going through the trouble of taking off work to get him. You guys really are the best."

"It's no trouble at all," Liam assured. "We've been wanting to spend more time with Cameron ourselves."

*Now that we've finally figured out what he is,* Mateo thought. *This has become more urgent than ever and we need to tell Amara the truth about the palisyfum. With Cameron in town, at least she'll have someone closer to her than she thought in the first place to confide in other than us.*

After learning from Amara that Cameron got into what should've been a fatal accident the same week that her grandmother died and additional details surrounding the circumstances of his survival, Mateo and Liam had a solid theory about what Cameron might be and they were ready to confront him about it.

～

Samuel and David were set to meet at Joey's Tavern so Samuel could break the curse inflicted on David from Amara's notebook. It had been weeks since the two of them last met and the curse had taken a toll on David's health.

"It's about time," David griped as he approached Samuel in the alley to the side of the bar.

Samuel ignored his attitude and and leaned against the brick building with a smug look on his face. "Do you have my payment?"

"Are you going to break this curse?"

"Yeah, yeah…" Samuel waved dismissively. "Don't worry. When I'm done, you won't have to worry about a curse ever again."

"Great, because I've been feeding like crazy and it's been impossible for me to focus on anything else."

"'Anything else,' like what? Your Palisyfum hunt?"

"Exactly."

"You seem rather desperate for a mythical flower."

"I think you and I both agree that the palisyfum isn't 'mythical,'" David countered. "And remember how I told you about Haze? The palisyfum lotus is real and I need its power."

"For what, exactly?" Samuel questioned.

David eyes brightened and turned a glowing red with his excitement. "Whatever the fuck I want, just because I'll be able to! Haze is an idiot for not using her powers to their full potential. First, I'm going to turn myself human so that I'm no longer a slave to this unquenchable thirst, nor will I need to worry about wearing this fucking ring to survive the sun! However, I plan to maintain my enhanced senses and abilities…" He drifted off. "Wait, why the hell am I speaking so freely with you?" Suddenly, David caught whiff of a familiar scent. Before he could flee, a pair of arms wrapped around him and a head rested on his shoulder.

"Long time, no see," Haze's velvety voice caressed his ears and David's resistance immediately ceased. However, he was still visibly in fear, trembling in her embrace.

"H-Haze? I didn't know that you..."

"Shut the fuck up, David," she spat. "You talk too much."

An entertained smirk pulled Samuel's lips "Have I ever told you how much I enjoy watching you do that? You really do live up to your name, Haze."

"H-how?"

David was once again cut off. This time, Haze hooked her fingers into his mouth and dug her sharp nails into the bottom of it.

"Didn't I tell you to shut the fuck up?" she hissed. "And what the hell do you mean 'how'? You're running your mouth about me holding the power of a palisyfum, but did you forget why my name is 'Haze' in the first place?"

"Aw, it looks like you've pissed her off," Samuel teased as he watched her hook her other hand at the roof of David's mouth. As much as the vampire wanted to fight back, he couldn't.

Even before she gained Palisyfum power, Haze was already a special-grade vampire. While the ability to charm was common among their kind, Haze had a more intense effect on her targets, capable of putting them in a hazy state of mind, powerful enough to hypnotize them.

Thus, she earned the name Haze.

"I'm not pissed," she replied calmly. "I simply forgot to tie up a loose end..." Just when she began pulling David's mouth apart, tearing him at his cheeks, Samuel stopped her.

"Wait..." Samuel raised his hand. "I need to see his reaction when he learns that the Palisyfum was under his nose the entire time."

Haze huffed her annoyance and released David's mouth, allowing it to immediately heal, so he could look at Samuel as he spoke.

"The Palisyfum isn't a flower, you idiot," Samuel scolded. "Think about the lore that you claim you've read and remove every instance of 'flower' or 'lotus' or replace them with the word 'being.'"

David's eyes darted in several directions before they finally landed on Samuel again. "But they're magically engineered..."

"Magically engineered *beings*," Haze added. "They were created solely to act as an amplifier... You're a vampire, are you not? Then you should know the power that blood holds beyond our food supply. Blood magic is the most powerful magic that there is, so powerful that even non-warlocks can cast potent spells using it."

"I'll give you a quick lesson in magic," Samuel began. "Blood is an intense amplifier. The better the quality of blood, the mightier the spell. So, imagine when you take samples from as many magical and ethereal beings as possible—witches, warlocks, fairies, pagan gods and goddesses, elves, unicorns... hell, even the Phoenix—and combine them all to create a single being..."

David's eyes grew wider as he listened to Samuel's explanation and started putting more of the pieces together on his own.

"And so, the Palisyfum was born!" he announced with a mocking exuberance in his speech as he went on. "That's right, the most powerful magical amplifier to ever exist being pure blood and flesh in a single being. But no! That wasn't enough for the greedy Assembly that created them. They wanted more. Just one problem, though... each time they wanted to create a Palisyfum, they needed to gather thousands of samples and go through the process again. Do you get where I'm going, yet?"

"So fucking annoying when he gets like this," Haze muttered. "The narcissist loves to give a damn speech."

Samuel grew more entertained with the increasing awareness on David's face and went on about the story of the Palisyfum. "To solve that problem, the Assembly figured why not allow the Palisyfum to procreate with humans? And so they did, birthing a whole new race of beings that grew into a population of thousands over centuries... The arrogant fucks thought their lies that Palisyfum were incapable of magic and prohibiting them from practicing it would be enough. It only took about a century before the Palisyfum gave magic a shot anyway. And when they did, it awakened their abilities—essentially making them witches and warlocks on steroids.

"When the Assembly *did* find out about their little *experiments* doing experiments of their own. They decide to take the genocide route. So, before many of the Palisyfum could realize their true potential, they were killed. But, of course a group as sloppy and power-drunk as The Assembly 'missed' some Palisyfum. Or conveniently left stragglers behind."

Samuel scanned over David's face and then looked into his mind and saw Amara's image before giving him a sarcastic applause.

"Finally, you've figured it out! That's right, Amara Jenkins, PhD candidate is a Palisyfum witch. All you had to do was feed from her and you would've been as powerful as Haze!"

David gulped, pure bewilderment on his face as he learned all this information from Samuel. "What?"

"I imagine that she didn't smell like a witch because she put some sort of sealing on herself to hide it. You would've figured that out if you weren't such an idiot... Anyway," Samuel sighed, now seemingly bored with the conversation. "I was nice enough to give you a history lesson so you'd know the truth behind the Palisyfum before dying, so you should thank m-"

He was cut off when David suddenly released a blood-curdling scream as Haze tore his face in half, finishing the move she'd started earlier. She dropped his body to free one of her hands and with a snap of her fingers, it was set ablaze before she threw the remnants of his head into the fire as well.

When Haze's eyes went from the pile of ash to Samuel's, she raised an amused brow.

"What? You gave your speech... The rest was just fluff even more unnecessary than telling him about the Palisyfum in the first place."

"Whatever," Samuel huffed and rolled his eyes. "I've been bored all day in this bumfuck town of Masoncrest and his reaction to knowing he had the Palisyfum in his grasp this entire time was my appetizer for the evening... But I see you wanted to rush straight to dinner."

In the blink of an eye, he had Haze pressed against the wall, pinned by her neck with her legs wrapped around his waist. "You know I don't like being rushed, Haze," he rasped against her ear. "I think you were trying to piss me off just now."

"And why the hell would I do that?" she challenged.

"Because you want me to fuck you into oblivion, of course."

# THIRTY-SIX

Amara carried a subtle frown as she dragged herself across campus to the Humanities building where she would be teaching dance workshops for the entire first half of the day. Cameron was arriving that morning and Liam and Mateo were on their way to pick him up.

Amara wanted nothing more than to spend time with them all, but she'd already committed to doing the dance workshops just a few days before students and faculty were to be released for Thanksgiving break. Fortunately, dance was one of the things Amara loved most and she knew that as soon as she started, she would temporarily forget all she was missing out on with Cameron, Liam, and Mateo.

"You're here!" Sarah Finch, the head of the Fine Arts Department who hired Amara to teach dance, beamed when she walked into the studio.

"Yes!" Amara returned her greeting with a big smile. "I'm here and I'm excited to get started."

"Excellent! Well, everyone is mostly stretched out, as you can see." Sarah gestured around the packed room where students and faculty were already at the barre or on the floor, much to Amara's surprise. She was also confused as to why there were sheets draped over the mirrors.

"Wow! I thought this was a mix of beginners and long-time dancers, but everyone knew to stretch?"

"No, one of the people taking your workshop today came in and took the lead on getting everyone started on their stretches... She even had us cover the mirror with a cloth so that the people who were a bit shy or nervous could stretch without being distracted by our reflections. Very professional."

"Interesting... Who is it? Was it one of the other instructors?"

"Oh, no... She actually doesn't have ties to the university, but she said she lives in Masoncrest. Considering it's a very small town and she had such a distinct look, I'm surprised I've never seen her off campus before. Beautiful woman with long braids and some of the straightest, whitest teeth I've seen in my life. And her voice was oddly soothing, putting everyone in the room at ease."

"So, a stranger came in here and convinced everyone in the room to just stretch?" Amara questioned skeptically.

"Well, when you put it like that, it *does* sound weird." Sarah chuckled. "I don't know, I'm feeling a bit hazy, to be honest, but I guess we're all just in great spirits ahead of the holiday and excited about this workshop."

"I'd love to meet this stranger and thank her," Amara said, looking around the studio.

"Right, of course!" Sarah also scanned over the room searching for the woman who seemed to have disappeared. "That's weird... I don't see her. She was standing right in front of the room just before you got here. Maybe she went to the bathroom or something?"

"Hm, well I guess I'll have a proper chance to thank her at the end of class before moving on to the next workshop."

Amara walked over to the speaker in the room and connected her phone's Bluetooth. She did quick stretches and jumped to warm up before returning to the front and waving for the group's attention.

"Hi, everyone and thank you for coming to today's workshop. Today, we're going to focus on musicality. I'll teach a brief routine to one song and then I want you to try fitting it to others..."

As Amara explained the work shop, she noticed from the corner of her eye a figure in the doorway that gave her pause. It was a silhouette and it was only through her peripherals, but Amara found it hauntingly familiar. She went to the door to look outside the studio, up and down the hallway, but no one was there other than a handful of students.

"Are you okay, Amara?" Sarah asked.

"Y-yeah, I'm fine..." Amara replied, turning back to the class, but now with her face tightened and eyes on the floor. "Sorry about that. Let's get started."

LIAM AND MATEO were anxious as they sat across from Cameron in a secluded part of the Seattle restaurant. The time had finally come for them to confront him about their theories regarding his nature and Amara's. They understood that due to the blood promise he mentioned, Cameron likely wouldn't be able to provide details or confirm or deny their suspicions. However, the answer would be in his response, or lack thereof, to their words.

Other than exchanging routine greetings, the three men hadn't spoken much since picking up Cameron from the airport, mostly a combination of their nerves and his hunger.

"You were right, Mateo," Cameron said with food still in his mouth. "The veggie burger is amazing."

Mateo chuckled nervously and rubbed the back of his neck. "Yes, well... Amara told us that you are a strict vegan and considering we were out here anyway to pick you up from the airport, I knew just the spot."

"Ehhh, I wouldn't call myself 'strict,'" Cameron clarified. "One thing I can't get enough of are milkshakes and the vegan substitutes just don't do it for me... So, now that we've all eaten and Liam doesn't look so pale anymore, are you guys ready to tell me what you wanted to talk about?"

"Yes, right, of course!" Liam replied quickly, still nervous.

Mateo leaned in toward Cameron with a sharp gaze. "We believe we've figured you out what Amara could be and what you are."

Cameron nodded with pursed lips. "Even if you have figured it out, I wouldn't be able to confirm or deny anything."

"That won't be necessary because we are pretty confident," Liam added.

Cameron readjusted in his seat and rested his arms on the table. "Fair enough. So, what conclusions have you come to."

Liam and Mateo looked at each other and then looked at him before saying it unison.

"Amara is Palisyfum."

Cameron was physically unable to react, only giving them a blank stare.

"And if we recall correctly," Mateo continued. "Palisyfum somehow managed to be a line of witches and warlocks with familiars—something many of us don't have. Amara has mentioned on several occasions a pet rabbit she and her grandmother had by the name of Xivan."

Again, Cameron was unable to physically respond to them with much, but he did wince when he heard the name.

"You told us that your case is rare, almost unheard of and we deduced that it was likely the result of a spell that requires several conditions to be met," Liam stated. "We were also made aware that this 'Cameron' got into an accident—and upon further research—was declared brain dead. However, by some miracle, he made it through and was a changed man, miraculously cured of alcohol addiction."

"We also learned that this happened the same week, if not the same day, that Amara's grandmother and her pet rabbit Xivan died... Taking all of that into consideration, it made it easy to narrow down the list of possible spells since there is only one that can turn a familiar into a human and based on the information we had, all of the criteria had been met.

"You and Cameron likely died at the exact same moment and his body, which was still habitable since he was considered brain dead, was within the distance in which your soul could travel. Cases like yours are unheard of because they require the stars to align in a way that is nearly impossible. It has to be less than a one-in-a-million chance of something like that happening."

By the time Mateo and Liam finished their explanation, Cameron had a single tear running down from his right eye.

"Based on this lack of reaction, we have to assume we are correct. There's no other way to explain it, given the information we currently have."

"However," Liam cautioned. "Something we haven't been able to figure out is why you remained in Georgia rather than coming here with Amara. We know that you convinced Evelyn to move to Masoncrest a few years prior to Amara, setting her up to have someone that you were connected to by her side. But all of that begs the question of why staying in Georgia was more important to you than following Amara."

"Have you discussed any of this with Amara?" Cameron questioned.

Mateo shook his head. "We wanted to speak with you first. And we wanted you to be here when we revealed it to her. The other question that we have is why her grandmother told her nothing, and why she seems to be blocking something that is in Amara's head. We saw the 'medicine' that she makes for her nightmares.

"Based on the mix, it's clearly made to suppress her abilities and keep her hidden from beings that may sense her true nature. There are also memory erasure elements that we don't quite understand. We assume all of this is an effort to keep her safe considering she'd be at the top of every hunting list if anyone found out. However, we have mixed up a potion that will allow her to have access to her magic while also cloaking its scent and scrambling any distinctly Palisyfum identifiers."

"Yes," Liam confirmed. "And we have another potion to clear her system of the one she's currently taking."

"No!" Cameron interjected, his face washed with terror. "Amara cannot be taken off of that medicine."

"What do you mean? Liam and I, while our magic is a bit inconsistent at the moment, are perfectly capable of helping her understand her abilities."

"It's not that," Cameron shook his head urgently. "She

absolutely cannot have access to her m-" He choked before he could finish his sentence. When he tried to speak again to explain, he was physically unable to do so and realized that his blood promise with Glenda also blocked his ability to explain the true purpose of Amara's medicine.

*Damnit, Glenda!* he thought to himself. *All this shit you did to protect her is only hurting her!*

"You can't say it, can you?"

Cameron's shoulders slouched and he looked down at the table. "I cannot... Just please don't take her off of that medicine."

"I NEVER DID GET to thank that woman who got everyone stretched," Amara said to herself as she exited the building after finishing the final dance workshop. When she checked her messages for the first time since starting the classes, Amara groaned at the text she saw from Liam.

> We're still in the city. Promise not to keep you waiting long.

Amara frowned, knowing that she wouldn't see them for almost an hour considering Masoncrest was at least forty-five minutes from Seattle. She had a mind to call them and scold the men for leaving her out, but decided against it. To her, it was a sign that they were getting along, which took care of one of her biggest fears that Cameron wouldn't like her men or vice versa.

> Okay, but please hurry. I miss you guys.

> Of course. Are you still on campus?

> Yeah, getting in my car now.

> Great, we will do the same.

> That'll still put you at like 30 minutes away when I get to the house.

> Considering how long you take to shower, we'll be arriving before you finish.

> I move faster when you two aren't interrupting me…

> Can you blame us?

> Just hurry!

Amara got into her car and began her route to Mateo and Liam's house just fifteen minutes from campus. Although Amara was sheltered for most of her life, her grandmother's paranoia still influenced her. As a result, Amara was constantly aware of her surroundings.

When she pulled out of the parking lot, she realized a black car seemed to have pulled out at the same time. She figured that it was nothing, but kept an eye on the vehicle, anyway, as it appeared to be following her for several minutes.

In an effort to be extra careful, Amara took a route that would've circled back to campus and if the car was still behind her, then she'd be sure that it was following her.

However, her concerns were washed away when she made a left that was heading back toward Masoncrest University and the black vehicle continued straight. Exhaling her relief, Amara returned to her route to go to Mateo and Liam's house, though she kept an eye on her rearview mirror to be sure she wasn't being followed anymore.

When Amara arrived to the house, she was still

cautious. Despite not seeing the black car anymore, she had a strange feeling in her gut that made her uneasy and she wasn't sure why.

"Whatever," she muttered to herself. "I'm just being paranoid."

She took out her phone and looked at the time, hoping that her detour would've cut down the length of her wait at home until Mateo, Liam, and Cameron arrived. She texted Liam again.

> How long until you guys get here?

> Mateo is driving, and you know how he is about the speed limit...

Amara smiled to herself because she knew that Mateo had an odd habit of always following the speed limit, and most of the time going under it.

> Oh god...

> We will be there in 15 minutes. Did you already finish your shower?

> Not yet. I just got to the house.

> What? Was there traffic or something?

> No... just a bit of a detour. I got paranoid that someone was following me, but it turned out to be nothing.

As soon as she hit send, her phone started ringing and it was Liam calling her.

"Hey, did you mean to call me?"

"Are you okay?" Liam asked urgently and Amara burst out laughing.

"Yes, I'm okay, Liam," she replied still giggling. "I told you it turned out to be nothing."

She heard him clear his throat on the other side of the phone before his tone calmed. "Right. I just wanted to make sure."

"There's no need to worry. I'll hop in the shower and you'll be here for sure by the time I get out."

"Of course. Sorry for panicking like that."

"It's okay," Amara assured. "I know you're just worried about me. I'll see you soon, okay?"

"Yes. Okay," Liam replied before they ended the call.

Amara looked at her phone with an amused smirk. "Always so adorable... Maybe I am in love."

"Adorable, indeed..." A deep voice with a slight rasp said, startling Amara.

She turned to where the voice was coming from and sitting on the living room couch was a familiar, yet completely foreign face.

"What?" he questioned before he was suddenly in front of Amara, towering over her with his face in perfect view. "Did you need a closer look?"

Amara was frozen as she examined the man before her. If not for the tattoos that covered his body and the scar on his lip, he'd be an exact replica of Liam—oddly dark blue eyes, chiseled features, and even his haircut were identical to Amara's lover.

Amara gulped, finally able to speak, her voice just as shaky as her body.

"S-Samuel?"

# THIRTY-SEVEN

Amara stood there trembling, looking up into the eyes of a man who shared a face with one of her lovers.

"What's wrong, little flower?" Samuel sneered mischievously. "You're not happy to meet your Fated's twin? Girls always loved comparing us growing up, though I'd always win as the more attractive brother."

Her hands shaky, Amara tried to dial Liam on her phone when it was snatched from her.

"No, no, no," Samuel wagged his finger before crushing Amara's phone in his hand. "Why in such a rush to have a family reunion?"

Suddenly, Amara bolted toward the front door of the house and Samuel rolled his eyes before waving his hand and sealing it along with all the other exits in the house. When she redirected herself and continued running to try to escape, Samuel found it odd that she decided on non-magical means before coming to the conclusion that Amara was unable to use her abilities for some reason.

"Ahhhh, so our little flower likes to be chased," he

teased as Amara scrambled around the house urgently searching for a way out. "You can't use your abilities, huh? I'll play! You're the mouse and I'll be the cat!"

Samuel's words weren't registering to a panicking Amara, whose eyes were filled with tears and heart beating almost inhumanly fast. After running to the backdoor and then trying and failing to open any windows, she determined that there was no way out of the house. Her only choice was to stall for as long as she could until Mateo and Liam arrived.

She'd lost sight of Samuel when she went up the stairs and from the sounds of the floorboard on the first floor, he wasn't running after her. Amara went into Liam and Mateo's office and hid under the desk. The room was already cluttered and she hoped that if Samuel was tracking her, he wouldn't notice any disturbance in the room.

"Little flower..." Samuel sang as he slowly walked up the steps. "Where are you, little flower? I only want to pluck off your petals..."

Amara curled up tighter under the desk and pressed her hand firmly over her mouth. She took shallow breaths in an effort to mute the sounds of her breathing.

"First cat and mouse and now hide-and-go-seek?" Samuel griped playfully. "You have to tell me when you're going to change things up."

Amara tried to keep herself from making noise with her cries and stayed as silent as she could possibly be. She heard Samuel's steps in the upstairs hallway creeping closer and closer to the office door until they grew distant again and it sounded like he'd passed it. Mateo's door creaking open gave Amara a slight bit of hope that Samuel would waste more time going into the wrong rooms and Liam and Mateo might arrive before he could take her.

However, her hope was quickly diminished when Samuel suddenly appeared crouched down in front of her behind the desk. Amara kicked and fought and screamed as he dragged her from under the desk.

"Oh, you are feisty one, aren't you?" Samuel taunted. "Don't be too sad, little flower... You never stood a chance. You should know that I can see your thoughts... Though what's odd is that I can't sense your magic, nor are you using any..."

Amara didn't understand what he was saying when he referred to *her* magic, but based on the stories Liam had told her about Samuel, she figured it was just one of his frequent ramblings that she'd heard about.

Samuel dragged her back downstairs and threw her on the living room couch. He got close up to Amara and examined her with a raised brow and tilted his head to the side. "Aren't you a Palis-"

He was cut off when Amara head butted him as hard as she could, leaving blood dripping from her own forehead.

"Damn," Samuel replied as he rubbed his forehead. "Good on you for fighting back and all... Even if it is futile." He snapped his fingers and Amara was bound at her wrists and ankles.

She continued to struggle, trying to fight her way out of the restraints or strike Samuel again while he held her down with an amused smirk.

"Haze!" he called and Amara's eyes went wide at the name. She immediately recognized it from her dreams. "Come here and confirm for me that she is indeed a Palisyfum."

Amara hadn't even noticed that someone else was with Samuel and when she saw the woman appear out of seemingly nowhere, confusion was added to her panic. Haze was the woman from her nightmares.

"You're sleepy, aren't you?" Haze questioned, holding Amara's gaze. "Why don't you take a nap?" Her soothing voice calmed Amara, turning her mind cloudy and alleviating her distressed state. Haze's eyes then went from dark brown to a glowing purple and Amara's struggling stopped before she drifted off into a deep slumber.

Samuel groaned. "I really could've listened to her panicked cries a bit longer."

"Shut up," Haze told him sharply. "She'll be easier to transport this way."

"Wait," he cautioned with a raised hand. "You need to check if she's Palisyfum. I don't understand why she wasn't using her abilities."

Haze used a single finger to wipe the blood from Amara's forehead and put it in her mouth. As soon as the familiar taste hit her heightened senses, Haze's eyes flickered purple again and she released a satisfied hum.

"She is absolutely Palisyfum," Haze confirmed before her nose twitched and her eyes cut toward the door. "I smell two warlocks and a human."

"I know," Samuel shrugged casually. "Although I severed our connection, my twin and I do still sense each other when we're this close." He stretched out and cracked his neck just in time to make eye contact with his twin brother when the door flew open and Liam and Mateo stormed in, going straight for him.

"Get the fuck away from her!" Mateo shouted and just when he thought he'd reach Samuel, he and Liam were stopped in their tracks about ten feet away and unable to move.

The house began quaking and Liam's eyes turned gray

while Mateo's turned green as they tried to pry themselves from whatever spell was holding them in place. The floor under their feet cracked and crumbled only to immediately repair itself and Liam and Mateo felt their bodies becoming heavier with each time they tried to free themselves.

"That was easier than expected." Haze sighed. "I was hoping a Taylor and a Vazquez would be more challenging. Then again, I *have* already tamed one Taylor," she added with a confident smirk.

"Oh, please..." Samuel scoffed. "You don't talk shit like that when I'm balls deep inside your cunt."

"What the fuck are you doing here, Samuel?" Liam yelled as he still struggled to get free of the spell.

Samuel turned to his twin brother with a mocking grin on his face. "We haven't seen each other in over sixty years and that's how you greet me?"

"What do you want?" Liam questioned through clenched teeth.

"Well, I've been great, brother! Thank you so much for asking," Samuel replied sarcastically. "I've managed to visit every single country in the world and doing a few odd jobs here and there, I've gathered even more riches than our family has hoarded in all its millennia! No need to tell me about you. I've been keeping tabs."

"It looks like that intel we got about them from Petra was right," Haze noted. "She really did weaken them... By a lot, at that. I was expecting at least a little bit of a fight, especially since we're taking their Fated."

"They should've made curing themselves of the affliction more of a priority, but I imagine they were too occupied with this one," Samuel replied, looking down at an unconscious Amara. "Oh, and Haze... Will you do something about the human that's with them. I can't see what's in his head, but based on the parameter we set, he's doing something out there."

Haze huffed, expressionless as her eyes turned purple and she waved her hand to reopen the front door of the house. When her gaze latched on to Cameron, she simply snapped her fingers and he was inside, bound to the floor just a few feet behind Mateo and Liam.

Samuel titled his head to the side and examined Cameron curiously. "What a peculiar human... I can't seem to get inside of his head."

"Odd indeed..." Haze approached Cameron and held his face before sucking in a deep breath through her nose. "I don't smell any magic on him. Perhaps we can take him too. I'd love to try out some new experiments. I'm curious what effects his blood may have."

"Samuel... please," Liam winced, interrupting their conversation. "I'm not sure why you're here, but we can work this out"... Liam was silenced when Samuel's eyes flashed gray and both his and Mateo's mouths were sealed shut.

"Do not lie to me!" Samuel boomed. "You know exactly why I am here. To pick up your Palisyfum Fated, of course. And I'm a mix of relieved and disappointed about how easy this was for me. Do you want to hear why?"

"Oh fuck, here we go again," Haze mumbled and rolled her eyes. "Another speech."

"Let me tell you a little story," he began. "You see, our dear old friend Petra approached me not too long ago asking me to hunt down a Palisyfum... At first, I'll admit that I was skeptical, doubting my abilities and all that, but then I figured why the hell not! I mean, I *am* the best procurer of rare objects in the world, so why not see if a so-called 'extinct' group of people are still wandering around?

I decided Masoncrest would be a great place to start considering it is a former capital of our world and just like every former capital, the Assembly leaves their archives on the site—unable to relocate them because of their own shortsighted security measures."

"Anyway, we all know that it had to be Masoncrest because it was during that particular session of the Assembly that the Palisyfum were created. Funny enough, I also got called in for a job helping a vampire by the name of David, one of your Fated's colleagues. The stars seemed to align perfectly for me because one peek into his mind and I knew exactly who I was looking for. Seeing what's in people's heads is much better than hearing, brother.

"He told me about a girl who had all these notes on the Palisyfum and the journal where she kept them seemed to have a very strong protection spell embedded with a curse on it. In fact, it a spell so strong that only four lines of witches or warlocks could've done it. A Taylor, a Vazquez, a Vallis, or... A Palisyfum. You understand where I'm going here, right?

"And then, when I asked David about this colleague who he was working with on the Palisyfum, a very familiar face popped into his mind... It was the woman you'd been dreaming about since we turned eighteen! Would you look at my fucking luck? Like it was meant to be... Like it was *fated* to be!"

Samuel approached the couch, closing in on Amara who was still unconscious. Neither Liam nor Mateo could speak or advance from their spots, but tears fell from Liam's eyes while Mateo's nostrils flared and his hand turned to a tight fist.

"She's a once in a millennium opportunity, brother. And you mean to tell me she's your Fated?" He released an entertained laugh and clapped his hands. "All this time, I thought you were the unlucky one. Maybe I didn't have a Fated at all, but *you* and the rest of our siblings were stuck being fated to mortals who'd be nothing but a blip compared to the length of your lives. However, it looks like I was wrong..."

He leaned over and ran his knuckles over Amara's cheek."Her aura feels pure... Have the two of you not been performing well enough to corrupt her? Guess I'll have to be the one who-"

Suddenly, a bright light filled the room, blinding them along with a high-pitched ringing noise, sharp enough to cause their ears to bleed.

When Mateo and Liam could see again, Samuel had disappeared and Haze was sitting on the couch next to Amara, holding her face.

CHAPTER
# THIRTY-EIGHT

D eep in the sleep induced by Haze, Amara was thrown directly into an intense nightmare.

*"Here honey, you need to drink something," the purple-eyed woman reached across the bars to hand Amara a glass of water.*
*"No!" the eight-year-old protested, hitting the glass out of her mother's hand and allowing it to break on the floor. "Go away! I hate you!"*
*"Amara..."*
*"No!" the girl repeated. Her eyes momentarily flashed purple, but she didn't have the strength to do anything but fall on the floor and continue shouting at her mother as her tears blurred her vision. "Go away! I hope he drains you into nothing! I hate you!" Amara went on and on until her mother walked away as if the girl wasn't in obvious distress.*
*Amara cried softly, sitting on the concrete floor of the cell. For the past six days straight, her body had been mutilated and experimented on by the red-eyed man.*
*"Why did mom do this?" she winced quietly to herself. "And*

*dad... I don't feel him anymore..." She choked up remembering what Alistair said about killing her father.*

*Amara pulled her knees tighter to her chest feeling an anguish so intense that her heart was physically aching more than her body. When she lifted her head and wiped the tears from her eyes, her gaze landed on a large piece of the glass cup that had broken on the floor before.*

*She picked up the shard and squeezed it in her hand until it bled, realizing that even that pain couldn't surmount what she was feeling. Agony, torment, suffering—there weren't words strong enough to describe what the girl was going through.*

*She was also acutely aware that no one would be coming to save her. What she'd been experiencing for the past several months was her new reality.*

*And Amara could not accept that.*

*She knew simply bleeding her wrists wouldn't be enough for what she wanted to do, so instead, Amara held the glass shard to her throat with shaky hands and tears running down her face. Concerned that fear might hit her and keep her from following through with the entire cut, Amara decided that she would plunge the glass deep enough that she wouldn't need to drag it.*

*Amara closed her eyes, dug the shard into her neck, and fell forward on the ground so that it'd be pushed all the way into her throat. She choked on her own blood as it flowed from the wound.*

*Just when she was fading away, Amara heard the faint sound of someone calling her name.*

*"Amara! Amara!" the voice yelled urgently. "Get up!"*

*Suddenly, the girl felt herself being yanked up and cradled in a pair of cold arms. The shard was pulled from her throat, causing her to to bleed out faster until she felt a wet wrist being held to her lips.*

*"Drink, child..." the voice begged and as the liquid from the wrist begану to enter Amara's mouth, the wound started to heal.*

Amara's face twitched in her sleep and it was obvious what she was dreaming about was intense. Haze looked down at Amara with an indecipherable expression as she gently cradled her face.

"Don't touch her!" shouted a furious Mateo. With Samuel's disappearance, the spell that was keeping him and Liam quiet had been broken. He was still glued to his spot several feet away from the living room where Haze was sitting on the couch with Amara.

Liam stood there silent, feeling the most helpless he'd ever felt and it terrified him. Haze—a vampire who was somehow capable of magic—had managed to immobilize both him and Mateo. Even if it was temporary, it reminded him just how inadequate he and Mateo were to take care of Amara.

"Can't you see that they're horrified?" Cameron groaned. "You could at least let them loose, Haze."

Liam and Mateo were taken aback, unsure if they heard Cameron correctly.

"Not yet," Haze answered flatly, as she kept her eyes on Amara and moved her hair from her face. "As if the poor child hasn't been through enough, she gets stuck with two useless warlocks as her Fated. I was able to disable them with that single spell. They aren't suitable for her."

"Haze." Cameron sighed. "They aren't at their best right now, but they're working on fixing that."

"Obviously they're not working fast enough," she spat. "If not for me, the girl would've been taken to Petra, bled dry, and then ground to nothing but dust."

Mateo and Liam's eyes went wide when they heard Petra's name.

"Petra!" Liam exclaimed. "What could she-"

He was cut off yet again when Haze snapped her fingers and he and Mateo's mouths were sealed, just as they were when Samuel was present.

"Haze, please..." Cameron pleaded.

"Based on the fact that she couldn't counter any of Samuel's attacks, I assume Amara still does not know what she is?"

"She does not."

Haze sucked her teeth and rolled her eyes. "Fucking Glenda and her goddamn curses, spells, and blood promises. She could've told the girl without triggering her, and now everyone who knows her secret either can't say shit or is hunting her down."

"Not anymore," Cameron replied, to which Haze's gaze cut from Amara to him. "Mateo and Liam figured out what she is... And Samuel just confirmed it better than I could for them."

Haze's eyes flickered purple and her nostrils flared. "Then why the fuck didn't they tell her when they first assumed?" she snarled.

"They were going to do that today."

"Well, looks like they've got no fucking choice now, do they?" Haze turned her attention back to Mateo and Liam. "You're supposed to be from the *all powerful*"—a term Haze used mockingly-"Vazquez and Taylor families, yet I shut you down with ease," she scolded. "Why the fuck are you two so damn weak? Do you understand what it means to be fated to her?"

"Haze... You can't talk as if you've been around all this time protecting her."

"Because the girl isn't my responsibility! And Glenda told me to stay away the last time I saw her. She didn't want any of Amara's memories triggered."

"Glenda was always doing what she thought was best," Cameron explained. "The problem with that is she assumed she'd be alive long enough to tell Amara of her origins and train her when the time was right. But she died before that could happen."

"She also didn't take anyone's fucking input. Goddamn elderly witches always think they know everything. And she wasn't even that old for a witch... Technically, not much older than I am now if you count the years after I was turned."

"Okay, Haze... Now, can you let the men go before they die of the stress?"

"I have a few more things to say." Haze raised a silencing finger and spoke to Liam and Mateo. "I couldn't kill Samuel, so I banished him to the middle of Siberia. He doesn't have the supplies to do a long-distance transport spell, so he'll need to mostly go by foot to get out of the tundra. However, it won't take long. Also, as a result of helping you today, I won't be able to help you anymore." She held up her decaying arm.

"My body is not built to do such powerful magic. I may hold some—enough—of their power, but I am no Palisy-fum. Between the energy I had to use to put Amara to sleep, pin you two down, and get rid of Samuel, it'll take me months to fully recover." She then turned and looked down at Amara, whose face was still twitching. "And I can't feed from her. Which means you two are the only ones who can protect her... At least until she can learn to protect herself. And I expect you to teach her."

"There might be a slight problem there," Cameron suggested. "The potion that Glenda has Amara taking is blocking her powers and her memories. If they take her off of it, the impact could be..."

"Debilitating," Haze finished with a groan. "Well, it is what it is at this point. Now that Petra is after her, she needs access to her power. And I hope these warlocks of Amara's aren't as dumb as they are weak and can figure out a way to remove the power suppression while preserving the block on her memories."

She returned to addressing Liam and Mateo. "Before you ask—although it's not like you're able to, right now—I won't be able to tell you about Amara's past. Just like Xivan, I made a stupid fucking blood promise with Glenda. I'll make the rest of this quick before I use the last bit of my energy to take myself somewhere safe so your dear old twin doesn't rip me to shreds..."

Haze shifted in her seat, moving Amara's head to rest on her lap. "Petra says she's planning to kill all humans, but I think it's bullshit. It's not poetic enough for her. The witch is known for her theatrics. It's how she got the cult following she has now. Either way, she needs the blood and flesh of a Palisyfum. I'd planned to play the role of Samuel's sidekick and get in closer with her to stop her. I hoped you two would be strong enough to take Samuel and I so that we'd be forced to retreat and I could continue to play along. However, you turned out to be let downs and I had to give myself away."

Haze sighed, shaking her head, the disappointment clear in her face. "You have two options: Play keep away for the rest of Amara's life as Glenda did or kill Petra, and actually get the job done this time." She turned to Cameron.

"Xivan… You might be human now, but it doesn't mean you're completely useless. Do what you can."

When Haze rose from the chair as she prepared to leave, Cameron called to her.

"Wait! Can't you stay with us? You can still help."

"No," she replied curtly. Haze knew that they were better off without her in her weakened state. Using her good hand, she snapped her fingers and once again, a light blinded everyone in the room.

After she disappeared, Cameron, Mateo, and Liam were freed from their bindings.

Liam and Mateo rushed over to Amara to wake her up and when her eyes fluttered open, she was in a state of panic as she was before Haze put her to sleep. Screaming to the top of her lungs, her arms flailed and she hit both men, still fighting as if Samuel were there.

"Amara! Amara!" Mateo called, holding her arms down. "It's us, amor. It's us."

Amara looked between the two men apprehensively as she hyperventilated before wrapping her arms around both of their necks and embracing them with tears running from her eyes.

"He was going to take me!" Amara cried hysterically. "What did he want? Why?"

Liam rubbed Amara's back in a comforting motion, unable to make eye contact with her due to the shame that he felt. "I'm sorry, Amara… I'm so sorry."

"He kept talking about the Palisyfum," she said urgently. "Did he want my research? Is it actually a magical flower? A powerful one like in the stories?" Amara came to a sudden pause before she gasped. "No! Wait… He asked that woman Haze… To check if I was a Palisyfum. What does that mean?"

"About that..."

"It is time we explain to you the truth about the Palisyfum."

# THIRTY-NINE

Amara paced the living room anxiously, her arms crossed with one raised to rub her chest as if it would somehow ease the tightening of it that came with the information she just learned. After Mateo and Liam explained the story of the Palisyfum to Amara, a suffocating tension filled the room and it didn't take Liam's telepathy to know that she was furious.

"You know how obsessed I've been with the Palisyfum. It's at the center of my research! I've been so stressed out about not having any breakthroughs and you knew this entire time, but let me go on like some idiot?"

Mateo shook his head. "Amara, you're not an idiot."

"It doesn't change the fact that I feel like one, Mateo!" Neither of her lovers had ever seen Amara so angry before and Cameron hadn't seen her in such a state since she was a teenager and he was still in his form as Xivan.

"An entire race of people meant to be nothing but live-stock..." she said softly, eyes wide staring at her feet as they moved across the floor.

Liam's mouth twisted and he gulped. It was a practice

that he'd been ashamed of since learning about it—especially knowing that his ancestor played a role in the decision to exterminate the Palisyfum before he was born. "Amara... when you say it like that..."

"But I'm saying what it is!" Amara shouted. "People! These are *people* created just to use for your spells. You bleed them dry and use their flesh until it's nothing!"

"That practice ended close to two-thousand years ago, but it is still indefensible," Mateo noted.

"'Indefensible' is an understatement! It's absolutely insidious! You're saying that the Palisyfum are living beings with feelings, with the ability to care, to love, to feel emotional and physical pain, build relationships and families, and register all of that... And then when they just wanted to be treated with dignity and respect and not like damn ingredients, they became targets for genocide?"

Mateo and Liam simply nodded as Cameron continued to sit still, unable to respond.

"You said I'm one of them... These people who were supposedly eradicated and you're saying I'm one of them?"

"Yes..."

"But how? I don't understand..." Amara held out her shaking hands and looked over her palms. "I can't do magic."

Mateo nodded. "We believe that the medicine you take for your nightmares could be blocking your magic."

"But that's a remedy that my grandma taught me. I didn't start taking that medicine until I was like eleven or twelve, so I would've remembered doing magic before then. I've never done it and my grandma never did it before either."

"Right..." Liam replied. "Some of your memories may have been altered."

"Who would do something like that?"

"We believe your grandmother likely altered them. We're just not sure why."

"No! Grandma wouldn't do that. She couldn't do that... Could she?"

"It's possible," Mateo confirmed. "Palisyfum are a very powerful line, so there wouldn't be much that she *couldn't* do."

Amara chewed at her fingernails and continued pacing as the room again fell silent.

*I'm a witch?* she thought to herself. *A Palisyfum witch? This flower—well, not flower—I've spent all these years studying? The one that grandma kept telling me about. All these stories and truth was that it wasn't a flower... It was us? Or what if Mateo and Liam are wrong? Maybe they made a mistake and I'm not one. If we were, then grandma would've told me, right? But then again, she was always overprotective and kept us isolated. It did feel like we were in hiding now that I think about it, but it had become so normal to me at that time. But still... I would've at least seen her do magic, right? Or I would've had at least one odd occurrence by now, wouldn't I? There's also...*

"Mateo, Liam... I remember you guys telling me that some lines of witches and warlocks eyes glow when they do magic. Vazquez eyes turn green and Taylor eyes turn gray... Do Palisyfum eyes turn as well?"

"They do," Liam answered. "But for Palisyfum, it's not only when they do that magic. Palisyfum actually have to go out of their way to keep their eyes from turning. Their distinct eye color used to be a way to easily identify or keep track of them, but they eventually learned how to keep them covered. Either through continuous spells or potions."

"And was their eye color..." Amara gulped before finishing. "Purple?"

"Yes."

*Just like the woman who's my mother in the nightmares. But grandma had pictures of mom and dad and mom doesn't look like that woman... How is any of this real? How is any of this happening? Does this mean that my nightmares could have something to do with this? Fuck! It's like a ten-thousand piece puzzle and the pieces are scrambled for miles. I believe them, but at the same time, I don't understand.*

Liam was concerned about the purple-eyed woman from her dreams that Amara was thinking about. It only added to their concerns that the nightmares she'd been having weren't dreams, but possibly memories. However, she was already deeply upset and he didn't want to make it worse by digging further into her dreams in that moment.

Amara continued to pace around the room and had reached the point of circling the men on the couch. As her mind continued to register all that had been revealed to her, Amara could barely look Mateo and Liam in the eyes with her anger toward them for not telling her the truth about the Palisyfum. And she was also confused as to why Cameron was allowed to be present for the conversation and his lack of reaction.

"You guys never answered me when you started your explanation of the Palisyfum about why it's okay for Cameron to hear this stuff even though you've told me to keep magic a secret from everyone else... And why haven't you said a word, Cam? You seem so unfazed by all of this! I was freaking out when I learned."

"That's because Cameron knows about our world," Mateo replied.

Amara turned to Cameron with a glare. "You knew all of

this stuff? About the Palisyfum and everything? Did you know I could be one? How come you never said anything? And why are you still being so damn stoic right now, Cam? You're like a statue."

"Cameron can't exactly engage in the conversation we're having," Liam explained. "We're actually lucky that he's able to listen to it without incident."

Amara rubbed her temples and closed her eyes. "I don't understand."

"Cameron made what is called a blood promise. It's a very powerful magical pact and whatever terms you commit to, you're physically unable to break them, even if you try. They're pretty foolproof in that way. Other such pledges usually mean if you break them, you die, thus giving the choice to break said promise. However, what we've deduced from Cameron's commitments, he's unable to discuss your origins or his. Even if he wanted to, he wouldn't be able to."

Amara's mouth pulled to a deep frown. "I'm only more confused."

Mateo took a deep breath as he tried to steady his nerves. Now that he and Liam were finally sharing this information with Amara, Mateo felt even more guilt than he did before about keeping it all from her. "We think Cameron made a blood promise with your grandmother not to tell you or anyone about your origins, Amara."

"What?" Amara shakily breathed out. "Cameron doesn't know my grandma. I met him after she'd already died."

"Not exactly..."

"We have strong reason to believe that Cameron is actually Xivan. Your pet rabbit from your childhood."

Amara's eyes nearly doubled in size at Mateo's words.

"What the hell? I guess I can't say that makes no sense because not much is making sense to me here."

"Amara," he began. "You told us that your grandmother and Xivan died the same day. And upon further digging, Liam and I came to realize that those deaths likely happened at the same time as Cameron's car accident that should've left him brain dead. We've explained to you what a familiar is, right?"

"Yes," Amara nodded. "Like a companion for witches and warlocks, right? But I thought you said they're not much of a thing anymore."

"They're not. Mostly because very few lines of witches and warlocks can have familiars. It just so happened that the Palisyfum—despite being a relatively short-lived line— was one of the few.

"It seems that Xivan was probably your grandmother's familiar and so it makes sense that they would die together. However, there exists one spell that can turn a familiar to a human and on the night of your grandmother and Xivan's deaths, all the conditions of that spell were met. We concluded that Xivan and Cameron died at the exact same moment, but Xivan's soul, which was more resilient than an average human, could still travel up to a certain distance even after the death of the physical body.

"As part of the spell, any viable host bodies—that is, those who experienced death at the same moment as the familiar and still had a habitable physical form—act as a magnet for the soul of the familiar. If the familiar's soul makes it to that body before fizzling out, then it takes over."

Amara's brows furrowed and her eyes moved rapidly between the three men. "So you're saying that my best friend of these past seven years is actually Xivan, my pet rabbit who was really my grandma's familiar? Xivan is possessing Cameron's body?"

"Possessing isn't the best term here," Liam clarified. "Cameron is dead and so his body is now Xivan's. Xivan is now Cameron."

"Is that not possession?"

"Well, possession has a bad connotation."

"Oh!" Amara cringed and turned to Cameron. "I didn't mean to insult you Cam! Er... Xivan?"

He chuckled at her very characteristic reaction—it was the first light-hearted moment of the night. "I actually like the name Cam. And it's the only name I've been able to answer to since-"

Cameron was cut off when Amara suddenly threw her arms around him and pulled him into a tight hug. She buried her face against his chest and he didn't realize it until he felt his shirt getting wet that she was crying. The reality had finally hit her that one of the only two people who'd known her since childhood—the only family that she knew—was still alive and reentered her life as a brother figure.

"You've been here with me this whole time," she winced. "When you and grandma died, I lost my entire world... But you're here. And you've stayed with me... Still looking out for me."

Tears began to roll down Cameron's face and he tightened his embrace with Amara. "I'm sorry that I couldn't tell you. I'm sorry that I *still* can't tell you all that you need to know..."

Amara shook her head. "It's not your fault. You didn't hide the truth from me on purpose... What about the woman- er vampire who saved me? Mateo and Liam said you knew her? I remember Samuel saying her name was Haze."

"I'm sorry Amara, but I can't talk about that either. All I can say is that Haze is someone we can trust."

"I've seen her in my dreams before... She's in the nightmares I get sometimes."

Both Mateo and Liam's faces washed with a mix of worry and surprise while Cameron's nose scrunched.

"What was she doing in your nightmares?"

"Well, I'm still pretty fuzzy on a lot of the details of my nightmares and I don't always remember them, but I do recall her arguing with a purple-eyed woman who I keep calling mom... But the woman doesn't look like my mom, Cam—nothing like that photo grandma had of my parents."

"I see..." Cameron stroked his chin thoughtfully. "And do you feel anything toward Haze in these nightmares? Does she do anything to you?"

"I don't know. I can't really place exactly what I feel toward her. Do you know why she might be in my dreams?"

"I'm sorry, Amara." Cameron shook his head. "I can't say."

Amara looked down as she ground her teeth. She was afraid to say it aloud or think too far into it. She had a theory about her nightmares. A theory that they weren't nightmares at all.

"Why does my life just feel like a bunch of unanswered questions?" Amara groaned before turning her attention back to Mateo and Liam and her voice turned cold.

"Mateo, Liam... How long have you suspected that I am Palisyfum?" she asked with her arms crossed.

Mateo and Liam both hesitated.

"I said... How long have you suspected?" she repeated through clenched teeth.

Mateo's jaw tensed as he searched for the words, while Liam ended up choking them out.

"I-it's been a couple of weeks since we first suspected."

"Couple of weeks?" Amara questioned. "Couple of weeks? Couple of weeks! You suspected all this time and didn't say anything to me?" She collapsed to her knees and buried her face in her hands as she began sobbing.

When Liam approached to put a comforting hand on her shoulder, Amara snatched herself away.

"Don't touch me!" she snapped. "I'm upset with both of you right now and I don't want you touching me. I can't believe you kept this from me for so long!"

"Amara, please..." Mateo pleaded. "We were going to tell you."

"But why didn't you tell me sooner?" she cried. "At least I could've been more cautious or you could've taught me ways to defend myself! What if Samuel actually would've taken me! I was helpless! All I could do was run around this house and hide. And it was completely pointless because all he had to do was snap his fingers to appear exactly where I was hiding."

"We're sorry, love. We really are..."

The men felt helpless once again as they watched Amara sitting on the floor crying hysterically, in the most distressed state they'd ever seen her. Cameron was the only one she allowed to touch her and he simply stayed by her side with his arm wrapped around her. Mateo and Liam were also feeling Amara's pain to a certain extent through the connection of the Fated on top of their own feelings about failing her.

It was a torturous fifteen minutes of Amara sobbing

until her cries grew quieter and she was now sniffling on Cameron's shoulder while the two remained on the floor by couch.

"Amara…" Mateo said softly and she finally lifted her head to look at him. He felt his heart crumbling at the sight of how distraught she was.

"We know that you've already been through so much and I hate to do this right now, but we must leave Masoncrest immediately."

She looked at him apprehensively. "Because of Samuel?"

"Yes." Liam nodded. "Because of Samuel and a witch by the name of Petra. They're hunting you. And now that they know you're in Masoncrest, it's no longer safe for you to be here."

"Who's that? And let me guess, they want to use me as an ingredient for a spell?"

Mateo and Liam exchanged a glance before looking at Amara hesitantly, only further agitating her.

"Seriously? Still with the secrets? Why can't you guys just tell me the truth?"

"Amara, we've told you so much already," Liam reasoned. "Perhaps we could tell you another time?"

"No! You tell me that your twin brother and some witch are hunting me and proceed to say you'll tell me about her 'another time.' What the hell?" Amara scolded. "Tell me now! I deserve to know what I'm up against."

The men took deep sighs and paused for several moments until Mateo finally spoke up.

"It's better if we show you."

# FORTY

Samuel treaded his way through the Siberian tundra, grumbling to himself.

"Goddamn bloodsucker double-crossed me. I should've known... This isn't the first time she's done it. All of that Palisyfum magic must've went to her fucking cunt because it's impossible for me to think straight when it comes to her."

He saw a light in the distance and it appeared he was coming up on a small village. He figured that once he reached it, he could find a human to sacrifice for a long-distance transportation spell, as well as make contact with Petra.

Samuel continued walking for what felt like hours, but the light didn't appear to be getting any closer. He'd already been going for days and was growing physically tired and had already run out of magical energy after using it to summon food and clothing to keep himself warm.

As he continued, Samuel realized that the light he'd been seeing was probably an illusion, considering he wasn't making any progress toward it. It seemed that as part of the spell Haze used to throw him into the tundra, she also likely planted something in Samuel's mind that would cause hallucinations.

"Fuck!" Samuel shouted his frustration. Just as he was about to collapse into the snow to wait for the spell to wear off, his fall was stopped by an invisible force and he was lifted back to his feet.

"It's a good thing I put that tracking spell on you, isn't it?"

In front of him appeared a woman with pale skin and long blonde hair that fell almost waist length. She approached and her icy blue eyes bore into Samuel's as she examined the state of him.

"Well," Samuel gleamed. "If it isn't my current employer, the famous Petra Vallis, finally making her appearance. About time you showed up. How many human sacrifices did you have to make to give yourself enough strength to travel to me?"

"Who did this to you, Samuel?" she asked softly.

"Take a wild guess," he spat. "Never trust a fucking vampire."

"So, it was Haze, I presume?"

"Yes, the conniving bloodsucker betrayed me as soon as we secured the Palisyfum. She's probably feeding on her as we speak."

Petra's expression turned to a glare and her nostrils flared. "Is she going to kill it?"

"No." Samuel shook his head. "It wouldn't benefit her to bleed the Palisyfum dry. She's likely taken her some-where to keep her captive and feed off regularly."

"I see... So, Haze isn't reckless enough with hunger to kill what is presumably the last Palisyfum left? That's good news for us. How quickly do you think we can track them down and retrieve it?"

"Well, Haze is a fucking genius when it comes to hiding... She'll have to come up eventually because I know she wouldn't leave her club behind forever, but that could still be months or years from now. And even if we found her, I'm not sure we'd be able to get much information out of her."

"Is this the arrogant Samuel Taylor showing doubt in his abilities?" Petra questioned, her arms crossed while the challenge was clear in her expression.

Samuel dusted the snow off himself. "Absolutely not." He scoffed. "I said she's a fucking genius. But you best believe that I'm *still* smarter. Plus, we have multiple connections to this Palisyfum that could aid us with tracking it."

"What do you mean by that?"

"Oh? You haven't figured out why I asked you for information on my brother and Mateo?"

Petra shrugged casually. "I assumed that they were still doing your mother's bidding and you worried they may try to stop you if they'd learned you were hunting a Palisyfum —even if the elites believe they're all dead."

Samuel opened his mouth wide and started laughing. "C'mon, Petra! That was your best guess? I know you're smarter than-" His speech paused when a binding wrapped tightly around his neck.

"I may not be at full strength, but if you disrespect me again, you will lose your head." Petra's voice was low and haunting by the time she got to the final part of her sentence. Well-aware of her resolve, Samuel straightened himself up and began to explain to Petra what he'd learned about the Palisyfum he'd been hunting.

"The Palisyfum goes by the name of Amara Jenkins and it turns out that she is Liam and Mateo's Fated. So, I had the opportunity for a nice little reunion with my twin brother."

"Hm," Petra hummed, looking down pensively. "It's not surprising when you think about it. It is unheard of to be fated to two members of the elite families, so it'd make sense that their Fated is something as strong as a Palisyfum... At least a lot more sense than a human being fated to them."

Suddenly, her eyes glowed yellow and a wide smile came to her face. "This couldn't be anymore perfect. Almost poetic, even! Once I gain more strength, I can use my connection with Liam and Mateo to track them down. And then once I have them, I can use their connection with their Fated to track the Palisyfum down. Or even better, they'd have retrieved her by that time and I'll snatch her right out of their hands as soon as they think all is well.

"... And it'll be all to finish the job they so rudely interrupted decades ago," she finished.

"She's also not so strong, by the way," Samuel clarified. "I captured her with ease. I'm not quite sure what it is, but it seemed this Palisyfum was unable to use any magic. In fact, I didn't sense an ounce of power on her."

"So how do you know that she's Palisyfum?"

"Haze confirmed..."

"And you trust that confirmation?"

"Haze wouldn't have gone through the trouble of setting me up and then banishing me if that woman *wasn't* Palisyfum."

"Fair enough. Well, it looks like I will finally have my revenge."

# FORTY-ONE

Amara sat on the floor of Mateo and Liam's office with her legs crossed facing the two of them. Meanwhile, Cameron was looking through the lore that Mateo and Liam had shared with him, which served as the basis for their ideas on how to free him of the blood promise he'd made with Glenda.

The men had just finished explaining to Amara that it's possible for them to share memories with her through a specific spell. It was the most thorough and the quickest way for Mateo and Liam to explain to her what happened with Petra. While the memory might be an entire day's worth of recollections, only a few seconds would pass in their current reality.

"So, I would be able to see your memories?" Amara questioned. "Like, I would be in your head or something?"

"More like we would be putting something in your head. Because the three of us are Fated and it was a day that Mateo and I experienced together, we should be able to share it with you by compensating our current lack of magic with extra concentration and our existing connection."

"Amara," Mateo continued from where Liam left off. "We understand that you are still upset with us and don't want us touching you... However, for the connection aspect of this spell to work, we will need to hold hands while we focus on delivering the memories to you."

Amara looked between the two of them before her gaze went to the floor and she fidgeted with her fingers. "Will it work even if our connection is a bit rocky at the moment?"

As soon as she asked the question, both men's hearts fell. It was easy for them to sense how angry she was with the two of them and they regretted keeping so much from her for so long.

"We can at least give it a try, amor. If it's okay with you, that is."

Amara hesitated for several moments without making eye contact with the men before she reached both of her hands out with her palms up.

"Fine," she surrendered.

Mateo and Liam placed their hands in hers cautiously, afraid that if she were filled with too much rage, it could disrupt their connection as they tried to complete the spell.

"Because our magic is not at its best right now, we won't be able to get down to any specific time," Mateo explained. "So we'll just have to share the entire day with you, amor."

"Wait," Liam whispered sharply. "Don't you remember that morning?"

Mateo looked at him apprehensively as he tried to recollect what occurred until it finally hit him. "Ohhhh, *that* was the same day."

"Secrets," Amara huffed, not hiding the frustration in her tone.

Both men turned to her with awkward smiles.

"Well," Liam started. "You see, the day of our Petra incident was also a day that we..." he trailed off as he failed to find the words.

"Don't worry, mi alma," Mateo assured. "You're going to see everything that happened that day when we share these memories with you, so there won't be any secrets, okay? This is the most transparent we can can possibly be."

"I understand," Amara replied before she interlocked her fingers with theirs and closed her eyes. "Now let's get to this concentrating thing so I can see."

"Right," Mateo and Liam said softly in unison.

The three of them closed their eyes as the men concentrated their energy and thoughts on sharing their memories with Amara while she focused on keeping her mind open to receive them.

London, 1970

LIAM LEANED FORWARD to press his lips against Mateo's and slowly eased his length into him. As they attempted to get into their moment, Liam was turned off by the feeling of Mateo's facial hair and Mateo didn't like the way Liam's kissing felt like a weak—and failed—attempt to take charge.

Finally, Liam broke away to suck Mateo's neck while Mateo looked up at the ceiling expressionless, hoping that at some point he would start to feel pleasure from the experience.

He and Liam had learned nearly one hundred years prior that their Fated would be a mortal who they wouldn't meet until two-thousand ten. Their families saw it as a misfortune and Mateo and Liam held the same sentiment in some respects, but they were still excited to meet her someday.

Considering they were also fated to be with each other and got along well as friends, Mateo and Liam figured it was time to see if they might also be romantically and sexually compatible. The two never found themselves attracted to each other in such a way, but thought they could at least give it a try.

"Perhaps we should try with you on the bottom?" Mateo sighed. "I just don't think this is working. It is not enjoyable."

Liam pulled out and sat back on his heels while Mateo rose up to meet him face-to-face.

"Are you saying I am not doing a good job?" questioned an offended Liam. "The women I sleep with have no complaints."

Mateo rolled his eyes and huffed his annoyance. "I only said it was not enjoyable to me. It could be that I am not meant to be the one receiving, which is why I suggested you try it... And besides, you couldn't even seem to stay hard inside me."

"Oh, I see," Liam nodded thoughtfully. "I will take the potion to prepare and be back shortly."

Once Liam left the room, Mateo began stroking his length in an attempt to get himself hard, as he'd been soft the entire time he and Liam were attempting to be intimate.

"Alright, let's get on with it," Liam said when he

returned to the room. He got on his back in the bed and opened his legs.

Mateo sat up once he finally got hard enough for penetration and positioned himself at Liam's entrance after lubricating.

"Wait," Liam held his hand against Mateo's torso, who in turn looked down at him with a confused brow raised. "Be gentle," he cautioned.

"Yes, yes. Of course I will be gentle. I am not an animal, Liam."

"You say that because you've never witnessed the way in which you have sex. You get quite rough. Remember when we were practicing on that mortal to prepare for our Fated and you almost seriously injured the woman?"

"You are grossly exaggerating what occurred," Mateo groaned. "I simply forgot that mortals aren't as durable as our kind and got a bit carried away... Damnit!" he spat and looked down at his length in his hand. "You've gone and made me soft."

"At least when I was on top, I kept myself decently hard," Liam muttered.

"Shut up." Mateo started stroking himself again in an attempt to get his erection back, but it wasn't working. "Liam, maybe you could help."

"No!" Liam exclaimed. "I told you that I will not perform fellatio."

"I wasn't going to ask you that. I was just suggesting that you could at least lend a hand..." Mateo trailed off when he saw Liam holding a blank stare. "Is your mother really mind-linking you at a time like this?"

Liam raised a silencing finger as he received his mother's message and once she was finished, he got up from the bed and started getting dressed.

"My mother needs some help and we're the closest to the problem, Mateo," he said. "Get dressed. We have to go deal with Petra of the Vallis family."

"So, what is this job that your mother has pulled us into?" Mateo asked as he and Liam walked through the streets of London. *And thank goodness she did because that was* not *a pleasant experience,* he thought to himself.

Liam cut his eyes at Mateo. "I can read your mind, you know?"

"And it was your choice to do so," Mateo countered. "Don't go poking around in my head, perhaps? We are one hundred sixteen years old and I know you can control your powers by now."

"Of course I can. I was only curious to see what was going on in your mind after what just occurred."

"Or, you could've just asked me and I would've answered honestly. You and I are not compatible physically. That was made very obvious."

"Excellent." Liam nodded. "I'm glad we're on the same page. This century cannot end soon enough. My fantasies about our Fated are only building."

"I feel the same. My ideas for her are already immense. It is a shame that she will be a mortal and unaware of our world. It means we will need to court her and eventually explain the Fated to her. I do hope she will understand, and quickly at that since we won't have much time with her relative to our own lives..."

"Yes, but let's take our minds off that and I will answer your initial question, Mateo. My mother made contact about Petra Vallis of the Vallis family. You know they always choose to be the difficult ones out of the three of ours. Even down to the nature of their powers, they are innately divergent."

"Not an enjoyer of necromancy, are you?" Mateo questioned sarcastically.

"Why the hell would I be? My family is the family of minds. Your family is the family of seers. Meanwhile, the Vallis family are the family of the dead." Liam shook his head. "I still don't understand how they've reached our caliber."

"Their magic is just as powerful as ours, even if they are quite strange..." Mateo replied.

"Anyway, on to the subject at hand as you already know, Petra has managed to develop a following for her ideas, which—I must admit—aren't exactly outlandish," Liam explained. "She believes us as the superior beings and questions why we hide our gifts and our world from the mortals. That they should be the ones that fear us."

"She makes valid arguments." Mateo shrugged. "But I say we continue to allow the mortals to have at it. Watching their pettiness can be quite entertaining at times and we have our own troubles to address. Expanding our authority wouldn't do any good."

"You're right, which is why we need to stop Petra. Her followers consist of a mix of human, witches, warlocks, vampires, and so on around the world—it's why she'd been able to hide from the Assembly up until now. My mother said an informant contacted her about a big ritual Petra was holding just outside of London."

"And what might that ritual be?"

"It was something about thirty sacrifices—volunteers at that—for her to absorb their life energy. She intends to make herself more powerful."

"Hell!" Mateo exclaimed. "Absorbing just one would be

a significant boost to her power, but *thirty*? She will be unstoppable."

"Exactly. And with such power along with her relationship with the dead, she'll likely be strong enough to take sizable action against these mortals that she hates so much... or even us. Which is why we need to move more quickly..." As soon as the words crossed Liam's lips, the men felt a burst of energy coming from the direction they were heading toward and immediately started running with magically-enhanced speed.

"It would be much easier if we'd visited this location before and we could just teleport."

"Well, we can't, so let's go!" Liam urged and both men hit their top speed.

However, despite arriving in less than a minute after they'd detected Petra's magic, it appeared they were too late.

Petra was on her knees in the middle of the secluded field far outside the city, surrounded by thirty corpses that'd already been sacrificed. From the bodies, energy flowed into Petra and she dug her fingers into the dirt as she absorbed that overwhelming power.

Her eyes glowed their signature Vallis yellow and her veins illuminated the same color. The magic in the air was heavy and had Mateo and Liam come from lesser families, they wouldn't have been able to advance toward her with the strong resistance.

"Stay back!" Petra's distorted voice rumbled the entire field. The warning behind her words combined with the sheer power that they could sense from her intimidated Mateo and Liam to the point that they considered whether they should have brought more help.

The Vallis were just as powerful as the Vazquez and

Taylor families, and their relationship with life and death gave them an advantage—whether it be communicating with the dead, controlling them, or the ability to forge a spell that absorbed life force. Petra was more than a formidable opponent for Liam and Mateo combined.

"We need to stop her," Mateo said to Liam as he sensed his doubt. "If we don't do it now while the power is still settling within her, she will truly be unstoppable."

"I know that, but she appears to have already achieved this 'unstoppable' that we fear-" Liam was interrupted when he and Mateo were thrown to opposite sides of the field.

"I said stay back!" Petra repeated. "This is for the good of our kind! Can't you see it? The mortals must all die!"

"We can't let you do this, Petra!" Mateo shouted. "Surrender now and we can ensure that your punishment is not be as severe."

"Please, Petra! I'm sure we can find a more amicable way to address this. Killing all mortals is monstrous and pointless!"

"'Monstrous,' you say?" Petra challenged. "That is what the mortals say about us. However, *they* are the scourge on this planet!"

"And our kind has our own history with that as well," Liam rebutted. "Now please, put a stop to this hypocritical madness."

"I will not!"

With her outburst, another layer of protection surrounded Petra as she continued to absorb the energy of her sacrifices. Mateo and Liam teleported back to the positions they held previously.

Liam scanned over the scene, trying to assess the situation. "We need to disrupt this, but the forcefield around her is quite powerful and acts as an offense and defense."

"You're right, but we are more powerful," Mateo assured. He snapped his fingers and before them appeared an alter along with several herbs and a large bowl.

Petra saw what they were doing and just when she sent an attack their way, Liam dispelled it with a flick of his wrist and formed a magical cocoon around himself and Mateo for protection. She continued to attack with bursts of energy strong enough to cause the ground below them to rumble despite their shield.

"We must hurry. I'm not sure how long this protection spell will be able to withstand her strikes. They are growing stronger with each one."

"Right." Mateo split his palm open to allow his blood to pour into the bowl where he'd already mixed the necessary herbs. "We will need to do a draining spell and absorb the power ourselves. All of that energy has to go somewhere and we'd make the best vessels for it. Since she is currently channeling it into herself, we just need to disrupt the path and redirect it here."

"But how will we do that? This is Petra's spell and she has complete control over it."

"Yes, which means we will need to create a connection with Petra. And we already have one, remember? From when we were kids. We can use that."

"That sounds both risky and difficult."

"Because it is. But what other choice do we have with our lack of backup and time? I estimate it'll take less than ten minutes before she's finished with this spell and too powerful to fight."

"All valid points," Liam agreed. "My best guess is that we expand on this slight connection with Petra through reflection on our childhood memories with her and gathering as much as we can on how it felt whenever our magic would interact with hers."

"That is exactly the plan. And this potion I've mixed up will make our memories more vivid, considering there is nothing particularly distinct we have of Petra. Now, add your blood to it, too."

Liam sliced his hand and as soon as his blood made contact with Mateo's inside of the potion, both men's eyes glowed—Liam's in the Taylor gray and Mateo's in the Vazquez green.

Through concentration mixed with their spell, the men were able to expand the small connection they had with Petra until it was strong enough for them to have an impact on her spell.

The life forces flowing to Petra began to split off and redirect toward Mateo and Liam.

"No!" Petra roared, sending ripples of energy through the air that finally broke the protection spell that Liam put up. However, both men held their ground.

Suddenly, Mateo felt a blunt pain at the core of his body and toppled over, gasping for air. "What... the hell... is that?" he questioned as he struggled to catch his breath.

"Mateo! What-" Liam was cut off when the same thing happened to him and he found himself on the ground.

"You didn't think I had a backup plan?" Petra's voice echoed in their minds. "Such a connection can work both ways and by accessing my powers, you've turned into willing participants in an exchange."

"Fuck... I didn't expect her... to be in a state... to turn this... back on us," Mateo choked out. "I thought... enough guards... were up in... the spell."

"I have... an idea..." Liam reached out and took Mateo's

hand before he began chanting something under his breath.

"Wait!" Mateo interrupted when he realized what Liam was doing. "Do we have any other options?" He had already run out of ideas, but hoped Liam at least had an alternative to what he was currently doing.

Liam shook his head. "It's the only thing... that will work," he explained. "Or... she will win... We can always... find a way... to retrieve our power."

"Fine... Do it."

Following Mateo's affirmation, Liam continued chanting until an orb manifested between the men and Petra. It began to glow as the energy that was being exchanged started flowing into it.

Petra tried to strike the orb with the same bolts of energy she'd been using against Mateo and Liam before, but her attacks proved ineffective and she was growing weaker by the minute—as were the men.

The spell that Liam used acted as a magnet for the magical and life energy that were swarming about in the exchange and pulled from both men as well as Petra.

It was a big risk, as the orb collected power from Petra, her sacrifices, Liam, and Mateo, and should she somehow get hold of it and be able to absorb that energy, she'd be the most powerful being in existence.

But it had also turned into their only chance of ensuring Petra's plan would fail by changing the energy into a solid matter that could be destroyed without redistribution.

Finally, Petra moved from her position at the center of the field and bolted toward the orb, falling right into Liam's trap. Just as she neared the large deposit, Liam used the final bit of power that he could muster to make it explode.

A blinding light spread through the field, disintegrating

everything in its path. As the magical explosion approached Liam and Mateo, the men were suddenly transported to their shared flat in London where they'd started their day.

Just as Liam had expected when he initiated that dangerous spell, Mateo managed to gather enough strength to transport them before they were destroyed.

Laying on their stomachs on the floor of the flat, both men already knew that their debacle with Petra would result in long-term damage to them, but were too weak to begin to think about just what that damage would look like.

"You really trusted that I would have enough power to make such a move?" Mateo said softly.

"I didn't have a choice."

That was their last exchange before both men passed out.

# CHAPTER
# FORTY-TWO

Only a few seconds had passed in their reality, but with the memory-sharing spell, Amara lived out that entire day with Mateo and Liam. When the spell ended and she opened her eyes, the first thing Amara did was burst out laughing, despite the dire end to Liam and Mateo's story.

"I'm sorry, guys," she said through her hysterical laughs. "I know this is extremely serious. It's just that you two... When you tried to have sex-" Amara was giggling so hard at the flashback that she couldn't finish finish her sentence.

Both men were embarrassed—Liam's face a subtle hint of pink and Mateo with a red undertone to his light brown skin. However, they also felt slightly less tense to see how amused Amara was in that moment.

Upon learning the truth about the Palisyfum and that Mateo and Liam kept the truth from her, Amara was the angriest they had ever seen her. And both men could sense that there was a rift between them and her following the revelation. However, seeing her with a wide smile and hearing her laughter fill the room as amused tears brimmed her eyes, the men found hope that their relationship wasn't beyond repair.

"Mateo! You weren't into it at all, you even seemed annoyed!" Amara continued. "And Liam! You were so turned off, but casual about it, treating it like a chore!"

Amara's laughing went on for several more minutes to the point that even Cameron had come to check on her before promptly being told by Mateo and Liam to go back downstairs as not to reveal exactly what it was Amara was so amused about.

When she finally calmed down enough to communicate more clearly with the men. "I'm sorry," Amara said after a long exhale. "What happened after you passed out?"

"Well," Liam began. "My mother eventually retrieved us from our shared flat and took us to some healers. Even with their help, Mateo and I were out for months. And when we finally woke up, or powers were out of wack even worse than we expected."

"We knew that we would lose some of our strength considering it was decimated," Mateo continued. "But our inherited abilities were also affected... My visions were less accurate and more difficult to trigger."

"And I lost control of my telepathy, no longer able to turn it off when I wanted. The first few decades of having it like this, I thought sure I'd lose my mind. It was like being in a crowded mall any time I'm in public."

"Years later, we learned that Petra survived the incident, but was severely injured as a result. It also explained why our powers were still in such a poor state—we still have a connection with her somehow, but we haven't figured out how to sever it."

"If you're connected, couldn't you track her and finish the job?" Amara asked.

"We gave that a try on several occasions, but it didn't work. Either Petra herself or whomever was hiding her found a way to scramble her magical signature, so even with our connection, our attempts to track her misled us. As such, we did the same with our own magical signatures to avoid the risk of her ambushing us."

After the men answered her questions, Amara's initial entertained reaction to their memory of that day wore off and she was hit with a wave of emotions over what she saw from their fight with Petra. Because Amara was reliving the memory with Mateo and Liam through their connection, she also felt the panic that they felt along with the pain as their power was being drained.

Although they were strong, if anything had gone wrong after Liam initiated that final spell, they could've been destroyed. And when Amara was faced with that fact, she was reminded of just how deeply she cared for the men. The idea of them no longer existing or having never met Mateo and Liam in the first place terrified Amara more than anything.

Suddenly, she threw her arms around them and held Mateo and Liam in a tight hug.

"I'm glad that you survived... I can't believe you made such huge sacrifices to save mortals..."

Mateo and Liam returned her embrace and rested their heads on each of her shoulders.

"Trust us when we say it was worth it."

"What if we go back to my grandma's house in Georgia where I grew up?" Amara suggested as she packed her suitcase. Amara, Mateo, Liam, and Cameron were in her room in the home that she and Evelyn shared while Evelyn was out on a date with James.

The four of them were trying to determine where Amara could go to hide from Petra and Samuel and neither of the men's families were an option. They did not feel comfortable revealing Amara's origins to anyone out of fear that the information could spread wider as to the identity of who was likely the last Palisyfum in existence.

"What?" Mateo and Liam questioned in unison.

"Well, doesn't it make sense? My grandma kept us there hidden. There were never any incidents when I was growing up... Then again, my memories have apparently been altered, so I could be wrong, but I think we would've at least relocated if there were an incident."

"What about a paper trail?"

"Grandma was paranoid and the house is so rural that our closest 'neighbors' were like a half mile from us," Amara explained. "I moved away after she died, and used that apartment address for everything. But I couldn't bare to sell the house, so it's just sitting there looking abandoned. I would drive by sometimes, just to see it when I was feeling lonely or after visiting her grave, but I still don't think it can be connected to me."

The three men pondered her words before Cameron finally spoke up.

"That house is probably the safest place for you right now."

"That does sounds like a good idea," Mateo agreed. "The fact that you two of the Palisyfum line were able to live there without anyone finding you gives me assurance that the place is likely effectively cloaked and secluded."

"Great." Liam nodded. "Then we will go there."

"Okay," Amara took a deep breath and pulled out her phone. "I'll book us plane tickets for tonight."

"We can't fly," Liam said softly. "It'll have to be another way."

"What? Why not? I thought you two couldn't teleport to places you'd never been and even if you could, you don't have the power to do something that big right now."

"That's not what we're saying. We will need to travel using another, less traceable means... Like by car."

"By car? This is the twenty-first century and this is urgent... Why can't we fly to Georgia?"

"For one, magical beings still use nonmagical means to get jobs done at times—including monitoring something as easy to track as air travel. If Petra or Samuel do that, then they'll be able to easily determine where we are traveling. And secondly..." Liam's voice softened once again. "I'm afraid of flying."

Amara slowly blinked and Cameron pursed his lips.

"What?"

"I'm afraid of flying," Liam repeated with almost a mumble. Meanwhile, Mateo pressed his fingers to his forehead and lowered his head.

"You're... afraid... of flying?" questioned a baffled Amara.

Liam gulped. "Yes."

Cameron snorted before covering his mouth to avoid laughing while Amara swallowed and tilted her head as she scanned over Liam.

She wondered to herself why an immortal warlock would be afraid of airplanes. Amara noticed how Liam hung his head in shame at the revelation of his phobia and walked up closer to him and gave him the assurance he needed.

"It's okay, Liam. We can drive... I've always wanted to go on a road trip, anyway. Though, I didn't expect these circumstances."

Liam's eyes came up to meet hers with a small smile. "I appreciate it."

"There's also another issue," Amara said. "I know that I don't really have a choice but to leave, but can I at least talk to Dr. Minnow about working out something for my studies? I'm not going to stop pursuing my PhD, even if I do need to make adjustments in my research."

"Fine," Mateo said with a sigh. "But we'll need to tell him it's an emergency and you'll have to do it over the phone. We will also need to make sure it's untraceable and you can't tell him the truth about your location. Also, you can't tell him you're with us."

Amara took notice of the way both men seemed uneasy the moment she said James' name.

"Why do you guys look so uncomfortable...? Wait! Don't tell me that James is a vampire or evil warlock or something!"

"No, he's human..." Mateo clarified. "But quite obsessed with the supernatural. There have been a couple of times where Liam and I have helped him out after he attempted spells that went awry."

"Wait, so James knows that you're warlocks?"

"Yes, but he doesn't seem to know the truth of the Palisyfum. Though it's clear that he's trying."

"What about Evelyn? Is she in danger?" Amara asked.

Liam shook his head. "James is harmless. It's not unlike humans who know of magic to want to try it and obsess over it. They often assume it will help them achieve whatever it is that they want. We'll be sure to put a protection charm on Evelyn to protect her from anyone intending to harm her."

"Understood," Amara affirmed. "... And if it helps make that protection stronger, you can use my... my blood."

"It will. Thank you, love."

Amara returned to throwing clothes in her suitcase as she spoke. "There's so much to talk about, but I guess we'll have plenty of time while the four of us are on the road."

"You mean three," Cameron corrected. "I'm going to take my flight as planned and I also need to cover for you with Evelyn and figure out some excuse that won't be too alarming for her. Besides, I'm useless in this state and hopefully you'll be fine with Mateo and Liam."

Amara pouted, but didn't bother arguing considering the predicament they were in. "Fine." She sighed. "I guess it'll just be the three of us."

CHAPTER

# FORTY-THREE

Amara sat in the backseat of the car while Liam and Mateo were up front. She leaned her head against the window looking out at the blurred scenery as they drove by. After three days of driving and motels, it was their last full day on the road and they would arrive to their destination the next day. As they got closer to Georgia, more of Amara's memories of her final weeks at her grandmother's house flooded her mind.

*"I'll be eighteen next week and can do what I want!" Amara shouted at Glenda. The two had been arguing for almost a half hour after Amara informed her grandmother that she would be leaving their isolated home to live on her own in what she described as 'the real world.'*

*"Not yet, Amara! It's not safe for you... The world is a dangerous place and people cannot be trusted."*

*"You always say that, but you're the one who has been keeping things from me. You've isolated me from the world. I*

*never had friends or got to go to real school. It's like I've been a prisoner my whole life."*

*"Trust me when I tell you that this is* not *a prison. I'm doing what's best for you, Amara," Glenda explained. "I just want you to be safe."*

*"Trust you? You're still being so cryptic. How can keeping things from me be 'what's best' for me?"*

*"Please, Amara. I promise that I will explain everything to you soon. Just stay here and I'll tell you everything."*

*"No! I'm leaving next week and there's nothing you can do about it, grandma! I need to live my life and you've been preventing me from doing that for as long as I can remember by keeping me cooped up here."*

*"That's not true, honey. I have been helping you live. Do you really think I intend to harm you at all?"*

*"How is completely isolating me from the real world helping me live?"*

*"Do you really think I want to do that? Do you think I've enjoyed seeing the way you've suffered from being sheltered here?"*

*"No..." Amara replied softly, breaking eyes contact with Glenda. "I don't think you want to hurt me, grandma. I know that you love me and care about me. But, I think that you're just too paranoid and overprotective... I know that the world isn't a safe place and that it comes with hardships, but I have to experience those. All of it is part of life."*

*"I just need more time, Amara... I'm not stopping you from going out, but I have to equip you with the skills and knowledge you need before making such a decision."*

*"You've had my whole life to tell me whatever this thing is that you've been keeping from me and you haven't said anything yet. You're just using it to trick me into staying here. There's probably nothing," Amara spat.*

*"There is! It's just not easy to explain..."*

*Amara paused for a long time and analyzed her grandmother's face. Tears brimmed her eyelids and her gaze on Amara was filled with desperation.*

*"Fine... I don't turn eighteen until next week anyway. But if you don't tell me by then, I'm leaving, grandma. I'll be an adult and you won't be able to keep me here."*

*"It's a deal," Glenda nodded and they went on with the rest of their day with the tension between them being somewhat eased, though Glenda was stressed about the looming deadline of Amara's eighteenth birthday.*

*Later that night after the two of them went to bed, Amara couldn't manage to fall asleep, as Glenda kept having coughing fits.*

*"She conveniently always gets sick whenever I talk about leaving," Amara whispered sharply as she rose from her bed to check on Glenda.*

*"Grandma," she called, walking down the hall to her room and knocking on the door. "Are you okay?"*

*There was no response, but she could hear her grandmother's ongoing coughing fit. Amara cracked open the door and saw Glenda sitting at the edge of her bed, coughing hard into her hand with her veins popping from her forehead and her face showing a red undertone with the intensity.*

*Also, Glenda's eyes were barely open, and Amara wasn't sure if she'd seen correctly, but she could've sworn that they appeared to be purple.*

*"I'll go downstairs and mix up your medicine," Amara said softly.*

*As the teen went through the kitchen drawers and cabinets to gather the herbs she needed to make the remedy for her grandmother's coughing fits, Amara heard a scratching sound from the living room. She ignored it, continuing to make the medicine, until she heard another distinct noise that she knew could only be Xivan.*

*Carrying the bowl with her, Amara went around the corner to look into the living room and saw a struggling Xivan scratching desperately at the latch on his cage. He was still making that odd sound, similar to the one he'd made when Amara told Glenda about the black rabbit from her dream, and appeared to be in distress trying to escape the cage.*

*"Xivan? What's wrong?" When Amara approached and reached for the latch to the door, Xivan slightly calmed down and stopped his scratching to wait for her to open it. As soon as he was free, the gray rabbit moved with unreal speed up the steps before Amara could even rise to her feet.*

*"Did he know that grandma was sick or something? Xivan is such an odd rabbit..."*

*Amara went back to the kitchen to put the herbal mix into a few capsules before she returned to her grandmother's room and saw Xivan sitting on the bed next to her, curled up by her leg.*

*"I think Xivan knew you were sick, grandma," she said as she handed Glenda the medicine with a cup of water. "He rushed up here so quickly."*

*Glenda couldn't respond through her coughs and quickly got up to go to the bathroom and Xivan followed behind her. Before Amara could go in with them, the door closed behind Glenda and Amara heard the sound of it locking.*

*"Grandma! Are you okay? Why did you lock the door?" Amara knocked urgently until she heard Glenda's coughing cease and the sink in the bathroom begin to run.*

*"I'm fine, Amara," Glenda called from the other side and soon after her assurance, she opened the door and meet Amara with a weak smile. "Thank you, sweetie... These coughing spells have been getting worse and worse lately."*

*"I wonder why..." Amara mumbled under her breath.*

"And what's that supposed to mean?" Glenda questioned.

"It's just..." Amara hesitated for several moments, twisting her mouth and pulling at her fingers. "You always seem to get sick when I talk about leaving..."

"Really, Amara?" Glenda glared at her granddaughter. "Are you implying that I'm faking this?"

"I'm just saying, it's..." Amara trailed off.

It was true that her grandmother was normally in great health, but whenever Amara would mention plans to leave, Glenda would become ill. However, after seeing Glenda's reaction to her accusation, Amara felt guilty about bringing it up.

"Sorry, grandma..."

"Amara... I know it's frustrating, but all I'm asking is for you to give me a little bit more time."

"Right," Amara sighed before locking eyes with Glenda. "And grandma..."

"Yes?"

"When you were coughing, your eyes looked kind of weird... They were a strange color, like a... Purple."

Glenda's mouth went agape before her face relaxed and she shook her head. "It's late, Amara... Why don't you go to sleep? You're just seeing things because you're tired."

Although Amara knew it was very unlikely that her grandmother's eyes turned purple, something about Glenda's response to the teen didn't feel genuine and she huffed her annoyance.

"Whatever... Goodnight, grandma."

"Good night, sweetie. And thank you again."

Glenda watched as Amara turned away and went back to her room. She knew that time was running out to tell her granddaughter everything and although she'd had years to do so or at least prepare, it wasn't as simple as she'd hoped. She was afraid that by telling Amara the truth, it could trigger debilitating *memories that Glenda had locked away and she couldn't bare to see her in such a state again.*

*However, Glenda accepted that it was long overdue for Amara to know the whole truth, because that truth would be important to her survival. She picked up Xivan and held him in her arms.*

*"I'll tell her everything, Xivan... I'll finally do it first thing tomorrow morning. I promise."*

*In her room, Amara continued to toss and turn, despite the silence that fell over the house after Glenda went to sleep. She'd been restless for the past month in anticipation of her eighteenth birthday and plans to finally leave and live on her own, to the point that she'd already had a bag packed and ready to go.*

*Amara had also been saving for the past eight years money that her grandmother would give her whenever they went into town for groceries or other necessities, and that added up to exactly $1,357.86 in cash. She figured it would be enough for her to find a place to live for at least a month or two until she could find enough work to sustain herself.*

*Amara sat up in bed and looked aimlessly into the pitch blackness in deep thought, whispering to herself.*

*"I want to go now... I've been stuck in this prison for my whole life and if grandma hasn't told me whatever it is that she had to tell me by now, then is it really going to make a difference? After holding out for so long, I doubt one week will be enough to change her. I just want to be free..."*

*A tear fell down Amara's face as she reflected on her secluded lifestyle and how she spent all of it longing for friends or to see other parts of the outside world that weren't just the small town that she and Glenda would go to twice each month.*

*I do love grandma and Xivan and I wouldn't say I'm running away from them... I just need to live. I need to live life on my own and make my own choices...*

*Suddenly, the teen got out of her bed, grabbed her backpack from the closet, and escaped the house without making a sound.*

AMARA NOW WONDERED if the thing that her grandmother wanted to tell her was the truth about the Palisyfum and that she was a witch. She also pondered if maybe Glenda's overprotectiveness wasn't totally unwarranted and if perhaps she was worried about them being hunted considering the history of the Palisyfum.

"Are you okay, love?" Liam, who was in the passenger seat, turned to look at Amara and placed his hand on her leg. They'd made progress over the course of their trip and the men were permitted to touch her again, though she still wanted Liam to stay out of her head. "You seem in distress."

"I'm fine," Amara assured. "Just memories that have kind of been dulled down are coming back up the closer we get to home..."

"If it's too much for you, we can figure something else out," Mateo suggested as he pulled into the hotel parking lot. "We could look at other options for where to stay."

"N-no... It's fine. I can do this. And my grandma put so many guards up, I think this really will be the best place for us to lay low and figure things out."

"Understood. Just let us know if you at any point want to leave and we will."

"Th-thanks, guys... You know, despite the circumstances and the fact that half of this road trip was spent in awkward silence, I'm actually glad we did this... As weird as it sounds."

"I understand what you mean. Even with all that is hanging over our heads, these past few days have just been the three of us, this car, and our hotel rooms."

"I agree with you, love. It is very strange, but this was sort of like a getaway."

"We are so weird." Amara giggled. "We should be in panic mode, shouldn't we?"

"Yes, we probably should, but let's enjoy this odd state we're in while we can."

# FORTY-FOUR

"We've arrived, mi alma," Mateo said as the three of them pulled into the driveway of Amara's childhood home. While she was still living in Georgia, Amara would occasionally visit the house to do some upkeep so that it wouldn't look completely abandoned, but it still wasn't always in the best shape.

However, to her surprise when they got out of the car, the house didn't look as bad as she expected, especially considering she'd been away for close to six months. The lawn wasn't overgrown and the potted ferns outside the front door were still a lush and healthy green. There also appeared to be an almost fresh coat of dark blue paint on the house—a hue that her grandmother was adamant about keeping, even when a young Amara insisted they tried another, less depressing color like yellow or even a lighter blue.

"Cam must've been coming here to take care of it," Amara said softly as she approached the door. She pulled out her keys with a shaky hand and tried to unlock the door, but her trembling was too strong and she ended up dropping them.

Liam picked up the keys for her and rubbed her back in a comforting motion. "Are you okay, love? I'm sure this is... a lot."

After Amara nodded, Liam went to unlock the door for her, but as soon as the key made contact, he was blown back by a wave of energy while Amara was unaffected.

He lay spread out on the ground and Mateo ran up to him while Amara shouted as she hurried over from the door.

"Liam!" she called. "Are you okay?"

He slowly lifted himself up to a sitting position and Mateo crouched to meet him at eye-level with a hand on his shoulder.

"What are you feeling?" Mateo questioned, analyzing his friend's face.

"Drained," Liam answered as he rubbed the back of his head. "It must be some sort of guard her grandmother put up."

"Liam!" When Amara reached him, she sat on the ground beside him and took his hand into hers. "I'm so sorry! I didn't think something like this would happen."

"No, no... It's alright. We should've considered there'd be some sort of protective spell on the house... Even if she's not here anymore."

"Are you sure?" Amara asked as she held up his arm and started looking over him and feeling his body to check for soreness. "Does anything hurt?"

"No," he assured. "I'm just suddenly exhausted, is all. It feels as if that blast used my own energy against me. But I'm sure I'll be fine."

"Amara," Mateo said as he helped Liam stand. "How

about you go inside? It seems that the house is the only thing that blocks us. I already checked the backyard and didn't face any issues."

Amara nodded. "Right. I know that we'd planned to use one of the doors in the house for your spell, but there is a shed back there we used for gardening tools. If it doesn't blow you away, then maybe try it for the spell you had planned?"

"Great, that should work for us. It'll take two days for our home to manifest completely, but after that, we can at least use the same house we had in Masoncrest."

"Oh, right... That's why we didn't do it while we were traveling. But where will we sleep since you two can't come inside? Another hotel?"

"We can talk about it later," Liam replied. "Go take a look inside the house and Mateo will get started with the spell."

"Okay." Amara turned and walked toward the home. When she reached the door, she cautiously touched the nob, hoping she wouldn't somehow experience the same fate as Liam. "Of course I wouldn't," she whispered to herself with a slight huff. "I need to get it together."

Slowly turning the nob and opening the door, Amara stepped through the threshold of the house and as soon as she entered and looked around the living room by the entrance, she blinked several times. The place was much cleaner than she anticipated and again, she figured that Cameron was likely behind it.

She'd expected her heart to be heavy when she got inside, but a small smile came her face knowing that Cameron was still taking care of the home that they shared while he was still in his form as Xivan.

Amara took her time walking through the house. The

couch that divided the living room from the kitchen reminded her of when she would sit on the floor while her grandmother braided her hair. The coffee table in the middle of the room brought back memories of the "tea parties" she would have with Glenda growing up—it was a Sunday ritual of theirs that she looked forward to up until her teens. She looked over at an empty corner in the room where they used to keep Xivan's cage and shook her head thinking about all the times she'd try to teach him new tricks and how the stubborn rabbit would never cooperate.

Going up the stairs that creaked with each step that she took, Amara's heart was pounding in her ears and she was barely breathing. The sounds triggered memories of the day that her grandmother died... Or at least the day Amara learned that she died.

*"This isn't as terrible as grandma made it seem," Amara said to herself as she entered the small motel room. It had a single queen-sized bed with a green and gold comforter, the off-white wall was covered in marks and holes that revealed the insulation behind it. The burgundy carpet was covered in stains and had a high smell that Amara did not want to name. Despite her efforts to clean the carpet over the week she'd been on her own, the scent never left.*

*"It's my first birthday without Grandma or Xivan, but I'm too exhausted to do anything but sleep." Amara fell back into bed. She'd gotten a job bussing tables at a diner near the rural motel where she was staying and despite the place not getting a ton of business, she still felt like they were working her to the bone.*

*"I can't believe a whole week has already passed since I left... I'm surprised grandma hasn't found me yet. I miss her and*

*Xivan a lot, but I'll give it another three weeks before I go back home so I can show her that I was able to live out in the real world on my own for a whole month. I'm sure she's worried about me, but once she sees how well I'm doing for myself, she'll realize she was wrong about everything and maybe she won't be as stressed about me being away."*

*However, despite her desire to prove to Glenda that she was fine on her own, Amara was still plagued with thoughts of how worried her grandmother might be and the guilt of running away from home was weighing on her.*

*"Maybe I could just call her from the payphone so that she knows I'm alive and okay and then I'll promise her that I'll see her in just a few weeks." Amara nodded to herself as she pondered the idea aloud before getting out of bed and heading outside and down the stairs to one of the three pay phones at the motel.*

*She put her quarters in the first one only to realize that it wasn't working. Amara let out a deep sigh. Her budget was extremely tight and although she was working at the diner, her pay was only five dollars and twenty-five cents an hour, so she was forced to supplement it with her savings more than she'd expected.*

*Going to the next phone, Amara pushed several of the buttons and didn't hear a sound, realizing that it was also out of order. She looked over to the third and saw another resident using it. Based on the intensity of the conversation and the fact that the woman had brought out a folding chair and was sitting in it, Amara figured she would be there for a long time.*

*"I guess I can just call another time," the teen whispered to herself as she turned back toward the building before pausing when she walked past the check-in area. Something in her caused Amara a strong need to call Glenda and she felt like she shouldn't push it back any further. So, she changed her route and*

went toward the motel check-in counter to ask about using the phone.

Delilah, the motel owner was sitting at the counter and focused on the magazine she was reading. The woman was in her mid- to late-fifties and had gray streaks throughout her dark brown hair and she was oddly pale despite the Georgia sun. Also, while Delilah was nice enough to Amara—in the way a business owner would be to a customer—there always seemed to be an underlying uneasiness she caused Amara that she couldn't quite identify.

"Excuse me, Ms. Delilah," Amara said, pulling the woman's attention from her magazine. "May I please use your phone? Two of the three outside aren't working and another tenant is using the other one."

"You can't wait for the other tenant to finish or make your call later?" Delilah asked coldly.

Amara swallowed, put off by Delilah's tone. "I just need to make a quick call. It won't take long. I promise."

Delilah analyzed the girl's face and noticed the worry in it. She put the phone up on the higher part of the counter in front of Amara.

"Fine, but it'll cost you. Three dollars flat fee and then seventy-five cents for each minute."

"Seventy-five cents?" Amara questioned with a gasp. "But the pay phones are only twenty-five cents per minute and the flat rate is two dollars."

"Yeah, but you're asking for premium service here since you won't wait for the payphone, meaning you pay premium prices."

Amara's looked at Delilah curiously before she was reminded that the woman was running a business and based on what she'd already seen at the diner, people would look for any reason to get every last dime out of their customers.

"Fine," the teen surrendered, putting three dollars and

*seventy-five cents on the counter. "It'll only take me one minute, anyway."*

*Delilah took the money and gestured to the phone for Amara to make her call. She dialed her grandmother's phone and the line trilled and trilled and trilled until it cut out. Glenda didn't believe in voicemail, so there was no way for Amara to leave a message.*

*"That call was so important but no one picked up?" Delilah commented when Amara hung up the phone.*

*Amara simply shrugged, not wanting to engage further with Delilah and went outside and upstairs to return to her room.*

*"Between that broken payphone and using the motel phone, I spent two days' budget worth of food." Amara shook her head and sat in bed. "I guess I'll see if they're willing to share any returned orders or scraps with me at the diner... It's weird that grandma didn't answer, though. I wonder if she's out looking for me. Or maybe she's in town getting food or something. I'll try again tomorrow."*

*As the days went on, Amara continued her attempts to call her grandmother and grew increasingly worried when she couldn't seem to get ahold of her and by the end of her second weekend, she decided she needed to go back home and check on Glenda and Xivan.*

*Amara had just finished her Saturday afternoon shift at the diner and went to speak to her boss, Paul, about taking a personal day on Sunday so that she could visit her grandmother. Although she'd only been working for two weeks, she hoped that he would be understanding, especially given that she'd gone above and beyond her duties at the restaurant.*

*She approached the man, who stood at about six feet with a burly build. He had dirty blonde hair with a matching beard and blue eyes. Similar to Delilah, despite Paul being reasonably nice* to Amara, there was still something about him that didn't sit well with her.

"Mr. Paul," she started. "I know that I haven't been working here long, but I was wondering if I could take off tomorrow? I'm worried about my grandma who lives alone and I want to go and check on her. She's in a rural area not too far from Augusta."

Paul gave her a confused look and tilted his head. "Are you really asking me this right now?"

"Yes." Amara nodded. "I've been worried about my grandma and I just want to make sure she's alright. I promise I'll be back the next day and can even work a double."

Paul shook his head. "That's not going to work. You can't take off tomorrow."

"W-why?" Amara asked. "It's just one day and like I said, I'll be be back Monday and can work a double. Heck, I can work doubles the whole week if that'll make up for it. I just really need-"

"Some advice for you, girl..." interrupted an agitated Paul. "When you're working a job, you can't just ask for time off the next day. You need to give advanced warning. Otherwise, how am I supposed to find someone to cover for you, hm?"

Amara nodded without making eye contact. She didn't like the way he called her 'girl,' not only was it condescending, but it also felt demeaning, as if hate or disgust accompanied the word when he addressed her as such. Paul's attitude was just as cold as Delilah's when Amara asked about using the phone and she found it odd how they were nice enough to her when she was a paying customer or hardworking employee, but when she asked for any other support, it was like they turned into completely different people with her.

"Right..." the teen said softly, still looking away. "I understand. Could I try the following Sunday, in that case? And I can help with looking for someone to cover me, for what it's worth."

*"Yeah," Paul replied. "But good luck finding someone. We're already pretty short on staff. That's why we hired you on the spot."*

*Amara didn't respond again and put her backpack on and left the restaurant to start her twenty-minute walk back to the motel. She was deeply concerned about her grandmother and with each day, Amara was regretting her decision to leave more and more.*

*By the time she got back to the motel, Amara was ready to take a shower—one of the only things she could look forward to about the place. If it had nothing else going for it, it had hot water.*

*When Amara got to her room, she went straight to the bathroom to turn on the shower, but as soon as she did, she noticed brown water coming out of the faucet and a repugnant smell that came with it.*

*"Why is this happening today?" she groaned before trying the sink only to experience the same thing.*

*Fed up with what was already a long and difficult day to cap a stressful and demoralizing week, Amara stormed downstairs to speak with Delilah in the lobby. As always, the woman was tied up in her magazine, not even lifting her head at the sound of the door opening.*

*Amara took a deep breath before speaking. "Delilah, there's something wrong with the water in my room. It's brown and smells awful."*

*Without removing her eyes from the magazine, Delilah responded to Amara. "Right, we're having issues with the water in your building, but someone will be coming to fix it in a few days."*

*"What am I supposed to do until then? I need to clean myself. I also use that water to drink and to cook."*

*"That's not my problem." Delilah shrugged, still looking down at the magazine.*

*"But you own the place! And you said it was just my building. So does that mean the other one is fine? Could you maybe move me to a room over there until the water in the building where I'm staying is fixed?"*

*"No, I can't."*

*"And why not?"*

*The woman finally looked up from her magazine and narrowed her eyes at Amara. "Because, that other building is for special clientele and you don't fit the criteria."*

*"What the hell does that mean?" Amara snapped. She was completely fed up with Delilah's attitude. The teen was also already on edge after being denied a day off and dealing with the ongoing stress of not knowing what was happening with her grandmother. "I'm a paying customer and the space you rented out to me isn't livable with that water. I demand another room with functioning water until mine is fixed!"*

*Delilah shot to her feet and glared at Amara with pure hate in her eyes. "Don't get that tone with me, girl!" she spat.*

There it goes again, *Amara thought to herself.* The way she and Paul call me 'girl' just doesn't feel right.

*"I have every right to kick you out of here for getting aggressive and intimidating me," Delilah continued. "Do I need to call the authorities?"*

*Amara was taken aback, not understanding how or why that escalated so quickly to the point that Delilah was threatening to call the police and at that point, the teen had enough.*

*"No, just give me a refund for the next two weeks that I paid ahead on. I'm leaving tonight."*

*"You didn't read the contract?" Delilah questioned with a snide smirk. "There are no refunds. And besides, I won't be able*

*to make that money back since I can't rent your room out until the water is fixed."*

*"What contract? You didn't give me a-" Amara stopped herself as she felt the anger well up inside her. Something internally was telling her that things would end badly if she continued to argue with Delilah.*

*"Whatever." The teen threw her arms in the air and went back to her room to pack her bags without saying another word.*

*It was still summer, so despite it being seven in the evening, the sun was out and Amara could at least walk the forty-five minutes to the bus stop while it was mostly light outside. However, she knew that the summer heat would be relentless and for obvious reasons, she couldn't fill up her water bottle before starting the journey.*

*"It all went all downhill so fast," Amara muttered to herself as she walked along the side of the road. "It's crazy how quickly everyone seemed to change and just turned on me. Maybe grandma was right."*

*Amara managed to survive her trip to the bus station and once she arrived, she went straight to the vending machine and purchased a few bottles of water. She went up to the counter to buy a ticket home and lucky for her, there was a bus leaving in just fifteen minutes that would get her there before midnight.*

*She slept the whole three hours of the trip and she was dropped off in the rural town not far from her grandmother's house, which was about thirty minutes away on foot. Despite it being dark out, Amara knew the area well, and based on her experience when she first ran away, she felt safe enough continuing to the house.*

*Amara exhaled a long breath when she finally arrived at the door of the house. She knew she'd be in big trouble with her grandmother. However, she was prepared to handle the consequences. Amara recognized that her grandmother was likely* worried sick and probably was out looking for her all the times she tried to call her.

Slowly turning the knob and opening the door, Amara was smacked in the face by a strong stench that she couldn't quite identify. It was late and she didn't want to wake Glenda, so rather than calling her to find out what the smell was, Amara followed it to find its source.

As she entered the house further, the smell grew stronger and she gagged while she followed it up the stairs and toward the end of the hall where her grandmother's room was located. It was dark, and even the single lamp that her grandmother used to keep on was turned off.

By the time she reached Glenda's doorway, Amara realized that the source of the odor was likely coming from that room and when she held her arm up to knock on the door, a chill suddenly went up her spine and a cold heaviness came over her body. Suddenly, she felt a sense of urgency and opened the door without knocking, barging in and turning on the light to see an sight that was more devastating that she could fathom.

A lifeless Glenda was flat on her back with her eyes closed and Xivan resting on her stomach. A drop of dried blood was at the side of her mouth and her hands were covered in it. Glenda's skin appeared to have been sinking in, closer to her bones and her flesh graying. As Amara scanned over them, she realized that Xivan also didn't appear to be breathing.

Amara was speechless and frozen in place, her eyes wide, and a lump growing in her throat. The overbearing odor no longer seemed to be noticeable as she tried to process what she was seeing. She stared at the two of them and several attempts to speak were failed until she finally called out to her grandmother.

"Grandma!" Amara wailed hysterically, running over to the bed and putting her hands on Glenda's shoulders before she started shaking her. "Wake up!

*Glenda and Xivan were unresponsive no matter how loud Amara yelled or hard she shook her grandmother.*

*"I'm sorry!" Amara cried. "I'm sorry I ran away. Please, grandma! Please... Please wake up."*

*Amara sobbed and shouted and begged for her grandmother and for Xivan for nearly an hour, hoping that they would wake up. When she finally realized that wouldn't be happening, Amara got into bed next to them and lay at their side, facing the only family she'd ever known.*

*Amara stayed in that bed for days in silence until she was finally able to drag herself out of it to a local funeral home that Glenda would sometimes assist with services to bury her grandmother.*

AMARA WRAPPED her arms around herself looking at the room. Like the rest of the house, it was thoroughly cleaned and natural light flowed in from the open blinds. At first sight, it didn't look like the space that held Amara's worst memory.

In the center of her grandmother's perfectly-made bed, Amara saw Glenda's large, leather-bound journal with a small piece of paper attached to it. Hesitantly, Amara approached, sat on the bed, and read the note stuck to the front of it.

Amara,

Given my current state, I can't say what I want to, but now that you know part of the truth, I hope this can help you figure out the rest.

~ Cameron

The book felt heavy in her hands as she picked it up and unlatched it to open it. Amara had seen the book numerous times growing up with her grandmother, often when she was teaching her about various herbal remedies. While Glenda had several notebooks, and even one that Amara kept with her, this was by far the thickest of them all.

Flipping through the journal, Amara realized that information on botany only took up about one-third of it as she got further into the book, she found pages of writing that she didn't quite understand. The words appeared odd, yet familiar and she noticed how close they seemed to Spanish.

"Is this... Latin?" she said to herself as she went through the pages. "I guess that would make sense. Mateo and Liam use Latin for their spells."

Suddenly she shot to her feet.

"Oh my god! It's a... It's... Could it be...?"

Amara ran downstairs and out the back door to Mateo and Liam who were sitting in lawn chairs by shed. As soon as she came outside, they both turned to look at her with wide smiles driven by Amara's contagious energy.

"What is it, love?"

With a cheesing grin, Amara held up the journal. "I found a... I think grandma had a book of spells! A grimoire!"

Amara sped over to the men in no time and sat in Mateo's lap before flipping to the second half of the book to show them what she'd found. "You speak Latin for your spells, right? Well, this whole second half of the book is in Latin! I think it's all spells."

"That's interesting. I wonder if it's a family grimoire of sorts." Liam reached out to take the book from her and Mateo raised a cautioning hand. "Perhaps we should try to avoid touching any of Amara's grandmother's belongings...

We're not sure what may or may not have a protection spell."

"Fair enough," Liam agreed with a sigh. "Show us what you've found."

"Right!" Amara held the open book up to show the men her findings, but her smile slowly fell when they looked at her with confused expressions.

"What? Why are you looking at me like that?"

"Cariño, we don't see anything on the pages."

"What do you mean you don't see anything? They're full of words and I am like ninety-nine percent sure it's Latin!" Amara looked at the pages again to confirm that words were indeed there and she still saw them. "But I see words— *oh*... Magic?"

Both men nodded.

"Magic," they said in unison.

Amara let out a deep, agitated sigh and stood from Mateo's lap. Her jaw tensed and she shook her head quickly as she looked to the ground. "It's like grandma was prepared for everything except telling me! She kept so much from me and then blocked off anyone else who could've told me anything! She had me here my whole life and didn't say a word about magic, lying to me all those years!"

As Amara ranted, Mateo and Liam started to feel consumed with her rage as well as another energy that they couldn't quite identify. The air felt heavy and they noticed slight breezes that went in the direction opposite of the rest of the wind.

"How do you—as a witch yourself—not tell your granddaughter witch, that she's a witch too? And then she lies to me about the Palisyfum knowing how obsessed I became with it! Never once did she tell me the truth. Why would she do something like this? I don't understand!"

A wave of energy strong enough to make them shudder rippled through Mateo and Liam. They'd seen Amara in an extreme emotional state one time before—when they first revealed the truth of the Palisyfum to her, but this felt like a different level.

"Why?" Amara said with tears running down her face. "I don't understand!" she repeated and her eyes flickered purple for a split second and both Mateo and Liam rushed up to her.

"Your eyes, Amara," Liam said softly, cradling her face. "They just..."

"Why did she keep everything from me?" she cried one last time before burying her face in his chest and sobbing."

While Liam held Amara, Mateo rubbed her back.

"We'll figure this out, amor."

"He's right. And we'll start your training right now."

CHAPTER

# FORTY-FIVE

A month had passed since they arrived in Georgia and the men still weren't able to enter her grandmother's house, but for Amara, that was better. She didn't want to spend all day and all night in the home that held one of her worst memories. Instead, using a spell that took two days for them to complete, Mateo and Liam manifested an exact duplicate of their Masoncrest home hidden inside the shack in the backyard.

Amara lay sleeping in bed between Mateo and Liam. Her body was tense and her fingers dug into the sheets as she experienced one of her graphic nightmares for the third night in a row.

*Young Amara sat on the floor of the cell looking down at her mangled legs. It was another day of experiments with Alistair, the vampire who'd taken her family five months ago. The child had grown numb recently—it was the only way she could make it through the days. Three months into their imprisonment, Alistair killed her father and the girl had never been able to fully process that or her mother's betrayal.*

*"It looks like I won't be able to walk for a few days," she said softly. The screams of her mother could be heard from the other room, but those sounds no longer fazed Amara. "At least, that lady will have it worse..."*

*Amara stopped referring to her mother as such and instead began calling her "that lady." She also refused to acknowledge the woman, even when she tried to speak with Amara.*

*She looked around the empty cell and it appeared the same as it did every day. A plastic cup within arm's reach of her—her captors stopped giving her access to glass following her suicide attempt. Small puddles were scattered throughout the room— during a rainy day, water had leaked in through the ceiling. A plate of rotted food sat in the corner of the cell—Amara had stopped eating partially in protest and partially hoping it would be her demise, but starvation couldn't seem to kill her.*

*Almost in sync with the dripping water, Amara heard familiar steps coming in her direction, though it was an unusual time for that particular visitor. Amara didn't bother to look up into the visitor's eyes, but she saw the black tennis shoes and pair of dark wash jeans.*

*"Amara..." The woman's voice was always particularly soothing to the girl despite the horrific circumstances of her current existence. However, Amara didn't respond.*

*"Amara..." the woman repeated. "Please, just look at me."*

*"Why bother asking?" Amara replied, still examining the floor of the cell. "You can get me to do it if you want to."*

*When the girl heard the sound of keys, she lifted her head and met the face of the vampire using them to unlock Amara's cell. Her hands were shaky, though she managed to get the key into the lock and open the door.*

*"What are you doing, Haze?" Amara questioned, looking up at her expressionless.*

*"I'm going to get you out of here." Haze ran up to Amara and*

*examined her legs, seeing that they couldn't be used. "There's not enough time for me to heal you. I'll need to carry you."*

*"Whatever," the girl replied. "Is this one of his games?" The child refused to use Alistair's name. "Why now? You didn't help before..."*

*Haze felt an ache in her chest at the state that Amara was in. "I don't expect you to forgive me, child... But I want you to know that I am sorry for my complacency up until now. I promise-"*

*The vampire was interrupted by an uproar coming from the room where Amara's mother was being tortured and they felt a wave of energy from that direction.*

*"That's my cue," Haze said before scooping up Amara in her arms and running at full speed. The child didn't react. She'd lost the ability to feel anything at all—physically or emotionally—after being held prisoner and tortured for so long.*

*With the speed at which Haze was running, Amara could feel the wind on her face as she looked expressionless at the scene above her. A panicked Haze and blurred background.*

*Suddenly, Amara felt a sharp pain in her side, followed by the feeling of drops of blood hitting her cheek and seeing it pour from Haze's mouth.*

*"Did you really think this plan of your would work, Haze?" Alistair's voice boomed. "I own you. I'll always own you. You can't escape me, and neither can the girl."*

*Despite the injury, Haze continued to move until she came to a abrupt halt and Amara saw a familiar hand wrap around the vampire's neck before she dropped the girl. Haze was thrown across the room and in no time, hovering over Amara was Alistair's face. It appeared that he'd been cut across his forehead, but the wound was healing before Amara's eyes.*

*"You see... You'll never escape me. Just like H-"*

*An explosion interrupted him and Amara could feel and smell her own flesh burning—a pain that she'd encountered for the first time.*

"It burns!" Amara screamed to the top of her lungs and shot up out of bed, startling Mateo and Liam. She'd thrown herself to the opposite side of the room and was on her hands and knees sobbing and touching her skin, reassuring herself that what she'd experienced was just a dream. However, with the confirmation that Haze existed, and saved her from Samuel, Amara knew that her nightmare had some truth to them, she just wasn't sure what truths they held.

In the month since they'd arrived in Georgia, the men had been weening Amara off of the medicine that sealed her powers. As a result, her nightmares had grown more frequent and she was often waking up in a panic in the middle of the night because of them.

Mateo and Liam hated seeing Amara like that, but it was necessary to take her off of the medicine to start her training. They'd told her about their suspicions that the medicine also likely blocked her memories and offered a potion that could continue to do so, but Amara was adamant about gaining access to as much information about herself as possible.

The men were by her side in no time—Mateo on her left and Liam on her right.

"I'm... sorry," Amara said through heavy breaths. "It seems like I'm waking you guys up with this every night lately."

"It's alright, amor," Mateo assured. "Besides, it is six o'clock and this just gives us an excuse to start with some early morning training."

"You're right. The more training I can do, the better. I

feel like I'm moving so slow in trying to get a hang of this magic stuff..."

"Well, it's not something one can learn overnight, love," Liam said as he rubbed her cheek. "And it's clear that you're making progress."

"What? You mean making stuff barely levitate and one of my eyes being purple now?"

"That's great progress for your first month!"

"But it's not nearly enough to be ready for Petra... We can't be on the run forever and she's going to keep looking for me. And didn't you guys say she has some sort of following? I bet even if she sent one of her weakest followers after me, I wouldn't stand a chance."

"Don't be so hard on yourself, mi alma. This isn't easy stuff and you are new to magic. Of course there'll be a learning curve, but I promise that it'll click one day and you'll see how quickly you can progress after that. I'm sure of it."

"I hope so."


"AMAZING!" Liam beamed as he watched the full cup of water float steadily in the air. Amara was working on not only levitating it, but also moving it in Liam's direction. After she placed the cup in his hand, Liam brought it up to his lips and took a sip.

"Wonderful job, love."

"Yeah," Amara sighed.

"What's wrong? This is exciting!"

"I just put a cup in your hand, Liam. It feels simple. I've been training for a whole month and it feels like I should be able to do more. At this rate, how am I going to catch up to people who have over a hundred years of experience?"

Liam nodded and held a finger to his chin and he thought about Amara's words. "Then let's try something else."

"Like what?"

"Well, now that I've stopped taking the potion that prevented you from interacting with my telepathy, perhaps we could explore why that is. I'm sure it has to do with your powers. It could maybe give us some insights on your special ability."

"You think so?"

"I do. Even with us being fated to each other, it is still unusual for one's Fated to have such an effect."

"Hmmm…" Amara rubbed the side of her neck and looked down thoughtfully as she tried to figure out what her special ability might be. "Do you think I like activate powers or something?"

"Something like that, but with you being of the Palisyfum line, I think it has to be more complex."

"I see. I hope it's something that'll be useful for my defense or offense."

Liam held Amara's face and looked her in the eyes, examining her and admiring her beauty. And as he continued, his mind began to wander. Despite their current predicament, he still wanted her every minute of every day. He and Mateo did wait over one hundred years to meet Amara, after all. "How about we do some practice with it?"

"How so?"

"By duplicating what we did last time it happened, of course."

Liam slowly backed Amara against the wall. She looked up at him with a smile on her face, knowing his mischievous expression.

"Liam, Mateo told us to focus on training while he's gone."

"We are focusing, love," he said as he placed one hand on her hip and the other flat against the wall beside her head. "You remember our first kiss, right?"

Amara nodded. "When I could hear your thoughts and I thought I was going crazy?"

"That's right." Liam started rubbing his thumb against her hip and leaned in closer. "So let's practice more of that."

"The kissing or me reading your thoughts?"

"I want you to do more than read my thoughts. I want you feel them."

"Feeling thoughts? I never understood exactly what the meant."

"Which is why we should practice. Thoughts have various textures to them that can give you more insights on a person. I suspect that the more physical contact we have, the more you'll be able to use my powers."

"Is that so?" Amara challenged. "But that doesn't seem to work when we have sex."

"Fair point, but are you focusing on reading my thoughts when we're having sex?"

"No. I'm distracted by... other things."

"So, let's try this with you focused on trying to read my thoughts."

Amara giggled as Liam began placing gentle kisses on her neck. "Why do I feel like there are some ulterior motives here, Mr. Taylor?"

"This is simply part of your training. Focus on getting into my head."

"Kind of hard to do that right now..."

"Think about our connection, Amara. Just focus on that."

Amara tried to do what Liam told her and focused on their connection, as well as tried to recollect how she felt the first time they kissed and she got into his head. She closed her eyes and leaned her head back against the wall while Liam's mouth explored her neck before he worked his way back up to her jaw and then their lips brushed against each other.

When Liam closed the distance, Amara continued to try to focus on the connection rather the heat rushing to her core.

*You can do it, Amara… Just focus on—*

Amara's eyes popped open when she heard Liam's thoughts and she broke away from their kiss. "I heard your thoughts! It was like last time! I mean, a little bit spotty, and cut off at the end, but I heard them!"

"Good job. And what about texture? Did you feel anything?"

"Well… I can hear decent enough, but I still don't exactly feel the thoughts. What would they feel like?"

"Let's try again," Liam rasped before his lips returned to Amara's and he pressed his body against hers. He put one of his legs between Amara's and she ground against it as the two of them continued.

*Focus*, he thought.

*Your thigh between my legs isn't it making it that easy.*

Liam broke the kiss and scanned Amara's face. "Or perhaps I need to kiss you elsewhere."

WHILE AMARA TRAINED WITH LIAM, Mateo went off to make contact with his sister Camila. He spoke to her every week, no matter what.

"So, how is life with your Fated, Mateo?" Camila asked him.

"Life is as wonderful as can be," he replied. It was partially a lie given the looming issue of Petra and Samuel hunting Amara, but even then, Mateo was the happiest he'd ever been now that he and Liam were finally with their Fated. "I now understand what you meant when you wouldn't shut up about yourself and Nico. By the way, how are they?"

"Nico is great! It's been fifty-seven years, but they finally adjusted to the immortality. You know the ritual was quite difficult for them."

"Right, that was rough on them, especially as all they could do was watch the rest of their family age and..." Mateo gulped just thinking about it. He never considered how cruel the ways of their world was until he was fated to what he thought would be a human at the time. "Do you ever think about how cruel it is, hermanita? To give our Fated immortality and then force them to watch their loved ones wither away while they go on, solely to be with us?"

"Of course I do," Camila responded. "Especially after watching Nico go through it. It's a shame that the Vazquez family lost our spot on the Assembly. We were the only ones who spoke up for reforms in our systems. I say we get rid of this immortality completely."

"I'm sure the end of immortality will come soon enough —whether we want it to or not."

"Ah yes, the mortals' assault on this earth will likely do us all in soon enough."

Mateo shook his head with an amused smile.

"Speaking of the end of the world," Camila continued. "I've been hearing rumors that Petra is on the move. Have you heard the same? Maybe you can hunt her down, kill her, and finally sever that connection of yours so you're not the weak sibling anymore."

"En serio? Did you really need that last part?" Mateo questioned. "Anyway, yes, I've heard, but she's not an easy witch to track. She still has a following, you know?"

"That is right... And I imagine they're hiding her. Well, maybe you and Liam should give your Fated a break and put some effort into hunting Petra to finish things once and for all."

"What do you mean 'give our Fated a break?'"

"Oh, you know what I mean..." The suggestiveness was heavy in Camila's tone. "Remember that the woman is mortal and she must be able to use her legs for at least a few more years, now. Besides, I still have yet to meet her and I'd love to host her at my home for a few days."

"Whatever," Mateo grumbled. "But yes, the day will come when you can finally meet her in person. I've told her about you and I think the two of you would get along."

"I'm sure we will, plus I'm excited to interact with a mortal who seems to have no intention of exploiting our kind. It's quite rare, you know."

"Excellent. We'll have to arrange something. Oh! There was one more thing I wanted to ask you..."

"Yes?"

"Your ability to see into someone's past. Do you know if you're able to access it, even if the individual is not? Have you ever tried it on someone with amnesia or someone who might have a... magical block on their memories?"

"Well... I can see the past of people with amnesia. But if they're under a spell or curse... I'm not completely sure. Why do you ask?"

"Oh um... Just curious. Have a good night. I'll talk to you later."

"Let me know when you're ready to tell me the truth. I love you. Bye."

"Love you too."

After hanging up the phone Mateo took a deep breath trying to relax himself as he ran his fingers through his hair. He, Liam, and Amara figured Amara's nightmares were most likely flashbacks and she'd been remembering them more and more since reducing her medicine.

From what she did explain to them and the state in which she'd wake up from those nightmares, Mateo figured that whatever she'd experienced was traumatizing and that could be why her grandmother put a block on those memories. He hoped that if his sister could see Amara's past, the men could better understand what she went through and help her cope. He also wondered if maybe there could be some information that could help with her training.

Mateo looked down at his watch to see that evening had already arrived at it'd be best for him to get back to the house to assist Liam with Amara's training.

"I better return to them. Hopefully Liam didn't goof off too much today."

# FORTY-SIX

Petra's temporary residence was a penthouse on the Vegas strip. After her followers located her and woke her from a comatose state, they brought her to the bustling, touristic city, that also acted as a hub for the shady dealings of their world. There also existed a strong community of humans who knew of the supernatural and worshipped them. The same way she viewed many of her followers, they were simply a means to an end.

As Petra lounged on a loveseat, Samuel sat not far away at the bar in the penthouse with a bottle of vodka in his hand ranting about Haze. While Petra was working on regaining her strength, Samuel had spent that time obsessing over the vampire who sold him out.

"Haze is im-fucking-possible to hunt down..." he griped. "Maybe if I wreak havoc at that fucking club of hers that she's been neglecting to hide from me, it'll bring her out of whatever hole she crawled into."

"And piss off more than half of the magical world? You know every heathen loves that place," Petra challenged. "Even *you* are not crazy enough to do that. Besides, it has been months and you are still brooding about over being betrayed by a vampire? What did you expect to happen?"

"Do not speak to me like that, Petra, unless you intend to pay extra," Samuel replied without looking at her. "Haze and I have an... *understanding*."

"It sounds like that 'understanding' might be one-sided."

Samuel shot to his feet and his brows were tense with anger. "Keep it up and-"

"Do not threaten Petra!" One of her followers interrupted him and held a knife to Samuel's neck.

Ignoring the human, Samuel directed a question at Petra. "Why do you allow these pests into your space? They're obviously also idiots considering this one is attempting to threaten me."

The follower let out a bloodcurdling scream and the feeling of his hands dissolving. Petra watched and shook her head with disapproval.

"Please, Samuel... Show him some mercy." Petra's plea was unconvincing, her tone dry and noncommittal.

"What?" Samuel chuckled. "This is my favorite spell. It's a fun go-to."

"Well, you need that energy to help me restart our Palisyfum hunt. Even with the passive approach we've been taking using mortals' technology, there's been no progress. I've restored enough of my strength to get by and now it is time we take a more aggressive approach. That Palisyfum will be key to completing my spell."

An excited Samuel released his spell. "About damn time!"

"I'm glad you're excited. You can do our transport to Masoncrest."

"Why there? I've already told you the only useful information that came from there was realizing that my brother is still alive and he and Mateo are likely on the run with their Fated and possibly Haze. I only surmised as much because when I tried to get into the Palisyfum's home or near her roommate, I was incapable. The only answer would be that they put a protection spell on both and considering my brother and Mateo are weak right now, I imagine they used the Palisyfum's blood since I can't break it."

Samuel pushed himself away from the bar and stood to his feet. "Who would've thought my sensitive idiot of a brother would be smart enough to cover so many tracks? The other people at the university who supposedly worked with her were useless. Those three clearly did a much weaker version the Taylor family spell and seemed to have modified the memories of everyone who knows the Palisyfum."

"Remind me of that spell again."

"Our family spell in its strongest form can modify the memories of every living thing in the world. I assume Liam and Mateo mustered up enough strength to do that to anyone who came in contact with their Fated knowing that you or I would make our rounds. Now, everyone has some bullshit story about them all getting job offers at some other university and moving there together."

"Thats fine," replied an unfazed Petra. "I still have a few ideas on how this trip will aid our hunt."

CHAPTER

# FORTY-SEVEN

Amara and Mateo were in the office of the home while Liam was off to make contact with his family so that they wouldn't be worried about the lack of contact and him severing the connection that would allow his mother to track him.

"You are progressing at amazing speeds, amor!" Mateo commented with a big grin on his face as he watched Amara use magic to put together a broken wine bottle. She figured that the best way to practice controlling her magic was to do exercises that required the utmost precision, and that approach was working.

"Right?" replied an energetic Amara. "And it's like the more I've gotten a grip on this magic stuff, the more I've been able to read from grandma's spell book. I'm still inter-preting it, but I think it might help me figure out a way to allow you and Liam into her house."

"There's no pressure. I wouldn't want you to risk removing the protection completely just to allow the two of us into the house. We are fine here in this duplicate of our Masoncrest home."

"I know, I know... It just that not all my memories from that house are bad. There are things I wanted to show you guys, like my room and stuff, but in person instead of just pictures..." Suddenly, Amara perked up even more with a wide smile. "I also found something else that was super exciting!"

Mateo looked at his Fated and couldn't help but adore every bit of her, especially when she got enthusiastic in the way she was at that moment, it brought his heart a warmness he didn't know possible.

"What is it, mi alma?"

"Well... I came across this one spell that I think can restore my memories! It's um... It's exciting... But also terrifying."

Mateo's face fell from gleaming to concern immediately and he took her hand. "Amara... I know you want to know more about your past, but-"

"I know," she interrupted. "Like I said, it's also terrifying because even if you and Liam haven't said it aloud, I know you've been thinking the same thing I have about my nightmares. You think they might be those memories that my grandma blocked off. Right?"

Mateo slowly nodded. "I know you don't remember much from them, but what you have remembered... the flashes of the imprisonment and torture... Maybe we should be careful about-"

"Mateo, these memories have been kept from me without my consent! I'm already aware they will be bad, but they belong to me, they are somewhere in my brain, being withheld. Do you know what the feels like?"

"I don't, but there are some memories that maybe we should allow to be forgotten. Especially based on the way you wake up from those nightmares. It's really, really bad."

"You don't think I know that? But you know what's worse than 'really, really bad?' Not knowing a damn thing about my parents or what happened to them. My grandma gave me the generic line of them dying in an accident, but based on my nightmares, it's obviously a lie. I need to know the truth of what happened!"

"Amara, please... Just give it some more time. You're doing great with magic, but we need to make sure a spell like this, that involves dealing with the brain, is as stable as possible. We also need to be prepared for what might show up in those memories."

"But Mateo -"

"Trust me, you'll want to think about this... You just might unlock memories you don't want. There are some I wish I could get rid of."

Amara reached out to place a comforting hand on Mateo's cheek. "Your mom?"

He sighed and nodded as his expression fell.

"That's also why you're still taking that potion, right? The one that keeps me from interacting with your powers?"

Again, Mateo nodded. He hadn't been having many visions after he and Liam fought Petra and since then, his visions were rare and inconsistent. And before they finally met Amara, most of those visions were about her.

In the months that they'd been together, Mateo only had a handful of visions—the one about Samuel coming to get Amara and more mundane premonitions about daily occurrences such as meals or smaller interactions with Amara or Liam.

"I can't risk seeing you-" Mateo choked up at the thought and he didn't need to finish the sentence for Amara to know what he was referring to.

Amara wrapped her arms around his waist and pulled

him in for a tight hug as she leaned her head against his chest. Mateo, though he could be uptight at times compared to Liam, was often relaxed under his proper demeanor. However, the warlock was cursed with a memory that would haunt him and his relationships forever.

"I know," Amara said softly.

Mateo took a deep breath and pulled away so that he could look at Amara's face as he gently rubbed her cheek with his thumb. "How about we get back on topic and return to your training?"

Amara looked up at him with a grin. "I *do* have something else fun that I wanted to try."

"Oh? You are full of surprises today. What is it?"

"Okay, so don't make fun of me for trying something like this, but I could not resist."

"Now I'm really looking forward to this. Show me."

"Alright, so here it goes..." Amara kept her hold on Mateo and closed her eyes as she went into deep concentration. A warm energy began to fill the room, circling the two of them and as it picked up speed, their feet hovered off the floor and the pair began floating.

Amara felt the movements of Mateo's chest as he attempted to silence his chuckling.

"I said don't make fun of me. I thought it'd be fun."

"I'm not... making fun... of you, amor... not at all." Mateo's attempt to give Amara assurance was unconvincing as he continued to laugh.

"Tell the truth." Amara was smiling herself, unable to keep up her offended act for long.

"I'm not! Really, I'm proud of you. I'm proud of how far you've come so quickly. You are an incredible woman, Amara."

Amara's heart fluttered and she looked into his deep brown eyes, taking in Mateo's sincerity. He and Liam had similar, yet distinct effects on her. However, they both felt like home. Mateo came with a smolder that triggered a fire deep in Amara's belly, enveloping her in a warmness that felt both safe and invigorating.

"Oh shit!" she blurted, realizing she'd lost concentration for too long. Before Mateo could stop it, they both fell down. He was on his back and Amara was on top of him.

"Mateo! Are you okay? I'm sorry, I-"

"There's no need to apologize." He reached up and held her face, admiring it. From her brown skin, to her wide nose, to her full lips, to her tightly coiled hair, everything about the woman he was looking up at was perfect to Mateo.

"What?" Amara asked. "Are you still getting used to this weird thing with one of my eyes being purple? It's been a couple months now. I thought about contacts, but-"

She was cut off when Mateo pulled her in for a deep kiss. As the two of them went on, Mateo moved his hands from Amara's face and began to explore her body. Heat came over both of them and Amara was the first to break the kiss as her lips made a path to his neck.

"There's more that I've learned," she whispered before snapping her fingers and removing Mateo's shirt and jeans.

"You never cease to amaze me." Mateo snapped his fingers and Amara was completely nude. Her clothes were neatly folded on the chair just a few feet away from them. He gave her a wink and said, "I'll teach you that one day."

"I'm telling you now, Mr. Vazquez, I'm going to need a lot of practice to learn such a complicated spell."

Mateo placed his hand on the back of Amara's head and turned them over so that he was on top. Between placing soft kisses down her body, he spoke to her. "I'll be sure... to give you... plenty of lessons."

Amara gasped and her back arched when Mateo's mouth latched onto one of her nipples and he used his fingers to toy with the other. He circled and flicked his tongue on her sensitive bud before switching to the other one and Amara began to release more audible moans.

She looked down at him with a small smile on her face as his kisses trailed lower until he reached her bare core. Mateo started by kissing and gently sucking her inner thighs as he fingered her and when Amara's spasms turned more frequent, his lips met her lower ones.

Mateo enjoyed eating her out and he had a sense of pride that he was the first one who gave Amara that experience. From her taste to her sounds to the way her fingers would tangle in his hair and she'd pull it as her back arched from the bliss he put her in, Mateo received his own pleasure from the act. The feeling of her thighs shaking on each side of his head as she approached her climax emboldened him and he sped up his movements.

"Mateo!" The sound of her saying his name when she hit her orgasm never failed to set him off and by the time she was coming down from her high, she opened her eyes to see him hovering above her and already positioned at her entrance.

Smirking up at him, Amara held her hands against his chest to stop him and the pair were suddenly in an accent chair in the living room.

"Impressive," Mateo muttered, before placing kisses on her body as she straddled him. Amara pulled away to get down on her knees in front of him. She held his member and licked up and down his length before taking him into her mouth.

Mateo's head fell back and he let out a groan of pleasure as Amara's head began to bob. He felt her open her mouth wider and when she took him further down and started choking on him, he forced himself to stop her as not to come too soon.

Bringing her back up to his lap, Amara again straddled Mateo and she eased herself down on him. She slowly rocked her hips to get into a rhythm and had a loud outburst when Mateo slipped the tip of his finger into her ass.

"Do you like it, amor?" he rasped and in response, Amara nodded and started bouncing up and down his dick.

Mateo thrusted his hips up to meet her as he continued to finger her from behind and he could feel from the way she spasmed and the way her wetness was starting to coat his groin that Amara was enjoying it.

"More," she moaned and Mateo added a second finger while she continued to ride him. "Oh fuck," Amara let out with a shaky breath and her body vibrated at her climax.

Sensing her fatigue, Mateo lifted Amara up and turned them so that she was sitting at the edge of the chair with her legs on his shoulders while he held on to the back of it for leverage and pounded into her.

It didn't take long for his own body to start trembling when he hit his orgasm and came inside of her.

Before he could collapse, the two of them were teleported to Mateo's bed and they lay there together.

"We'll... clean up soon... I promise," he whispered through his exhausted breaths.

"Thank you," Amara replied softly, with her eyes closed. "... my love."

The last part was barely audible, but Mateo heard it. He knew that it wasn't the equivalent of her saying those three words he and Liam wanted to hear so badly, but it was the first time she'd gone as far as using that term for him.

And it made the moment with her that much more cherished for him.

"I THINK we should consider telling some of our family about Amara," Mateo suggested. He and Liam were sitting out in the backyard while Amara was inside their house studying. "She's becoming more antsy about unlocking her memories and I think either my sister or your younger brother could help."

"What do you mean?"

"Well, she was telling me this morning about how she may have found a spell in her grandmother's book that could unlock her memories. While I'm sure Glenda was powerful and Amara is learning quickly, she still has a ways to go and I don't want to risk her mustering up an unstable spell, especially considering that her mind is involved."

"My sister can look into the past," Mateo continued. "And I know that your little brother inherited that strong trait that only comes along every few generations, right? He can quite literally get into someone's head and look at their memories, as well as other aspects of their mind. One of these options will at least provide us a controlled environment."

Liam scratched at his facial hair, a nervous tick he'd developed now that he was growing it out for the first time in his life, mostly because of the underlying, yet overwhelming stress of Amara being hunted.

"You make a point... However, while I do think my younger brother, Gabe, would be perfect for this, he would never keep such important information from my mother.

And with her being on the Assembly, I don't expect it would go well if she knew."

"That's right, your mother, she..."

"The Assembly will always come first for her, no matter what," Liam finished. "It's part of the reason Samuel ended up the way he did."

"Well then, I think we should try our luck with Camila. As you know, my family has no problem keeping secrets from the Assembly."

"Yes, but it's not just the Assembly from whom we need to hide this."

"You're right, it is a risk. But the chances of her sharing are so low... And if she can help us unlock Amara's memories..."

"You know what?" Liam as he abruptly stood up straight. "We have to stop doing this. This exact thing is what got us in trouble before. We need to stop making decisions about Amara without consulting her."

Mateo let out a deep breath and stepped back to turn toward the shack. "You make an excellent point, Liam. Let's just bring this to her."

The two of them walked through the door that led into their duplicate house, but it was oddly silent and they sensed a lingering energy that matched Amara's magic.

"Amara!" Liam called. He grew more worried when he realized he wasn't hearing her thoughts when they entered the house. "Amara! Love, where are you?!"

Both men quickly searched the house for her and Mateo's heart stopped when he reached the shared office and found a passed out Amara.

"Amara!" Mateo shouted urgently when he saw her laying on the floor. He rushed up to her and immediately checked her. She was breathing, but unconscious.

Suddenly, Liam appeared in the room, just as panicked as Mateo. "What happened?! What's wrong with her?!"

"I just came in here and she was like this." Mateo scanned over the room and his eyes landed on the spell book sitting on the table beside Amara. It still appeared blank to him and Liam, but Amara was becoming increasingly able to read it as she unlocked more of her powers.

"Look," Mateo pointed at the book. "That spell I told you she was thinking about. She may have-"

Amara's phone rang and when the men saw it was Cameron, they quickly picked it up and hoped he could be of some help.

"Cameron!" Liam answered. "Your timing is impeccable, Amara-"

"Have you heard from Evelyn?" he interrupted. "I've been trying to call her for days and can't get ahold of her."

Liam and Mateo exchanged a confused glance.

"It can't be anything too urgent, right?" Liam whispered to Mateo. "We put that protection spell on her using some of Amara's blood and I'm certain neither Samuel nor Petra are strong enough to get through it, let alone any weaker beings."

"Unless that weaker being is a human. We couldn't repel them, remember? Otherwise, she wouldn't be able to interact with anyone."

"But we accounted for the possibility that Petra might send one of her human followers after Evelyn and repelled anyone baring that cultish mark."

"Unless she sent someone else..."

"Hello," Cameron called from the other side of the phone. "Have you heard from her? And why are you picking up Amara's phone?"

"About that..." Liam started. "Amara is unconscious right now."

"What?" Cameron began chuckling. "Too much training?"

"No, we believe she tried a spell to unlock her memories and it's put her in sort of a coma."

"M-memories?" Cameron's fear was palpable from his tone.

"Yes, she said she found a spell in her grandmother's book and-"

"Oh no..." Cameron cut in with a gasp. "I'm on my way now."

# FORTY-EIGHT

**LATE FEBRUARY 1993**

Young Amara was playing with her rabbit Chel in the backyard of her parents' house. Her dark brown hair was in plaits with yellow ball bows at the top and white butterfly clips at the bottom. She'd built an obstacle course that the black bunny went through with supernatural speed and Amara laughed with amusement. From the back porch, her parents watched her with smiles on their faces, happy to see how much fun she was having.

Amara's mother, Victoria Jenkins, had shoulder-length dark brown natural hair that she wore parted down the middle. It was summer time and she often wore flowing sundresses that fell below her knees and she'd even make Amara matching sets. Today, the two of them matched with a sunflower pattern.

Amara's father, Miles Jenkins, was a tall man with a brawny build. He kept his hair cut short with his hairline perfectly-shaped. His warm ebony skin was without blemishes and his hazel eyes that covered his purple ones were more pronounced in contrast.

"That was great work, Chel!" the girl complimented, scooping the rabbit off the ground. "Now, I'm going to make it harder and you can try that next."

"Hey, baby girl!" Miles called, walking over to his daughter. "Why don't you give Chel some rest? She looks tired."

"No she's not." Amara stubbornly shook her head. "If she was tired, I would know, right? You said that we are connected... like in our brain?"

"It goes deeper than that," Miles explained. "You know how grandma has Xivan, I have Cora, and your mom has Roz?"

The little girl nodded.

"They're what some people call familiars, but we call them companions. We are connected to them from birth. What they feel, we feel and vice versa."

"You already told me that, daddy, and that's how I know Chel isn't tired. Look!" Amara held the rabbit up to show her father that she was still full of energy, but Miles knew that it was Chel's effort to satisfy Amara.

"I'm not so sure about that. You see, it's going to take some years for the connection between you two to build, and then you'll have a more nuanced understanding."

Amara scrunched her face up. "Nuanced? What's that word?"

"Hmm..." Miles held his finger to his chin thoughtfully and crouched down to meet his daughter at eye-level. "It means when something is more complex than can be explained."

"Oh, okay?" the child replied.

Miles patted Amara on the head with an entertained smirk. "Still don't understand, do you?"

Amara shook her head. "No."

"Well..." Miles stood back up straight and stretched his arms out. "You'll have plenty of time to understand what I mean while we're on this road trip."

A big smile grew on Amara's face and she ran over to take down the obstacle course. "I can't wait! I'm going to meet more kids like me? And you'll have grown up friends like you?"

"That's right, honey!" Victoria called out when she heard her daughter. "We've got to hurry up so that we get there in time to meet everyone before they close things down."

Miles turned to his wife and walked over to her as skepticism decorated his face. "Are you sure we're doing the right thing? I mean, maybe we should consider what my mom was saying. She's really against it."

"I understand, love." Victoria held her husband's face. "But it's a risk worth taking. This entire time, we thought we were the last of our kind—my parents were hunted down by soldiers serving the Assembly, with me being the sole survivor... I was lucky enough to be fated to you, and so I found more Palisyfum in you and your mother... But when I first heard that there was this community, it gave me hope —hope that we wouldn't have to keep hiding."

"But what if it's a trap?"

"I get your concern, but you met Claire and her husband. We confirmed that they are both Palisyfum! I don't think they would set us up like this."

"What if we at least leave Amara behind with my mom? Just to be safe. And then we can come back and get her."

"It's not that simple. They move camps and we won't be able to leave for a while—they can't risk people going in and out. Learning of Claire's existence was pure luck. We just so happened to be doing spells within proximity of each other and our powers resonated with one another... If we leave Amara here, it may be a year or more before we see her again."

Miles sighed and leaned against the railing on the deck. "I don't want to be away from her for that long either... Claire and Arthur were nice and I didn't sense any bad intentions with them."

"See! And we're still allowed to have contact with your mom, if she doesn't hear that established code between us, she'll know something is wrong."

"You do have a point," Miles agreed. "It *would* be be nice proving her wrong if all goes well. And I'm feeling optimistic for the first time in a long time."

"Thank you for being open to this, love." Victoria pecked her husband on the lips and rubbed his cheek. "There's also Amara... I feel horrible about isolating her like this. A life of hiding isn't a life at all. And I want to give her a better one than what you and I had."

"Hey!" Miles chuckled. "My life wasn't too bad. I knew at least five people other than my parents growing up."

"That's three more than I knew," Victoria countered. "And Amara will actually have kids to spend time with instead of putting all of our companions through obstacle courses."

"You say that like the companions on that compound won't also fall victim to her tests."

"I can't argue with that, knowing our stubborn little one."

• • •

Amara sat in the back of the van with Chel in her lap, petting the rabbit's soft black fur. Her short legs that hung over the seat were swinging as she hummed a tune that her mother would often sing to her. Across from her in the back of the van was her mother, who looked at Amara with a small, peaceful smile on her face. At the front was her father who was driving them to meet with the other Palisyfum he and Victoria had met.

"Are you excited, Amara?" Victoria asked her daughter.

"Mhm," she nodded happily. "I'm going to meet other kids like me. I can finally meet people other than you, daddy, and grandma."

"That's exactly what we want for you, honey. We want to make sure you don't grow up as sheltered as your dad and I were. We have to be safe, but that doesn't mean you shouldn't have a life outside of us."

Amara smiled before her face fell and she looked back down at her rabbit.

"What's wrong, Amara?"

"Do you think grandma and Xivan are going to be lonely without us?"

Victoria sighed and reached out to take her daughter's hand. "They'll be okay, Amara. And don't worry... We can call them regularly."

Amara pursed her lips, still looking down at Chel as the rabbit slept peacefully. "Okay..."

Victoria leaned back in her seat and kept her eyes on Amara. She knew how close the little girl was with Glenda and she felt guilty about leaving them behind, but Victoria also wanted a better life for Amara—one where she could at least interact with other Palisyfum children her age and grow up with them.

As the ride went on, Victoria finally relaxed enough to go

to sleep, but Amara's excitement was too strong for her to do the same. The child had daydreams of what her new life would be like playing with other kids and she wondered if their rabbits would be willing to do obstacle courses like the ones she built for Chel and the other familiars in her family.

"You doing alright back there, baby girl? Your mom went to sleep, didn't she?"

"Mhm," Amara hummed. "How much longer until we get there, daddy?"

Miles chuckled and shook his head at his daughter's excitement. He hadn't seen her like that for some time.

"Not much longer. Just count back from one million and we will be there."

"One million?" The little girl gasped. "I don't know if I can count that high!"

"Of course you can! You could count to a billion, too, if you tried. Why don't you try?"

"That's too many." Amara crossed her arms and pouted. "I'll start with one thousand."

"I'll take it!" Miles chimed.

Amara began counting aloud, but she stopped when she noticed her mother's eyes turn purple without changing back. Her parents were always serious about keeping their eye color hidden, even when they were home alone with just each other.

"Mommy, your eyes," she said, pointing to her. However, Victoria did not respond and simply stared ahead blankly. "Mommy," Amara repeated, waving her hands in front of her face.

Suddenly, the van came to an abrupt stop and when Amara looked toward the front seat to search for her father, there was no sign of him.

"Dad!" she called, but she was met with silence. With the lack of responsiveness from both of her parents, Amara could feel in the pit of her stomach that something wasn't right.

"What's going on?" Amara turned to look down at Chel and saw that the rabbit had woken up and appeared uneasy. It hopped out of her lap and around in a circle urgently before going over and hitting her paws against the back door of the van.

Amara followed and before she could reach for the handle, the door flung open and there stood a red-eyed man towering over her. Immediately, the girl felt a chill go up her spine and she quickly turned and ran over to her mother who was sitting still and staring blankly.

"Mommy," she grabbed her mother's shoulders and shook her. "Mommy! What's happening-"

The child was cut off when she was snatched out of the back of the van by the red-eyed man who held her up and examined her with pure greed in his eyes. "So, my plan worked... And this time, there's a child. I wonder what I might learn from you in my experiments. And your blood, it smells slightly different... Perhaps because your powers haven't fully developed."

"Get away!" Amara held up both hands and a spark of energy flew from her. It was enough to catch the red-eyed man off guard and he dropped the girl, but he was otherwise unaffected.

"Mommy! Daddy!" Amara struggled to get up and ran back to the van to try to wake her mother up, knowing she'd be strong enough to defend them. "Mommy! Please, wake up!"

"Yes, Vicky," Alistair said. "Why don't you wake up?"

Her eyes still purple and her expression blank, Victoria finally moved and looked at Amara.

Amara tilted her head to the side and tensed her brows. "Mommy?"

"Come, child... We are going to change the world." Victoria picked up her daughter and carried her out of the van. As she started walking toward Alistair, Amara struggled against her, trying to pry herself from her hold.

"No! Mommy, please!" she cried. "He's scary."

"We're changing the world," Victoria replied calmly, seemingly in a trance. "We will save everyone."

Feeding off of Amara's panicked state, Chel's body contorted and the rabbit bounced over to Victoria, attempting to disrupt her path.

"Would you look at that..." Alistair laughed as he lifted the rabbit by the nape of its neck and held it up. "Vicky, where's yours?"

Victoria's arm slowly rose straight behind her and she pointed toward the back of the van where her familiar was sitting calmly under the seat.

"Excellent. I will feed on that one later. And as for this one..." Alistair looked over Chel. "It is weak, I can barely sense any magic here. It'll do for a decent snack, maybe."

"What are you doing?" Amara cried. "Mommy, what's happening? Where's daddy?"

"I told you, honey. We're changing the world."

Amara suddenly felt a sharp pain in her heart and she lost the strength to struggle against her mother. Her eyes glided over to where Alistair was standing and the vampire had already sunk his teeth inside of Chel. As the rabbits life left it's body, Amara could feel energy leaving hers and she rested her head on her mother's shoulder. More tears fell from her eyes before the girl drifted off to an unconscious state.

"I AM GOING to be the most powerful creature who ever existed!" Alistair gleamed as he fell into the large leather seat that sat in the middle of the warehouse. His headquarters were located in an abandoned warehouse with a basement that acted as a holding place for Amara, Victoria, and Miles. The three of them were unconscious after being captured by Alistair and his small pack of vampires.

"You sure you won't fuck this one up too?" questioned one of the vampires who served him. She was leaned against a wall across the dark room. Her silhouette showed long braids that fell to her waist and from the darkness, her red eyes pierced through.

"Oh Haze..." Alistair sighed. "My once favorite creation continues to mouth off. If you think that'll make me give you the pleasure of death, you are wrong. I much prefer watching you starve and forcing you to comply."

"And if I threaten to find Petra and tell her about your betrayal? She hired you to secure Palisyfum for her and you've been simply practicing your own greed. Will you kill me then?"

Alistair's eyes flashed purple and Haze appeared in front of him as he held her in the air by her neck. "Have you forgotten that I *own* you?" A glowing chain from Haze's neck that attached to Alistair's wrist became visible. "I may have gotten carried away with my last few Palisyfum experiments, but I was still able to absorb some power from that previous batch. You weren't a match for me before and you're definitely not a match for me now."

Haze used her sharp nails to claw at Alistair's arm for

him to let her go, but it was ineffective. Before he fed from his first Palisyfum, she was at least able to cause him some injury, but now, Alistair's skin had become impenetrable.

Alistair cackled at Haze's struggling. "That's useless. And even if you somehow got beyond the handful of locations I allow you to go to, and told Petra what I did, do you really think she'd be able to do anything about it? She's been weakened since the nineteen-seventies!" He threw Haze across the room back into the wall where she was standing before and she remained on the ground, motionless.

"However..." he continued and pointed down toward the basement where Amara and her parents were being kept. "Petra thought she'd regain her strength by rounding up a few Palisyfum and using them for some spell or potion to get back to who she was... But you know what she conveniently left out when telling me about these beings I needed to hunt? That when a vampire feeds from them, it's like magical steroids! Some of her intelligence must have left with her strength because she had to predict that I'd figure it out at some point. She was even dumb enough to give me that amulet to control Palisyfum."

"Why so quiet now?" Alistair pouted playfully and strolled up to Haze before crouching down to look over her. A smirk pulled to the left side of his face when he realized why she wasn't moving. "Damn!" He clapped his hands and stood up straight again. "Even that child's little rabbit supercharged me! You can't move because all of your bones are broken just from me throwing you across the room, isn't that right?"

Haze simply stared up at him.

"Aw, giving me the silent treatment now? Don't be so upset. You are still one of my creations and you heal slightly better than other vampires. You'll be fine and ready to do my bidding in just a few days... In fact, being the generous god that I am, how about I give you a snack to speed up the process?" Alistair snapped his fingers and moments later, the sound of a man's muffled screams could be heard getting closer to him and Haze.

Only able to move her eyes, Haze honed in on what was approaching her. One of Alistair's henchmen was dragging over a young man—appearing to be in his late-teens or early twenties—who was bound at his wrists and mouth covered with duct tape. Haze's red eyes glowed with even more intensity the closer they got.

"This is hilarious, Haze! Remember when I first changed you and you thought you'd be able to survive on animal blood because you didn't want to kill humans? Now look at you! You're so starved that you could probably lunge yourself at this young man to feed, even with your bones crushed! Speaking of which..." Alistair crouched back down again and held Haze's face. Her mouth was bloody and her teeth were also destroyed from when he threw her across the room. "Let me show you another ability I've developed thanks to this Palisyfum blood I've taken."

Alistair placed his hand over Haze's mouth and his eyes went purple. A few moments passed and when he removed his hand and pulled Haze's lips apart, it showed perfectly-white, straight teeth.

"You know what? That God the humans worship has nothing on me. I mean, look at your teeth now, Haze. After your transformation, they were still a bit crooked and off-white, but now..." Alistair bought his fingertips to his lips for a chef's kiss. "Beautiful! Much better than the old ones! Give me her food." Alistair waved over the henchman who dropped the young man's body into his arms.

"See this, Haze? Am I not—as the humans would say—an 'awesome God?'" he mocked, holding the man in front of her as he struggled. "You can smell it, can't you? He's terrified! And his blood, it smells appetizing, does it not? The prime of youth, a man of twenty-one, had an... eventful birthday celebration that resulted in him and his four friends going missing!"

The hostage winced and tears fell from his eyes at Alistair's account.

"However, I must say, Haze, some of your colleagues got a bit greedy and fed on them while you were gone on what you thought was your little runaway, but I saved the birthday boy for you. Here!" Alistair placed the young man in front of Haze, so he was close enough for her stretch her neck out and reach him. With inhuman speed, Haze sunk her teeth into him and his struggling subsided with the more she drank.

"That's a good girl," Alistair said softly, rubbing her head as she fed. "Build your strength. We have a lot of work ahead of us."

On the floor of the cell, Miles held Amara in his arms while Victoria stood opposite the two. Amara was still unconscious following the energy she exerted trying to resist Alistair and her companion rabbit Chel's death. Victoria—positioned in front of the bars of the cell—stared expressionless at the dark basement hallway.

In the hours since they'd been captured, Miles had already pleaded countless times with his wife, begging for an explanation as to their predicament, but her only words for him were, "we're going to change the world" without further discussion. From their interaction with Alastair,

Miles deduced that the vampire already had Palisyfum abilities. And considering Alastair was strong enough to seal Miles' powers, he likely fed from numerous of the Palisyfum line.

An often mild-mannered man, the anger within Miles was growing by the minute and for the first time in his life, he felt true rage. After gently placing Amara on the floor, using his shirt as a pillow for her, Miles rose to his feet and approached the love of his life. Victoria had always had a natural purity about her, a softness that spoke to Miles' own. However, her entire aura in the moment felt unrecognizable—it was cold, detached, unfamiliar yet some small part of her was still present—as if she were only a shell of herself.

As Miles neared Victoria, waves of energy scattered throughout the entire warehouse basement where the cells were located, similar the feeling of strong winds.

"Victoria," Miles said sternly. "Tell me what has happened here? Who is that vampire? Why does it seem like you're serving him?"

"We're going to change the world," Victoria replied emotionlessly, as she had since they were captured. Still her eyes remained focused on the hall outside the cell.

"What do you mean by that?"

"We're going to change the wor-" Victoria was cut off when Miles grabbed her by her shoulders and turned her around to face him.

"Victoria!" he boomed. "Answer me! Tell see why we are here. Why did you betray us?"

The energy in the space grew more intense until the building began to shake and debris started falling from the ceiling.

"Victoria!" Miles repeated. "Snap out of whatever the

hell is going on with you. What happened with Claire and her husband? We met them! They were real! Where are they? This is the exact address they told us to go to!"

"We are going to-"

"Look at where we are, Victoria!" Miles interrupted as he began to shake her and his eyes glowed purple. "How the hell are we going to change the world from here? What's happened to you? You're not you!"

A tear fell from Victoria's eye while her demeanor remained otherwise despondent and she continued to say, "we're... going... to change... the world..."

"Please, Victoria!" Miles begged, a crack in his voice accompanying his glossy eyes. "Please, answer me, please just snap out-"

He paused when he felt a pair of small arms wrap around his leg and looked down to see his teary-eyed daughter looking up at him with the plea clear in her face.

"Daddy, I'm scared," Amara cried. "Something's wrong with mommy. Don't hurt her."

Immediately, his shoulders slacked and he let out a long breath before placing a comforting hand on Amara's head. "I won't hurt her, Amara. I'm trying to see what's wrong. Your mother isn't like herself... You notice it too, don't you?"

Amara's eyes slowly inched their way up toward her mother's face, but as soon as she met Victoria's despondent gaze, Amara quickly looked to the ground by her father's foot. Without speaking, the girl nodded and Miles could feel her tears starting to dampen his pants leg.

"Come here," he said softly as he lifted his daughter into his arms and walked back to the other side of the cell. "It's okay baby girl, we're going to figure out what's wrong with your mom and help her, okay?"

Amara nodded a sniffled agreement as her father wiped the tears from her face.

"So..." Miles began. "We first need to figure out what type of sealing spell was used on us because we need to undo it. From there, were can help your mom."

"D-daddy... why did they seal our powers? What will they do to us?"

Miles gulped. He'd hoped his daughter's inquisitive nature wouldn't come out in their current emergency. Considering they were of the Palisyfum line and had been captured alive instead of immediately killed and drained, he figured the worst was afoot. Usually when Palisyfum were captured, they knew that it was in their best interest to immediately die before they'd be forced to be used as blood farms or experimented on.

However, Miles couldn't imagine doing that to his daughter or even his wife who'd presumably betrayed them. He was determined to get them out of their predicament without resorting to killing his loved ones.

Miles kneeled down to meet Amara at eye level and placed his hands on both of her shoulders. Looking straight at her with a determined expression, he said, "They want to hurt us really bad. And with our current state, they probably will be able to do so. But I want you to know that you're getting out of this alive. That, I can promise with every fiber of my being. And when you do, I want you to live a full life, Amara. Not the one in hiding that we've forced ourselves to for so long. Do you understand?"

At the time, the young girl didn't understand the weight of her father's words, but she knew that she would need to be strong. She wiped away her own tears and halted her crying.

Amara nodded with a sniff. "I understand. I can be strong."

For the first time since they'd been taken prisoner, a small smile came to Miles' face and Amara felt truly comforted.

However, the moment was short-lived when the sound of clapping and a maniacal laugh interrupted their moment and Miles and Amara turned toward the hallway to see red eyes glowing in the darkness. Immediately, Miles stood up and pushed Amara behind him as she held on to his leg.

"Would you look at that! A heartfelt father-daughter moment," Alistair taunted as he looked down at them from the other side of the bars. "'I can be strong,'" he added, mocking Amara who in turn held her father tighter. "You can't be 'strong' while hiding behind your daddy like that."

"Do not speak to her," Miles spat.

"And what will you do about it?"

"Do you really believe you're unstoppable, bloodsucker?"

"Do you really believe you're able to threaten me?" Alistair challenged.

"I have no need to threaten you. At the end of this all, you will die. That is a promise."

"Who says it has to end? You're the last of your kind, as far as I know. I have to keep you going for all eternity. You can't get old and fizzle out like the others. Promise me that, okay?"

"The others?"

"Yes," Alistair replied as his eyes flashed purple. "Clearly, I have fed from your kind before. You don't remember Arthur and Claire who told you about this wonderful, safe place? I know all about you Palisyfum. I've studied you in great detail. You'd be perfect, godlike beings if you weren't created just to be ingredients. I mean, sure you learned magic and all, but there still exist ways for even the lowliest of creatures to control you—like this amulet of mine..." Alistair held up a gold chain with an oval-shaped pendant hanging from it. "Though too bad it only works on one at a time."

Miles looked over to Victoria. His anger toward her had completely dissipated, turning into a mix of guilt that he actually believed she betrayed them and anguish that she was being controlled. Alistair had in his possession an amulet that the creators of Palisyfum created to manipulate them. While many were destroyed in the Palisyfum uprising, a handful still remained.

After returning the amulet to his pocket, Alistair continued. "There's also the lack of immortality despite your blood being used to achieve just that for those three warlock families... it's always so frustrating when you Palisyfum get too old and die. Even worse that I can't just turn you into a so-called 'bloodsucker' like myself."

"If you've fed from our kind, then you already carry our power. What more do you need?"

"Do you think I'm stupid? The more I feed from you Palisyfum, the more powerful I get. Why should I ever stop?"

"If you're so smart, then you would know of the risks."

"I'm smart enough to mitigate those. Like I said, I've studied your kind in great depth and... Why the fuck am I explaining myself to you?" Alistair snapped his fingers and Miles appeared beside him with his hands and feet bound.

"Daddy!" Amara cried and ran over to the bars of the cell, desperately reaching through them toward her father. "Give him back!"

Ignoring Amara, Alistair turned to Miles. "Since you're

so curious about how I can continue this work, you'll go first. And I've got grand p-" The vampire was cut off when Miles head butted him hard enough make him stagger back.

Alistair chuckled and grabbed Miles by his face, analyzing the way his forehead was bleeding with the force he'd used. "Did you really think that would do anything?" the vampire said before taking Miles with him.

Amara's cries could still be heard in the background as her father was taken away.

# FORTY-NINE

"Liam!" Mateo shouted franticly as the two of them stood over Amara. Hours had passed since they found her unconscious and they'd put her in the bed while they desperately searched for a spell or potion that could wake her up. However, Liam stopped out of nowhere and Mateo noticed the way he appeared hauntingly pale. "What's going on, Liam? I thought you said you couldn't hear her thoughts! Now you look like you're in distress. And I can feel it!"

"It's her memories." Liam began sobbing and tears started rolling down his face. "I can't hear much, but I can feel them... I've never experienced a pain like this, Mateo. Not ever."

"That's it!" Mateo boomed. "All these spells we have tried are useless and we still can't read her grandmother's spell book. I am contacting my sister."

"What will your sister do? She can look into pasts, but she can't wake Amara! What about my mother, I'm sure there's a spell for this."

"Your mother is part of the very Assembly that orchestrated the execution of Amara's people! I don't trust it. And besides, my sister is at least a Vazquez who is at full strength. It will help."

"Amara is our Fated, maybe my mother wouldn't betray that just for the Assembly! Please! It's our best bet to get her out of this and it hurts, Mateo. If this is what I'm feeling, then I know it's even worse for her."

A few moments passed of Mateo analyzing Liam's face before surrendering. "Fine. If it's our best bet. It's a risk we'll have to take. Cameron should be here soon and..." Mateo was interrupted by urgent knocking on the door. "That's him."

"Amara!" Cameron called out when he entered the home after Mateo let him in. "Where is she? Everything has gone to shit! Please tell me you guys have figured out something. Shit. Shit. Shit!"

He and Mateo quickly went upstairs to the room where Amara was in bed and Liam was in a chair next to it holding her hand.

"Do you hear anything?" Cameron asked and Liam shook his head as he winced.

"I only feel... pain."

"Damnit! What are we going to do? Fucking Glenda! There are other ways this could've been handled and now here we are! Exactly what she feared..."

"We can take her to my mother. I'm sure she can help-"

"No!" Cameron protested. "Not a Taylor... Liam, I trust you as an individual, but we will not bring Amara to someone on the Assembly. Let alone the head of the body. They are at the root of all this shit."

Liam shot to his feet and stormed up to Cameron. "She's our best bet and my mother would never betray us!"

"I don't trust it. The Taylors played a role in the decision to slaughter Palisyfum!"

"My mother is not like that!" Liam snapped. "And we don't have many options. Amara is in so much pain and we need to help her as soon as possible!"

"And bringing her to the Assembly will make things worse! Are you ready for them to kill-"

"Do not finish that fucking sentence!"

"Both of you shut up!" Mateo shouted. "Let's see my sister. She's a Vazquez at full strength, not on the Assembly, and may have a chance at waking Amara. Or at least giving us answers. She can see into a subject's past."

"Fine," Cameron huffed. "We will go with that. And it needs to be done quickly because we have another crisis on our hands..."

"And that is?"

"Evelyn," Cameron gulped. "She's been taken."

"What do you mean Evelyn's been taken?" Mateo questioned with disbelief.

Cameron held up his phone, showing a message from Evelyn. In it, there was a photo of her bound to a chair and knocked out with text that said, "Bring Amara back to Masoncrest. We know what she is."

"That's it? Was there anything else indicating whom it could've been behind this?"

"No," Cameron replied, shaking his head. "That's all there was."

"I know one thing," Liam added. "It's not Samuel. There would've been a lot more boasting there. But still, this doesn't mean that Petra isn't involved."

Mateo stroked his beard as he looked down thoughtfully. "What about James? He and Evelyn have been dating and he's obsessed with magic."

"Possibly," Liam agreed. "However, when and how could he have found out the truth? Especially given that we changed everyone's memories of Amara. Then again, even with Amara's blood, we *did* rush the spell. And I'm not powerful enough alone to do it."

"Fuck!" Mateo shouted. "Everything is going to shit. So much is broken and it all needs to be fixed urgently."

Cameron looked at Mateo, then Liam, and ultimately to an unconscious Amara. "Amara must come first here. She's the key to all of it. Handing her over to them unconscious like this means they will surely win. If she's awake, then we could have a chance... Unless her memories are too much."

Liam, who'd been looking down at Amara while Cameron was speaking, snapped his gaze back up to meet Cameron's eyes. "What do you mean by that?"

"Thanks to this blood promise with Glenda, I can't go into much detail, but Amara's memories were locked away for a reason... What she went through, it was... traumatizing to say the least."

Mateo straightened up, pulled his phone from his pocket, and started walking toward the door. "Well then, now that we know Amara absolutely needs to be awakened before anything else, we must contact my sister. She can examine pasts. Surely she'll be able to see Amara's."

"But what will that achieve as far as waking her?" Liam asked.

"Maybe... just maybe if we know the details of the past that Amara is experiencing, we can figure out a way to get through to her... connect with her somehow and pull her out of this state."

"That is a good point, Mateo. You know, my younger brother works quite well with minds, so perhaps we can see if he's willing to take a walk into her head."

"I wouldn't bet on it," Cameron replied. "With the lock that Glenda put there, the only one powerful enough to see into Amara's past would be another of the Palisyfum line... and there are none."

"Can we catch a fucking break?" Mateo exclaimed before throwing his phone across the room. "What the hell are we supposed to do now? Every time we seem to so much as think we have a plan, we learn that Amara's grandmother has done something to thwart it long ago."

"This is why I say we go to my family!" Liam suggested. "Even if we are not the level of the Palisyfum, we still have a lot of power. And we know the mind more than any being ever could or ever did. We may be able to outmaneuver Glenda with the help of my mother and siblings."

Mateo shook his head in response. "But it still runs a high risk. We can't bring our Palisyfum Fated to a member of the very organization that implemented the indiscriminate execution of-"

"Then what will we do?" Liam interjected. Low vibrations went through the room as his eyes faded to gray. "We could at least try to trust my mother. Amara's life depends on it..."

"Wait..." Cameron lifted a cautioning hand and turned to Mateo. "We should still call your sister, Mateo. I think she can still help."

"But you just said that Glenda-"

"I know what I said, but... we do have one more option. And I think I can track it down... Just... Just contact your sister, Mateo. And have her meet us outside of Lenrod City."

CHAPTER

# FIFTY

"So, to what do I owe the visit of two useless warlocks?"

With a calm demeanor, Haze watched Mateo, Liam, and Cameron slowly enter the living room of the small safe house where she'd been hiding and healing herself since the incident with Samuel months prior. Haze was seated on the left end of a wide sofa with her legs crossed in the chair. Her decaying arm was wrapped in an off-white cloth with symbols on it that neither warlock recognized and in her healthy hand, she held a smoothie of sorts that was a deep red color.

"... or should I say, to whom?" Haze shifted her gaze to focus directly on Cameron who was several feet behind with an awkward half smile and mopey eyes.

"Haze," Cameron greeted. "You look like you're healing up nicely, despite how much energy you expended."

"This is not a casual visit, so quit acting like it is one," Haze replied sharply before cutting her eyes back at Mateo and Liam. "Where is the girl? Do not tell me that despite my

396

efforts, you two still ended up losing her to Samuel and Petra."

"No," Liam replied quickly. "Amara is somewhere safe..."

"Ah, so the girl realized that she was safer without two painfully weak lovers holding her back and left you behind?"

Liam's nostrils flared as his expression turned into a glare at Haze. Before he could say anything, Mateo spoke up.

"We're here because we need your help, Haze."

The vampire's lips pulled until they reached an open-mouthed smile and she cackled as she shook her head. "And why the hell would I help you?"

"Because Amara's life depends on it."

Immediately, Haze ceased laughing and turned to Cameron with a questioning brow raised. "What does he mean, Xivan?"

"He means what he says, Haze," Cameron answered. "We need your help to save Amara."

Haze gritted her teeth and looked away. Her voice shifted down to almost mumble. "I've already done that."

"And you'll do it again. Just as you've done before."

"Please," Liam added with a wince. "She did some spell from her grandmother's journal and passed out. Now she won't wake up. We think she... She might be reliving the memories that were locked away from her."

Haze closed her eyes. Despite spending nearly a half century as a vampire, she still found herself with human tendencies that were unnecessary for her, including exhaling her distress. Haze reflected on what she knew of Amara's past—those months when their lives overlapped and the girl and her family were prisoners to Alistair, the vampire who'd enslaved her.

"We're begging you here, Haze," Liam pleaded. "We're running out of options... Amara is running out of options."

Avoiding eye contact with her unwelcome guests, Haze finally parted her lips to respond.

"How many times must I save the child? Why must she constantly end up in these predicaments? First with *him*. And now she's being hunted by *the* Petra Vallis and Samuel-fucking-Taylor. To fuck with her luck even more, despite being fated to two warlocks from the elite three families, she ends up with the weakest of them all. Maybe the girl is just not meant to live-"

"Shut up, Haze!" Cameron snapped. "Would you just admit that you care about her? Glenda has been gone for years now and you've maintained contact with me to keep tabs on Amara. You and I have even grown close enough for me to find you here. You don't need to continue lying to yourself, and it's not like you were convincing anyone else before that. You care about Amara. You always have."

Haze's eyes finally connected with Cameron's as her mouth went agape for seconds—seemingly attempting to form words, but nothing escaping her until she closed her mouth, swallowed and tried again.

"I... simply did what Glenda asked of me... I wanted the power of the Palisyfum, and she promised that in exchange for the night that... well... you know I can't say it."

"And what about that time you retrieved that prism, despite Glenda being unable to pay you."

"We had a fruitful working relationship and I wanted to maintain it."

"And when you came to deliver that prism and strategically made it so that Amara would find you before Glenda could detect you. I know you were angry when she interrupted..."

"Enough!" Haze shouted. She brought the deep red smoothie she'd been holding to her lips and drank it down in three big gulps before slamming the cup on the table next to her sofa. "Your fucking point has been made. Now... tell me what I need to do."

Cameron huffed and shook his head. He mumbled under his breath, "Why'd it have to take convincing in the first place?"

"Did you think I wouldn't hear that, rabbit?" Haze slowly stood up, crossing her arms as she walked toward Mateo and Liam with pursed lips and narrowed eyes. "Tell me what you need from me."

"To come with us," Mateo replied quickly. "We have Amara in a safe place not far from here."

"You left the girl alone?" Haze's tone was low and cold.

"I said she's in a safe place. And my sister, Camila, is with her."

"I hope your sister is more powerful than you... Even then, she probably wouldn't be enough for Samuel should he track wherever you've hidden the girl."

"Myself, Liam, and Camila used Amara's blood when we casted the cloaking spell for where they're hidden. All that power combined, even Samuel wouldn't be able to find the place."

"Humph... Back to my question... what do you need from me?"

"Your memories," Liam replied. "If we could just learn the details of Amara's past, it could give us a chance to connect with her deeply enough to break her from the comatose state she's in."

"While there might be a block on your ability to tell us

what happened, there's not a block on your memories in the same way Glenda blocked Amara's..." Mateo added. "Where I can see into the future, my sister can experience pasts."

"And you want your sister to look into my memories to glean what Glenda was hiding about Amara's past?"

Mateo nodded urgently. "Yes! We can use that information to connect with her or figure out some other way to wake her."

"Humph. And you think that'll work? Glenda was smart enough to put enough barriers up as part of that blood promise so that the thoughts on Amara's past can't be read out of me either."

"But memories differ from thoughts. And while memories can be altered or even guarded, the experiences themselves cannot. The way my sister's power works when it comes to pasts, is it leverages the way your body physically stores memories. Remember the word I used? *Experience.* My sister doesn't just see pasts. She experiences them in the way the person being read has."

Haze tilted her head to the side while sizing up Mateo. "Then why hasn't she tried that on Amara? Or even Xivan... though he wasn't..." she immediately stopped in an involuntary move before cursing under her breath. "Fucking blood promise."

"She did," Mateo confirmed. "But the block on Amara's memories scrambles it. And while she was able to pull some very limited details from Cameron, we couldn't get enough that would allow us to connect with Amara as deeply as we need to."

Haze shook her head as she walked toward the door ahead of the men. "I'm still not convinced this is the right approach, but if there's even the slightest chance that it could wake the girl, then I'll help you."

"Let's go."


HAZE, Mateo, Liam, and Cameron arrived to the abandoned apartment building where they were keeping Amara. It was isolated enough that they wouldn't have to worry about non-magical beings stumbling upon the building by accident and had enough units so that if Samuel or someone else hunting Amara found it, they had a spell in place to continuously change which unit Amara was being kept.

The entire thirty-minute drive from Haze's safe house to complex was silent, and that silence continued when they entered the building and made their way up the steps until Liam's curiosity got the best of him and he spoke up.

"Haze..." Liam called softly. "If you don't mind me asking... How hasn't Samuel found you by now? You betrayed him when he had Amara in his hands. I'm sure he wouldn't have just let that go. And he is the type to hold a grudge, trust me."

"Samuel?" Haze said with a chuckle. "Samuel is busy trying to make sure he gets whatever payout he can from Petra. And besides... No matter how unruly he might be, he'd never kill me."

"What makes you so sure? Is it because you hold the power of a Palisyfum?"

"Well..." Haze turned and looked down at Liam who was a few steps behind her with a smirk on her face. "Similar to the Palisyfum, it is the influence of what many refer to as a flower."

Liam's brows tensed in response, but he didn't pry

further. While he knew his twin brother to be an indulgent man, he also knew him as the type who lacked leniency, especially when it came to disrespect. However, his dynamic with Haze seemed different. They worked together on a mission as important as hunting Amara and he didn't immediately hunt down and kill the vampire after she betrayed him.

His musings came to a stop when they arrived on the sixth floor and stood in front of an empty wall.

"Revelare," Mateo said and a door was revealed to them. It was barely a studio apartment, made up of only two rooms—the main living space where Amara was in a bed furthest from the door and a bathroom that set off to the left of the entrance.

His sister, Camila, stood there at the door. She looked just like him—dark brown eyes with tightly curled hair to match and light brown skin, though she differed from her brother with freckles that spread across her face cheek-to-cheek. Camila examined Haze as the four of them entered the room. Even if Mateo didn't already explain who Haze was, Camila would've sensed something abnormal about the vampire. While her magical energy wasn't immediately apparent, Haze had an intimidating air about her that told Camila's natural instincts not to challenge her, even in the vampire's injured state.

Mateo extended his hand to introduce Camila. "Haze, this is my sister. We must be quick, so if you could let her..." he drifted off as he, Cameron, Liam, and Camila watched Haze completely ignore him and walk toward the bed where Amara was laying in a motion that appeared instinctual.

Her eyes on Amara the entire time, Haze approached and sat on the bed next to her. She studied Amara's tightly wound face and the twitching of her bottom lip. It was clear she was in distress. And from what the men explained to her on their way to the hideout, Haze was sure that Amara was reliving the events they'd experienced together. And as a result, Haze began having flashbacks of her own.

She reached over to hold Amara's cheek. Haze hadn't known the feeling of a beating heart in decades and her years as a vampire had surpassed her years living, but in that moment, she felt a pain in her chest. She then noticed a warmness brimming her eyes before it fell down her cheek.

"Damnit," she whispered through gritted teeth. "What is it with this one that makes me..."

With her back to the others, they couldn't see the blood tears running down Haze's face, though they could sense a tenseness in the air.

"Haze," Cameron called as he slowly made his way toward her. "We don't have time to wait."

"Take another step closer and I will turn you back into a rabbit," Haze said coldly.

Cameron huffed his annoyance. "Then what do you want?"

"Give me fifteen seconds. That amount of time is incon-sequential... And I'm not asking."

The room fell silent. Camila looked to her brother inquisitively, and then to Liam who read her thoughts.

*This is odd behavior of a vampire. Is she... unsettled? Can you read her mind?*

Liam shook his head in response. While he in theory *could* read Haze's mind, the vampire had a constant block that seemed to act as a passive defense spell that kept him from getting into her head.

Meanwhile, Haze took the fifteen seconds to clear her face of tears and any proof that they had fallen from her eyes. She took one more look at Amara before getting up and walking up to Camila.

"Camila Vazquez," she said calmly. "I don't think introductions are necessary. Your brother tells me you can see into pasts, and I'm sure he's already told you everything he thinks he knows about me. I understand that the plan here is for you to look into my past where it overlaps with Amara, correct?"

Camila hesitated before she nodded. Haze's presence shook her. Even in her current state, Camila could sense Haze's power. She never encountered a being outside of the three major families she thought could overpower her, and the unknowns of a vampire with the power of the Palisyfum created a wildcard that at one point seemed impossible. "Y-yes."

"Simple enough. I'll let down my guard just for this purpose."

"G-great! That's great. I just need to um... to take your hands in mine." Camila lifted both of her hands with the palms up and Haze placed her cold hands in Camila's.

"I'll also be joining," Liam added. "While Camila is going through your memories of that time, I will be reading her mind."

"Right. So once you close your eyes and let your guard down, Haze, I am going to close my eyes and connect with you. It's not like the Taylor family where they're reading your mind. It's more like the parts of your mind, body, and soul that have experienced your life will tell me what they went through... and I feel it as if I were in your body when you had those experiences."

"Fine," Haze sighed. "Then we should do this sitting down... let's hope you have a decent enough pain tolerance, Camila Vazquez... You'll need it."

# FIFTY-ONE

"No!" Camila cried. She had just begun her search into Haze's past and the physical sensations were too much for her. The burning of flesh, breaking of bones, prodding with knives and needles—even with Camila jumping around to different parts of Haze's past as she searched for when it overlapped with Amara's, the horrors seemed endless.

Liam held her shoulders firmly, offer Camila some stability. Her shirt grew wet with her sweat as she experienced what Liam could tell were traumatizing memories of being subjected to various experiments conducted by a sadistic vampire.

Several minutes passed before Camila finally communicated with him in more coherent thoughts.

*This... little girl... looks like... a small... Amara,* Camila thought and Liam let out a brief sigh of relief that she'd finally reached the memories they'd been searching for. *She is with her parents... but her mother... something isn't right... Vampire... Alistair... amulet... to control Palisyfum... he already has Palisyfum powers... wants more...*

The slight relief Liam experienced was cut short when Camila let out a bloodcurdling scream and immediately let go of Haze. Her breaths were short and rapid and she grabbed at her chest, looking at Haze with wide eyes that signaled a mix of disbelief and pity.

"What happened?" exclaimed a panicked Mateo as he rushed over to his sister with a cup of water in hand. I know you were having a hard time with her past, but I've never seen you fall out of one like this before.

Unable to answer her brother, Camila attempted to slow her breathing by taking deeper inhales and longer exhales before accepting the water from Mateo and taking small sips in between long breaths.

Haze—whose body was visibly tense from reliving some of her worst memories—eyed Camila curiously. "She made it through snippets of what were essentially live autopsy, but shattering every bone in the body is what scared her... Just when we'd gotten to the correct time, too."

"Hermana," Mateo said as he rubbed Camila's arm. "Que pasó? Can you go back in?"

"I— I'm sorry," Camila choked out. "I d-don't think I can... I can't handle it."

"What do you mean?" questioned an agitated Haze. "Take your break and then come back into my head. I lived through the pain. So can you."

"No... Not when I can't focus... And that pain... I don't know how anyone could... under those conditions."

Haze's gaze sharpened as she leaned toward Camila who in turn cowered back and grabbed her brother's arm. "What do you mean you can't focus? You're immortal. Older than me. And you can't handle a bit of pain?"

"A *bit* of pain? You were dissected while conscious... and then this memory... Every bone in your body..."

"Was shattered," Haze finished. "That was life with Alistair. And even worse when he was high on Palisyfum blood."

"What do we do now?" Liam let out with a shaky breath, finally breaking his silence. "This was..." He gulped as tears brimmed his eyes. "This was our last hope."

"It can't be!" Cameron cried out. He was sitting on the bed next to Amara holding her hand. He used his free hand to grab Amara's shoulder and started shaking her. "Wake up, Amara! Please... We're here. The people who love you are here with you!"

To his surprise, he felt a cold hand squeezing his arm to stop him and Cameron turned to see Haze looking down at him. "That wasn't our last hope... We still have one final option."

The confusion was brief before Cameron saw Haze's eyes fade to purple and panic came over him again. "Haze, no! Not that... You don't know if it'll work."

"What else can we do, Xivan?"

"It could..." Cameron lowered his voice even more—aware that they were under the watchful eyes of Mateo and Liam. "Kill her. In fact, the spell depends on her meeting a certain death."

Haze spoke calmly as she removed a knife from her pocket and opened it. "Move, Xivan."

"No."

"What's happening?" Mateo questioned when he saw the way Cameron began spreading himself across Amara's body, as if covering her from Haze.

"Xivan," Haze repeated. "Move."

"Y-you can't possibly-"

"Move!" the vampire shouted and that was when chaos ensued.

Mateo and Liam sensed the imminent danger and attempted to summon magic that was immediately locked down by a purple-eyed Haze. Cameron was thrown off of Amara, colliding with the wall beside the bed and knocked unconscious. Camila—who had more power than Mateo or Liam—was still recovering from the physical trauma of experiencing Haze's past and couldn't muster enough energy to attack.

Getting on top of Amara, Haze held the knife tightly with both hands and her arms extended above her with the blade facing Amara's chest. The sounds of Mateo and Liam shouting were drowned out by a beating sound in Haze's ears resembling that of a heart.

"You better be in there, old witch," she whispered before bringing down the blade, driving it toward Amara's heart.

Just when the knife pierced Amara's skin, Haze was blown away across the apartment as a light grew out of Amara's body and a high-pitched noise deafened everyone in the room.

Amara's eyes flew open and she immediately sat up with a deep breath. A bright light disrupting her vision, Amara blinked several times and rubbed at her eyes until her vision was clear enough to see where she was.

Coloring pages and cutouts of flowers from text books and magazines lined the off-white walls. On the dresser to her right sat a pot with an orchid and ice cubes atop the soil, the one large window setting a backdrop. Looking up, she saw the ceiling fan moving at its slowest speed. A small smile came to her face that it wasn't making the annoying squeaking sound it often did on its highest level. To her left was a small nightstand with a cup of water and a jar containing the medicine for her nightmares.

Finally turning her gaze forward, Amara saw a familiar figure sitting at the end of her bed. The woman wore a black bonnet with pieces of her gray hair sticking out along with a dark green nightgown that was too big for her small frame. The smoothness of the dark brown skin on her arms could be seen as they rested on each side of her. Her head turned as she admired the orchid, Amara could see the half smile on her face.

Even without the view of her side-profile, Amara would've known the woman sitting there. Tears flowed from her eyes and she gulped before she said...

"Grandma?"

# FIFTY-TWO

"Grandma?"

Watering eyes blurring her vision, Amara stared at the woman, who sat just a few feet away from her on the edge of the bed. The woman turned her body toward Amara to give her a full view of her face. Her round eyes were low as she gave her a lazy smile and nodded. "Hello, Amara... It's been a while."

"Grandma!" Amara cried and crawled over to Glenda to wrap her in a tight hug. "I don't understand. How is this possible? How are you here?"

Returning Amara's embrace, Glenda answered, "It seems the protection spell I put on you was triggered... I put a piece of my own life into you so that if you were to face imminent death, you'd have one more chance."

"I... died?"

"Well... thanks to this spell, you haven't."

After they parted from the hug, Glenda looked to Amara's face, expecting to see her still teary-eyed with a small smile. However, she was met with a purple-eyed glare more intense than she had ever seen from her granddaughter. There was an immediate shift in the energy between them. A witch as keen as Glenda knew exactly what was afoot and before it could happen, she grabbed hold of Amara's arm.

"Amara..." she said calmly as waves of energy flew past her, powerful enough to blow the bonnet off of her head and reveal her gray and dark brown hair. "I can feel your anger. You must calm down."

"Calm down?" challenged and exacerbated Amara. "You're telling me to calm down? You kept everything from me. Palisyfum *lotus*? You manipulated my memories! Hid them from me! And my powers! You kept me locked up and hidden away my whole life! Nothing! I knew nothing about myself. It was all a lie. My dreams that you made that 'medicine' to suppress, they were memories! They were *my* memories! And you told me nothing! You knew!"

"Please, just calm down, Amara," Glenda pleaded. "I've never seen you like this."

"Tell me everything!" Amara snarled. Even for Glenda—who'd raised Amara through her most difficult times—had never seen her show such aggression. It was an unusual sight, and one she couldn't have imagined she'd ever witness.

"It's easier if I show you..." When Glenda reached out toward her, Amara pulled back defensively. "Do you really think I would hurt you?"

"What if you try to manipulate my memories again? What if this is a trick to make me forget everything?"

"Please, Amara... I won't do that. You've already tapped into your powers. You've seen much of your time as a prisoner and while reconnecting with those memories has affected your behavior, you're not shut down like you were in the past."

"What do you mean by that?" Amara questioned. "Shut down like how?"

"Shut down in a way anyone could expect of a child who went through what you went through... That's why I put the block on your memories, Amara. You couldn't function with them."

"I don't understand. Couldn't function?"

"You were in a constant state of shock and despondent, unless you were triggered," Glenda said. "The few times you would sleep—often once you body refused to stay up—your slumbers didn't last long because of the nightmares. Screaming, crying, fighting... You destroyed your room more times than I could count..."

Her eyes wide as she trembled, Amara dug her fingers into the bed comforter as she listened to Glenda.

"Amara, I didn't want to manipulate your mind in the way that I did, but it reached a point where I had to. You were like that for months... And no matter what I did, as long as you had access to your memories, there was no improvement. Finally, you had one final outburst where you nearly destroyed the house, it injured Xivan and I... That was when I realized that you'd never be able to live a healthy life if you continued to have access to your memories from that time. So I put a spell on you to block them... And when you kept having nightmares is when I created that medicine to erase those dreams and calm you down."

"I..." Amara exhaled a shaky breath. "I hurt you and Xivan?"

"You were in a lot of pain, Amara. You didn't do it intentionally."

There was a pause of silence before Amara's sobbing broke it and she repeated, "I hurt you and Xivan?"

With tensed brows, Glenda analyzed her granddaughter. Everything about her demeanor was screaming distress—trembling, eyes darting around the room, tense shoulders, short and fast breaths. "It's okay, Amara," Glenda assured. "We were fine. Don't say you're doubting my abilities—clearly we were healed expertly."

Glenda's attempt at a light joke to ease the tension fell flat. There was another shift in Amara's energy—her distress switching from terror in its overtones to agitation once again.

"Was my whole life a lie? You hid everything. So much. There's so much I don't know about my life! *My* life!"

"If you just allow me to show you, I can reveal everything..." When Glenda extended her arm toward Amara, Amara again pulled away. She then stood up and began walking around the room, making erratic steps.

"No! I don't trust you to get into my head! You've ruined it enough! Tell me! Just say it! Tell me! Explain everything! No more of you using magic on my head!"

Concern decorating her face, Glenda watched Amara without saying a word—trying to figure out where and how to start. She was also worried about the behavior Amara was showing. She'd seen her granddaughter grow furious in the years of raising her in isolation, but nothing like this.

Clearly distressed, Amara dug her fingers in her hair before pulling at it as she continued to walk around the room. Her breathing was heavy and fast, the sounds of sobs escaping her with each exhale.

"Tell me!" Amara repeated. "Tell me! Tell me! Tell me! I saw everything with that vampire! And then Haze, she was running with me! Explosion! The vampire again... He had me. Then burning! Tell me the rest!"

Glenda cleared her throat before swallowing the lump

in it. Amara's erratic speech showed clear signs of her unnerved mental state. "Right... Haze helped me save you. In exchange for our power without the side-effects that Alistair dealt with..."

"I don't care about your deal with Haze! Tell me what happened in the escape! What happened to... that lady?"

"Y-you mean Victoria?"

"Yes! Her!"

It was clear that Amara's patience was less than thin and Glenda wasn't sure what her granddaughter was capable of in this state. But she knew that it was best for her to be transparent and get to the point.

"Your mother-"

"No! Don't call her that!"

Glenda's shoulders fell. "V-victoria... She didn't *choose* to betray you and Miles..." There was a brief pause at the sound of Amara wincing at her father's name. "She was being controlled by an amulet used against our kind. Most had been destroyed, but Alistair managed to find one. It can only be used on one Palisyfum at a time and Victoria was the target. So she lured you two. She didn't mean to, she just..."

Amara interrupted her grandmother, tears running down her face as she shouted repeatedly, "I don't care! I don't care! I don't care! I don't care!"

"Amara..."

"No! S-she still betrayed us! I don't... c-care about some a-amulet! If she loved us..." Amara sucked in a long breath through her nose to steady her breathing before she continued. "If she loved us, it shouldn't have worked, right? Why didn't she fight for us? She didn't fight for-"

Amara was cut off and stopped in her tracks when Glenda appeared in front of her and grabbed both of her hands. Looking into her grandmother's worried eyes up close, Amara couldn't bring herself to fight back, even with the boiling anger inside of her. "Please, Amara... Listen to what I have to say."

Her head trembling with the rest of her body overcome with emotions, Amara slowly nodded for Glenda to continue.

"Victoria *did* fight for you in the end. That memory you referenced about your escape, you said you felt a burning after the vampire, Alistair, recaptured you... That was your mother. She came in at the last minute and saved you... It resulted in her death as well, but she *did* break free of the control of that amulet in the end, and it was just in time to make your rescue a success."

Although the traumatic memories had returned to Amara, they were still jumbled and not fully clear to her. She replayed what she could piece together about the escape—Haze running away with her, Alistair attacking Haze and taking Amara back, the burning sensation when Alistair fell again and let Amara go. *'I'm sorry.'* The words were faint in Amara's chaotic memory, but following Glenda's explanation, it was all making more sense.

Several minutes passed while Amara calmed herself through breathing exercises and a light meditation to center herself. When she was finally able to find a small piece of calm, she spoke to Glenda.

"Grandma, there's something else I need to know...

"And what is that?"

"How did you die?"

Glenda let go of Amara's hands and sat back at the edge of the bed to look up at her. "Well, Amara... It's a continuation of the Alistair saga and even connects to what you're going through now."

"What do you mean?"

"My death was at the hands of Petra Vallis."

Breathless and in a shock deeper than she thought possible, Amara's mouth was open as her lips quivered to repeat the name. "Petra? Petra Vallis?"

"Yes," Glenda replied with a nod. "The same witch who is hunting you now."

"How do you know about that?"

"She's been hunting you for some time... I thought I'd gotten rid of her, but it wasn't enough."

"What do you mean?"

"Let me show you..." When she brought her hands up to hold Amara's head, Amara flinched away from Glenda. "It's okay, Amara. This time, *you'll* be in *my* mind."

Amara settled down and allowed Glenda to initiate the spell, sharing her memories with Amara.

# FIFTY-THREE

FEBRUARY 2003

Unable to hear anything beyond her own heartbeat and breaths crossing through her nose, Glenda rushed through the small house desperately, calling for her granddaughter.

"Xivan! I can't sense her," she yelled. "Where is Amara?"

When she reached the staircase, she paused at the feeling of pain in her chest and covered her mouth before she began violently coughing.

After wiping the blood from her hand on her nightgown, Glenda held tight to the rail of the steps and began descending them as quickly as she could. Once she got to the bottom, she made a path straight for the dining room table. On her way there, she grabbed a knife, tore a map of the United States off the wall, and snapped her fingers to light the candles in the dining room.

The sound of bones cracking could be heard approaching Glenda as Xivan shape-shifted from his rabbit state into the only other form he was cable of—a copy of Glenda.

Glenda huffed when she saw him take shape. "Must you play games right now, Xivan? Amara has left us. I need to find her!"

"I'm not playing games. You barely take me seriously when I'm in my natural form. However, when you're looking into a mirror, you're somehow more inclined to listen to me."

"Please, Xivan! Enough of that! I need to focus on locating Amara... I can't believe she'd do this! I know staying here wasn't easy but... but... I just needed one more day... not even that! I was going to tell her in the morning and now she's gone."

Xivan crossed his arms and sighed before replying. "Glenda, what did you expect? You kept her locked away here for a decade now. And as far as Amara knows thanks to the changes you made to her memories, it's been like this her whole life. That's not far off, either, considering when Miles and Victoria were still alive, they were also isolated here."

"No! I did it to keep her safe! She experienced what happens when our kind is exposed, and it traumatized her. There was no easy way to tell her. That's why it's taken me so long. But I'd planned to tell her. I was going to do it when we woke up. Now it's too late. She's gone..."

"Even though you're not at full strength now, do you have enough in you to do a tracking spell?"

Glenda gestured down to the map that she'd laid out on the table. "And what exactly does it look like I have here? Of course I'm doing a tracking spell."

Looking over the materials laid out, Xivan realized

Glenda was down an important item. "You're missing something of Amara's. I can get it."

Immediately, both Xivan and Glenda paused when they felt an intense presence just outside the house. As her familiar, Xivan could communicate with Glenda telepathically and was the first to make contact.

*Glenda, did you sense what I just did?*

*Yes.*

*Could it be that someone from the Assembly finally found us?*

*This presence is strong, but not Assembly strong...*

Glenda and Xivan both turned their attention toward the backdoor when they heard the creaking of the porch steps.

*Whomever it is, they were able to make it through my protection spell.*

"Am I seeing double?" asked an unfamiliar voice.

Mouths wide with disbelief, Glenda and Xivan looked to the front door and saw who the question had come from. Standing in the doorway was a blonde-haired woman with pale skin and unnaturally light blue eyes. Her frail figure was barely visible under the green dress that she wore, her eyes had dark bags under them, and her lips were dry and peeling.

Despite her decrepit appearance, it was clear the woman was a force to be reckoned with considering she'd made it through Glenda's protections over the house seemingly unscathed.

"I'm not seeing double," the woman followed up casually, scanning over Glenda and Xivan. "I forgot that you Palisyfum get familiars who can morph into you. Your species never ceases to amaze me."

"Who the hell are y-" Xivan was cut off when the

woman flicked her wrist and his body was thrown into a wall, knocking him unconscious.

Just when Glenda was about to summon her magic, she was overtaken by another coughing fit that had her hacking up blood.

*Look at how pathetic I've become*, Glenda thought to herself as she tried to regain her composure. By the time she was able to look up again, the woman was already seated at the end of the dining room table tapping her fingers against the surface.

"You clearly don't have much fight left in you," the woman commented. "Good. Getting past those protective spells took enough sacrifices. Now, let's get straight to the point, shall we?"

"I know who you are," Glenda said. She hid the blood that was on her hand by balling it into a fist and holding it at her side. "Petra Vallis of the Vallis family of necro-mancers. At one point, I heard you were dead, but I knew it couldn't be. Between your necromancy and the special privileges you get along with the Taylor and Vazquez fami-lies, there was no way."

Petra clapped in response as she leaned back in her seat. "Well, that was a much better introduction than I had planned for myself, so thank you for that, Glenda Jenkins."

Glenda wasn't nearly at the strength she'd needed to be able to fight Petra and live, so she needed to bide her time a she figured out a strategy. "Why are you here? What do you want?"

"Years ago, I sent Alistair on a mission to find whatever Palisyfum were left and bring them to me so I could restore my power. But it was my fault... Even though I promised him a taste of the Palisyfum, and warned of the risks of feeding on them too much, he still betrayed me for his own gain. Typical of a bloodsucker."

"And you think I'd go with you willingly?"

"Oh. I'm not here for you—you're all shriveled up and I can sense that you are missing a piece of your life." Petra waved her hand in a dismissive motion and got up to walk around the dining room until she stopped in front of a corner table with a photo of Amara sitting on it. "What I came for is the girl. The child whose mother killed Alistair..."

"You're out of luck," Glenda spat. "She died in the explosion that killed Alistair, along with her mother and father."

"Do not lie to me, old witch," Petra's voice reverberated through the room and sent a shiver down Glenda's spine. "I know that the child lives. You wouldn't have left that place without her. And besides, there were no signs—no magical signatures—indicating she died. Everyone else's residuals were there. Alistair, all his vampires except one, and two adult Palisyfum."

"I told you, the girl d-" Glenda was cut off when her mouth sealed shut and she was bound.

"I told you not to lie to me! And don't assume just because I'm not a full power that I'm incapable of incapacitating you. That bit of life you're missing has you weaker than me in this state. Let me guess... You put it inside the girl? Tell me, was it to save her life? Or a protection to give her another one?"

Following Petra's questions, Glenda's mouth was freed from the spell to talk, but she refused.

"Alistair's experiments weren't for naught, I will say that... He was missing a few pieces of the puzzle, mostly in magical history, otherwise he'd see... Your granddaughter, she's quite special. Did you know that?"

Glenda kept her lips firmly together and her gaze straight ahead, ignoring Petra's efforts to get her to speak.

"From your silence, I assume the answer is yes, you do know your granddaughter is special. She has a keen ability when it comes to... abilities. Your granddaughter has the power of powers."

Still, Glenda remained silent, the stubbornness clear in her face.

"You hear me?" Petra suddenly appeared in front of Glenda, her ice cold gaze piercing Glenda's. "You granddaughter can control and manipulate powers! She can absorb them, pass them to another, cancel them, combine them... The girl is the ultimate Palisyfum. All that magical DNA inside your kind... It all culminated to her. It's poetic, even... Considering she'll be the last one."

Glenda began straining, her face tense and redness showing on her brown skin. Veins in her neck became more visible and she struggled to get out of the seat.

Xivan had just awakened from his unconscious state and bolted toward Petra. However, her reflexes were too fast for him. Petra grabbed the knife that had been sitting on the table for the spell and sunk the blade into Xivan's neck. He immediately returned to his rabbit form, but the wound remained.

Using the split second that Petra was distracted by Xivan, Glenda initiated her attack. She grabbed Petra by both arms and sunk her nails into them. Petra's thin skin gave into Glenda's grip as her nails dug until they drew blood. Petra tried to fight back, but it wasn't enough to overcome Glenda's determination.

"Let go of me!" Petra shouted as she tried to shake Glenda off of her.

Summoning every bit of power that was still left in her, Glenda's eyes turned purple and Petra came under the burden of a significant weight that made it more difficult for her to move. Drops of blood from her arm began to gather on the floor between them. Glenda bit the inside of her cheek until it bled and spit the blood on the floor with Petra's before she began chanting.

Petra's moves grew more urgent when she realized what Glenda was doing.

"The hell are you doing, old witch? That spell will kill you!"

Glenda tightened her grip on Petra even more and started chanting faster.

Petra shrieked with agony—dust started to build up under her and she looked down to see that her body was dissolving.

"This still isn't enough to kill me! You're not at your best! You're too weak! This won't work! Let me go and I'll let you live! I only need that granddaughter of yours!"

By the time Petra finished her pleas, half of her body was gone.

"You'll die before you finish that spell!" Petra continued. "And all I need is one particle of myself to reconstruct! And then I'll just come for her again! This is useless."

Glenda finished the incantation of the spell and as the final pieces of Petra turned to dust, she said, "You may well come for her in the future, but you will not win."

"You're dying. I'll be speaking with you soon, Glenda Jenkins," were Petra's last words before disappearing completely.

Glenda's eyes remained purple after the spell. She couldn't risk wasting a drop of her final bit of magic by covering them. Before her body could register the toll that the spell had, she rushed over to Xivan. Sensing that there was still life in him, Glenda wiped the blood from her nose using two fingers and swiped it across the rabbit's back, making two parallel lines.

"Fate must align for this to work," she whispered to herself. The spell she was casting was the only way to turn a familiar into a full-fledged human. For it to work, Xivan's final moments had to align with that of a human within a three-mile radius whose body was still habitable.

With all she had left in her, the purple of Glenda's eyes glowed one last time and a small light expelled from Xivan's body. She watched it shoot out of the house as a single tear dropped from her eye before turning to pick up the rabbit.

"I know Amara..." Glenda said to herself as she held Xivan's corpse and limped up the stairs toward her room. "She'll come back. And she can't know I died in an attack... I just hope that... Xivan's soul has made it to another body... I hope... he'll be around to look out for her... As for me... Amara must believe I died in peace. She can't blame herself..."

After entering her room, Glenda made her final steps toward the bed before laying in the center on her back, her head rested on a pillow, with Xivan's body cradled in her arms.


## CURRENT DAY

By the end of the flashback, Amara was hysterical. She experienced it just as Glenda had. The panic of searching for Amara. The deep, intense regret she felt about keeping so many secrets from her. The pain of knowing that she had failed Amara. The remorse that she wouldn't be the person who told Amara the truth about everything. The determination she felt when she protected Amara one last time by fighting Petra.

"Grandma," Amara cried before falling on Glenda's shoulder while she in turn held her granddaughter. "If I was there, I could've... I could've done something."

"Don't blame yourself, Amara," Glenda assured. "This was my doing. I should've told you the truth sooner, I should've taught you to use your powers, I should've believed in you, believed in your resilience."

"But still..."

"But nothing. I am sorry, Amara... I truly thought I was doing the right thing by hiding your past from you. I hoped you could live a more normal life if you didn't know the truth. And by the time I realized I was wrong, it was too late."

"I left you and you died," Amara whispered.

Glenda pulled away to look Amara in the eyes. "None of it is your fault. If Petra is nothing else, she is tenacious."

"Speaking of her... you said she's a necromancer. And when you were dying, she said she'd see you soon. Has she been contacting you? Torturing you?"

Glenda shook her head. "No. A piece of me has still been alive all this time. In you. Through this spell."

"Then what happens next, grandma?"

"When I finish fading, you mean?"

Amara nodded.

"Then her inherited necromancer abilities can reach me, but it doesn't mean they'll work." Glenda tilted her head to the side and gave Amara a small smile. "I've still got some fight in me."

The minutes that passed after those words felt like an eternity, yet still too short for Glenda as she felt herself fading more and more. Reluctantly breaking the silence, she spoke to her granddaughter.

"Amara, I wish we could talk more, but there's not much time left. This spell uses the part of me that stored in you to restore your life. It'll be done soon."

"No! Please, I can kind of use my magic now. Is there anything I can do? I want to bring you back..."

With mournful eyes, Glenda shook her head as she maintained eye contact with Amara. "I'm sorry that's not possible..." She reached up to hold Amara's cheek. "But there is one last thing I can leave you with... Please, just give me your trust one last time."

Amara nodded without hesitation and Glenda brought her other hand up to hold Amara's face in both hands before closing her eyes and humming a tune that sounded vaguely familiar to Amara. It was the one her mother used to sing to her.

A light began to dance around Amara, leaving sparkles in its path and she could feel her tense muscles relaxing while energy within her that used to exist in pockets started to flow freely, now as an intrinsic part of her existence.

"It's time you realized your full potential, Amara..."

# FIFTY-FOUR

Mere seconds had passed since Haze stabbed Amara and triggered the bright light from her body.

Cameron was still unconscious and so was Haze following the blowback from Glenda's protection spell on Amara. There was a collective gasp followed by sighs of relief from Liam, Mateo, and Camila when Amara rose to a sitting position, seemingly unfazed by the attack she'd just experienced.

Mateo and Liam were over to her in no time, holding her hands on each side of the bed.

"You're awake!"

"Are you okay?"

"Are you hurt?"

"What did that vampire do to you?"

"Was it some sort of spell that repelled her?"

"I don't see any blood."

"No scars, either."

The onslaught of questions and comments came to an

immediate halt when Amara pulled both of the men toward her for tight hugs.

"It's me," she said through a shaky breath. "I'm back."

Elated, both men held her tight—Liam holding back tears and Mateo with his face buried in her neck.

"My love."

"Mi alma."

Letting go of the two men, Amara got out of the bed and went straight to Cameron and he woke up when she touched his forehead. Giving him a small smile, she nodded assuringly before walking across the room toward Haze and kneeling down over her. As she did with Cameron, Amara touched Haze's forehead and the vampire woke from her unconscious state.

Haze gasped when she opened her eyes to see Amara hovering above her. "It... It worked..."

As Haze continued to look at her in disbelief, Amara examined the vampire's arm that was wrapped in cloth with strange writing on it. With a whisper, Amara fluidly read the incantation on the bandage and it began to glow. Moments later the cloth dissolved to reveal Haze's fully-healed arm.

Getting up from her kneeling position and looking back at Mateo, Liam, Cameron, and Camila, Amara took a deep breath.

"I need to kill Petra Vallis."

Amara said the words with such conviction that both Liam and Mateo's mouths went agape. This was on top of a noticeable difference in her composure. In the few moments since she woke up, Amara maneuvered through the room with purpose, effortlessly using healing magic on Cameron and Haze before looking back at all who were there and stating such a considerable goal with confidence.

Mateo was the first to speak up. "Amara... Taking care of Petra is of course important, but you're different. Can you start by telling us what happened? How are you awake?"

"Grandma," Amara replied, her tone detached. "Another one of her... *preparations*. Now, we need to find Petra. Now I know a spell that can locate her."

As Amara turned away from them and started toward the door, Liam took her arm.

"Please, Amara!" Liam pleaded. "Please, can you give us more than that? I was in your head... or at least tried to be for part of it. You were in a lot of pain. And now you wake up and tell us you need to kill Petra. No explanation or anything. Please... Just give us more. Please... Tell us more."

Amara looked toward Haze then Cameron, thinking about all her grandmother revealed and the memories of them from her time with Alistair and her childhood with Glenda. Anger boiled within her, and she knew if she went on to explain aloud everything that she had learned, she'd have to deal with all the emotions that came with them. Thoughts began to run through her mind almost faster than Liam could keep up with.

*Everything is Petra's fault. No! It's the Assembly! They created Palisyfum. Then they wanted to destroy us. I was angry when I learned about that. It's worse now. My whole life was spent in hiding. My whole life I've been hunted. Petra is behind it all. She hired Alistair. Amulet... To control my mom and lure her with me and dad. Held us all prisoner. Experiments. Torture. Killed my dad. Escape. Haze helped. Then my... mom broke free and saved us. Me and grandma and Xivan. We were the last. I am the last Palisyfum. Petra killed grandma.*

Again, Liam's mouth went agape after hearing what he could pick up from Amara's thoughts. When he could feel

Mateo about to speak again, he put a hand on his shoulder. "I'll explain later," he whispered. "We need to help Amara."

"Did you hear it, Liam?" Amara said softly. "You understand?"

"I... I think so. But what about now?" Liam questioned and then gulped. "We saw Haze stab you in your heart."

Fidgeting with her hands, Amara shook her head quickly. "No. Haze isn't an enemy."

"I had to do it to wake the girl," Haze explained. "Otherwise, who knows how long she would have remained in that state. It was admittedly a bit of a gamble, but knowing how much Glenda cared for her and that she was the type to have a spell in anticipation of almost anything, I figured she'd have used *that* spell on Amara to give her a second chance of life should she face imminent death some day. It's a good thing I was right."

"Hey..." Cameron walked over to Amara, keeping enough distance as he could sense her need for space in that moment. "Did you see her, Amara? Glenda? Is that why you can... Is it why you can use your powers now?"

Amara nodded without saying anything. Although she continued to fidget with her fingers, her movements eased.

Cameron sighed with a small smile. "Finally, at least she made the right decision in the end."

"Cam..." Amara winced as she slowly looked up from her hands to him. "I saw everything. I know everything... How do I... What do I... Is there a way to bring them back, Cam?"

"No. But you know that too, don't you?"

"It had to be hard for her... for grandma... to know all these spells, have all this power... and to still lose everyone... I was so... I was so ungrateful!"

Cameron stepped in closer to Amara and held her arm. "You didn't know, Amara. You can't fault yourself for that."

"But I left you two alone..."

"Don't go there!" Cameron argued. "You say you saw what happened. If you were there, the outcome would've been the same, if not worse. Glenda—although her decisions weren't always the right ones—did everything for you. She wanted you to live. She still would've done the same thing. She still would've sacrificed herself for you."

"But if I knew magic. Maybe I could've helped."

"But you *didn't* know magic. Amara, please. Think about everything you've learned from what Glenda gave you. Does it really look like any of this is your fault?"

There was a long pause. Mateo, Liam, Camila, and Haze looked at Amara apprehensively.

Amara put her hand over Cameron's that was on her arm and squeezed it. "No," she said, shaking her head. "Petra... It's all Petra. I need to kill her, Cam. Not just stop her. Not incapacitate her. I need to *kill* her... Everything is because of her."

"You know you can't do that alone, right?"

"Right..." Amara looked at each person in the room, pausing when her eyes landed on Camila. "Mateo, is this your sister? Er— I mean, I guess I could just ask you... Are you Camila?"

Blinking several times, Camila nodded. "Y-yes. I'm Camila. Mateo's sister. It is nice to finally meet you, cuñada."

There was finally a break in the tension that came with Amara's awakening and she giggled nervously at the last word. "Oh! I... I'm not married to Mateo yet— I'm not married to Mateo and Liam, I mean... We're not. We will— I mean... I think... I don't know... I want... Er—"

"It's okay," Camila assured. "We sometimes use it even without marriage. But you are his Fated, so you are now just as much family to me as he is. I was brought here to help wake you, though I did fail."

"Oh! Right yes... I'm sorry we had to meet like this..."

"I am just happy you are alive."

"T-thanks..." Amara then awkwardly looked at Haze, unsure what to say to her, but she found relief when the vampire spoke first.

"That crazy witch Petra is planning to wipe out our food supply," Haze lamented. "I'll help you... Anything involving Samuel Taylor as a part of the plan is vulnerable to my persuasion," she added with a smirk.

"Do you think you could locate him?" Amara asked. "Even if Petra is hiding with him?"

"We don't have to worry about Petra hiding..." Cameron interjected as he pulled his phone from his pocket and showed Amara. "She's ready for us to come to her. They have Evelyn."

Amara's eyes went purple and waves of energy surged through the space, causing Camila to shudder with its intensity. Meanwhile Mateo and Liam grew more tense, the bond with Amara affecting them.

"Evelyn? How? Mateo and Liam put that protection spell on her! They even used my blood! I don't understand!"

"The spell only works if the individual has ill-intent or bares the mark of the cult that follows Petra," Cameron explained.

"Abduction isn't ill-intent?"

"Not if the interaction started as something other than that... Like a date."

"That's very specific..."

"Well, after talking it through with Mateo and Liam on our way here, we determined that with James' obsession with magic and the Palisyfum specifically—a shared goal with Petra—it's possible they may have conspired together."

"I can't believe James would do that to Evelyn..."

"His obsession with magic always seemed desperate, unsettling," Liam commented. "He was good at covering that side of himself."

"I see..." Amara had been avoiding their gaze for the past several minutes, but she knew it was time to tell Mateo and Liam everything. Now that she had full control of her magic and all of Glenda's knowledge, she knew that she would be at her strongest when in sync with her Fated.

"Hey guys," Amara said, turning her attention to Mateo and Liam. "Can we... Can we talk in private?"

"Of course!" the two said at the same time.

Walking over to the door of the apartment, Amara grabbed the nob and her eyes flashed purple before she opened it to show the duplicate of their Masoncrest home —a spell that took days to finish when the men cast it before.

The men looked in disbelief at their fully-manifested home through the doorway.

"We won't take long," Amara said to the others as she walked through the door and the men followed behind her.

SITTING in the living room of their home, Amara explained everything that occurred while she was passed out to the men—her memories coming back, Glenda's death at the hands of Petra, and Glenda transferring every bit of knowledge she had to Amara so that she could realize her full potential.

"Wait," Mateo raised a cautioning hand. "So Petra went from wanting *any* Palisyfum to *you* specifically? Why is that?"

"Well for one, grandma and I were the last ones left, and I was much younger than grandma but also..." Amara gulped before finishing. "It's for my ability."

"Ability?"

"Yeah... So do you remember when we first met? When we touched hands and I could see one of your visions?"

Mateo nodded.

"And Liam, do you remember when we first kissed and I could read your mind?"

Liam nodded.

"My ability is that I can manipulate abilities. If I make physical contact with them, I can use someone's special ability. I can also take it away and give it to someone else. There are also amplification spells to strengthen their ability, or make it disperse to others."

Mateo gasped. "That is... incredible. It's unheard of. That type of power. Your power..."

"It's almost godlike," Liam added enthusiastically. "It is godlike."

"C-could we not say that?" Amara cautioned. "It feels weird."

"Oh! Yes! Of course, love. I'm sorry."

A silence ensued between the three of them as Mateo and Liam processed everything and Amara began thinking through next steps. Suddenly, her nose scrunched up and she lifted her arm over her head and sniffed herself.

"I need a shower," she said, breaking the tension, and the men—who'd both been looking at the floor pensively—

turned their gazes to her. "You didn't at least wash me while I was passed out?"

"It seemed too intimate of a task without your consent," Mateo answered. He then walked toward her with a small smile on his face and pecked her forehead. "We would be happy to oblige now, if you want us to. Right, Liam?"

"Absolutely," Liam replied. "Would you like that, love?"

Amara nodded. "I'd like that a lot."

AMARA CLOSED her eyes with a subtle smile and leaned her head back against Liam's shoulder as water fell down her body, rinsing the soap away. She gasped when she felt Mateo's hand brush her inner thigh.

"Amor... we've practiced enough self-control, haven't we?"

Relaxed and full of desire, Amara, Mateo, and Liam were in total contrast to what they were merely thirty minutes prior. But they'd learned quickly that such shifts when together were their normal, especially after leaving Masoncrest. Even when they were in hiding, they could still find moments in the madness where it felt like it was just the three of them in their own world.

Amara opened her eyes to meet Mateo's gaze. "I think so," she replied softly.

Mateo leaned forward toward her to whisper in Amara's ear while Liam placed kisses against her shoulder and his hands joined Mateo's in wondering Amara's body. "Close your eyes. Focus on how this feels."

Amara did as she was told. The water from the shower was cut off. Fingertips danced across her breast, along the curve of her hip, up the inside of her thigh, and from her ribs to her waist. One set of lips made a trail from her shoulder to her neck while another lightly brushed against her own, just enough to tease her, before moving down to the other side of her neck. Meanwhile, Amara reached back to tangle her fingers in Liam's hair and used her other hand to caress Mateo's bicep.

She felt the fingers that were at her inner thigh finally reach her pussy, touching her briefly before gliding down to the inside of her other thigh. Amara let out a frustrated huff and soon felt a hand gently wrap around her neck.

"Why so eager, Amara?"

A palm flattened against her stomach and she felt Liam's length press against her lower back. "Enjoy this with us, love," he whispered.

Teeth caught her earlobe in a gentle grip, lips brushed against hers again, pressing just enough for her to want more before pulling her bottom lip. A hand cupped her breast while a thumb teased her nipple. Another hand returned to her core, putting light pressure against it, but not enough for Amara. When she tried to move her hips to create more friction, the hand moved back down to her thigh.

Another frustrated sigh from Amara was met with hands dropping behind each of her knees and lifting her legs up to wrap around what she knew were Mateo's hips, his length lightly brushing her pussy. Eyes still closed, Amara turned her head to meet Liam's lips.

More moans came from Amara as Mateo and Liam continued to tease her. For a third time, a hand was against her core. This time, two fingers slipped inside before they were slowly pulled out of her and brought to her lips. She opened her mouth as she and Mateo savored her essence.

Her chin was taken, turning her head to meet Liam's lips again.

Two hands grabbed her ass and pulled her in. Mateo's member pressed against her core, moving slowly against her.

Suddenly, they were transported to the bedroom—Amara still sandwiched between them, but the men now switched, Liam in front of her and Mateo behind. Amara and Mateo's lips moved against each other while Liam kissed his way down to her breasts, flicking his tongue against her nipple. Arching her back, Amara rubbed her ass against Mateo while Liam's tip occasionally brushed against her core as she moved her hips.

Again, the three repositioned—Liam with his face buried between Amara's thighs as his mouth moved eagerly while Mateo remained level with her, holding her gaze.

"We missed you," Mateo whispered to Amara.

Her moans grew more intense as Liam continued to eat her out. His fingers dug into her thighs and he let out a satisfied hum at the taste of her. One of Mateo's hands drifted down to gently toy with her other entrance under her. When Liam sat up to position his member at her core, Amara placed a hand against his lower stomach.

"I... I want both of you," she said through labored breaths. "... at the same time."

Both men looking her in the eyes, Mateo held her chin. "Are you sure?"

"There's no pressure, love," Liam assured.

"I know. I want this. And I don't need a potion to *prepare* anymore." Amara closed her eyes momentarily before opening them again. "It's done."

And with that, the three of them repositioned so that Liam was on his back and Amara was on top straddling him while Mateo was behind her. Taking Liam first, he slid into Amara's soaking pussy. Mateo summoned a bottle of lubricant and toyed with her other entrance as Liam pumped in and out of her, slowly adding more fingers as she relaxed.

"Mateo..." Amara called after hitting another climax. "I'm ready... please."

He didn't need more prompting than that. After covering his length with lube while he continued to finger her entrance as Liam slowed his strokes, Mateo then positioned his tip against Amara's ass.

Amara let out a loud moan as Mateo eased himself into her and for the first time, she had both men inside of her.

"We'll start slow," Mateo rasped. He placed one hand on her shoulder and the other on her waist while both of Liam's hands held her hips. The men moved in and out of her slowly as she grew accustom to taking them at the same time.

Her body quivered and her moans were uncontrollable as they got into a rhythm. Meanwhile, the men couldn't keep their own moans at bay. When Amara started moving with them, Liam squeezed his eyes shut, struggling to hold himself from coming while Mateo leaned back to watch the way Amara's ass moved up and down his length while he grabbed one cheek and smacked the other.

"You feel... so good..." Liam choked out. "I don't know how long I'll..."

"You're taking us so well," Mateo cooed.

Knowing he was at his limit, Amara leaned forward and kissed Liam, swallowing his grunts as he came inside of her. She soon felt Mateo tighten his grip on her shoulder as his strokes sped up before he released a low, strangled moan and finished inside her.

Amara rested on top of Liam and Mateo fell to his side

after pulling out of her. The three of them were completely spent.

Amara extended her arms above her head and stretched her legs under the covers letting out a relieved sigh. She savored the moments like that she, Mateo, and Liam had together—the only times it didn't feel like their world was falling apart.

Looking at the bedroom door, Amara shook her head. "I told them we wouldn't be long... They're probably wondering what's taking us."

Mateo chuckled and kissed her arm. "I'm sure they've guessed it by now."

Suddenly, Liam rose quickly from the bed and held his fingers to his ears as he cringed, startling Amara and Mateo. "Fucking hell! I thought I blocked the mind linking! She broke through somehow!"

Amara and Mateo watched him with concern as he walked across the room and leaned against the dresser by the door.

*Liam,* Scarlet's voice echoed in his mind. *I'm sure this hurts quite a bit. It takes a stronger mind link when I have blockage spells to get through, which you've seem to put up against me.*

*Then... perhaps you could... stop?*

*Too urgent. I need you to report here immediately... with your Fated.*

*Why?*

*I just need you here as soon as possible.*

The three of them looked to the door when Haze burst through. Amara and Mateo covered themselves with the bedsheets, but Liam was too distracted by his mother's painful mind link. Unfazed, Haze's eyes quickly searched the room before landing on Liam.

"Are you mind linking your mother? Cut it off now!"

Liam struggled to get words out through the discomfort of the ringing in his ears. "I—I wish I could but..."

"Amara!" Haze called. "Cut them off, now."

Without hesitation, Amara snapped her fingers and Liam released a sigh of relief and let go of his ears.

"What the hell is happening?" Liam questioned. "My mother asked for all of us to come to her immediately."

"Don't do that unless you want her to to kill Amara."

"What?"

Haze straightened her stance and stood against the doorframe with her arms crossed. "The secret is out. 'Rumors' are swirling that the Palisyfum isn't a flower, it's a people with unlimited abilities thanks to their blood, flesh, and bones. There's only one left and she's fated to Mateo Vazquez and Liam Taylor. Last seen being taken by the vampire Haze, who's believed to have fallen to the warlocks."

Mateo closed his eyes and massaged his temples. "What the hell? What are you saying? How could this get out?"

"My guess? Petra released the information to force Amara out of hiding. Now, the best of the best magical mercenaries and government officials—including the Assembly—are actively hunting her."

"Doesn't that make more competition for Petra?" Liam asked.

"She just wants to draw Amara out," Haze explained. "This many beings hunting her means you're likely to use stronger magic more frequently while being on the run— easier to track and you're bound to slip up. And even if someone else catches Amara, Petra probably thinks she has a better chance of getting Amara through them…”

Feeling a weight of tension overcome the room, Haze turned to Amara who was sat up in the bed fuming with her eyes glowing strongly with the Palisyfum purple.

“It's time we end this.”

# AUTHOR'S NOTE

Thank you. Thank you for giving this book a chance in the first place. Thank you for making it to the end. Thank you for giving your time and energy to reading it.

Thank you to the very special cafe where I spent MONTHS working on edits for this story. Thank you to the friends who were always up for co-working sessions. Thank you to my sister for listening to my ideas whenever I was trying to think through things vocally.

I remember when I first started this story, I had no idea where it would go (or if it would go anywhere, tbh). But as I continued, the plot and characters took on lives of their own. By the time I reached the end, I was *satisfied*. More than that, I was damn proud of how the story turned out.

Stay tuned for a novella featuring Samuel and Haze as the leads next. Then, there will be the second and final book of The Last Petal.